"So I'm your prisoner?" Isobel snapped. "I wonder what my father will think of this?"

"He'll take a strap to yer arse when I tell him about yer behavior."

Her face flushed, and her mouth flattened. Philip was afraid she might explode. He stared back at her, brows raised.

"Perhaps you should save him the trouble," she said.

A wicked grin pulled at his lips as he imagined it. "All you have to do is ask, lass—I'd be happy to oblige."

My
Wicked
Highlander

THE
MacDonell Brides
TRILOGY

My Wicked Highlander

Jen Holling

POCKET BOOKS
New York   London   Toronto   Sydney

An *Original* Publication of POCKET BOOKS

POCKET BOOKS, a division of Simon & Schuster, Inc.
1230 Avenue of the Americas, New York, NY 10020

ISBN: 0-7394-5448-X

Cover design by Min Choi; cover illustration by Alan Ayers

Manufactured in the United States of America

For Michele, the sister of my heart

For more than twenty years of friendship,
support, and encouragement

This one's for you

Chapter 1

England, 1597

For Isobel MacDonell being a witch was hell. Living in constant fear that what she said or did would send her to the gallows. The image of hanging by the neck until dead caused an involuntary tightening of her throat muscles. It was an especially frightening thought after reading that horrific pamphlet detailing the torture and execution of witches just across the border. Lord and Lady Attmore had gone to great lengths to keep the pamphlet from her, but Isobel had finally managed to acquire one and read it with morbid fascination. But then everything about Scotland was fascinating to Isobel.

Still, fear of discovery did not deter Isobel from her chosen path. She hurried through the forest, glancing repeatedly over her shoulder, worried someone had followed her. She shouldn't be doing such things. In his letters had her father not cautioned her repeatedly to have a care? To be mindful of all her mother had suffered?

I am careful! But those atrocities happened in Scotland—another world, it seemed, and one she barely remembered most days. She paused, her palm on the silvery gray trunk of an ash, and peered into the trees behind her. She stood in silence, listening, feeling. She was alone. Besides, there was no real harm in visiting Ceri. If caught, it would earn her a stern lecture and perhaps even punishment from Lord Attmore, but so long as no one discovered why she really frequented the witch's cottage—or how often—she would suffer no serious repercussions.

Her hand slid down the tree as she gazed up into the branches, through the green clusters of buds, at the gray sky. A storm was coming. The air felt damp and heavy. Thunder rumbled in the distance.

Her fingers moved over deep grooves in the wood, and longing filled her—sharp, passionate. She dropped her hand and stepped back, inspecting the tree. A heart was carved into the gray wood. Inside the heart the names *Anne and Dan* were deeply carved. Isobel smiled, passing her hand over the carving again, enjoying the youthful passion that passed through her. Dan had labored over this carving . . . many years ago. Because this was wood—and living wood at that—she'd never learn more than feelings mixed with the soft, warm hum of the tree itself. She would have liked to learn more about this Anne and Dan, but it wasn't to be.

With a deep, wistful sigh, Isobel continued on her way. The underbrush was thick, bush and scrub sprouting their first green buds, but Isobel had worn a trail over the years with her comings and goings and merely swished her skirts right and left to avoid catching them on the spiny branches.

Soon Ceri's cottage was in sight, nestled in a clearing. Isobel paused, waiting. She couldn't chance being seen if Ceri wasn't alone, so she must always wait. The damp wind blew at her, plastering her skirts against her legs and pulling her hair from its severe plait. She scanned the clearing but saw no horse or mule.

The cottage door opened abruptly. Isobel ducked behind the thick trunk of an ancient oak. Voices carried to her, one nasal and masculine, the other sharp and feminine. Isobel peered around the tree to see the vicar trotting into the trees, his shiny pate gleaming in the dull light just before he slapped a cap over it, and his dark robe flapping about his ankles.

Ceri stood at her door staring after him for a long moment. A strong wind gusted through the yard, disturbing old leaves and setting the penned chickens to clucking. Ceri's graying black hair swirled loose about her narrow shoulders.

She turned toward Isobel's hiding place. "You can come out now—and be quick, afore you're caught in the rain." Ceri pulled her wrap over her head just as a raindrop plopped onto Isobel's nose.

Isobel lifted her skirts and ran through the clearing as the sky opened up, sending down a deluge. Ceri slammed the door and latched it behind them, then hurried to the window and closed the shutters.

Isobel shook out her skirts and unpinned her lace cap, spreading it out on the stone hearth to dry.

Ceri watched with disapproval. "What if the vicar comes back, lass? You shouldn't be here."

"I had to come! It's that . . . feeling—I still have it, and it's worse now. You're the only person I can talk to, the only person who understands."

Ceri sighed heavily. "Tell me."

Isobel lowered herself onto the hearth, putting her back to the warm fire so it could dry her bodice. The cottage was small and comfortable. The rich scent of rosemary and lamb floated to her from the cauldron in the fire behind her. She preferred Ceri's cottage to anywhere else in the world—except perhaps Lochlaire. But her childhood home was only a fond memory; she hadn't been there in more than a decade.

Ceri lit two lard candles and set them on the wooden table.

Isobel placed her hand over her belly, rubbing at the knotting, sinking sensation that had been with her for weeks. "Something . . . or *someone* is coming . . . but I don't know what. Something dreadful will happen." She fisted her hand, frustrated. "If only I knew what . . ."

Ceri chuckled. "You rely overmuch on your gift. Remember what I told you about dreams?"

"Dreams don't work for me. I must have something solid to touch."

"You don't try hard enough. You're like those who refuse to believe until they see—and yet you yourself are proof of what is possible."

Isobel nodded blandly. She'd heard this before. Ceri was convinced Isobel had many untapped gifts. Isobel had not believed her until recently—until she began to have this feeling of dread. That something . . . or someone was coming. And when this thing was upon her, it would bring bad things, things that would change her forever. But that was all she knew. She hated this lack of clarity. With her other visions, she could focus if she chose to, probe until she understood.

"But *your* dreams oft tell you nothing useful until it's too late," Isobel said.

Ceri nodded, unwrapping a loaf of bread. "Aye, but that is my failing. I'm still learning to read them. Sometimes things aren't what they seem in a dream. A toad doesn't always mean a toad. It can mean many different things." She grinned at Isobel; her wrinkled face softened to reveal the great beauty even age couldn't dim. "You've been a great help, you have."

Isobel smiled. It warmed her to hear Ceri's kind words. "I would do anything to help you—you're my only friend."

Ceri's smile faded to consternation. "I cannot bear to hear you say such things. You're so young, so lovely. 'Tis wrong you should spend more time with a moldering old bag of bones than with lads and lassies your own age."

Isobel shrugged and plucked at her skirt. "It doesn't matter. I know too much, and no one likes that." She thought of her foster brothers and sisters, most married and gone now, and how they had distanced themselves from her. "I can't help myself sometimes, not when I know I can change things, that maybe I can make a difference. I *am* getting better at keeping silent. But the past cannot be undone, and everyone already knows I'm different. But in time, mayhap they'll forget?"

Ceri raised a skeptical brow. "Not if you keep giving your warnings—"

"Suggestions. Nothing more. Anyone can make suggestions . . . right? I never give specifics anymore."

Ceri's brow creased with worry. "You *are* being more careful, aren't you?" She came to stand before Isobel, hands on hips. "You *must* learn to guard your tongue."

Isobel forced a smile. "Of course. I wear gloves most of the time, and now, unless I see something dreadful, I truly do keep it to myself . . . most of the time."

Ceri shook her head, lips pressed into a flat line, her gaze fixed on Isobel's hands—which were currently gloveless. "You should keep it to yourself *all* the time. Even if you see something dreadful. Serves them right to get back some of what they give out so freely. It's not for you to change their lot."

Isobel looked away, to the window. "Well, even *I* can't change some things." Memories of Benji's wee lifeless body as it was fished from the swollen river rose in her mind. She had seen it, clear as day, and yet had been unable to prevent it. That was often the curse of it. Sometimes she was too late.

Ceri touched Isobel's chin. Isobel met the pale gray eyes that smiled at her.

"The only lot I want to change, my lass, is yours." She patted Isobel's cheek and straightened. "Come, we've a wet day, let me cast your fortune, see if there's a man in your future."

Isobel straightened her shoulders and sighed ruefully. "There is no man—at least not until my father chooses him." Isobel frowned. "Do you think he's forgotten me? Perhaps he doesn't realize I'm now four-and-twenty—well past marriageable age. Surely if he remembered me, he wouldn't leave me here to become an old maid. It's been more than two years since he last visited."

"Your father hasn't forgotten you. He's looking for the right man, is all—you're not just any lassie, but an heiress, should aught happen to your uncle. And he has your sisters to worry about, too. Scotland isn't safe these days. He knows you're in good hands and is likely waiting for the time to be right." She nodded sagely. "That time soon approaches, methinks. I had a dream about you and just such a lad."

Isobel laughed, knowing Ceri jested, but wishing it was true. "What did he look like?"

Ceri cut bread for them and set bowls of stew on the table. She leaned forward. "Oh, he was handsome—a big man, not like these wispy Englishmen. He must be one of your kind—a brawny Highlander."

Isobel considered that while they ate. Her father, Alan MacDonell, was a big man, though not overtall. But all the other men she knew seemed frail and fine-featured compared to the chieftain of Clan MacDonell of Glen Laire, with his heavy brow and rugged features.

Ceri withdrew a scarf and laid it in the center of the table. Isobel sobered. "Who brought it?"

"The vicar."

Isobel stared hard at the fine linen scarf. Its edges were embroidered with bright red thread. A faint yellow stain marred a corner.

"What does he want?"

Ceri raised her brow. "He came to me yesterday asking for a love philter to keep his wife faithful. You've seen his wife—I told him it was likely unnecessary, but he was most insistent. So I advised him to bring me something of hers to use in the potion. He brought me this."

"You know there's no true love philter. Why do you agree to such things?"

"Because it's safe—safer than delivering babies." Ceri shuddered, eyes closed. "I thought my life was over when the sheriff's long-awaited son was stillborn. If not for the good vicar and your auntie, I'd be long gone. No more midwifery for me."

Isobel scowled. "It is the village's loss." She smiled and reached across the table to pat her friend's hand. "Besides, now you find things for people. That's safer, aye?"

Ceri opened her eyes and pinned Isobel with a hard look. "It is. But you know I couldn't locate things so quickly—if at all—without your help. And I'll not have you in such a situation as I was." She returned to her stew. "As for love philters, no one wants to admit they purchased one, so no one will accuse me of witchcraft. It's harmless."

Isobel shook her head, her gaze going back to the stained linen. "What happens when it doesn't work? It is a dangerous game you play."

"You play it too, my lassie. Now touch it and tell me if his wife is faithful so I know whether or not to make this philter."

Isobel took the scarf and held it between her palms. Sometimes the visions came fast, overwhelming her, other times she had to work for them. This would be one of those times. She felt nothing initially. She rubbed it rhythmically between her palms and closed her eyes, breathing deeply, clearing her mind of everything but the vicar's wife and the scarf she held.

When still that didn't work, she tried thinking of the vicar. Almost immediately she felt lust. Not like the longing and desire she'd felt at the ash tree. This was not a love affair like Dan and Anne. This was base, empty. As these feelings didn't reconcile with Isobel's knowledge of the vicar's wife, she frowned and dug deeper, probing through the feeling, looking for visions, not merely emotions.

A picture slowly materialized behind her eyelids, like a mist clearing away. Arms and legs entangled in a pile of filthy hay, hairy buttocks thrusting, a bald head shining in the candlelight. She strained to bring the vision into closer focus, to see it from other angles.

It was the vicar, his godly robes bunched up to free his movements. The woman beneath him was young, red-headed, her head thrown back, lips parted in pleasure. Rain tapped the roof above them.

Isobel's eyes sprang open, and she stared at Ceri in disbelief. "He's riding the baker's wife—well . . . he will be—this evening, I believe." She threw the scarf onto the table as if it had turned into a viper. Thunder crashed over head—as loud as a pack of horseman. "This isn't his wife's scarf, but Letty Baker's. Some man of God! First he visits a witch, then goes straight to commit adultery! I saw them—all covered in sweat and rutting like animals."

Ceri studied Isobel critically. "You're looking a bit flushed yourself, lass. Such things a maid should not be seeing."

Isobel pushed back the damp curls that had escaped her plait from her forehead with dignity. "It takes a lot out of me, you know that."

Ceri raised her brows censoriously.

"What shall you tell him?" Isobel asked.

Ceri smiled wickedly. "I'll tell him the philter rejected the scarf since it came from an adulterer."

Isobel shook her head. "Have a care. He might have saved you once, but he might not be so quick to if you anger him."

Ceri made a rude sound but before she could say another word someone hammered on the door so hard it shook in its frame. They both froze, staring at each other in disbelief. Who would be out visiting a witch in such a storm?

Ceri sprang into action. "Hurry! You must hide!"

She shooed Isobel to the back of the cottage, where a blanket hung. A small cot was concealed behind it.

"Get on the bed," Ceri said, shoving her family of cats to the floor. "They'll see your feet otherwise."

Isobel did as she was bid, her heart pounding against her ribs, excuses for why she was at the local witch's cottage chasing through her head. *She was lost in the woods and just happened by.* No one would believe that. She'd lived at Attmore Manor for twelve years and spent a great deal of time in these woods. *She had an ailment and sought Ceri for a cure.* Why come alone, then? She knew as well as any young lass she shouldn't be wandering the woods unescorted. She should have brought a servant—not that she ever did.

Her thoughts were interrupted by a deep voice that resonated through the blanket, into her very belly.

"Gude day, lady. We seek shelter from the storm."

A Scotsman. Isobel sat up straighter.

"I've but a humble cottage and no room for so many."

"There are but three of us, lady, and we vow to wipe our feet."

"I'm but a lone woman," Ceri continued to protest, but weakly now. She was no lady, as they all well knew, but being called one had softened her.

"We mean ye no harm. Only rest and a dram, for which I will give recompense."

But no ordinary Scotsman. He spoke well and had fine manners. Isobel sat cross-legged on the cot, straining to hear every word. Soon the scraping of boots was heard. True to his word the Scotsman and his men were cleaning their boots before entering. Ceri's cats returned to the bed, one stretching out on Isobel's lap and the other two lying on the other end of the cot. Isobel scratched their heads absently. Though many animals shied away from Isobel, cats rarely feared her, and these cats had come to know her from her frequent visits.

When the movement had quieted down, Ceri spoke again. "You're far from the road, sir. Whence are you headed?"

"Attmore Manor. I was told the way was quicker through the wood."

Isobel stiffened, the twisting in her gut growing fierce. Attmore Manor was *her* home. What business had he there?

Ceri's thoughts clearly mirrored Isobel's for she asked, "Attmore Manor? What business have you there?"

Silence drew out, then Ceri said, "I see."

What did she see? What had Isobel missed? She couldn't stand the suspense. She slowly placed her feet on the dirt floor.

"Could I at least have your name, sir?"

"Sir Philip Kilpatrick of Clan Colquhoun."

"A Highlander."

"Aye."

Ceri grunted insolently. "You don't look like a Highlander."

Isobel couldn't bear it. Setting the cat aside, she eased to her feet and tiptoed to the edge of the blanket. What did Ceri mean, he didn't look like a Highlander? He was small? Fine-featured? He didn't sound small. His voice was a deep, rumbling baritone—it conjured images of bears and lions.

She peeked around the blanket. Two large men crowded around the hearth. An enormous blond man sat on the stone ledge where Isobel had rested earlier, and a burly red-bearded man hovered close to the fire, trying to dry wet clothes. A third man sat away from the others, on the bench at Ceri's table. His back was to Isobel—and a broad back it was, heavy, too, filling out the buff jack he wore. His longish hair was sandy brown and damp at the crown. Even sitting he was more than a head taller than Ceri, who sat across from him.

Ceri saw her peeking out and her eyes widened, then narrowed. The man turned abruptly to see what Ceri peered at. Isobel drew back, her breath catching as she nearly fell on the cot. But she caught herself, teetering momentarily. The cats showed no interest in the fact she'd nearly squashed them. The large gray yawned.

"You are not alone?" the man asked. The bench scraped. His footsteps started toward the blanket.

Isobel whirled back to the blanket, her hand clamped to her mouth in horror.

Ceri said, "Cats—that's all. Getting into things." She was moving toward the blanket, too. The man's footsteps stopped, and a moment later Ceri joined Isobel behind it.

Isobel smiled sheepishly. Ceri pointed to the cot, giving Isobel a severe look, and scooped up Whiskers, a fat black cat. Isobel returned to the cot, and Ceri went back to her guests.

Isobel propped her chin on her fist and listened to Ceri chatter at Sir Philip. The old woman tried to discover his business, but he was not a talkative sort. Isobel thought about his eyes as she waited. She'd caught but a glimpse, but they'd been dark, deep-set. Ceri was right, he didn't have the harsh, rugged features of her father. His nose had been straight, his jaw wide, but elegant, in spite of the dark whiskers shadowing it. His lips had been full and smooth. By the time the rain ceased, she'd convinced herself he was devastatingly handsome. And this darkly beautiful knight was on his way to Attmore Manor. Why?

It had to do with her. The roiling in her gut had worsened since he'd arrived—so he must be the reason for it. Was he sent by her father? By the time the men departed a sense of urgency had filled Isobel. She must get to Attmore Manor before Sir Philip. She burst from behind the blanket.

"You best be getting home, lass," Ceri said, handing her the cap she'd removed earlier.

Isobel pinned it back on her head. "First—give me the cup he drank from."

Ceri quickly fetched a battered tin cup from the table and thrust it into Isobel's hands. Isobel knew immediately he'd come for her. Her father had finally sent for her. But she could glean nothing else from the cup, except a warm and faintly disturbing sense of his lips against the rim. He'd not held it very long, so little of him would be imprinted upon it, she understood this. Still, it frustrated her. She'd hope for some sense of him, but he was a mystery.

"Soon enough, lass, you'll know just what he wants," Ceri said, urging her to the door. "And then come back and tell me!"

Isobel stopped in the open door and turned back to her friend. "Is he the one? The one you dreamed of?"

Ceri shook her head. "I didn't have no dream, lass. That was a jest."

"Oh." Isobel's heart sank. "He was very handsome, wasn't he?"

"That he was, and such pretty manners. Now off with you, afore Lord Attmore sends someone to look for you!"

"Oh, you know he won't. He'll just ring the bell."

Ceri gave Isobel a firm look. "Just go afore you get in trouble."

Isobel stared at her friend, the heavy sensation of dread intensifying in her belly. Impulsively, she grabbed the crystal charm Ceri wore about her neck. Warmth filled her as she saw Ceri shuffling about her cottage, surrounded by her cats, older and content. Isobel smiled. At least the feeling had nothing to do with Ceri.

She squeezed her friend's hand and raced into the forest.

Chapter 2

Shortly after they left the old woman's cottage Philip and his friends emerged from the wood. A manor house was visible in the distance. Philip reined in Horse, stroking the dark chestnut coat and murmuring calming nonsense. The stallion's eyes rolled, still uneasy about something that had spooked him and the other horses in the wood. Philip had caught only a glimpse of it—a bit of golden red hair—before it vanished. A wood sprite, he'd think, if he believed in such fancies, which he did not. However, it did seem odd that Horse, usually a most steadfast beast, had become so fearful.

Stephen had wanted to give chase, but Philip had stayed the lad, they didn't have time for foolishness. It was probably just another oddity living in the forest, none of their concern.

Fergus and Stephen gathered around him as he considered Attmore Manor. Fergus stroked his thick red beard, fingering the narrow braids that adorned it. His dark eyes were resolute. It had not occurred to him to chase after their woods phantom—he knew Philip's ways by now. He would do whatever Philip asked, no questions.

"What are we waiting for?" Stephen asked impatiently.

Philip's gaze rested on the lad. Though he'd been with

Philip several years now, he still had a great deal to learn. But Philip did not question his loyalty, or his intelligence. It was his tongue, however, that often proved problematic. But he was only eighteen. Philip supposed he hadn't been much different at that age.

"Not a word about her father," he advised them, pointing his finger at Stephen, whose gregarious nature had gotten them all in trouble more times than they could count. "Or I'll thrash you. And this time you'll not sit a horse for a month"

Stephen nodded. "When will you tell her?"

"I'm not here to tell her anything. Our orders are to see her safely to Lochlaire, and that's all we're going to do." Philip spurred his horse.

Stephen sputtered indignantly behind him, but Fergus held his tongue. He would not naysay Philip. And though Stephen might argue, he would obey.

The red brick mansion loomed before them. Though it had a moat and a wooden bridge, they were merely for appearances. This far from the border, such a country house didn't need fortification. Large glazed windows surrounded the top floors, conical turrets adorned the corners, and octagonal chimneys sprouted from the expensive clay-shingled roof. Lord Attmore lacked for naught. After living in such comfort, Isobel MacDonell wouldn't know what to do with herself at Lochlaire. But then she was destined for an earl—a Scots one, but an earl nonetheless—so perhaps it was fitting.

According to her father, Alan MacDonell, chieftain of the MacDonells of Glen Laire, she'd lived with Lord Attmore and his family for twelve years. She was four-and-twenty now. More than a decade she'd lived in such sumptuous luxury. She was probably spoiled rotten and would whine and complain the whole journey north.

Philip sighed. It was for Alan that he did this—anyone else he would have refused. But he owed Alan a great deal. And besides, she wasn't Philip's problem, thank God. He was merely here to fetch her, then she was her father's problem, and Philip could get back to important matters.

They cantered over the bridge and into the statue and shrub-lined courtyard. Liveried servants rushed out to greet them and take their horses. They were led into an expansive entryway. The polished wood floor and paneled walls gleamed. A servant led them to a carpeted drawing room and abandoned them.

When the door closed Fergus whistled under his breath. "God's wounds!" He elbowed Stephen. "Yer uncle is an earl—do Scots nobles live like this?"

Stephen scratched at his head. His long blond hair was secured at the nape of his neck. "Uh . . . no. Not that he lives in a cave or anything." He wandered over to a curtained alcove and fingered a heavy tassel. "This is silk . . . and gold thread, too."

Philip frowned at the lad. He still stood where the servant had left them, his hands clasped hard behind his back. "Don't touch that—your hands are dirty."

Stephen grinned and rubbed the tassel against his blond-stubbled jaw. "Aye—maybe some bastard Scots will rub off on them."

The door opened. Stephen dropped the tassel and straightened, his expression grave.

A portly man entered, his face florid. He toyed with the small mustache that feathered his lips, eyeing them suspiciously. He was well dressed, but in comfortable attire and riding boots.

"Lord Attmore?" Philip queried.

"Yes? And who might you be?"

Philip unhooked his jack and withdrew a letter. "Sir Philip Kilpatrick of Colquhoun."

Attmore's eyes narrowed. "I've heard of you. Whom do you seek here?"

"I'm here on MacDonell of Glen Laire business."

Attmore sighed with relief and took the letter Philip proffered. He read it, his brow furrowed, but when he looked up his face was shining. "You're here for Isobel? She's finally going home?" His voice nearly trembled with joy.

Philip hesitated, not expecting such a reaction. MacDonell paid Lord Attmore well to ward her. He'd anticipated resistance, not elation. "Aye. She's to wed the earl of Kincreag in a fortnight, so haste must be made. We leave at dawn."

The sound of running feet caused them all to turn. A woman appeared in the open doorway. Her cheeks blazed from exercise, and reddish blond curls surrounded her face like a halo. A lace cap hung askew from her hair. Philip's eyes narrowed. It was the same type of cap he'd seen lying on the hearth in the old woman's cottage in the woods. He'd thought then that such finery was out of place in her rough cottage. His gaze dropped to the lass's feet. Cork-soled shoes, splattered with mud. The shoes he'd seen beneath the curtain, though cleaner, had been cork-soled. Not the slippers of a gentlewoman. Mud splattered the edge of her skirts, as if she'd been running through puddles.

By the time his gaze had traveled back up her willowy figure to her face, she'd composed herself and was trying to smooth down the unruly curls that had come loose from her plait. Red-gold hair. Though he couldn't see her back, he'd wager his life it hung in a thick ropelike braid. It seemed he'd found the wood sprite. Though why such a thing would alarm Horse was a mystery.

She carried kidskin gloves in one hand and after a moment

she slipped them on surreptitiously. "Lord Attmore," she said, her voice low. "I didn't realize we had visitors."

She was a liar and a sneak. She had known he was there—had raced them through the woods.

She pinned Philip with a warm green gaze. "I'm Isobel MacDonell."

Philip sucked in a surprised breath and coughed. Stephen was there, pounding on his back until he shrugged the lad off irritably. *"You* are Alan's daughter?" He'd not considered she might be his charge. Bloody hell. This was not at all what he'd expected. But now that he looked at her he could see she was a MacDonell. In fact, she looked remarkably like her mother, Lillian, who'd died twelve years before.

Her expression chilled at his incredulity. "Why, yes. I am."

Stephen crossed the room, seeking to smooth over their awkward beginning. "Mistress MacDonell, I am Stephen Ross, this is Fergus MacLean." He indicated Fergus, who nodded and mumbled a gruff greeting. "And this is Sir Philip Kilpatrick of Colquhoun."

Her cool green gaze swept Philip from head to toe. "A Keeper of the Dogs? Hmm . . . to what do we owe this honor?"

Philip frowned, unsettled that she knew Colquhoun history. After twelve years he hadn't expected Alan's daughter to even remember the Scots' tongue, let alone any history.

Lord Attmore answered before Philip could. "Your father has sent for you, my dear!" He went to her and grasped her hands tightly in his. "You're going home!"

Her eyes widened in disbelief. "Home?"

Attmore thrust the letter into her hands. "Yes, isn't it wonderful? You must leave first thing on the morrow. There's packing to be done . . . arrangements to be made . . ." His eyes moved rapidly as he thought of all that must be done.

"We'll have your things sent after you. Worry not. Just gather what you need for your journey." He patted Isobel's shoulder. "I'll see to the rest." He nodded happily at Philip and hurried from the room, leaving Isobel to read the missive in stunned disbelief.

Philip felt strangely annoyed at Attmore's good humor over the situation. She'd lived with the man for twelve years—he was a foster father to her. He shouldn't be so happy to see her go. Isobel didn't seem upset by his behavior. Perhaps she was accustomed to it. That disturbed him even more.

He watched her with narrowed eyes. She held the letter in her gloved hands, reading it over and over again. Gloves. Why would she put on gloves *inside,* when she'd not bothered with them outside?

Stephen roused Philip from his reverie with a hard slap on the shoulder. "Didn't Alan send *her* a letter?"

"Oh, aye." Philip retrieved it from his jack and crossed the room to her. She raised her head, and his heart seized. She was not at all what he'd imagined. He wasn't sure exactly what he'd expected, but not this fair, slender thing. She looked nothing at all like her father. Her face was narrow and fine-boned, her wide eyes were a pale, silvery green, and her hair . . . he'd never seen such a shade of red.

Her eyes seemed to shimmer as she stared at him, a question in them. "My father is bringing me home for my upcoming nuptials?"

Philip still held the packet Alan MacDonell had given him. He nodded, offering it to her.

"He has chosen a husband for me?"

"Aye."

Her gaze dropped to the packet, but she didn't reach for it. She licked her lips and swallowed. "Is it you?" she asked quietly.

Philip blinked, uncertain he'd heard her correctly. "What? Me? No. Good Lord, no." He spoke with more force than he'd intended—only because he'd feared the same thing when Alan had sent for him. He'd been greatly relieved that Alan had only this task in mind and not yoking Philip to one of his daughters.

Her gaze jerked back to his. "I see." She snatched the packet from his hand.

He'd insulted her. He'd not meant to. "I—no, I mean, that's—"

"I'll see you on the morrow." She spun around and left the room, with Philip still struggling to form a coherent apology.

He dropped his hands to his sides and exhaled. "That went well." He did not spend a great deal of time in the company of gentlewomen; nevertheless, he had never been so ill-mannered. The woman had set him off-balance from the moment she'd appeared in the doorway. He scowled, not liking any of this and wishing he could do it over.

Stephen slapped him on the back. "It doesna matter—remember? We've got our orders."

Stephen laughed at Philip's sour look.

"Where are you going?" he called after the hulking lad as he exited the room.

"I'm hungry. There's a kitchen about here somewhere."

When Fergus followed, Philip put out a hand to stop him. "I didn't mean to insult her. Surely you can see that."

Fergus smiled and gripped Philip's shoulder. "'Course I see that. Dinna fash—she'll get over it."

Stephen and Fergus were right. What did it matter? Why was he letting it trouble him at all? He shrugged it off and followed his men in search of dinner.

• • •

Isobel shut the door to her room firmly, then bolted it for good measure. She went to her bed and drew the bed curtains. With a candle and the pouch Sir Philip had given her, she crawled into the privacy she'd created. She unfastened the ties on the leather pouch, withdrew a letter and a small bone casket, decorated with knotwork and silver. Isobel recognized it. It had been her mother's.

She set both the letter and the casket on the bed with shaking hands and stared at them. Part of her was relieved her father had not forgotten her, excited to soon be reunited with him in her old home. But the sense of foreboding had not gone away—it had only intensified since Sir Philip's arrival. It must have something to do with her father. Something was wrong. She must discover what.

Slowly, she removed her gloves and set them aside. As soon as she took her father's letter in her hands the stone in her belly grew heavier. She held the missive between her palms, probing at the darkness that shrouded it. There was a sense of great weariness. An aching in her joints. Resignation.

Alarmed, she hurriedly broke the wax seal and spread it on the bed near the candle.

To My Loving Daughter Isobel,

How I've longed for this day to arrive, but now that it has there is so little time. Remember you Alasdair Lyon, Earl Kincreag? He was a good friend and lord to me. It has been many years since he passed on and his son, Nicholas, the current earl, is widowed. He agreed that a union between our families would be advantageous. He is a good man and will bring you much happiness.

I regret that I am unable to bring you home myself, but I am indisposed. I trust no man more than

*Sir Philip Kilpatrick. He will guard you with his life.
But you must have a care. He heeds not the stories of
your mother. I know you are ever like your mother in
all you do, and so you must exercise caution. Give
no one reason to suspect you are aught but what you
appear. I'm sending your mother's charm to you.
I've kept it close to me these many years since
Lillian's death, but it is yours now. Use it to remember why you must guard your secret with vigilance.*

  I count the days until your homecoming,

          A. MacDonell

Isobel frowned at the letter. It revealed nothing of why
this leaden weight of dread would not leave her. Why had
her father felt weary and resigned when he wrote it? Why
could she discover nothing from the parchment? As she
rubbed it between her palms, probing at it with her mind,
she wondered if her father had cast some sort of veiling
spell over the letter, for she could get little else from it. He
was not a powerful witch, but did know a few tricks from
being married to one and had an uncanny talent for knowing before anyone else if a woman was pregnant and
whether it was a girl or boy. He'd never been wrong, so far
as Isobel knew. He would know that Isobel would try to
discover all she could from anything he'd held.

What was so terrible that he must hide it? Disturbed,
Isobel set the letter aside and focused on the casket. She'd
seen it and the charm inside before, but had not held them
since her mother's death. She was afraid of what she'd see.

But her father wanted her to see it. So she took the casket in her hands. It was strong with her father's sadness and
love, and Isobel smiled, digging deeper. Her mother was
there, just as Isobel remembered her. Her face and her form,
looking happy and beautiful, delighting Isobel. She hardly

remembered what Lillian MacDonell had looked like, except that her hair had been reddish blond and her eyes green. Isobel held the casket reverently against her breast, seeing her mother in her mind. So lovely. But it was more than that, she felt her mother. The warmth of her love, her essence, captured in the casket for Isobel to unlock. Her love for her children was there, too, as well as a deep desire to protect her family. Isobel had never forgotten her mother's teachings, and as an adult, she'd come to understand them in a way she never could as a child. Isobel and her sisters were to use their gifts only for good, never for evil. Never for their own gain, but to help others. It had been important to Lillian that her children become white witches.

Lillian had given Isobel her own special warnings. Isobel possessed the same gift as Lillian MacDonell, and so she knew the temptations and dangers Isobel faced. *It is not your right to know another's mind. Just because you can, doesn't mean you should. Never look into another's soul unless you're certain you are welcome.*

Isobel had tried to follow her mother's teachings, though sometimes her curiosity got the best of her. She sighed, stroking her hands over the casket, wishing her mother was there now to guide her. Perhaps if her mother had been more willing to look into other's souls, she could have saved herself.

Isobel lifted the clasp holding the casket closed. Inside was the charm her mother had worn as protection from evil. She'd not been wearing it the day they'd taken her.

The rough-cut peridot lay in its silver setting, the watery green reflecting the candlelight. Her mother had always worn it on a green ribbon about her neck. The ribbon was still there, stained and ragged. Isobel swallowed and reached for the pale green stone. She'd barely laid hands on it when she saw her mother's face, tear-streaked and flushed from the proximity of the fire that blazed around her. The fire grew fierce, feeding on the branches thrown onto it. And then she was inside her mother, seeing through Lillian's eyes, feeling through her skin.

A mob surrounded the stake, their faces twisted, all running together, the air wavy from the intense heat. They shouted at her, cursed, and called her foul names.

"Alan!" her mother cried. "Alan!" *Where was he?* She searched the faces and beyond them, to the empty hillside. Why did he not come for her? Was she to die this way? Thoughts of her children and husband surged through her, causing waves of despair to crush her. Would her daughters be safe from the mob? Or would they be lynched, too? She focused all her power on her husband. *The children. Save them.*

Through her tears and the heat of the fire she saw a dark figure ride to the top of the hill and turn, looking back at her. He raised his hand and rode away. A flicker of recognition jolted her, quickly followed by horror.

"No!" Lillian screamed.

The wind gusted, and her face burned. Her red hair billowed out around her and caught. Lillian screamed as the fire seared her, agony and despair ripping through her.

It was dark, and someone hammered at her door. Isobel panted, uncertain of where she was. Her face was slick with cold sweat. She no longer held the charm. She felt its weight on her leg, where she'd dropped it. The candle had gone out and her hand burned. Her breath seemed loud in the closed dark.

Who was the figure on the horse and why, if Lillian had recognized him, was his identity hidden from Isobel? It made no sense. Isobel almost always knew most of what the subject of her visions thought and felt, at least during the period of time she saw, especially in a vision so vivid. And yet the horseman's identity was hidden from her, as if a wall of silver mist obscured his name and face.

The hammering began again.

"Mistress MacDonell! Answer me or I'll break down the door!"

Isobel scooted off the bed and through the bed curtains. The candelabra beside the door blazed. Isobel hurried on wobbly legs to the door and threw it open.

She was surprised to find Sir Philip outside her chambers, his handsome face thunderous. He looked her over quickly, then pushed past her into the room.

"You were screaming." He roamed the room, stopping to open the shutters and peer out the window.

Isobel watched him, speechless from his intrusion. He obviously took his duty very seriously. He paced to her bed and parted the bed curtains. Seeing nothing amiss, he turned back to her, hands on hips. "Why were you screaming? It sounded as if someone were killing you."

A shudder wracked her shoulders, but she forced a thin smile and rubbed her bare hands together. "I . . . must have fallen asleep. I . . . had a nightmare and burned my hand."

He crossed the room, frowning at her hands. "A woman your age should know better than to sleep with candles in bed."

A woman my age? Her spine stiffened, indignant anger chasing the chill away. He still bore down on her, gaze fixed on her hands. When she realized his intent, she backed away, hiding them behind her back.

"I'm fine."

His dark eyes were intent with purpose. "Let me see."

Isobel bumped into the wall. "It's unnecessary. You're no healer."

"You'd be surprised."

Trapped between him and the wall, Isobel could only stare at him, eyes wide. He was tall and beautiful in a dark, forbidding way. His nose was straight as a blade, his mouth firm and hard. His eyes were set deep below a smooth, straight forehead and thick brows. As he came closer she saw they were brown and thickly lashed. There was more there, too—a guardedness, a reserve that intrigued her.

She was trembling, afraid of him and uncertain why. He clearly meant her no harm and yet she wanted to flee. She remembered her foolish mistake of thinking him her betrothed, and her cheeks flamed. He'd been horrified at the very idea.

When he was before her she stared at his chest, since it was at eye level. He'd removed the buff jack, but still wore a quilted leather vest over his linen shirt, a thick sword belt yoked over his chest, so the ivory cross hilt was visible over his shoulder.

"Let me see your hands," he ordered, his gaze fixed on her, demanding.

Isobel fisted them behind her back.

He held his hands out, and she stared down at them, anything to avoid the intensity of his eyes. She couldn't think when she met his gaze. Strong, tanned hands reached toward her, dark hair dusting the back of them. He wore a ring on one finger; a tawny stone mounted in gold.

"Topaz," she said. "Protects the wearer and improves vision." She met his slitted gaze. "You do seem to squint. Does it help?"

His frown grew more pronounced. "I can see like an eagle."

"And you're modest, too."

"It is a family ring. I wear it because my father wishes me to. No other reason."

When he stepped away from her she let out the breath she'd been holding. She'd managed to distract him. His back was to her—broad and heavy with muscle. Her knees grew weaker. The vision of her mother's death had drained her. She needed rest. She wished he would just leave. His presence in her bedchamber was most disconcerting. It suddenly seemed small and close.

He ran a frustrated hand through his hair, then glanced at her over his shoulder. "You're certain you're fine?"

"Perfectly."

He nodded, scanning the room one last time. He started for the door.

"Sir Philip," Isobel called impulsively.

He stopped at the door and turned back to her.

"How is my father? Is he well?"

The dark eyes slanted away from her. "Aye—did he say otherwise in his letter?"

"No."

"There you are." He started out the door again, pulling it closed it behind him.

Before it latched she called, "Sir Philip?"

The door froze, then opened slowly inward again. His expression was bland and polite—expectant. He was impatient with her. He wanted to escape. That much was clear. Isobel was surprised that she felt slight amusement. She had little experience with men other than her foster family—and, in her opinion, they didn't count. The three men who'd come to fetch her interested her greatly—most especially this one.

"Perhaps he is withholding information from me," she suggested. "To protect me. Fathers do such things, you know."

He pinned her with a hard stare. "And if he were, it would not be my place to go against his wishes."

Isobel went to the door. "So there *might* be something amiss?"

"I didna say that."

"But you wouldn't, would you? Even if something *were* wrong."

His jaw hardened, and his dark eyes narrowed. "Everything is fine, Mistress MacDonell."

"Do you promise?"

He exhaled loudly through his nose. "I canna do that. What if something has happened since I left Lochlaire?"

"But you can vow to me that everything was well when you left it, can you not?"

His hand dropped from the door latch, and he rubbed at his right eyebrow. "I don't know all that goes on at Lochlaire—"

"But my father said in the letter he trusts you implicitly. Surely you are in his confidence."

He seemed quite disturbed now, which convinced Isobel something was definitely amiss. She quickly cataloged things that might be in Sir Philip's possession that her father might have also touched. Unfortunately, touching skin gave her no visions—it had to be an object. Her gaze went to his ring, glinting in the candlelight as he rubbed at his brow. He'd surely clasped hands with her father, but the contact would have been brief. It was unlikely she would learn anything useful—and she might discover something she didn't want to, that she had no business knowing. *It is not your right to know another's mind. Just because you can, doesn't mean you should.*

Isobel argued with herself, but when it became clear Sir Philip not only wouldn't answer her question but was also easing out the door again, she held out her burned hand.

He paused, staring down at the proffered limb.

"My burn. You wanted to see it."

After a moment's hesitation he came forward and took her hand in both of his. His hands were warm and strong. She shivered. She realized immediately he was in control, and she would not be able to touch his ring without being obvious. She glanced up at his face and her gaze snagged. He was so serious. Grim. Determined. His fingers were on her wrist as he turned her hand to see the palm, but she couldn't look away from the lashes, several shades darker than his hair, shadowing his cheeks.

His thumb stroked over the inside of her wrist and her breath caught. He met her gaze and held it. His eyes were searching, intense, and warm enough to turn her already weakened knees to water.

"It's not a bad burn," he said. "You'll be fine."

"Thank you," she whispered.

He released her hand abruptly and backed out the door, looking anywhere but at her. "Good evening, Mistress MacDonell."

"Good evening," she said to the closed door. She clasped her hand to her belly and closed her eyes. *Oh dear.* She had enjoyed that far too much. Her heart still galloped like a herd of crazed horses, and her face burned. She inhaled deeply and opened her eyes, gazing about the room.

Tomorrow morning she would leave all of this. Forever. She couldn't say she was sorry. She'd always been an outcast, despite the Attmores' reluctant kindness. But she would miss Ceri.

Ceri! She didn't even know Isobel was leaving. Isobel considered sneaking out, but Sir Philip was apparently nearby, perhaps even watching her room. Well, he would have to sleep sometime. She would slip out before dawn and be back before he knew it.

Chapter 3

Philip stopped by Isobel's room on his way down to the morning meal. He paused outside her door, debating what to do. It was unlike him to be so indecisive, and yet, he'd found their conversation last night disconcerting. It had been inappropriate for him to be in her bedchamber alone, but when he'd heard her scream he'd not been thinking at all, only responding. Odd, now that he thought of it, that no one else responded to her screams.

Besides all that, he'd dreamed of her. That troubled him more than aught else. In his dream, things he'd purposefully ignored about her last night, had come back to him vividly. The softness of her skin, her warm scent, the way her pulse had raced beneath his fingers. That moment he'd touched her hung suspended in his dream, allowing him to explore every nuance of her until he'd forced himself awake, disgusted. She was Alan's daughter and meant for another man. He had no business even thinking about her in such a manner. As Alan was like a father to him, he should view her as a sister.

Now that he was in a foul humor, thanks to her, the last thing he wanted to do was face her again. But he had his duty. He pounded on her door relentlessly, hoping she was asleep so he could rudely awaken her. His knocks went unanswered. When he eased the door open he found the room empty, the bed made. He didn't find her in the great hall either.

Stephen was at the long table with Lord Attmore, carrying on an animated—and apparently one-sided—conversation, a bowl of boiled eggs and a loaf of bread in front of him. Attmore simply watched Stephen yap and eat, a slightly bemused expression on his face. An older woman sat on the other side of Lord Attmore watching Stephen, her mouth pinched and white.

"Philip," Stephen said, after he washed down an entire egg eaten in one bite with some ale. "Tell these two my da did know Queen Mary." He pointed a peeled egg at Attmore. "He was even part of a plot to help her escape her English prison."

Philip sat beside Stephen, stealing an egg from his bowl. Stephen frowned at him and drew the bowl closer, putting a protective hand over it.

Philip nodded. "It's true."

Stephen nodded sagely.

"Though I suspect Stephen has taken some liberties with history."

Stephen scowled, but continued eating.

Lord Attmore shook his head as Stephen continued to eat voraciously. "You're a big lad, eh? Mine still aren't half so large and ate like birds."

Stephen swallowed his egg and took a long pull of ale. "It's me mother—she was but a common servant, daughter of a blacksmith. My da was the bastard son of the earl of Irvine—not a wee one in that family either."

The woman made a soft gasping sound and fumbled with the silver pomander about her neck, waving it under her nose. Lord Attmore seemed to just notice her and introduced her as his wife. She gave Philip a stiff smile and went back to shredding a piece of bread, keeping a careful eye on the hulking young man across the table from her. Stephen appeared oblivious to her unease as he grinned at her, but Philip knew better—he enjoyed making snobs like her uneasy.

"Where is Mistress MacDonell?" Philip asked. "I checked her room this morning, but she's not there."

Attmore stroked his mustache. "She's not? Hmm . . . She could be anywhere, I suppose." He didn't seem overly concerned as he placed a piece of herring on a slice of cheese and popped it in his mouth.

Philip was becoming annoyed at Lord Attmore's lack of interest in his charge. He was Alan MacDonell's representative, after all. And Isobel MacDonell was practically an heiress. The resources of Clan MacDonell were not insignificant—even to a rich Englishman such as Lord Attmore.

"It is important that she is located. I mean to leave within the hour."

Attmore and his wife exchanged alarmed glances.

"You'll not leave without her?" Lady Attmore asked.

Philip only stared at them silently, increasingly irritated at their attitude about Isobel. She couldn't be *that* bad.

"I'll find her at once," Attmore said, rising from the table.

Lady Attmore's smile was strained. "Worry not—we'll find her. We wouldn't want you to leave without her."

"I have no intention of leaving without her."

Lady Attmore laughed nervously. "Of course you don't."

Philip stared down at his egg, still uneaten. Then he pinned Lady Attmore with a hard look. "Am I the only one who heard Mistress MacDonell screaming last night?"

Lady Attmore seemed uncertain how to answer. "No . . ."

"Then why was I the only one to look in on her?"

She sighed wearily. "After a time, you'll come to pay her . . . *unusual* behavior no mind."

Stephen frowned, but continued shoving eggs and bread in his mouth and washing it down with ale.

"Screaming is alarming behavior. Not unusual. She burned herself, you know."

"Oh?" Lady Attmore seemed only mildly concerned. Seeing Philip's incredulity, she ventured, "She's unharmed, I trust?"

"Aye. Good of you to inquire."

Her mouth flattened at his sarcasm. Stephen stopped eating, eyebrows raised, recognizing Philip's growing anger.

"Prithee, take no offense, Sir Philip," Lady Attmore said, gathering her shredded bread into a neat pile. "You cannot understand what it's like to live with someone like her. I cannot say I'm sad to see her go. It would be a lie."

"Someone like her?" Philip repeated. "What mean you? She seems a normal, if not spirited lass."

Lady Attmore snorted delicately. "Hardly normal." She glanced at Stephen then sniffed. "I suppose I'll tell you, as you'll discover it for yourself soon enough, but it's always good to be forewarned." She paused, fixing Philip with a raised-brow look. "She's a witch."

"That is a dangerous accusation you make," Philip said softly. Not half as dangerous in England as it was in Scotland, but serious nonetheless.

Lady Attmore stared at Philip with hard eyes. "I do not wish for her to end up like her mother, I vow it, I do have a certain . . . fondness for her. But she *is* a witch. You will see."

A bell began to clang, and Lord Attmore appeared in the doorway. "Sir Philip? I cannot seem to locate her. When she hears the bell, she will return." Though his words were confident, sweat sheened Lord Attmore's face, and he couldn't seem to let his mustache alone.

Philip fought down his rising panic. She was not lost—just because they couldn't find her immediately, didn't mean she was lost. But logic rarely had any effect on his agitation—only action. In the event she truly *was* lost, he couldn't risk letting her trail go cold.

Fergus strode into the room, coming swiftly to Philip's side. Lady Attmore rose from the table and backed away from the enormous Scotsman, holding her pomander in front of her nose.

"Ready the horses," Philip ordered Fergus and Stephen. "We leave as soon as I return."

The lad was on his feet, stuffing the remaining eggs in a bag. Seeing that the Attmores appeared to be finished eating, Stephen gathered the rest of the food into his sack.

Philip jogged out of the hall. It was impossible for him to sit about idly and wait. Besides, that's what he did. He found people. He did not lose them. Well, not anymore.

He left the manor on foot, closely inspecting the grass on his way to the forest. The grass was long and he immediately found a fresh trail. The blades were bent forward, indicating she'd gone toward the wood. No dew dampened her trail, so she'd walked this way within the last few hours, wiping the moisture away with her shoes and skirts.

In the forest the trail was clearly visible—she'd come this way frequently. He hurried along, keeping an eye out for anything unusual. It led him to the cottage where the old woman who'd given them food and drink lived. The clang of the bell was muted, but if she'd been listening, she should have heard it.

He hammered on the door. After a bit of scuffling within, someone shouted, "Who's there?"

"Sir Philip Kilpatrick. I seek Mistress MacDonell."

After a moment the door opened a crack, and the old woman's face peeked out. "She ain't here."

"May I come in?"

The woman hesitated. "Why? I told you she ain't here."

Philip put his hand on the door and pushed. "I'd like to have a look, if ye dinna mind."

The woman clearly did mind, but seeing he meant to enter, she relented, swinging the door wide. "See? No one here but me and my cats."

Philip went straight to the blanket hung at the back of the cottage. The woman began to protest, but Philip pulled it aside. Isobel MacDonell sat cross-legged on the narrow cot, gazing up at him with wide green eyes.

The tension drained out of him, replaced with anger. How careless she was! A woman of gentle birth should not wander about the woods unattended. How could the Attmores allow this?

Isobel seemed to recover herself and gave him a smile. "Sir Philip! Why . . . you're up early this morn—"

She yelped as he grabbed her arm and hauled her off the bed. "What do you mean by running off and telling no one where you are?"

"What?" She tried her jerk her arm away, but he dragged her to the door. "I don't have to tell you where I go!"

"Oh dear," the old woman moaned, trailing after them. "She didn't do aught, sir. She was just coming to say good-bye to an old woman."

"Sir Philip! Release me at once!"

He released her arm, but only to push her in front of him. "Move. We should have been gone by now."

She whirled around, arms crossed under her breasts, and stared at him in disbelief. "I'm not finished saying good-bye to Ceri!"

He moved aside, and when she tried to walk past him, he caught her arm again. "Wave."

She huffed up at him.

"And get it over with—I havena time for this."

She exhaled through her nose, like a bull readying to charge. "Good-bye, Ceri! I shall miss you!"

The old woman dabbed her eyes with her apron and waved.

When Philip urged her forward she stumbled dramatically as if he'd pushed her.

"Ruffian!" She shrugged away from him.

Philip followed silently, amused by her behavior. But his amusement quickly died at the memory of her running off alone. Anything could have happened—then what would he tell Alan? Just imagining facing someone he so respected and telling him he had lost his daughter made him sick with anger. He would *never* do that again.

"From now on you will not leave my presence unless you are accompanied by Fergus or Stephen."

Her steps slowed a fraction, but she said nothing, keeping her back stiff.

"Do you understand?"

"Oh, I understand."

Philip didn't like being so harsh, but it was necessary. She was obviously reckless about her person, so he must take precautions. His anger slowly melted away on their return walk to Attmore Manor.

He watched how the sun streaming through the branches in shafts caught the coppery strands in her hair, glinting like metal. It hung loose down her back but for the narrow plaits at the side of her head, pulling it away from her face. Perhaps it was her age that led the Attmores to allow such behavior. After all, she was a full-grown woman—most lasses her age would have children by now. Alan had done her a disservice by leaving her a maid so long. A husband would have worked out all the kinks in her behavior long ago. She was probably set in her ways and would prove a most difficult companion. Philip was thankful that was someone else's problem. He only had to deal with her for a week, so long as the weather cooperated.

Of course, it was spring, not a terribly cooperative time of year. Though Philip was not averse to traveling in the rain, unfortunately he couldn't risk his charge's health. But all was clear today, and they should cover a lot of distance before nightfall.

They emerged from the wood, and Isobel immediately veered away from him. He tensed momentarily, ready to sprint after her, but relaxed as soon as he saw she didn't mean to bolt. She walked more slowly through the grasses, so she could walk beside him, though a dozen feet separated them.

"How did you know where I was?" she asked.

Oddly, Philip found he could only hold her gaze for seconds. She had the most amazing eyes. Soft sage, surrounded by thick auburn lashes. But it was more than the combination of extraordinary colors. It was the way she looked at him. Direct and bold. As if she could discern secrets in a person's eyes.

"You were there yesterday, hiding behind the curtain. I thought you might return."

Her pale brow crinkled questioningly. Her fair skin was a vibrant contrast to the reddish blond of her brows and hair. He looked away again.

"But how did you know it was *me?*"

He gestured to her feet. "Your shoes. I saw them beneath the curtains." He waved toward her head. "That . . . lace thing you wore on your hair yesterday, I saw it on the hearth drying. And your hair . . . it's an unusual color. I thought I saw it in the wood yesterday. You spooked my horse. And your shoes and skirts were covered with fresh mud—you'd raced us through the forest."

She stared at him, her mouth curved up on one side in a little smile, a dimple denting her left cheek. "How very clever. You're quite observant."

Suddenly Philip felt ridiculous. He'd not been fishing for compliments, yet he felt as if he were—and he was inordinately pleased that he'd gotten one. He cut his gaze away, fixing it on the manor in the distance.

"I wouldn't be very good at what I do if I didn't notice things."

"What do you do?" She drifted closer; he could sense that without looking at her.

"I find people."

"You find people? Whatever do you mean? Lost people?"

His chest tightened fractionally. He nodded. "Aye. Sometimes they're lost, but usually they've run away."

"Run away from what?"

Philip shrugged. "Criminals running from justice. Men running from their debts. Wives from their husbands . . . once even a husband from his wife."

"I see. You're some sort of seeker. Hmm . . . like a sleuth dog. It's fitting, you being a Kilpatrick of Colquhoun."

Philip narrowed his eyes at her and wished he hadn't. She teased him. Her expression was lively, her mouth curved in a smile. She had very straight, white teeth.

He was not accustomed to being teased. At least, not by a woman.

"How do you know so much about Clan Colquhoun?"

Her smile widened. "You fostered with my father. You think I don't remember you?"

Philip stopped, surprised. "You remember me?"

She walked a few more steps, then turned to face him, hands on her hips. "Aye. I didna at first—not until I'd thought aboot it. But clearly ye dinna remember me."

Philip grunted at her put-on Scottish burr. "Even if I

did, I wouldna recognize you anymore. You're more English than Scots now."

He started walking again, and she strode beside him, silent for a long moment. "Coming from you, I think that's an insult." When he didn't respond, she said, "You don't look like a Highlander. Where's your tartan or trews?"

"I'm not fool enough to wear such things outside of the Highlands"

"Why?"

"No one likes Highlanders, and I have no desire to call unwanted attention to myself."

Her brow creased, but she fell silent. He wondered what she was thinking but didn't dare ask. She was far too forward for a lass—he shouldn't encourage her.

"Do you know my betrothed, the earl of Kincreag?"

"I know of him."

"Have you *seen* him?"

"Aye."

She turned toward him, hands clasped before her, eyes alight with interest. "Really? What's he like?"

Philip groaned inwardly. This was not a subject he had any business discussing with her. "Your father thinks well of him."

She raised a brow. "I didn't ask what my father thought of him. I asked what *you* think."

"It's not my place to make judgments on great lords."

Her brow furrowed. "I see. You don't like him."

"I didna say that."

"But all you do is equivocate. If you liked the man, you'd say so. However, you have apparently been taught good manners and will not disparage a man to his betrothed. That is admirable of you."

Philip stopped in his tracks, hands on hips. "I'd rather not discuss Lord Kincreag with you—that is all. Whatever

I might say—good or bad—could color your opinion in ways I canna imagine. I won't do that."

She gave him an impish grin. "I'm not foolish enough to let someone color my opinion of my husband before I even meet him. After all, if I'm going to spend the rest of my life with him, it's only fair I allow him to do the coloring—don't you agree?"

"Then why ask me?"

"Because I'm curious! Wouldn't you be? I just found out last night I'm to be married to a man I don't even know. It would be nice to at least know what he looks like."

Philip sighed and started walking again. "Verra well. He's a tall man . . . Rather large, too. He's swarthy and . . . er . . . quiet."

"Like you?"

"I'm not swarthy."

"No, but you're rather quiet. What's wrong with swarthy? I think I'd like a dark man—the men in England are so pale. So feminine." She slid him an appreciative sidelong look that slid from his head to his toes, her auburn lashes shading her eyes like fans of copper.

Philip's groin tightened involuntarily. He ground his teeth together. The little minx had no idea what she was playing at. He hadn't the time or inclination for games of this sort.

"Then you'll be pleased with your betrothed, for he is very dark."

She smiled at him. "I'm certain I will be. How old is he? Is he older than you?"

"By at least five years."

"And how old is that?"

"I'm nine-and-twenty . . . so he's at least five-and-thirty. Mayhap older."

"Mmhmm."

He glanced at her. She'd picked a wildflower from the

grasses as they walked and was plucking the petals away, her expression dreamy. It annoyed him inexplicably.

"My father said he's widowed. What was his wife like?"

This was what Philip wanted to avoid. "She was very beautiful," he said curtly, hoping to discourage further questions.

"Oh."

She seemed troubled, and he wanted to assure her she had nothing to fear, she was far lovelier than the countess of Kincreag had been, but he held his tongue.

"Were they married long?"

"I know not."

"Any children?"

"No."

"So he's in need of an heir."

"Aye, it seems so." Philip was desperate to end this conversation. He stared fixedly at the manor looming closer, lengthening his stride.

"Did you ever see them together?"

"Look," Philip said, "we're back." They were several yards away from the wooden drawbridge, but Philip jogged to it. Fergus and Stephen waited in the courtyard with the horses. Though she said not another word about Lord Kincreag, Philip knew the conversation was far from over. He stopped at the door and waited for her to catch up. She took her time, strolling toward him. She stopped to exchange a few words with Fergus, who held the reins of a cream-colored mare. She stroked the horse's nose, and Fergus nodded emphatically. The other horses shied and snorted as she walked past, and Horse even managed to jerk free of Stephen's hold and trot away. Stephen swore, chasing the beast across the courtyard.

Isobel didn't seem to notice. When she finally joined Philip, he opened the door for her.

"I need to gather a few things. Am I allowed to go up to my room alone?"

"Aye—just hurry. We must leave."

He watched her disappear around a corner, then joined his men.

"Where was she?" Stephen asked when he returned with a nervous Horse.

Philip frowned at his mount, stroking his neck until he calmed. "Never mind—just listen carefully. No one is to speak to her about her betrothed, Lord Kincreag. Do you understand?"

Fergus nodded, but Stephen scowled.

"I canna talk about her father. I canna talk about her husband. What *can* I talk to her about?"

"I don't see any reason why you must speak to her at all."

Fergus made a choking noise as Stephen just stared at Philip in disbelief. Philip sighed, realizing how absurd it was for him to forbid Stephen to speak to her. *Especially* Stephen, who spoke to anyone who stood still long enough to listen.

"Talk about yourself—you're good at that. Talk about Fergus."

"Me?" Fergus said gruffly, smoothing his hair down self-consciously. "What would ye say aboot me?"

Stephen grinned. "I'll tell her how your wife is always winking at me when you're not looking—Ah!"

Fergus grabbed Stephen's sack of food and sent it sailing across the courtyard.

"Little bastard," Fergus grumbled, when Stephen ran off to fetch his bag, still grinning. He turned back to Philip. "Don't you think someone ought to tell her *something?*"

"No. Not our place."

Stephen returned with his sack. "Our duty is to find the people and deliver them to the lion's den—but never tell them what awaits them."

Philip shrugged. "If the lion pays in gold, what do I care what he does with his prey?"

"Spoken like a true Highlander."

Philip whirled at the voice behind him. Isobel was there, a small black-and-red checked arisaid draped around her shoulders and secured at the breast with the MacDonell of Glen Laire brooch—a griffin and a dragon, their tails entwined. Her gloves were on, and she carried a small leather satchel. She smiled at his dumfounded expression.

"What are you wearing?" he managed to choke out. It was unusually small, hanging barely to her waist and rather strained about her shoulders. It took him a moment to realize it was a child's arisaid.

She walked past him and mounted her horse. Stephen and Fergus gripped the other horses' bridles as they tossed their heads and skittered away from her, eyes rolling.

"What does it look like? It's what all the Highland women wear, isn't it?" She tapped the horse's sides and cantered across the courtyard before reining in to look back at the men still staring after her.

"Come on. I want to go home."

Stephen couldn't get his horse to stand still long enough to mount and was berating the beast in an ear-singeing stream of obscenity.

Isobel nodded her head at the horses. "Don't worry, they'll get used to me and stop that soon enough."

Philip stared narrowly at her a long moment, hands on hips, wondering why—or more appropriately, *how* she frightened their horses. Bizarre. Her own horse was docile as a cow.

He scanned the courtyard. No one had come to see her off. Some of the servants watched her departure warily, but not one friendly face. With a quick nod to Stephen and Fergus, they finally managed to mount and leave Attmore Manor behind.

Chapter 4

Isobel hadn't gone far when the sound of galloping hooves quickly surrounded her. She said, not looking at the man beside her, "We *are* cutting through the forest? It's quicker, you know."

"Aye." Sir Philip made some gesture that Isobel didn't quite catch, since she was pointedly trying to ignore him. Stephen and Fergus rode ahead.

She adjusted her arisaid self-consciously; still embarrassed from the way he had looked at her. She must not be wearing it correctly. It wasn't her fault. It had been twelve years since she'd worn the thing. A horrible thought struck her. What if they were no longer the fashion in Scotland, and he thought her a fool?

She tightened her jaw. He could think her a fool all he wanted, she didn't care.

"Have you no lady?"

Isobel frowned at him. "Lady?"

"A female servant?"

"Oh . . . no." She didn't add that she hadn't had one for years—the Attmores couldn't find anyone willing to be a personal servant to her. They were all afraid. He seemed troubled—no doubt by the prospect of three men and one woman traveling alone. Isobel wasn't concerned. If her father trusted them, so did she.

"Why are you wearing that?" he asked, his voice low.

"Because we are going to Scotland, are we not? This is what I wore when I left. It only seems right that I wear it when I return."

"That is . . . uh . . . the verra same one, too, aye?"

She shot him a narrow look. "It is."

He was silent for a moment, then said, "You must remove it. We cannot travel through England and the lowlands looking like redshanks."

"I am not ashamed of what I am."

His large, gloved hand rested on his thigh, the reins gripped loosely in his other. He certainly looked nothing like a Highlander. Not that she'd seen many in the past decade. Her father was the most recent, two years past, and he always brought a few clansmen. When he visited he didn't wear the belted plaid, or breacan, as he called it. He wore plaid leggings, or trews, and a plaid about his shoulders like a cloak. But he still looked a Highlander. Sir Philip was dressed like a common knight; nothing, but perhaps his overlong hair and faint Scottish burr marked him as aught else. He could easily pass for a lowland Scot.

"You're implying that I am ashamed?" he asked.

She shrugged. "You're dressed like an Englishman."

"I'm in England."

"You shouldn't pretend to be something you're not." She bit her lip and looked away. She sounded like a self-righteous ninny—and a hypocrite at that. She certainly didn't go about advertising she was a witch. She hoped the conversation would go no further—perhaps he would forget she'd said that.

But she was not so lucky. "You shouldn't wear an arisaid if you dinna know how. And if you're going to wear one, at least wear one made for a woman."

Isobel's face flamed. She fingered the black-and-red fringe of the arisaid, keeping her eyes averted. "It's been a long time since I wore it."

"Take it off," he said gruffly. "You brought a cloak, I trust?"

"What? I don't want to."

"I dinna care. You can think what you want of me—it's nothing to me. However, I have no intention of being attacked or killed because you dinna ken any better. Now take it off."

Isobel puffed incredulously. "You expect me to believe someone would kill me because I'm wearing this? That's absurd!"

"I dinna care what you believe." His voice froze her. His dark eyes glinted beneath thick brows. "I will not take any chances."

Isobel knew she should obey him—her father said he trusted Sir Philip above all men, so he must know what he was doing. But dammit! She felt humiliated and angry. And at the moment she hated him. He was cold and unpleasant and nasty. He thought she was a fool for wearing a child's arisaid and she felt like one now.

But she'd never been one to let on how she truly felt. Unfortunately, she couldn't control the heat that had flushed through her, burning her cheeks and undoubtedly staining them crimson. But that could be attributed to any number of emotions. She chose to let him believe it was anger—which she was feeling in no small amount.

"No."

When he didn't respond she glanced at him. He stared straight ahead, his narrowed gaze fixed on the distant forest, his whiskered jaw bulging. He looked dangerous and capable of great violence. A frisson of fear ran through her, and she looked forward quickly, her heart tapping insistently in her throat.

"Did you say no?" He sounded as if he spoke through clenched teeth.

"I did."

A muscle ticked in his jaw. His gaze cut to her, sharp as steel. "Why would you say no?"

Pleased she was affecting him, however adversely, she ran her gaze quickly up and down him, and said, "I don't like your behavior."

"So you defy me?"

"You are not my sire."

"But I have your sire's authority—you read the letter. You are my charge until we reach Lochlaire."

"Oh, such conceit! Does everyone bow in obeisance to your great authority, Sir Philip?" When he just stared at her, speechless, she plunged on, "Well, I am neither impressed by nor afraid of you. And I do not think anyone will murder me in my sleep for wearing a plaid about my shoulders. That, sir, is the end of it."

He stared straight ahead. After a moment he gave a jerky nod, as if he were in some silent conversation with himself, and spurred his horse forward, leaving her alone.

Isobel closed her eyes quickly and let out a shuddering sigh of relief. Her heart pounded and sweat dewed her upper lip and forehead. It trickled between her breasts. What a difficult man! She quickly opened her eyes again, lest he look back and think he'd upset her.

He was conversing with Stephen and Fergus, and after a moment Stephen reined in his horse while Sir Philip and Fergus continued onward. Stephen's mount pranced impatiently, waiting for Isobel to catch up.

When they were riding side by side, Isobel turned to look at the young man. He was broad-shouldered and heavy-chested. A wildflower was tucked incongruously into a hole in the sleeve of his jack, the bright purple brilliant against the buff leather. Sandy whiskers covered his chin. His thick blond hair was pulled back from his face and secured at his neck with a leather tie. Like Fergus and Sir Philip, he was bareheaded.

"For men who are trying to blend in you're remarkably ignorant of the English love of hats."

"Och—not ignorant, Miss. I just hate them."

Seeing Stephen had a ready and friendly smile, Isobel relaxed. After a moment, she said tentatively, "Am I wearing the arisaid wrong?"

Stephen's pale blue gaze inspected her, then he shrugged. "I dinna really pay much attention to such things, but aye, it seems so. You'll have to ask Fergus or Philip. I'm not a redshank myself."

"You're not?"

They entered the cool dark of the forest.

"My uncle is what you might call a frontier lord—or at least that's how he likes to style himself. His lands are close to the Highlands, and so the king often calls on him to deal with the more unpleasant redshanks. But my uncle prefers to make friends with them, and so sent me to foster with the one of the Colquhoun clans."

Isobel's eyebrows shot up. "Sir Philip is a chieftain?"

"Nay—not yet, at least. Perhaps not ever, though he is heir."

"Why are you with Sir Philip then and not with his father?"

Stephen shrugged. "Because I'd rather be, and since no one at Sgor Dubh seemed to care what I was doing—I'm with Philip. He can teach me more than his sire ever could."

Isobel snorted, causing Stephen to raise a brow in amusement.

"You dinna believe it? He can find anything."

"I can find things, too," Isobel said. In fact, she was rather good at it. Probably better than Sir Philip.

Stephen shook his head. "No, I mean really find things—well, mostly people, but he found some sleuth dogs once and a stolen cow. He's so good, people pay him. Lots."

"Why is the son of a chieftain tracking beasts and criminals?"

Stephen looked thoughtful, then said, "It's probably because of his sister. She's the only person he's never found. But then, so far as I know, he wasn't in the business when she was lost."

"His sister?"

"He doesn't talk about it much, but Fergus has told me some, and I did hear a good bit of it from his stepmother when I was at Sgor Dubh." He grimaced as if the memory were extremely unpleasant.

Isobel fell silent, thinking about this new piece of Sir Philip. She wanted to know more, but Fergus and Sir Philip had fallen back a bit. Sir Philip twisted around in his saddle, watching them both suspiciously.

Stephen noticed Sir Philip and cleared his throat. "Uhm . . . .I was wondering if you might not wear that . . . thing?"

Isobel shot a poison glance at Sir Philip. He faced forward abruptly.

"So you were sent to charm me into removing the arisaid."

Stephen grinned rakishly. "Am I? Charming?"

Isobel couldn't help but laugh.

He laughed, too, but kept at her. "I pray you—take it off. If I don't succeed, I vow he will thrash me tonight so I canna sit a horse."

Isobel sobered immediately. "What? That's horrible! He would beat you for something he couldn't do himself?"

Stephen nodded emphatically. "That and more."

Isobel hesitated a moment, but Stephen's expression was so earnest she unfastened the brooch securing the plaid and swung it off her shoulders. She folded it neatly and laid it across her lap. The forest was cool, but she'd always enjoyed the chill bite of the forest air. She breathed in deeply the scent of trees and damp leaves and earth.

"There," she said. "That should satisfy his majesty."

"Oh, aye." Stephen grinned and withdrew the purple flower from his sleeve, offering it to her gallantly. "My thanks, Mistress MacDonell, you're a kind woman."

Isobel accepted the flower, her cheeks warm. "Think nothing of it."

"When I saw it, I thought how bonny it would look in your hair."

Isobel's face was in full flame now. She obligingly tucked the flower behind her ear and preened momentarily. He nodded admiringly.

"I don't understand all this fuss about a plaid."

Stephen grew serious. "Well, he's right to make a fuss of it. I'm a lowlander, but the redshanks are my neighbors—I ken." He tugged on his reins, bringing his horse closer to hers, as if to tell a secret. He tilted his head toward her, his eyes fixed on the men in front of them. "People have a verra low opinion of the redshanks. I did, too, ye see, so 'tis no lie I'm telling you. The mountains are like a great wall, keeping the redshanks in and us out. And the lowlanders like it that way. But sometimes redshanks do come out, and when they do, folks assume it's to cause mayhem. And well, most of the time they're right."

When she just frowned at him, he said, "When folks see a Highlander outside the Highlands, he must be guilty of whatever crime has been committed recently. And if none has been committed, well, then he must be minding to. So they're quick to put a stop to it. So you see, as soon as a redshank is spotted outside the Highlands, people expect trouble and are on the defensive—often attacking afore asking questions." Stephen shrugged, straightening in his saddle. "We dinna need that kind of trouble. So it makes sense to look like everyone else."

"That does make good sense," Isobel admitted grudgingly.

Stephen grinned and winked. "I knew you'd understand if someone just explained it to ye. Dinna blame Philip—he's not good at that kind of thing."

"What kind of thing? Explaining obscure orders?"

"That . . . and conversation in general—until he knows ye real well, that is. He's an honorable man, Mistress MacDonell, and will guard you with his life, I vow it. But he doesna often see why he needs to explain himself to others."

"My thanks for not being as obtuse as your leader."

Stephen chuckled.

"Now that that's out of the way, tell me, how was my father when last you saw him?"

The humor fled from Stephen's face and a blush crept slowly up his neck. "He was . . . uh . . ." He seemed to struggle for a word, then his eyes lit up. "He was verra talkative. He had lots to say. Instructions, warnings—the like."

"Warnings?"

"Oh, you know. 'Take care of my daughter,' that type of thing."

Isobel opened her mouth to ask another question, but Stephen blurted out, "Did I tell you my da knew the Scots Queen Mary? The one your queen beheaded?"

Isobel's brow furrowed. "My queen? I'm Scots, too!"

"Oh, sorry. I canna stop thinking you're English. Anyway, the one the English queen beheaded?"

Isobel sighed. "No, you did not tell me."

Stephen excitedly launched into the tale of his plotting father and uncles, and Isobel resigned herself to learning no more about her father. Sir Philip set a grueling pace that Isobel was unaccustomed to, and soon they left the forest behind. Though her bum and thighs ached, and her face was gritty with road dust, she refused to complain. She would not give Sir Philip any more ammunition to judge her with.

Stephen was an entertaining companion and made the hours go by more quickly, but soon the pressure in her bladder and the gnawing in her belly caused her to speak up.

"Stephen?" she interrupted.

"Aye?"

Isobel watched Sir Philip's broad shoulders ahead of her. He didn't look the slightest bit weary. Did he not function like a normal person? "Will we be stopping soon?"

"Not likely."

Isobel tried not to slump dejectedly. "I'm so hungry— don't you eat?"

"Och, aye," he said, digging around in a sack tied to his saddle. He came up with an egg and some bread. "Here."

Isobel smiled weakly, accepting the gifts. "Thank you." She hesitated, then added, "That's not all. I have other . . . pressing needs."

"Ohh . . ." Stephen said, looking very wise. Then before she could say another word he yelled, "Philip—we need to stop." When Philip reined in and fixed a thunderous frown on Stephen, the lad jerked his head at her meaningfully. " 'Tis a woman thing."

Isobel nailed her smile to her face and merely raised her brows in question. Philip sighed and scanned the sky briefly. "Verra well."

They left the rutted road and dismounted. Isobel trudged through the tall grasses heading for a particularly large, flowered shrub a dozen yards away. It took her a moment to realize she was being followed. She turned to find Sir Philip a few steps behind.

"Could I have a moment?"

He nodded at the bush. "I'll wait on the other side."

Isobel gaped at him. "What is this? I cannot relieve myself without you or one of your henchman hovering over me?"

His brow lowered threateningly. "Lord Attmore might have let you run wild, but I won't."

Isobel flung her arm toward her bush. "I'm merely want to squat behind the bush, not burn it."

"Nevertheless, I am responsible for your safety."

Isobel gave the bush a considering perusal. "I suspect the bush has no designs on me—but you can never be too sure." She snatched up a tree branch and batted at the leaves experimentally. White flowers showered to the ground. "See, it's perfectly harmless. No heathens hiding within."

He watched her antics with thinly veiled annoyance. "You may jest if you like, but I'm going nowhere. Finish your business so we can carry on."

Temper simmering, Isobel shoved her egg and bread at him, and hurried around behind the bush. She was horribly embarrassed and so talked loudly. "I trust I saved Stephen a thrashing?"

"A thrashing?" came his voice through the bush.

Isobel waved away the buzzing insects. "Yes. He said if he didn't succeed in getting me to remove the arisaid, you would thrash him so he couldn't sit a horse."

There was a moment of silence, then she heard a deep rumbling. It took her a moment to realize he was laughing.

She struggled with her garments, but by the time she'd rounded the bush he was sober again, only a faint softening to his firm mouth hinting that he had ever experienced humor.

"I'd wondered why he winked at me."

"So it was a lie?" she said. "A trick?"

"Stephen is good at sweetening the lassies—though I'll admit I expected you to be a bit old to fall for pretty words." He reached toward her hair, the large, gloved fingers brushing her cheek accidentally as he touched the flower. Purple petals fluttered to the ground. "And childish gifts."

Isobel removed the wilted flower from her hair and threw it on the ground. "I am not yet a hag!" She brushed the stray curls away from her hot face and tried to summon some dignity, though considering her situation, it was becoming increasingly difficult. She snatched her food from him. "And I felt pity for him. I never want to be responsible for another's hurt."

He seemed taken aback by her outburst. "I did not call you a hag. You're just . . . mature for a maiden."

To her horror tears burned at the back of her eyes. "Apparently my betrothed is not so repulsed by my advanced age!"

"Well, you're practically an heiress after all—"

Isobel let out an enraged breath and whirled away from him, heading for her horse. It was worse that she'd thought these things herself—but to hear them from such a man was more than she could swallow.

She'd only gone a few paces when he caught her arm, swinging her back toward him. Before she could let loose the fury on the tip of her tongue, he said, "Forgive me— I've mucked this up. I meant none of that as it sounded. I vow it, I do not think you're a hag. Heiress or no, ye're verra . . . bonny."

Isobel's anger dissipated, and a different kind of heat crept up her neck. "Please don't choke on your lies for me."

His jaw hardened, and he closed his eyes briefly. "It's not a lie—I vow it, I just feel . . . foolish, saying it."

Isobel considered him from beneath her lashes. He still held her arm, his grip firm but not punishing. Her heart stuttered when she met the dark eyes gazing down at her. His wide mouth was compressed with regret, his eyes fixed intently on her. Waiting.

He released her abruptly, and she swayed, her watery knees almost giving way. She caught herself and smiled up at him. The moment was becoming awkward, but Isobel couldn't seem to form any words. *He thinks I'm bonny!*

He cleared his throat and looked at the horses. "May I ask a question?"

She nodded.

He frowned at his mount. "Did the Attmores treat you well?"

She nodded slowly. "Yes."

His frown deepened, and he fixed it on her. "They didna even come out to see you off. You lived with them for twelve years."

Isobel looked at the ground. She drew in a deep breath, wondering what to say. Her father's warning had found its mark. She'd been drained last night after Sir Philip had left her. Experiencing her mother's death had been harrowing, and she'd not realized how deeply it had affected her until she'd returned to her bed, exhausted from the vision and sparring with Sir Philip. It was often that way when she saw violence. Her father knew it. That was why he'd sent it. He wanted her to feel what would happen to her if anyone believed her a witch.

But her father's letter also indicated Sir Philip knew about Lillian MacDonell and didn't credit it. So long as he believed *she* didn't credit it either, she was safe from him.

She met his eyes and decided on the truth—or at least part of it. "They were afraid of me. It's not that they didn't care. They did, in their own way, and treated me with great kindness and consideration. But I was a constant reminder of . . . bad things that had happened."

"They think you're a witch."

She nodded.

He looked back to his horse, his brow furrowed meditatively. "Why are the horses afraid of you?"

"I know not."

Isobel couldn't take her eyes off him. He was the most beautiful man she'd ever seen. She wondered if her betrothed was as handsome.

When he turned back to her his expression had smoothed, was gentle almost. "Come," he said, tilting his head toward the horses. "We must be on our way."

Isobel nodded and followed him, her palms damp inside her gloves. She longed to take them off and decided she would once they were riding again. They stopped at her horse, a cream-colored mare her father had brought as a gift on his last visit. Philip looked around. Fergus examined his horse's hooves, but Stephen was nowhere in sight.

Philip stroked her horse. "We'll rest the horses here."

Not knowing what else to do, Isobel removed her gloves and began eating her bread. Philip had grown quiet, his hand absently resting on Jinny's withers. He stared at her hands.

She stopped eating, her heart leaping fearfully. Why would he stare at her hands so intently? She tried to remind herself that he had no reason to think her hands were any different than anyone else's, but the intensity of his gaze was almost a physical thing, as if he held them again, as he had last night, stroking at her wrist . . .

"Your burn is better?" he asked.

"Yes. I'd forgotten about it."

"I noticed yesterday—you wear gloves inside, but not outside."

"I've been wearing them outside all morning. I only took them off to eat."

"I'm not talking about today."

Irritated, she said, "My hands were cold."

"It was warmer inside Attmore Manor than outside—something you won't often find in Scotland, mind you."

Rather than address his question, she asked, "Why is that?"

"It's verra cold in the Highlands. The best you can hope for is to get out of the wet wind."

Isobel smiled. "Good, I love cold weather."

"It snows, too."

"How exciting! I think a snow-covered landscape is beautiful, don't you agree? And it's been years since I've engaged in a real snowball fight. The Attmores' sons and daughters were such mealymouthed boobs—too good to play anything fun."

The sides of his mouth twitched as if he were holding back a smile.

"Why, Sir Philip, I believe you think I'm not suited to your harsh Highland climate."

He turned his gaze on her, the corners of his mouth deepening into a smile. Her breath caught. Dimples dented both his cheeks. A smile transformed his whole face. "I think you'll do just fine, Mistress MacDonell."

"If we're to travel together, you must call me Isobel."

"I'd rather not. It's unseemly that you travel alone with us. I'll find a lass to tend you in the next village."

"I can tend myself, thank you. No need to waste any coin."

"Mistress MacDonell—"

"Prithee," Isobel said, an edge of irritation to her voice. The last thing she needed was a servant to reveal her secret. The men at least would keep an appropriate distance. "Call me Isobel. And I don't want a servant. My father trusts you with my life—he wouldn't do that if you weren't worthy."

He focused on her horse again, stroking it silently. She gazed at his profile, so strong and masculine, and asked, "What happened to your sister?"

He stiffened, his hand dropping from her horse. "Mount up."

Without sparing her another glance, he strode away from her, yelling at Stephen to get his arse back there posthaste.

Isobel sighed and stared down at her bare hands. Should she try to discover what she could of him? It ate at her, her curiosity about this man. She couldn't remember the last time she'd desired to know so much about another. Her hands curled into fists. She could not. Her mother had frowned on probing others without their knowledge.

She snapped out her gloves and pulled them on briskly. Besides, there was always the possibility she would discover something she didn't want to know.

Chapter 5

〜

It was nearly dark when they stopped for the night. Isobel's entire body throbbed, the lump of dread in her belly finally drowned out by something much more painful. She tried very hard to hide her discomfort, but knew, when Stephen grasped her elbow to help her to a blanket he'd spread out, that she fooled no one.

While the men tended the horses, Isobel tried to relax, surveying their campsite. They'd made good time, despite the muddy roads, but they were still in England. It was clear that Sir Philip hadn't wanted to stop. He'd argued with Stephen that there was no cover, but when Hadrian's Wall had come into sight, they'd ridden for it.

Isobel leaned against the crumbling wall that stretched away as far as she could see. She wondered how they were going to get over it. She had no recollection of the wall on the frenzied journey south twelve years ago. If they'd crossed it, surely she'd remember. It was as tall as Philip and thick with fuzzy moss, which served as nice padding, protecting her aching back from the stone. They were at the top of the rise, and in either direction she could see the wall ripple away into the distance like a ribbon.

Fergus built a fire. He smiled and nodded to her, but

went about his work silently. She could hear Stephen help-ing Philip with the horses, chattering nonstop. Isobel gazed up at the waxing moon. Soon it would be May Day. The thought brought forth a flood of May Days past. Her fondest memories were those in Scotland, before she'd been sent to England. Her mother always planned the local celebrations, and Isobel and her sisters would be put to work picking flowers. They did more playing than picking, but Lillian MacDonell never seemed to mind. Isobel sighed deeply and heartfelt, missing her sisters and regret-ting the years they'd lost. Her foster sisters had never filled the emptiness inside of her from being torn from her fam-ily. She wondered, as she oft did over the years, what her sisters, Gillian and Rose, were doing and where they were. Though she'd begged him for information, her father told her naught and wouldn't allow her to write them, for fear the letters would be intercepted. Would she see them again when she returned to Lochlaire? Her heart swelled at the thought, giving her a new sense of hopefulness about the journey.

"Tell me, Fergus," Isobel said, "does my father still cel-ebrate Beltane as he did when I was a child?"

Fergus glanced up at the moon. "Nay, lassie. Things have changed in Scotland—and prithee dinna call it Beltane—ye might make folks suspicious, and that's the last thing ye want to do. They've burned lasses for little more than suspicions."

Isobel's bones were as cold as the stones at her back. "We cannot even celebrate May Day?"

Fergus straightened, the fire blazing, and dusted off his huge hands. "Weel, I didna say that. Folks still do celebrate it. It's the kirk that doesna like it. They've stopped it in lots of places."

"Glen Laire?"

"Och, no—no one tells yer da what ter do. He stopped last year when . . ." He blew out a long breath, his cheeks above the copper beard reddening. "I better go see what Philip wants."

"But he didn't call you . . ." It was too late, Fergus was gone.

Isobel balled her gloved hands in frustration. There was definitely something odd going on. They were hiding something, and Isobel meant to find out what.

Stephen joined her moments later and eased down before the fire. He passed her some dried meat and fruit, and a skin of ale. Isobel practically ripped her gloves off. She took the skin between her hands and leaned back against the wall, as if she were merely resting, and closed her eyes. Many people had touched the skin, and she received a jumble of confusing pictures—the most surprising being Stephen and a young woman engaged in a passionate embrace. Isobel cracked an eye at the lad, but he was quiet for once, eating and staring into the fire.

Alan MacDonell. She focused on her father, imagining his face, his scent, his voice, but there was nothing. The visions dimmed to nothing.

"Are you going to eat that?" Stephen asked.

Isobel opened her eyes. He'd finished his meal and was eyeing hers. She put a protective hand over her food and nodded.

"Could I have a drink then?"

"Oh—yes." She passed him the skin, wondering who his lady friend was. She couldn't just ask—another frustrating aspect of her gift. To ask was to reveal she was privy to information she couldn't possibly know, and asking leading questions often grew tiresome before she ever learned anything.

The crunch of footsteps drew her attention to Fergus

and Sir Philip's approach. She watched Sir Philip beneath her lashes. His face was shadowed, thoughtful. He'd not spoken to her since she'd asked about his sister. She tried not to be disappointed, but it was hard. For a moment it had seemed as if he truly *liked* her. And that had made her inexplicably happy.

He lowered himself to the ground beside her, and it took her a moment to realize he watched her. She met his eyes questioningly.

"There's a village not far from here—half a day's ride—we passed through it on our way to fetch you. We'll stop there tomorrow so you can rest in a bed. Do ye think ye can hold out till then?"

Isobel shrugged. "I'm fine—don't stop on my account. I'll not slow you down."

Philip poked at the fire. "It's a little late for that."

Isobel straightened indignantly. "What mean you? I've not complained once. I've kept up just like a man!"

Philip snorted, dipping his hand into a sack and coming up with a handful of dried fruit. "Hardly. We've covered half the distance we would have without you."

Isobel looked at Stephen and Fergus, who both averted their eyes politely. She glared at Sir Philip. "Well, forgive me. I didn't ask you to ride at a snail's pace. That's your doing, so don't blame me."

"If we'd gone any faster, I'd have to carry you the rest of the way. You can barely walk."

"I'm perfectly fine. Just a little sore, but I'm sure it will be better tomorrow."

Philip chuckled, and had Isobel not been so angry, she might have swooned at the deep rumbling of his laughter and the way it lit his dark eyes. Instead, she asked harshly, "Why are you laughing at me?"

"You'll not feel better on the morrow—I vow it. In fact,

you'd best eat up and get some sleep. We're leaving at first light."

"In addition to being a bloodhound you are also the expert on sore arses?"

Stephen snorted through his nose, and even Fergus stifled a loud guffaw.

Sir Philip grinned unrepentantly. "I am at that."

Isobel tried to hold on to her anger—but it was difficult with him smiling at her like that. Her lips quivered to respond, so she looked away.

"As for sleep," she said, eating a dried berry, "I never retire so early."

Philip shook his head in amusement.

"I know," she said, sitting up, alert. "Someone tell a story." Stephen leaned forward eagerly, but Isobel cut him off. "Not you, Stephen. I'm sure we've heard all of yours. What about Fergus?"

Fergus shook his head gruffly. "Och, no—mine aren't fit for such gentle ears."

Isobel rolled her eyes and turned to Philip. "Sir Philip? Surely you have a story."

Philip didn't say anything for a long moment, staring at the ground thoughtfully. "No—I think I'd rather hear a story from you, Mistress MacDonell."

When he turned his dark gaze on her this time, her skin felt hot and prickly. He held her eyes until she felt sweat trickle between her breasts. "I . . . I don't know any stories." Her voice sounded breathless, unfamiliar.

"I think you do. Tell us what you know of Clan Colquhoun."

Isobel settled against the wall, drawing a blanket over her. It was quite cool out, despite the fact she was being assaulted with odd waves of warmth.

"I know Colquhoun is a small clan, and there are several

families that call themselves Colquhoun—several minor lairds and the chief, The Colquhoun—Sir Humphrey."

"Aye, my father is a chieftain who owes fealty to Sir Humphrey."

"I know you hate the MacGregors."

"And they hate us in equal measure."

"I remember . . . when I was ten, I think . . . you must have been fifteen."

The humor fled from Philip's face, and he watched her intently. "Aye."

"You were fostering with my father. I used to come out and watch the men train sometimes. I asked my father who you were, and he told me you were a Keeper of the Dogs. When I asked what that meant, he told me about some old law . . . if a person should kill another's hound he must either pay damages or guard the man's house himself for a year and a day. One day, a dog owned by the smith attacked a young boy. He killed it in the fight. The king condemned the boy to stand guard over the smith's possessions for a year and a day—that is how the lands where Sir Humphrey resides got its name."

Full dark had fallen. The fire crackled, limning their faces in red and orange. Philip continued to stare at her, his expression odd, wondering almost, but perhaps that was the fire and shadows.

"I remember you now," he said softly. "So much has happened since then . . . when I was fifteen, we still had Effie—everything was different then. Sometimes I forget what it was like . . ." His voice trailed off, his gaze traveling over her face, caressing her almost.

Isobel swallowed, her mouth like sand.

"Yes, I remember you now," he repeated more firmly, as if growing more confident in the memory. "And your sisters—such wee things, one dark, another with hair as red as Fergus's. And you . . ." He fell silent, his gaze fixed on her.

Isobel's throat grew tight, her body tense, awaiting his next words.

"You were the oldest—tall and willowy, with hair like a sunset, eyes like moss."

His eyes held her, a warm fire burning over her. Her heart throbbed painfully and her lips parted, but only a small breath escaped—a sigh almost. She'd never heard herself described so. It captivated her, to see herself as he'd seen her once.

Fergus cleared his throat meaningfully, and Philip looked away, scrubbing a hand over his face, then raking it through his hair.

"It was a long time ago," he said, his voice different now, hard.

Isobel stared into the fire, her cheeks hot, confused by the sullen ache in her chest.

She wanted to look at him but could not. She hadn't thought of him in years, but it came rushing back now. He wasn't the first lad she'd admired, but there had been something different about him. The girls had all sighed and giggled over him—Isobel included. He'd not seemed to notice any of them. But she'd been told he was known to visit a young MacDonell widow who'd taken shelter with her father. Isobel remembered not liking him after that. The widow had been nearly twice Isobel's age—several years older than Philip had been at the time. Isobel remembered the other lasses speculating on what they did when they were alone. She'd not paid much mind then, but now, the memories flooded her, and she imagined Philip in an intimate embrace with a woman.

"It certainly is warm, don't you think?" she commented.

Stephen and Fergus exchanged an odd look, and Sir Philip seemed intent on a knot in his leather gloves.

When no one seemed inclined to answer her, she held out her hand to Stephen, who was nursing the ale skin. "Could I have some?"

He passed it to her and she drank deeply. Her throat and mouth were parched and she was overwarm. What was wrong with her?

She lowered the skin and licked her lips and noticed Philip still watched her, but covertly, his dark lashes partially shading his eyes. But there was no doubt that his heated gaze was on her. Her heart tripped over itself. She looked away, murmuring something about being tired. She lay down, facing away from him, but she could almost feel his gaze scalding over her.

Someone stood abruptly, and Isobel looked over her shoulder in time to see the dark swallow Philip's tall muscular form.

"Where is he going?"

Stephen shrugged, lying back on his blanket and pulling another over top of him. "To inspect the perimeter. The borders are dangerous."

"Everything is dangerous," Isobel muttered, pillowing her head on her leather satchel.

"Aye, it seems that way," Fergus intoned from across the fire. "But dinna fash, lass, yer safe with us. Philip can smell trouble a mile away."

Isobel turned to face the two men. "What do you mean?"

"You were right when you called him a bloodhound," Fergus said. "Mind you a dog when it senses something that a man canna? Its ears prick up—sometimes it growls or goes to investigate. Well, he's like that. Sometimes his ears prick and let us know there's trouble."

Interesting. "So, you're saying, he *senses* trouble?"

Fergus nodded. "Aye, it seems so."

Isobel liked that. It comforted her. Her eyes drifted shut.

Though she felt safe and secure with these men, she could not sleep. The ground was hard, and she was sore. Her mind turned back to her father and the unease she felt about him. It would be a week or more before she was at Lochlaire; she didn't know if she could bear it. She must find a way to discover what Sir Philip hid from her.

Philip returned, and the men conversed softly. Philip's deep voice carried to her, but not his words. After a moment she heard him settle down near her. Her heart pumped in her chest, her throat tight. How odd that a mere look from him, or his nearness, seemed to send her body into some sort of frenzy. She did not like it at all and wished it would stop.

The night grew quiet except for the buzzing of insects and Fergus's soft snores. Isobel stared at the mossy wall before her, gray in the moonlight. Her mind worked on how to trick one of the men into revealing something. She considered using her gift to discover something, but was coming to the conclusion that they were not nearly as preoccupied with her father as she was and therefore touching things they held would be useless.

Except for Philip. An image of him formed in her mind, and she shut her eyes against it, but she still saw him behind her eyelids, toying with his gloves and watching her surreptitiously, his expression unfathomable. *His gloves.*

She strained, listening for any clue that they were still awake. Hearing nothing, she turned slowly. They formed a square around the fire. Philip lay beside her, his boots closest to her head. He lay on his side, facing the fire, his eyes closed, arms crossed over his chest. His hands were bare. The gloves were beside him on the blanket.

She got onto all fours, licking her lips nervously. She darted a look around the small camp. The night pressed in on them, black beyond the glow of the fire's light. Stephen lay on his stomach, his face turned away from her. Fergus was on his back, the firelight glinting in the copper of his beard, arms folded over his chest. She turned back to her quarry. He was so still he could be dead. But so peaceful.

She advanced, cringing at the swish of grass beneath her skirts. She froze, waiting for one of them to wake up, but no one moved. She let out a shuddering sigh and moved forward again. *Too loud!* Philip hadn't moved—not even a twitch. Was he perhaps *too* still?

Dammit! Her muscles were locked with fear. What would she say if one of them woke? She looked wildly around and spied the small stack of branches Stephen had piled near the fire. She'd say she wanted to build up the fire. That was all. No harm in that.

Still, she was afraid to move forward. The gloves were within reach if she lay on her belly. So slowly, she straightened her body, lowering herself to the ground. She reached out, but the gloves were still half a finger's length out of reach.

She gritted her teeth and wormed forward. Her fingertip touched the worn leather. Another wiggle and she had it. She snagged a finger. A hand clamped down on her wrist. Too terrified to scream, her head jerked up, meeting the dark narrowed eyes, her mouth opened in horror.

"What in the hell do you think yer doing?" he whispered.

Isobel swallowed convulsively, trying to calm her racing heart. "Th-the fire was dying."

"You thought my gloves would help?"

"Gloves?" She squinted at the gloves, tugging experimentally on her wrist. His grip was a vise. "I thought those were branches. It's so dark, and I cannot claim to have eagle eyes such as you."

He propped himself on his elbow and leaned closer to her. "You're lying."

"What? How dare you accuse me of lying. I'm cold. It's nothing more than that."

One well-formed brow rose. "If you seek warmth, I can oblige." He'd been whispering before, but his tone turned silky now, like fine whisky. His eyes were the color of whisky, too, she noticed. The fire reflected the amber lights, the heavy lashes that seemed to weight down his lids.

"What do you . . . ?" Her breath snagged. His hand on her wrist turned caressing, rubbing at her galloping pulse.

"Are you really so innocent, Isobel?"

As his meaning dawned on her, heat flooded her cheeks. "Why . . . I'm betrothed . . . I cannot—"

His mouth flattened, and he released her wrist. "Go to sleep." He lay back down, folding his arms over his chest again, his gloves trapped against his chest, as if to protect them from her. "On your own blanket."

Confused and embarrassed, Isobel crawled back to her own blanket and curled up beneath the coarse wool. She tried to force her mind clear so sleep would come, but she couldn't shake the feeling she'd woken a sleeping dragon— and rather than being terrified, she was fascinated.

Chapter 6

Isobel hated to admit it, but Philip had been right. Her body ached worse than it had the night before. She clenched her teeth with every jarring step Jinny took, but kept her face stoic. Stephen kept up a stream of chatter, and Isobel was glad for the sympathetic company. They followed the wall for a mile or so until they came to a crumbling gap, then headed north again.

Philip stopped frequently, to rest the horses, he said, but she knew it was to let her dismount and hobble about. He made no mention of the night before and seemed so indifferent to her she began to wonder if she'd imagined how he'd looked at her. That gave her a strange mixture of relief and disappointment. Though she couldn't remember ever having met Nicholas Lyon, he was nevertheless her betrothed and already she felt a sense of loyalty to him. She had no business engaging in flirtations with anyone. And yet, she couldn't deny she'd secretly fancied the idea of Philip desiring her.

True to his word, midafternoon they stopped in a village, and Philip rented rooms. He sent Isobel up to rest, and she didn't argue. She had no idea how long she slept, but the light outside the window was fading when she

woke. After tidying herself at the basin, she headed down
the steps to the tavern. The air was close and stank of lard
candles, sweat, and stale ale.

She peered through the gloom, searching for her com-
panions. Before she reached the foot of the steps Stephen
called to her. The three men sat at a table near the back.
Two women and a man were with them. One of the women
held a small child on her lap. His hair was a mass of dark
curls, and his face was smudged with dirt.

Isobel slid onto the bench next to Stephen.

"You look better," he said. He hailed a serving lass and
told her to bring Isobel some ale and a bowl of stew.

"I do feel better—thank you. Who are these people?"

Philip was in low conversation with the man. The
younger of the two women stared openly at Isobel. Her dark
hair was knotted at her neck and covered with a snood.

Stephen said, "Grace, meet Mistress Isobel MacDonell,
daughter of MacDonell of Glen Laire."

Isobel smiled uncertainly. "Pleased to meet you."

"Aye, Miss."

Stephen grinned. "She's your new maid."

"My what?"

"Philip said you needed a maid, and so here she is."

Isobel opened her mouth and closed it. What could she
say? "Surely such a young woman doesn't wish to leave
her family."

"Och, I'm not young, Miss. I'm sixteen—almost seventeen. Old enough to be wed." She slid Stephen a suggestive
look that he seemed oblivious to. "Sir Philip says that if
the MacDonell canna find a position for me at Lochlaire,
he'd find me one at Sgor Dubh."

"How kind of him," Isobel said, feeling strangely
uncharitable. She watched Philip impatiently. She was irritated he'd completely ignored her wish not to have a maid.

The other woman was apparently Grace's mother. The small child was growing restless and struggled down from his mother's lap, disappearing beneath the table. Isobel had not thought Philip even noticed, but when the child emerged from the other side, he caught the boy's arm. Lifting him under the arms, he passed him over the table, back to his mother. The woman accepted the child with a wan smile.

"He's a busy wee lad, aye?" Stephen observed, reaching across Grace to muss the boy's hair.

"Oh, aye," Grace said. "He's into everything. Mum canna get a moment's peace."

Isobel made a sympathetic sound. "Whatever will she do without your help?"

Grace frowned and looked at her mother uncertainly.

Isobel plowed forward. "Your mother must rely on you a great deal. I feel awful depriving her of your help."

"I'm sure the coin Sir Philip is paying her father will be of some comfort," Stephen said, holding his tankard out when the tavern lass returned with Isobel's stew.

Grace nodded. "Oh, aye, we do need the coin."

Isobel gritted her teeth but held her tongue. If she carried it any further, it would be obvious she was trying to rid herself of Grace's services.

Sir Philip and Grace's father stood and left the tavern. Isobel watched them disappear through the door, chewing her lip. She could think of no way to convince the stubborn man to forget about a maid, so she might as well resign herself to it.

The child slipped away from his mother again and crawled about under the table by Isobel's feet. He grabbed handfuls of her skirt to pull himself up and toddled to the next table to pull on a man's cloak. Everyone seemed to find the child amusing, Isobel included.

"He certainly is a handful," Isobel commented as the boy reached for a stranger's ale and took a drink, sloshing it down the front of his gown.

The men laughed and plucked the tankard from the lad's chubby fingers. The child frowned at his empty hands and moved on to the next table.

"Aye." The woman sighed, smiling fondly at the boy. "But he always makes us laugh—and there's little of that these days."

Stephen asked if there had been many witch trials, launching Grace and her mother into a detailed description of a grisly lynching a fortnight past. Isobel grew silent, the sick feeling in her belly curling and twisting. It was all everyone talked about in England, too—the witch-hunts in Scotland.

By the time Philip returned, Isobel was staring at her congealing meal and the child was across the tavern, giggling hysterically as an old man produced nuts from behind his ears. His mother never took her eyes off him, but seemed relieved that someone else was entertaining the child for a change.

Philip passed the child, paused, and retraced his steps. He hefted the child up and carried him across the tavern. The woman seemed astonished when he thrust her son into her arms.

"He's but a wean," Philip said, his voice sharp as a blade. "You canna let him wander about at will. It takes but a second's distraction, then he's gone."

The woman let out a surprised breath. "I never took my eyes off him, sir—"

"That's not true, and we both know it. You were quite involved in your conversation with Stephen when I walked in."

She became flustered. "I—I know most everyone here—"

"*Most* everyone? But not everyone?"

She shook her head. "But—"

"*But* a lot of strangers pass through this village, and all of them are not so nice. What if they had a taste for little boys, aye? I've known more than a few who do. Hell, I could snatch him up and you'd never see him again. Trust me—you'd never ken what happened if I'd a mind for evil."

The woman began to cry silently, clutching her son to her breast. Her husband cleared his throat. "That's enough, Sir Philip."

Both Fergus and Stephen watched the proceedings warily, but with no surprise. Isobel, however, was flabbergasted. She'd never seen a man give a woman such a tongue-lashing for her mothering skills. Philip turned on the man as if to give him an earful when Isobel stood, removing her gloves and placing her hand softly on Philip's arm.

"No harm's done," she said. "I was minding the lad, too. She watched him carefully, I vow it."

Isobel could feel the tension thrumming through him. When he still didn't seem inclined to let the matter drop, she squeezed his arm. His muscles were bunched tight, as if ready to spring. His whisky eyes were hazy with some long-ago pain. She felt it just from touching him, or his jack, actually; clothes retained something of their owners, though some fabrics were better than others for giving clear visions. Leather was more difficult and usually only gave her feelings.

"Sir Philip, walk with me. I need some air."

He turned to her, startled. He looked down at her hand on his arm, then back to her eyes.

She smiled encouragingly.

He took a deep breath, glancing back at the man and his

wife before nodding and letting her lead him from the tavern. Isobel was certain Stephen would smooth the situation over while they were gone; in the meantime, she meant to find out why Philip would scold a complete stranger in such a manner—and about this old pain she sensed.

Philip stopped right outside the tavern door. "What?"

"Can we not walk?"

Philip looked up and down the dusty street, filled with villagers going about their business, his fine mouth set with impatience. "I don't want to walk." He turned back toward the door, but Isobel caught hold of his arm again.

"Do not go back in there angry." She glanced around, then pulled him to the narrow alley between the buildings. He followed reluctantly. It was dark in the alley, and it smelled of rotting food and urine. He crossed his arms over his chest and stared down at her expectantly.

"Whyever would you rebuke someone like that? The lad was in no danger."

"You dinna understand. There are people out there that take bairns."

"I'm sure there are, but we were all watching the boy."

"It doesna matter!" His hand swept through the air violently, cutting off further argument. "If someone has a mind to, it doesna matter. Don't you understand?"

Isobel put her fingers to her lips and gazed up at him. Tall and dark, and quite suddenly, vulnerable. Though she didn't touch him, she felt strongly that this was about the sister Stephen had mentioned. "What happened to your sister?"

A shutter closed over his face. "That's none of your concern."

"Someone hurt her?" Perhaps his sister disappeared and was later found dead. Such things happened all the time. It had happened to the Attmores. And she'd not been able to stop it.

Philip ran a hand over his face, staring upward as if he were about to open up to her. She clasped her hands together, waiting. Then he shook his head. "Finish your dinner and go to your room. Lock the door."

"What?" He tried to walk away, but she caught his arm again. "Philip—"

"I mean it, Isobel. Do as I say."

Isobel stood in the alley, frustrated and hurt. Why wouldn't he talk to her? She left the alley and started to follow him into the tavern, but stopped. She still wanted a walk. It was too hot and close in there. And for some reason she felt as if a beehive sat in her belly every time she was near Sir Philip. After two days on horseback the last thing she wanted to do was lock herself in a dingy rented room. Besides, she'd slept all afternoon. She wasn't tired.

If she went back inside, he'd probably force her upstairs and set a guard on her. She'd just take a short stroll—down the street and back, perhaps stopping at the bakers to see if they had anything sweet left. Her mouth watered at the very thought, and that decided it. She was in dire need of something sweet. She'd be back before he even noticed she was gone.

When Philip returned to their table at the tavern Grace and her parents were gone. Philip stared at their empty places, hands on his hips, and sighed deeply.

"I suppose it's foolishness to hope they're taking Grace home to pack."

Fergus set the small bag of coins on the tabletop. "They said it wasna worth it. Grace feared ye'd harm her if she displeased ye."

Philip slumped down on the bench. He'd not meant to

get so angry, but couldn't help himself. He didn't understand what was wrong with people—didn't they understand how precious and fragile the life of a child was?

He spied Isobel's untouched bowl of stew and twisted
around to stare at the door. "Did she come in?" He glanced
at the empty stairs.

"Nay," Stephen answered readily. "She's still out there."

Philip sighed again, watching the door. She was being
stubborn and difficult because he'd refused to walk with
her. How tiresome. He didn't want to go after her. She disturbed him. Besides her being achingly beautiful, there
was something else about her that stirred him. Since he'd
first seen her at Attmore Manor he'd been preoccupied
with her, and her innocent interest in him was not helping
matters. He recognized the signs even if she didn't—the
darkening of her eyes, the shallowness of her breath, the
slow flush that stained her pale, flawless skin. If she
dragged him into another alley, he couldn't be responsible
for what he did.

He jerked his head at Stephen "Go get her."

Stephen slid off the bench eagerly and left. Philip
frowned after the lad. He'd certainly taken a liking to her.
Why that bothered Philip was a mystery. God's bones—
she was betrothed. It mattered little what he or anyone else
thought. She belonged to another man.

Stephen returned to the doorway. He caught Philip's
eye and shrugged.

Philip was on his feet. "Go check the room in case we
missed her," he ordered Fergus as he headed for the door.

"She said she wanted to go for a walk," Stephen said
when Philip joined him outside. "I'm sure that's where she
is. She'll be right back."

"Wait here in case she returns." Philip looked up and
down the street, trying to decide which way she'd gone.

He headed west, stopping in each doorway, scanning the interiors for her distinctive autumn gold curls. He didn't sense her presence until he arrived at the baker's. The front of the shop was empty. The counters were picked over, just a few hard rolls left. The soft murmur of voices could be heard from the back room.

Philip started for the door to the back when it opened. Isobel came out, her mossy eyes blank, empty. She held a bun glistening with honey in one hand, half-eaten, and in the other she held a wooden box, banded with iron and locked with a stout iron padlock. She clasped it oddly: against her middle, with her bare hand cupping the padlock. Two people entered from the room behind her, a fat balding man and his equally fat wife. If the flour coating their hands and clothes was any indication, they were the bakers. Both watched Isobel anxiously.

"What the hell are you doing?" Philip asked, moving between her and the bakers, scowling at them. He didn't like how they looked at her.

Isobel hushed him, not even turning her glassy eyes on him. She walked to one of the counters and stood there, her back to Philip. He'd had enough of her antics and grabbed her arm, swinging her around to face him. The box crashed to the ground, and her bun flew across the room.

Her expression immediately cleared. She blinked, then glared at Philip. "Look at what you've done. You'll buy me another bun, Sir Philip."

"Why did you leave? Did I not make myself clear yesterday? You are not to go anywhere unaccompanied."

"Let me go!" She looked over her shoulder at the bakers. They watched the proceedings worriedly.

"She was just helping us, sir," the man said. "Dinna fash, you can have another sticky bun—I'll not charge you. Can you find the key?"

"Mayhap—if this great beast will release me."

Philip reluctantly released her, his curiosity aroused. "What's going on here? What key?"

Isobel walked the perimeter of the room until she reached the stale rolls. Her hand hovered over them, finally grabbing one. She dug her fingers into it, ripping it in half. Something gray tumbled to the ground. She picked it up, holding it out for the couple to see. It was a small iron key.

"You dropped it in the dough this morning."

The baker came forward and took the key from her fingers. "Thank ye, Miss! I canna even remember having it near the dough."

Isobel stood several inches taller than the man and patted him on the shoulder. "It's no wonder, with that daughter of yours. You thought she was safe in bed this morning when you got up to make the bread—and she comes sneaking in. Out all night."

He opened his mouth and looked at his wife in amazement. "She's right. I did have the key then. That *is* the last time I saw it!" He smacked a hand over his face. "Thank the Good Lord no one bought these today!"

His wife scooped up the box and hurried into the back room. "I'll be right back with your sticky bun, lassie. I'll bring one for your lad, too."

Isobel's face lit up. She slanted Philip a sly look, and said in a low voice, "I get both."

Philip shook his head. "You get neither. We're leaving." He took her arm again, dragging her out the door. He didn't understand what was going on, but whatever it was, he had a bad feeling about it. The bakers seemed like decent folk, but it took precious little to rile people into a hysterical lather these days. All they'd have to do is tell someone with witch-fever about how Isobel miraculously found their key and she could find herself in a great deal of trouble. In Scotland, suspicion equaled guilt.

"Wait!" Isobel cried, but it was too late, he had her out the door and was dragging her back up the street. She tried to dig in her heels, but he clamped a hand on the back of her neck and forced her to walk beside him.

"Let go of me," she growled.

"Let's not make a spectacle of ourselves," Philip said, smiling and nodding to a frowning woman who passed.

Stephen waited outside the tavern for them. He took one look at Isobel's face and his grin faded. Once inside the tavern Philip led her to their table. "Finish your stew."

"I don't want it." She glared straight ahead, her shoulders rigid.

"I see. You only want bread."

She turned her icy green stare on him. "No—I just want you to stop shoving me around."

Philip's temper flared. He'd *never* harmed a woman. "I wasn't shoving you."

She made a rude sound. "If you're finished *pushing* me around, I'd like to go."

Philip wanted to shake her, but Stephen appeared. "I'll, uh, take her to her room." He slid between Isobel and Philip as if he were afraid Philip might snatch her away.

"Fine. And make sure she stays there."

"So I'm your prisoner?" she snapped. "I wonder what my father will think of this?"

"He'll take a strap to yer arse when I tell him about yer behavior."

Her face flushed, and her mouth flattened. Philip was afraid she might explode. He stared back at her, brows raised.

"Perhaps you should save him the trouble."

A wicked grin pulled at his lips as he imagined her bottom beneath his hand. "All you have to do is ask, lass—I'd be happy to oblige."

The innuendo was lost on her however. She glared at him and thrust out her chin. "Go ahead! I'm not afraid of you."

Philip gave Stephen a meaningful look. People were beginning to stare. At Stephen's prompting, she finally turned and went upstairs. Philip let out the breath he'd been holding. Damn, she was a hellion. Alan had warned him that she could be difficult, but he'd not anticipated these kinds of difficulties. What the hell had she been doing at the bakers? Damned if it didn't look like some kind of sorcery. That kind of behavior was deadly.

Philip ran a weary hand through his hair as Fergus joined him. He took the bottle of whisky his friend sympathetically offered. The sooner they arrived at Lochlaire the better. He didn't care if she was bruised from head to toe, there would be no more special rests for Isobel MacDonell.

Isobel was famished. She paced her tiny room, wishing for her sticky buns—even the cold stew was beginning to sound appetizing. It was well past midnight. Her single candle would soon gutter out. Isobel crossed to the window and stared down at the nearly deserted street. An old man lay on the ground outside a building across the way. A night watchman roamed the streets with a lantern, his silhouette hazy in the thickening fog.

Isobel's stomach growled painfully. Last time she'd peeked out the door, Stephen had been slumped against the wall, guarding her. She'd struck up a conversation with him, but it was cut short minutes later by Philip yelling at him to shut up or else. But surely Philip was asleep by now—and she knew if she asked nicely Stephen would find her something to eat.

She eased the door open and peered into the corridor. No candles lit the inky darkness, though there was a gray patch of light at the far end, near the stairs, from a high open window. Her eyes narrowed, probing the darkness, but could discern nothing.

"Stephen?" she whispered. When she received no response, she called again. Maybe he'd fallen asleep? She slipped through the door and into the hallway, feeling in front of her for the spot where she'd last seen Stephen sitting.

He was gone.

"Stephen?" she called again, louder this time. No answer. There were several doors in the hallway, but she had no way of knowing which one might be his. She decided to venture down the stairs herself. Perhaps the ostler would be there— or she could sneak into the kitchen and find something.

She crept quietly toward the lessening of complete darkness that indicated the stairs, her hands on the wall. She was almost there when she heard the soft creak of boot leather and something blocked her vision. She put up her hands just as she bumped into something warm and solid.

"Stephen?" she said hopefully.

"I'm afraid not, Mistress MacDonell."

Isobel froze, her hands curling into the worn leather. *Sir Philip.*

She tried to push away, but he caught her shoulders, pulling her toward the stairs. When they were both in the shadowy gray light from the open window, he glared down at her. Isobel's heart lodged somewhere in her throat, cutting off her ability to speak. What would he do? She found herself clutching at his arms, afraid he meant to throw her down the stairs in his fury.

"Where are you going?"

"I—I was looking for Stephen."

"Why?" The single word was a growl.

Isobel's eyes widened. "I'm hungry . . . he always has food."

The muted moonlight shadowed his face, emphasizing the clean straight lines of forehead and nose, the firmness of his whiskered jaw, the swell of his bottom lip.

His punishing grip relaxed. "Why are you awake?"

"I don't sleep much . . . and since I slept earlier, I'm not tired."

His gaze raked over her face. After a moment he released her, but when she tried to slip away he planted his hands against the wall, his arms on either side of her, trapping her. She pressed her back into the wood, staring up at him. He leaned close to her, and she caught a whiff of whisky. She shivered with unease—he'd been drinking. That would only exacerbate his irritation with her.

His eyes glinted. "Where do ye think yer going?"

She smiled. "Back to my room." She slid down the wall, as if to slip under his arm, but he leaned down with her, his arm still blocking her. He was trying to intimidate her. He was succeeding, but there was no reason for him to know that.

She met his dark gaze. "Prithee, don't let me keep you from your bottle—from the stench, you'll soon forget this incident."

She saw a flash of white and his deep laughter rolled over her. He leaned even closer, as if to antagonize her with the scent of whisky. Unfortunately, his nearness did not have his intended effect. She could see how silky his hair was this close, how fine and dark his long whiskers were, several shades darker than his light brown hair. How soft his mouth looked.

She averted her eyes, staring instead at the leather-clad arm blocking her escape.

"I'll let you go—so I can get back to my cups," he said sarcastically, leading her to believe perhaps he had spilled the whisky on himself, for he seemed far from inebriated. "But first, you must answer one question."

She straightened, still pressed hard against the wall at her back. He did not straighten with her. In fact, he leaned closer, bracing his forearm on the wall near her head. Her heart fluttered and her skin felt flushed and warm, but she kept her face impassive, raising a bored brow, still refusing to look directly in his eyes.

"Very well."

"How did you know the key was in the roll?"

Her pulse leapt. She licked her lips and swallowed. "Simple, really. I went to the bakers', looking for something sweet, and found the baker and his wife searching their shop frantically. I asked questions about what they searched for. From their answers I deduced they'd lost the key to their moneybox in the wee hours of the morning. What does a baker do in the wee hours?"

His mouth curved slightly, dimples denting his cheeks. "Bake."

"See? It was naught but deductive reasoning."

His lashes lowered as his gaze traveled over her face. She found she was holding her breath and struggled to breathe normally. She'd never had a man stand so close to her. The last time she was this close to a male, she was fifteen, and that seemed like a lifetime ago. Philip unnerved her. She could smell him, warm and male beneath the lingering fragrance of whisky. She could feel the heat coming off him, warming her.

"But how did you know it was in that particular roll?"

She shrugged. "Lucky guess. They told me those were left over from their first batch. I would have ripped them all apart. If I didn't find it, I would've then advised them to visit each customer who'd bought bread from their earliest batches."

He considered her, suspicion still in his eyes. She'd known at the time she probably shouldn't have helped the baker and his wife, but she couldn't help herself. Sometimes the magic seemed to swell within her, demanding release. She'd known immediately that she could find the key by touching the padlock—and why not? It was simple enough. She'd done it hundreds of times and knew how to make it look like cleverness rather than cunning. So what if it was witchcraft and not deductive reasoning? Who had to know? She thought her story was a very convincing one, and it made her bold. She stared up at him expectantly, daring him to find a hole in her explanation.

"What about your eyes?" he said.

Isobel raised her brows questioningly, wishing for just another inch between their bodies. She felt closed in, surrounded by him. Her thoughts skittered about her mind, unable to stay on his questions, straying instead to his voice, his face, his warm breath wafting against her cheek. A delicious shiver moved slowly through her, from her nape to her heels, making her eyelids heavy. She hoped he didn't notice.

"My eyes? What do you mean?"

His brow furrowed slightly, as if he were recalling something troublesome. "You're eyes were . . . odd, as if you were blind."

Isobel looked away from him, her mind racing. She often *was* blind when having a vision. And now that he'd brought it up, she remembered that moment. She'd been following the baker in her mind. He'd been carrying a huge tray of rolls to the counter.

"I'm sure you were imagining it. I can see perfectly well—perhaps not like an eagle, but adequate."

His fingers, bare and warm, touched her chin. She sucked in her breath. He tilted her face up so she was forced to look into his eyes. She was breathing hard—not just frightened, but something else that tingled through her body, making her skin unnaturally sensitive. It seemed as if she could feel the soft touch of his fingers all over her body, burning her to her toes.

"I did not imagine it."

"Then that's just the way my eyes look. I'm sorry if you don't like it."

He shook his head slightly, his gaze never leaving her face, his thumb stroking the skin of her neck. Her breasts tightened and grew heavy. Her mind was sluggish.

"That is not how your eyes look . . . it's dark, and yet I can still see you in your eyes."

She tried to laugh at his words and tell him he was being foolish, but the sounds died in her throat. And then suddenly his mouth brushed over hers, stealing her breath. She met his gaze, astonished, a strange excitement coursing through her. She wanted him to do it again, but didn't know how to ask. Perhaps it had been an accident? She stared up at him, her breath shivering between her lips, begging him in her mind to do it again.

His gazed burned over her, lingering on her mouth. She licked her lips, her own gaze falling to his mouth, wide and sensual. It had happened so fast, she wasn't even certain what his mouth had felt like, and she so wanted to know.

He whispered something to her. *Baobh le suil uaine.* The Gaelic. It had been years since she'd heard the Highland tongue—longer since she'd spoken it herself.

Before she could dig into her memories for a translation, he leaned into her and this time when his lips touched hers she pressed herself toward him. His hand slid behind her head, holding her still as the pressure of his mouth grew more insistent. She thought fleetingly of her betrothed, Nicholas, but it quickly dissolved in the warmth of Philip's mouth, the sweetness of it piercing through her.

Her lips parted, and his tongue invaded, stroking against hers, coaxing her body to melt. His taste was potent—of whisky and man. Her arms came around his neck, clinging as if she would be washed away. She'd never been kissed like this. Warmth rippled through her. He pulled her away from the wall and his arms came around her, his mouth fierce and insistent. His hands slid down her back, cupping her bottom.

Isobel whimpered when he pressed her hard against his body, miserable that she couldn't seem to get any closer. She ached and burned for something she knew he could give her.

Then he thrust her away. She sagged against the wall, staring up at him, panting, her body vibrating with lust. She'd never felt anything like it, only knew that she wanted more. He covered his face with both hands.

"What is it? What's wrong?" she asked, startled by her voice, low and husky.

He dropped his hands, but turned his face away, his jaw rigid. "Forgive me . . . I—should not have done that. I dinna ken what I was thinking, but it wilna happen again, I vow it."

Isobel blinked, confused, bereft. She felt so cold, wanted his arms around her again. Why must she forgive him? She *wanted* him to do it again. Then she remembered the earl—her future husband—and her face flooded with shame.

She turned her face away. "It's forgotten. We'll not mention it."

He gave her a hard, almost angry look, but said nothing. Isobel didn't know what to do. Some foolish part of her didn't want to leave, but she was as good as married, she had no business standing out here kissing and wanting another man. Guilt stabbed her.

She moved away from him hesitantly. When he didn't stop her, she hurried back to her room. At the door she peered back down the corridor. He still stood where she had left him, in the shadowy patch of gray, arms crossed over his chest. It was too dark to tell, but she thought he stared after her.

Baobh le suil uaine, he'd whispered. She searched her mind for the old tongue, and stiffened when she realized what he'd called her. Green-eyed witch—or witch with green eyes. She shut the door to her room quickly, leaning against it, terror sending her heart racing. What did this mean? They were in Scotland, and he thought she was a witch. Would he act on his suspicion or did his loyalty to Alan MacDonell protect her? Her father had warned her to hide her gift, and she'd foolishly revealed herself. She'd tricked the bakers, but Philip was clearly not as gullible. She stared down at her hands. She wasn't even wearing gloves.

She tore open her satchel and searched for her mother's ivory casket. She gripped it hard, her mother's love washing over her. But that was not what she needed just then. She removed the peridot charm, clasped it between her palms and forced herself to experience her mother's death until she fell into an exhausted and troubled sleep.

Chapter 7

They set off the next morning with Philip determined to banish all thoughts of Isobel MacDonell. He'd been mad last night to kiss her—he still couldn't fathom what had possessed him. He'd only meant to intimidate her, to put her in her place. Instead, he'd kissed her. And damned if she hadn't kissed him back with far more enthusiasm than any maiden—*betrothed* maiden—should.

It'd been the whisky—there was no other explanation. He hadn't thought he'd drunk that much, but apparently he had. He'd never been one to act so impulsively, especially with a woman. Well, he knew better now. He wouldn't touch another drop of whisky until Isobel was safe in her betrothed's arms.

His gaze rested on her, riding beside Stephen a few yards ahead of him and Fergus. She looked pale and tired this morning, a shade of the woman who'd purred in his arms last night. Her hair was pulled back into a bulky braid and wrapped with some kind of filmy material so its burnished color was hidden. She'd hardly spoken to him this morning. Unlike all the other edicts and warnings he'd issued, she seemed to be taking his kiss seriously, as well she should. He had no wish to duel it out with her betrothed.

And still, she had no maid. He still cursed himself for bungling that. He would try again in the next village. Hawkirk was a good-sized border town with a weekly market. They'd stayed there on their journey to England. So long as he didn't fly into another fit of rage they shouldn't have a problem finding a proper servant for her.

Fergus cleared his throat. Philip glanced at his friend.

"I heard ye last night—ootside me door. And so I took a peek, just to make sure naught was amiss."

Philip stared at his friend, then looked away. "Aye?"

"That's all I'm saying."

Philip exhaled through his nose, his mouth grim. He'd said enough. "It won't happen again."

"I ken it won't. Her betrothed is an earl, Philip—ye canna amuse yerself wi' her."

Philip's eyes narrowed at Fergus. "Is that what you think I was doing? Amusing myself?"

"I hope it wasna more than that." When Philip didn't respond, Fergus's brows lowered. "Philip? What're ye thinking?"

Philip shook his head. He wanted to tell Fergus about the bakery, but wasn't certain how his friend would react. Fergus would never harm Isobel, but still, Philip couldn't allow anyone to look upon her with suspicion. Fergus was a very superstitious sort. He would keep the bakery incident to himself. Besides, the more he thought about it, the more her explanation made sense—however suspicious it had appeared.

"You needn't worry, Friend. My good sense is not between my legs."

Fergus searched Philip's face, then smiled. "I didna think so. It's not like you to lose yer good sense over a lass. Besides, if I recall, there's entertainment aplenty in the next town to take yer mind off her."

Fergus's devotion to his young wife kept him from indulging in such activities, but neither Philip nor Stephen had anything to deter them from a night of feminine sport.

"Oh, aye." Philip grinned and winked with more enthusiasm than he felt, but it was just what Fergus needed to set his mind at rest.

When the sun was high in the sky Philip finally called their party to a halt. There was a loch nearby. Philip ordered Fergus and Stephen to take the horses down for water.

Isobel started to follow them.

"Mistress MacDonell?" Philip called.

"Yes?"

"Hold. There's something I need to say."

When she turned to him, her paleness had fled. Rose bloomed in her cheeks. Burnished blond curls escaped their plait to feather against her temples and forehead, glinting copper in the sun. Lovely, even after hours in the saddle. If it hadn't been clear to him before, it was now—he was quite taken with Isobel MacDonell. It had been years since he'd longed for anything more in a woman than a creative bed partner, but she'd awakened a dull longing in his soul. Dull because of its futility. Oh, he could seduce her—he had no doubt that last night she would have willingly ruined herself. This morning she was clearly having regrets; but he was still confident, if he set himself to it, he could overcome her resistance. But to do such a thing would be foolish and cruel—not to mention a nasty affront to Alan MacDonell and the earl of Kincreag—possibly sparking a feud the Kilpatricks of Clan Colquhoun would not be pleased about.

These were not welcome realizations, and so he said, with more gruffness than he'd intended, "We'll be stopping in another village tomorrow. You are to help no one else. Understand?"

She stared at him, unblinking, her face expressionless. "Do you understand?"

"Don't you think you're taking this a bit too far?"

He planted hands on hips, scowling. "What?"

"The protector role. Surely my father didn't intend for you to smother me."

Anger flashed through him, hard and fast. He advanced on her. She didn't retreat, though her bland mask faltered.

"Were ye so coddled in England you heard naught of what goes on here in Scotland?"

Her gaze darted away, but quickly came back to hold his. "No. I heard."

"Did ye, now? And it means naught to ye?"

"I don't understand—"

"And therein lies the problem, Mistress MacDonell. Ye dinna understand, nor do ye try to. You're too set in your stubborn ways to think for a minute that by crossing a border your whole world has changed in ways you cannot possibly imagine."

Her mouth flattened, and her cheeks grew ruddy.

"Now listen with care. You will go nowhere unless you are accompanied by Fergus, Stephen, or myself. Is that understood?"

"Yes." The single word was clipped.

"You will not offer your . . . *deductive reasoning* skills to anyone else. Ever."

She laughed incredulously. "Ever? Your control over me extends only so far as Glen Laire, Sir Philip. After that I no longer answer to you."

"Then consider it well-intentioned advice. I dinna want to hear of you burning for witchcraft, Mistress MacDonell, I vow it. And there is nothing a group of village elders likes to do so much as burn a witch. And if ye think being the daughter of a chieftain offers you some protection, you have only to remember your poor mother. She was lynched and burned; else she'd be alive today. And that was back when only the king could burn a witch—today, however . . ."

The effort to maintain her air of unconcern was obviously a strain, if the way she clasped her hands together and bit the inside of her lip was any indication. He didn't wish to frighten her further. He'd hoped mentioning her mother's nightmarish death would be sufficient, but she said, "What? What else were you going to say?"

"Today it's much easier to burn a witch, as elders all over the country have discovered. Surely you've heard? The king gave commissions to local men to try and execute witches. That means anyone who has a quarrel with anyone else can cry witchcraft and have his revenge. Anyone looking for a scapegoat to blame for their misfortunes can pick out whatever sacrifice suits them. There doesna even have to be evidence—once the finger is pointed you're as good as dead. No Scotswoman with a shred of sense would go about divining for keys. Why don't ye just carry about a toad for a familiar and give folks the evil eye? It will have the same effect."

Her mask cracked, and she stepped away from him, her throat working as she swallowed. She hugged her elbows, watching him warily. "You think I'm a witch."

Philip put his hands out placatingly. "I did not say that. Besides, whatever I think, I'd never harm you. I'm trying to protect you. Let me."

"Are you afraid of witches?"

"I'm not afraid of you."

She raised a red-gold brow slightly and, to his surprise, she reached out, sliding her hand in his gloved hand. Her hands were bare this morning, her gloves tucked in the garter at her waist. The urge to curl his hand over hers and pull her close was strong, but he did nothing, staring down at their linked hands.

"A child was lost to you," she said, her voice far away.

His head jerked up, his eyes fixed on her face. A frisson of alarm ran through him. Her eyes were blank, hazy, staring straight through him.

"That's why you yelled at that woman, why her inattention to her son angered you. It reminded you of your sister."

Philip jerked away, rubbing his hands together as if he could rub her magic from him. "What the hell do you think you're doing?"

She blinked, her eyes focusing on him. "I thought you weren't afraid of me."

"I'm not." But he was deeply unsettled. She'd been so odd. He continued rubbing his gloves together compulsively.

"Then what are you afraid of?"

He pointed a finger at her. "Stop it. Right now. Before Stephen and Fergus come back. They're good men, but not as tolerant as I am about such nonsense."

She smiled lightly. "You consider yourself tolerant?"

His uneasieness began to fade as he realized what she was doing. How very clever. She turned his threats right back on him, showing him she wasn't powerless. She had told him nothing she hadn't *deduced* already by other means.

He advanced on her again, but this time she tilted her head up to him challengingly, a slight smile on her lips.

"This game you play at is dangerous."

"It's not a game."

"You wish people to believe you're a witch?"

She shook her head. "No . . . but if I can help someone, why shouldn't I? My mother always helped others and told me I should do the same."

"Find another means to help people—one that doesn't make folks wonder, aye?"

She gave him a considering look. Her insouciance was

back as she strolled away from him. "You have spoken, Sir Philip, and I have heard."

He ground his teeth in frustration. It was like talking to a rock—except she had a poison retort for everything.

"Another bit of advice," he called after her. "I may not know the earl of Kincreag well, but I know enough to say he will not tolerate this type of behavior."

She whirled around. "What does that mean?"

"It means, you'd be wise to learn your place before we reach Glen Laire."

Her eyes flashed with anger, but there was a touch of unease there, too. "My father would never marry me to a cruel man."

"Alan sees the best in his friends—and ignores all that is unpleasant."

Her gaze raked him from head to toe. "Obviously."

He was tempted to tell the little green-eyed minx everything he did know about Nicholas Lyon, but reined in his temper. He had a suspicion that she was trying to goad him into talking, and talking about the earl of Kincreag benefited no one.

He just shook his head. "I tried to warn you." And he left her, before he said something he knew he'd regret.

She'd really done it now. Not only had Philip stopped speaking to her, but if he chanced to meet her eyes he glared at her. Isobel didn't understand what had come over her. She'd given the Attmores a bit of trouble, it was true, but she'd never been rude to them. And yet she couldn't seem to help herself with Sir Philip—he infuriated her. That, coupled with her body's melting response to the mere thought of his heated mouth and hands on her, seemed to put her in a rare mood.

And worse—she had tried to frighten him! Isobel's face burned with shame. It went against everything her mother had taught her. And she couldn't even apologize, for that would be tantamount to admitting she was a witch. *Never again. Only for good.*

But could she even use it for good anymore? Was Nicholas Lyon really such a hard man, or had Philip tossed her own game back in her face, frightening her with half-truths? If only she could see into her own future—unfortunately, touching her own things gave her no visions. How she missed Ceri. Ceri would know what to do. But Isobel was on her own now. She had only her own wits to rely on. She slanted Stephen a considering look. He was deep in a tale of how he and a cousin saved their uncle's kine from a pack of heathen reivers, his hand waving about as he spoke.

"Stephen," Isobel said, cutting him off midstory. "Will you tell me about my betrothed, Lord Kincreag?"

Stephen's eyes, blue and clear as the sky, widened. He was not an innocent, but he was decent. And he liked her. With a little persuasion, she could get him to talk about her betrothed.

"What would ye like to know?" he asked cautiously.

Isobel twisted around in the saddle. Philip and Fergus were yards behind them, well out of earshot.

"What kind of man is he?"

"Well, he's an earl—but you already knew that. He's . . . a bit reserved. Many people fear him, but my uncle thinks well of him. He doesn't believe the stories."

"What stories?"

Stephen looked away with poorly feigned confusion. "Stories? Did I say that? I misspoke. And if there are any, I canna recall them."

Isobel gave him a severe look. His gaze met hers, then bounced away, scanned the sky. "The clouds seem heavy.

A storm is brewing. What think you? The air feels thick—
and look at the trees—"

"The only storm brewing is the one I'll let loose on you
if you don't tell me the truth about Lord Kincreag."

Stephen looked around uncertainly, as if he wished to
escape.

"I *know* you know something. I thought we were
friends. You must tell me what you know. How else will I
find out? My father won't tell me, and if it's really so bad,
I doubt Lord Kincreag will. You *must,* Stephen—it's only
fair. Must I go into this marriage blind? Knowing nothing
about my husband?"

Stephen's expression was pained. He looked surreptitiously over his shoulder at Philip and Fergus, then reined
his horse in closer. "I'll tell you what I know. But you must
remember it's only gossip, so take it as such—and you
canna tell Philip I told you."

Isobel nodded.

Stephen took a deep breath. "A few years past . . . his
wife . . . well, something happened to her."

"She's dead."

Stephen nodded. "Aye, she's dead. Castle Kincreag sits
on a cliff overlooking a vast river. Some of the paths are
dangerous. She . . . fell." His blond brows arched meaningfully.

"She fell? Or someone pushed her?"

Stephen said nothing, his mouth grim.

Isobel's heart thumped uncomfortably in her throat. She
told herself it was naught more than a rumor. It wasn't fair
to condemn the man before meeting him.

"But no one knows, you said. He probably didn't do it.
It's just an unhappy incident, and cruel people love pointing
fingers—especially at one so high up as Lord Kincreag.
They can't hurt him any other way, but with vicious talk."

Stephen nodded. "Perhaps. But . . . they were at court, not a week before her death. Now, Lady Kincreag was no saint, so dinna misunderstand. My uncle used to get sore angry at how poorly she used Lord Kincreag—he said when she died, that was the best thing that ever happened to Nicholas Lyon—but you wouldn't know it today. The man hardly ever leaves his castle. And when you do meet up with him, his eyes are so dark and evil, most men canna meet them for more than a second afore they look away in fear."

"What did Lady Kincreag do that was so horrible?"

"She cuckolded the poor earl with half a dozen men— some nobles, some commoners. He called a few out, but after a time it became absurd. She was a whore, plain and simple, and he was tired of killing men because of her base nature. As I was saying, less than a week afore she died, they were at court. The night afore they returned to Kincreag, they were seen arguing something terrible. He called her some vile names that I cannot repeat—oh, she was plently foul, too—make no mistake. And it's said that he threatened, 'I ought to kill you.'"

At her horrified expression, Stephen nodded sagely, brows raised. "Not even a sennight later, she's dead. Fell to her death from the cliff. And it's said she never was one to walk along the cliff path. So why was she there at all? Hmm?"

Isobel slapped a hand over her mouth. "Oh my God! He's a murderer! I'm going to marry a murderer!"

Stephen tried to shush her, panicked. "I told you, it's but gossip. And my uncle thinks it's rubbish—and he knows what's what. No one knows if he really did it."

Isobel looked at him incredulously. "Nicholas Lyon is an earl! He can do whatever he wants so long as the king favors him."

Stephen nodded thoughtfully. "My uncle has mentioned

that King James is rather fond of Lord Kincreag. The king always appreciates a pretty face. And all knew the king didn't like Lady Kincreag at all."

"Jesus Lord," Isobel moaned, rubbing at her temples. She felt faint.

"Now, dinna go fainting on me, Mistress MacDonell," Stephen said, looking over his shoulder again. The sound of hoofbeats grew louder behind them.

Isobel fought to compose herself, but it was impossible. Had her betrothed really murdered his wife? She didn't want to believe it, but insidious doubt twisted in her gut.

"It's nearly dark," Philip said from the other side of Stephen. "There's a forest ahead. We'll camp there."

Isobel stared straight ahead, her body cold, trying to hide her unease.

"What's the matter?" Philip asked. When Isobel didn't reply, he said, louder, "Mistress MacDonell—is aught amiss?"

Isobel nailed a smile to her face and shook her head. "Not a thing."

"She's just tired," Stephen said anxiously. "That's all."

There was a long silence, then Philip said, "Fergus, ride with Mistress MacDonell. Stephen, let's ride ahead and ready the camp."

Stephen darted Isobel a frantic look, but spurred his horse after Philip's. They soon disappeared into the trees.

"I wonder what that was all aboot," Fergus said, coming to ride beside her.

They arrived a short while later at a small clearing amid tall birch trees. Philip was nowhere in sight and Stephen sat on a stone trying start a fire. Isobel dismounted, handing Jinny over to Fergus, and joined Stephen.

He didn't look up from his assault on the tinderbox. "He knows I told you."

Isobel let out a disbelieving breath. "How?"

Stephen shook his head. "I should have known—ye canna get anything past that man."

"But he could not have heard us."

"It doesna matter. He got a *feeling*—and when Philip gets a feeling he's like damn shark. He won't let up until he shakes the truth from ye—because he already knows, see? So now he's angry at me because I told you—and because I tried to lie about it."

Isobel was still speechless, her mouth agape, when Stephen looked up apologetically.

"Oh, and I'm not supposed to talk to you, so I should just leave off."

"Surely you jest?"

Stephen just shrugged, his eyes on the fire that had finally caught.

Isobel blinked, incredulous. So now Sir Philip was forbidding people to even speak to her? He'd gone too far. And poor Stephen looked so miserable. Guilt tugged at Isobel. She shouldn't have forced him to tell her. And yet, it was wrong for Philip to withhold the truth from her. It was *her* life; she had a right to know.

She stood decisively. "Where is he?"

Stephen thrust his thumb at a light path worn through the trees. "There's a burn not far."

Isobel hurried down the path, following the gurgling of water, her anger and indignation galvanizing her. She would tell him just what she thought of men like him. He claimed to want to protect her. So why would he not even tell her about Lord Kincreag? Wouldn't knowledge be protection? She circled the thick flowering bushes that banked the stream.

He knelt beside the water, shirtless. Water glistened on his broad back. His damp hair was pushed from his face.

His stared into the stream, his hands braced on his thighs, deep in thought. His ring gleamed dully in the dying light. Isobel was reminded of his kiss, and a sudden weakness overcame her. Her eyes fluttered shut. She fought against these new and unwelcome feelings, trying to steel herself for a confrontation.

She opened her eyes. "Sir Philip?"

He turned, his dark eyes pinning her, then he stood, snagging his linen shirt off a patch of grass. His chest was heavy with muscle and furred with dark hair. Isobel couldn't seem to find the angry words that had been ready to fall from her lips just moments before. Sinew shifted and flowed beneath smooth skin. She thought of how his body had felt, hard and solid against her, how she'd felt surrounded, protected.

When he'd finally donned his shirt she was able to meet his eyes. The knowing look he gave her scalded her cheeks. He stood expectantly, jack and vest dangling from his fingertips, and sword belt slung over his shoulder. "You had something to say? Or did you just come to look?"

The eloquent speech in her head dissolved into helpless anger. After a moment of useless sputtering, she burst out, "You should have told me about Lord Kincreag!"

Philip sighed. "It's not my place."

She rushed forward. "What is your place? Do you even have one?"

"Not with you. I canna involve myself in your life."

"Why? You can't even give me a warning? Do you not even care?"

Philip searched her face, his smooth brow creased with worry. "I didna want to frighten you. Can ye not forget this and give the man a chance? There's no proof he did anything wrong. His wife probably killed herself."

"Why? Because he was so horrible she chose death

over marriage to him? She couldn't bear to look in his evil eyes? He sounds like the horny himself!"

One whiskered cheek dimpled in a half smile. "Stephen's tongue runs away with itself. Pay his tales no mind."

"Why would he make such a thing up? His uncle is an earl—that makes him privy to things even you don't know, Sir Philip."

"There's little Stephen knows that I don't by now—whether I wish to know it or not." He sighed wearily. "I dinna ken what happened to Lord Kincreag's wife. I thought you didn't care what anyone thought? You said you would judge him yourself."

"That was before I heard he might be a murderer—or—or a man who drives his wives to fling themselves from cliffs to escape his evil stare!"

Philip dropped his jack and sword belt to the ground and covered his face with his hands. "God's bones," came the muffled curse. He lowered his hands and considered her for a long moment. "This is my fault. I shouldn't have said anything to you about Lord Kincreag, but you have a way of pricking my temper, lass."

"I want to know the rest."

"What more is there to say? Stephen clearly left no ugly rumor untold."

"I want to know about my father. There's something wrong with him. I know it."

He shook his head and grabbed up his sword belt and jack, pushing past her.

She caught his arm, stopping him. "Please."

He held her gaze, his jaw rigid, then looked at the ground. He gave another hard shake of his head. "I canna."

"Why? Have you promised someone?"

He said nothing for a long time, then, "I have."

Isobel dropped her hand. "I see." It was bad, whatever it

was, if her father swore him to silence. And she knew now that Philip would not tell her. If he was anything, he was a man of his word.

She turned away from him.

His sword and jack dropped to the ground behind her. His hands cupped her shoulders. A shiver ran through her, settling at the nape of her neck. She turned and gazed up at him.

"Dinna look at me so. Your father only charged me with bringing you home. Nothing more."

"And so you don't care."

His fingers tightened on her shoulders. "I'm not supposed to care."

"What do you mean? If you care, you'll feel obligated to do something?"

"Isobel—you're *betrothed*. There's nothing I can do."

Isobel laughed shakily. "What do you think I'm asking of you? I ask only for friendship. I've not asked you to intervene between Lord Kincreag and me. Regardless of what I've learned today, I still intend to marry him."

He frowned deeply. "You do?"

Isobel smiled. "Of course. It's what my father wishes. And though I must admit I'm rather . . . shaken by these tidings, my father thinks he will be a good husband, and that is good enough for me."

Philip searched her face, still frowning slightly. "Good . . . that's good. Just remember, no one knows for certain what happened to Lady Kincreag."

Isobel nodded hesitantly, her belly tightening. "But you think he did it, don't you? Why else would you not tell me and forbid the others to speak of it?"

She saw the concession to her logic in his face, but he continued to deny it. "All I know is he's . . . odd. Reclusive. And I wanted to avoid any unpleasantness—

that's why I didn't tell you." He sighed, his hands sliding up her shoulders to her neck. "I canna see you with someone like him . . . but that doesn't mean it won't work. You'll bring light into his life, and he'll be glad for it." His hands cupped her neck warmly, holding her immobile.

She thought of kissing him again, and her heart snagged. Her lashes fluttered, though she fought to appear unaffected. She sensed he would retreat if he knew how she felt.

His hands stilled. "But what I spoke of before—your little games. I dinna believe they'll amuse Lord Kincreag."

She nodded jerkily. Nicholas Lyon was probably the kind of man who'd burn his own wife if he thought he had sufficient cause. She smiled up at Philip, her lips trembling slightly. She felt so odd, filled with miserable joy when he touched her. It clawed at her heart, to look at him. Why could her father not marry her to Sir Philip?

He seemed torn, gazing down at her with obvious concern. Whatever he saw in her face made him pull her against him, his arms going around her, pressing her head to his shoulder. "It will be fine. You'll see," he murmured against her hair.

Isobel closed her eyes, her hands flexing like a cat against his chest. She breathed in the scent of him, the warmth of his body. His heart beat strong and steady beneath her ear. Mayhap it would be like this with Nicholas. Stephen had said his first wife was horrid. She would be a good wife, and he would love her and hold her as Philip held her now. And perhaps she would even feel the same way in his arms.

As her palms rested against Philip's shirt, she felt his earnest desire to protect her, and it warmed her. She wanted to do something for him, to help him somehow.

She noted the change in the tempo of his heart, beating

faster, his breathing shallow. His hands were on her arms, setting her away from him. He stared down at her, his eyes dark and unfathomable.

"Philip," she said hesitantly. "Is your sister dead? Because I feel that she's not."

He started, dropping his hands and stepping back from her. "What do you mean?"

"Stephen told me how you sometimes just know things. That you get . . . feelings."

His eyes narrowed. "Aye."

"Well, that happens to me . . . and I've had . . . feelings about your sister. It was a long time ago, I know that, and yet, your . . . unhappiness over her has not lessened. It's as if you can't say good-bye. That happens sometimes when a loved one is lost, but that's not what I feel either. It's . . . a desperate, searching sort of—"

"Stop it, Isobel!"

She came at him, her hands out. "I want to help you. I can, if you'll let me."

His jaw was rigid, his eyes slightly wild. "You canna help me. Forget about it."

"Can you not even tell me what happened to her? *Is* she dead?"

He stared at her for a long moment, then shrugged. He leaned down, grabbing his jack and sword belt. "I know not. It's been twelve years since I lost her." He gave her a hard, angry look. "And when I say *lost* her, I am being specific. She was in my care, and I just lost her. A six-year-old child. Gone. Forever, it seems. My family believes she's dead, and that I—that I am . . ."

He glared at a tree trunk, then stalked past her. Isobel's heart ached for him and she reached out as he passed, but he jerked away and disappeared into the trees.

Chapter 8

They arrived at Hawkirk without any more problems. The streets were swollen with the merchants who collected here weekly to sell their wares. If they kept up this pace, Philip would have Isobel home in less than a week. He could hardly wait.

Philip made Stephen ride with him, and Fergus was Isobel's new riding companion. Philip no longer trusted himself with her, and so made certain they were never alone. There was definitely something . . . unusual about Isobel MacDonell. Philip had always considered himself a pragmatic sort of fellow. He'd had excellent tutors and even spent some time at the Université Paris. He did not believe the rustic superstitions that a goodly part of Scotland did not question. He didn't doubt there was evil in the world, but he felt it was of the flesh-and-blood variety. And though he was a God-fearing man, he didn't believe Satan meddled in the affairs of women—young or old. As for the confessions the Scottish witch prickers had collected in reams, he attributed that to ignorance and torture.

However . . .

Isobel MacDonell was making him reconsider a few long-held beliefs. And he did not like it at all. She'd also made him think about his sister—a subject he steered clear of even in thought. It was the reason he rarely went home, much to his father's chagrin. His stepmother made sure he never forgot that he'd lost her only child.

Philip settled them in rooms above a respectable tavern and put out inquiries about hiring a servant. The landlord remembered him from when they passed through less than a week before and soon had them in a corner table with mutton, bread, and ale.

Isobel ate quietly, but with relish. Philip smiled to himself, remembering her passion for sticky buns, and stopped the tavern wench as she went by. Unfortunately, she remembered him, too.

"Oh, Sir Philip—I was hoping ye'd stop and see me on your way back." She slid her arm around his neck and bent her lips to his ear. "I can stop by yer room later."

Unbidden, Philip's gaze was drawn across the table to where Isobel sat, watching Alice or Anne—he couldn't remember her name—whisper to him. Philip caught the hand toying with his hair and gently put the lass away from him. "Sorry, lass, not tonight."

She pouted, darting a glance at Isobel, who had returned to her meal.

"Bring some of those buns with honey on them."

"Verra well." She gave Philip a long look before moving away.

When Philip looked around the table, Fergus frowned at him. Philip said in explanation, "We have to find Mistress MacDonell a maid this evening—then early to bed. This is the last bed we'll be sleeping in until Lochlaire."

He felt foolish suddenly. Why was he turning away a perfectly willing lass? And if he didn't feel like a tumble, he didn't need to dig about for an excuse. But as his gaze fell on Isobel, he knew that wasn't it either. He itched to tumble *her.* If she'd noticed the lass's flirting—which he knew she had—she showed no indication of caring. That irritated him far more than it should.

"May I have some say in choosing my servant?" Isobel asked.

"No."

She hissed through her teeth, pinning him with one of her poison stares. But before she could reply, Anne or Alice was back with the sweet buns. A basketful was set in the center of the table, and the lass was gone again, without sparing Philip another look. Isobel's mouth tightened as she stared at the buns. She seemed determined to deny herself until Stephen grabbed three. When Fergus's hand started toward the bowl, Isobel quickly snatched two buns and settled back on the bench. Philip suppressed a smile.

He was taking a drink of ale when a man and woman appeared beside him.

"Sir Philip Kilpatrick?" the woman said querulously.

Philip turned to get a good look at the couple. The woman was well dressed, a thick shawl wrapped about her shoulders and velvet hat on her head. Red rimmed her eyes, and she wrung a lace handkerchief. The man beside her was more roughly attired in woolen work clothes and scuffed shoes, but his leather mantle was very fine. He scowled with impatience.

"The landlord said it was you. You find people—for payment?"

Philip glanced at Isobel, and said quickly, "I'm not taking any new assignments now. Sorry."

He started to turn away, but the woman caught his arm. "But you must! We can pay you—double your usual fee."

Philip smiled gently. "That is doubtful." They had no idea how much he charged and would probably have apoplexy if he told them—fine clothes and all. Great lords had been known to haggle with him—but Philip never budged—except in rare circumstances.

The man tried to pull the woman away, muttering that he'd told her so, but she wouldn't release Philip's sleeve.

"Please, sir!" she cried. "It's my daughter. She's been missing five days now—I fear if we dinna find her soon, we never will."

Something heavy sank to the bottom of Philip's gut. *Rare circumstances indeed.* He looked at Isobel. Her gaze was fixed on the man, sweet rolls forgotten. He turned back to the woman. Tears welled in her eyes, and he sighed, pulling another bench to their table.

"I wasna speaking false, madam, when I said I canna help you now. We have to leave in the morning, and there can be no delay. But tell me your story and perhaps there is something I can do tonight."

The man and woman slid onto the bench at the end of the rectangular table, between Philip and Isobel. Philip didn't like the man, who sat beside him. It came to him all at once when he looked at the man's close-set eyes. The man did not care about the missing girl; Philip knew that just looking at him. Isobel stroked the woman's shoulder with her gloved hand, murmuring soothing words to her.

"Tell me everything," Philip said to the woman.

She sniffed loudly, wiping her nose on her sleeve, rather than the fine handkerchief. "My name is Heather Kennedy, and this is my husband, Ewan. We're brewers—ye might've heard of us? Our ale even makes it into the Highlands."

Very successful brewers. He suspected Ewan's place in the business had come through Heather. He was likely her second—or third, husband.

"Laurie does some sewing for the Armstrongs. That was the last time I seen her. She went to help Rhona Armstrong with her daughter's new gowns and never returned. When I went to the Armstrongs that night to fetch her, they said she'd left hours before."

New tears tracked her cheeks. "She was but fourteen, sir—and we had no quarrels. Ewan thinks she ran off with the Wood lad, but she never showed no interest in him." She held up the handkerchief. "I found this out behind the brewhouse—so she must've come home at some time."

Ewan scowled. "That damn thing had probably been lying ootside for days."

"It had just been raining," Heather said. "Would it not be filthy? But it's fresh. I say she dropped it not long afore I found it."

"The Wood boy is also missing?" Philip asked.

"Aye," Ewan said, coming to life. He sat forward, his hands fisted on the tabletop. "I heard her talking about that boy several times—and seen her looking at him, too. All sweet, she was."

Heather looked at her husband in disbelief. "Why would she not tell me? We talked many times about who she'd like to wed. She never mentioned Roger Wood. It makes no sense."

"That's because she's a worthless whore."

Philip cleared his throat and Ewan settled back on the bench, his arms crossed angrily over his chest.

"Have you spoken to Roger's parents?"

"Aye," Heather said. "They've seen naught of him either. It's true they disappeared the same day, but I cannot believe the disappearances are related."

"What kind of lad was Roger?" Philip asked.

"He was a good lad." "He was trash." Heather and Ewan spoke simultaneously. Heather gave her husband an incredulous look. "How can you say Roger is trash after all the times he's helped you?"

"I saw how he sniffed around Laurie."

Philip leaned his elbows on the table, rubbing his jaw

meditatively as he inspected the Kennedys. There was something else at play here. He was sure of it. Something both Heather and Ewan were aware of. Unfortunately, with the limited time he had he knew he'd not be able to dig deep enough to help them. But he would try. He glanced at Isobel and found her staring at Ewan with narrowed eyes.

"You are not Laurie's father?" Philip asked Ewan.

Ewan shook his head. "I married her mum a year ago—but before that I worked for Heather's second husband."

"How did Laurie get on with her stepfather?"

Heather's gaze darted to her husband, who now looked at the tabletop. "She did not like me wedding Ewan, it's true. She understood why I wed Jock, my second husband. He was also a successful brewer, and our marriage was profitable to us both." Heather stared at her husband, a line between her brows. "She didn't understand that I love Ewan—that I no longer needed to make a profitable marriage."

"So she didn't like Ewan."

Heather shrugged, releasing the handkerchief and hiding her hands beneath the table. Ewan's head had turned to watch his wife.

"She was strange with Jock, too," Heather said. "I think it must be common for a girl to . . . resent her stepfathers." Her head jerked up suddenly, her eyes intense. "But she and I—we had no quarrel."

Heather carefully avoided meeting her husband's gaze.

"Tell me how Laurie behaved in the days leading up to her disappearance," Philip said to Heather.

"I dinna ken . . . If something was wrong, she'd tell me, I'm sure of it. But she had no quarrel with me, I tell you—just that morning she'd hugged me!"

Though her words sounded sincere, she frowned deeply, her eyes averted as if she remembered something distressful.

"Perhaps we shouldn't waste each other's time?" Philip said, straightening. "If I can aid you at all, I surely cannot if you lie to me."

Heather bit her lip, her gaze on her husband.

Ewan's head jerked up at Philip's words. "You accuse us of lying?"

"I think there are things I'm not being told."

"Mayhap she *was* acting a bit odd," Heather conceded.

Philip had noticed some time ago how Isobel's gaze fixed on the abandoned handkerchief. Her hands disappeared beneath the table, then reappeared bare, gloves gone. Philip's chest tightened with the beginning of panic. He didn't know why, either. Why should he care if she removed her gloves? So her hands were hot? What matter?

Her fingers crept across the table until she touched the handkerchief with her fingertips, then, slowly, she gathered it to herself, until her hand was fisted around it.

Philip's gaze jerked up to her face, but she did not see him. Her sage green eyes stared blankly ahead. Philip glanced around the table, but no one seemed to notice. In fact, Stephen's bored stare as he picked at his teeth resembled Isobel's—glassy and vacant. But Philip knew Isobel's was not a result of boredom.

Not wanting to call unwanted attention to her, he leaned forward, focusing more intently on Heather's description of her daughter's behavior before she disappeared. He extended his foot under the table until he kicked something soft. Fergus grunted and scowled at Stephen.

Then Stephen cried, "Ow!" And straightened. "Wha'd ye do that for?"

"You kicked me," Fergus said.

"He did it." The words were whispered, but their entire table fell silent as all heads turned to Isobel. Her face had drained of color, the green of her eyes stood out vividly.

Her gaze was locked on Ewan Kennedy. Sweat trickled down her temples, plastering coppery blond curls to the sides of her face. Her hands shook.

Philip tensed. He had been thinking the same thing—that Ewan was responsible somehow—but he'd never reveal his suspicions so soon, not without proof.

"What did she say?" Ewan said, his voice dangerously quiet.

Stephen's gaze turned on Ewan. The lad was generally good-natured, but could be dangerous if provoked. He stared at the older man now with glittering eyes. "She said, you did it."

Philip knew this could not be avoided, so he said, "Why do you think that?"

Her gaze turned toward him, empty, the handkerchief still gripped tightly in her hands. "She was coming home from the Armstrongs. She'd learned not to go out alone, or he would find her. She usually asked Roger to meet her. Ewan didn't bother her if she was with someone. But Roger wasn't there. So she walked alone. At home, Mum was gone, so she went out back to look for her."

Her voice changed, became softer, higher pitched. Her reddish brows rose anxiously, making her seem younger, childlike. A chill settled in Philip's bones as his fears and suspicions sprang to life before his eyes. She was a witch. A seer. A *taibhsear.*

"He was there . . . waiting. He was angry at me for avoiding him—so I ran. I could hear him breathing, and I ran faster, not paying attention to where I was going, just wanting to escape. He caught me in the woods. He beat at me, ripping my clothes off. Then I heard Roger calling. I screamed for Roger to help me. He—he attacked Ewan—but Ewan is bigger and stronger. He beat Roger over and over again, until Roger was limp and his head hung oddly. And then he came back to me . . ."

Her voice trailed off as everyone at the table gaped at her in horror. Hesitantly, Heather took hold of the handkerchief and pulled it from Isobel's fingers. Isobel's gaze focused on Philip. Tears streaked her face; she looked as if she might collapse. *He did it,* she mouthed at him. *He killed them both.*

Ewan seemed to come to himself. "That is a God damned lie!" He turned to his wife, who stared down at the handkerchief in horrified amazement. "She has no proof! She's a liar—or—or a witch—set to ruin me!"

Isobel's head jerked. "No! I can show you where he buried the bodies."

A jolt went through Philip. Ewan stared, mouth agape.

Philip stood and held his hand out to Isobel. "Show me."

It seemed to take her some effort to slide off the bench, but she came to him, putting her hand in his. "First, take us to the brewery."

"I thought you knew where her body was?" Ewan sneered. He turned to his wife, who frowned worriedly at the handkerchief. "Lies, I tell you! She knows nothing! They're redshanks—we cannot trust them!"

Heather stared at her husband silently, her expression unfathomable, then stood slowly. "Follow me."

They followed Heather up High Street. They had attracted some attention in the tavern, and a small group of villagers followed curiously. The whole situation made Philip uneasy, and yet he would not stop it. He'd never seen the like. He'd heard all the stories of witches, but he'd never seen anything that convinced him such a thing was possible. Until now.

Heather led them through the brewery, hundreds of wooden casks stacked upon each other and secured with rope, and through a back door. Isobel stopped, her hand tightening on Philip's.

"Where did you find the handkerchief?" she asked.

Heather pointed to a spot a few feet from them.

"I need it back."

Heather looked down at the square of linen, her fist tightening on it. She didn't want to know any more. She was having second thoughts. Philip didn't know how he knew these things, he just always did in such situations. And maybe he didn't really know, but he felt it so strongly that he often went with his gut. In this case his gut told him Heather Kennedy knew this would change her life forever and was frightened.

Philip said, "If you truly wish to learn your daughter's fate, you'll have to give her the handkerchief."

"You dinna have to, Heather," Ewan said. "This a trick— something evil, I say."

"If you're innocent," Fergus said, "what have ye then to fear?"

Heather searched the burly redhead's face as if Fergus held the answers she searched for. Fergus nodded toward Isobel, and said, "Go on."

Heather thrust the linen at Isobel. Isobel tried to draw her hand from Philip's, but he held fast. When she looked up at him questioningly he asked, "Need ye two hands?"

She shook her head and balled the handkerchief in her fist. "We'll need shovels."

Philip turned to Stephen and Fergus, both of whom appeared thoroughly enthralled, their gazes fixed on Isobel. "Fetch some shovels and the town elders—then catch up." The two hurried back into the brewhouse.

When Isobel's eyes went glassy this time Philip was thankful he had a hold on her. She started walking, leading the group away from the house. Stephen and Fergus caught up, each with a shovel, before they reached the trees. Two bearded men dressed entirely in black trailed after them. They'd gone about fifty feet into the trees when Isobel stopped. Philip looked down at her. She swayed, her face white and damp with sweat.

"It happened here," she said, her voice weak, barely a breath.

Philip looked around. The signs of a struggle were not obvious, but as he looked closer, he saw them. The ground was craggy, lichen- and moss-covered stone poking up through the bracken and wild grasses. Several stones showed deep scratches in the lichen, as if the side of a shoe or boot had been kicking or struggling for purchase. Flowers that grew between the stones were bent, some wilting. The moss and ivy that grew up the side of a nearby tree had been ripped off and trailed to the ground.

"They're buried here?" he asked.

She shook her head. "No." She began walking again. A hundred feet farther Philip saw the fresh earth, a dark scar in the grass- and lichen-covered ground. Isobel pointed, her eyes stark and frightening.

Stephen and Fergus set to it, the townspeople crowding around, watching in ominous silence. The elders stood in the front, hands clasped before them. Ewan hovered close to his wife, watching the digging, sweat running freely down his face.

When Laurie's mottled face was uncovered, Stephen stood back, staring down into the grave, his expression tight and grim. Heather stepped forward. She cried out, clutching at Stephen as sobs wracked her body. Stephen put his arm around her shoulders, his gaze locked on Ewan.

Soon Roger Wood's body was uncovered, and his mother began to wail, too. The anguished cries echoed through the forest, sending a dozen rooks flapping and screeching their annoyance. The elders bent their heads together, conversing silently, their gazes sliding between Ewan and Isobel.

Ewan went to his wife and tried to embrace her. "I didna do it, love! I swear, you must believe me! This is a trick—or—or witchcraft. You would truly believe these—these redshanks, naught but Highland scum, over me?"

She gazed up at her husband, unblinking.

Philip wished the man would stop blathering about witchcraft. It was clear witchcraft was involved; but as Isobel had helped, not harmed, he hoped that detail would be overlooked. It would not if Ewan Kennedy didn't shut his mouth.

Ewan whirled suddenly, his finger stabbing the air, straight at Philip. "It's them that did this! They were here when Laurie and Roger disappeared—remember? *They were here!* And now look! They've led us straight to the body, trying to pin the blame on me! They knew where the bodies were because they killed them! Now they want to ruin me! They are redshanks, dammit!"

Stephen exchanged an alarmed look with Philip, dropping his shovel and gripping the butt of the dag tucked into his belt. Philip grabbed the handkerchief from Isobel's hand and tossed it away. She sagged against him, her lashes fluttering down.

Ewan came forward, his face red with fury. "And what do ye plan to do wi' that lassie when yer done with her, eh? Rape and kill her, too?"

Isobel murmured something.

Philip leaned his head near her lips. "What did you say?"

"She scratched him . . . his neck—three long scratches. Roger hit him with a tree branch, across the back. He'll be bruised still."

Philip straightened, his arms circling Isobel protectively. "Remove your ruff, sir. Your stepdaughter scratched your neck when you attacked her. And Roger Wood struck you across the back with a branch. If these things are not true, you'll be unmarked."

The elders turned to Heather and Ewan. Ewan faced his wife, his eyes bleak. And Philip saw it there, in her eyes.

The war. She knew her husband was marked, knew his life was in her hands. Philip also understood she'd known all along what Ewan was doing—knew, and chose to ignore it, to remain ignorant. He saw the decision in her eyes.

Before she even spoke, Philip sent a warning glance to Stephen and Fergus.

"My husband bears no marks on his person. I see him unclothed every night—his skin is clear as a babe's." She turned her hard gaze on Philip. "It's true—she disappeared the same day these men passed through town."

Ewan's eyes closed, his shoulders sagging.

Isobel's head moved against Philip's shoulder. He looked down. She frowned, trying to push against him. Her lips were tinged with blue. "Not true. She lies . . . why is she lying?"

One of the elders stepped forward, his hand out to Philip. "Would you come with us, Sir Philip? We'd like to ask you some questions."

"We've answered your questions," Stephen said, his dag leveled at the elder. "If you have any more, I suggest ye direct them to Ewan Kennedy. We'll be leaving now."

Fergus had also drawn his dag. Philip slid his arm under Isobel's knees and swung her into his arms. They backed out of the trees. No one tried to follow, though Ewan, back in possession of his wits, yelled that they couldn't just let the murdering redshanks get away.

They jogged back to the brewhouse, Isobel's head thumping against his shoulder. "Get the horses," Philip said. "We have to hurry—when they get their wits about them they'll come after us with more than we can fight."

Philip rushed into the tavern and took the stairs two at a time. Isobel mumbled something again, but he didn't have time to listen. He placed her on her narrow bed and went around her room, stuffing the few things she had brought into her leather satchel. He hesitated, wondering if he should just leave her there while he gathered the rest of their things. Instead he picked her up again, carrying her to the room he'd shared with Fergus and Stephen. He started to lay her on the bed when her hand caught at his jack.

"Philip," she whispered, her lids half-opened. "He *did* do it."

He laid her gently on the straw-stuffed mattress and pushed the damp hair from her face. She was so cold. It frightened him. Only corpses were so cold.

"I know," he said.

With obvious effort, she opened her eyes fully, focusing on his face. "I am a witch."

"I know."

Her other hand came up, gripping his with surprising strength for how weakened she was. "I'm not evil—I vow it. I've never seen the devil. I don't—"

He hushed her, squeezing her hand in response. "Christ, Isobel, I ken. I ken."

She searched his face. "You don't want to burn me?"

"Bloody hell, no!" He pressed his mouth to her cold damp forehead. "No, no, no."

The door burst open. Philip jerked around. Stephen was there, breathing hard. "Let's go! They've come back from the wood. We haven't much time." Stephen hurried around the room, grabbing things and stuffing them into the canvas sack. "Fergus has the horses outside—but if they mean to grab him, there's not much he can do alone."

Philip stood, hefting Isobel in his arms. "Leave the rest—let's go."

Though the elders called after them to stop, they didn't try to follow. Ewan Kennedy was being led into a tall stately home near the center of town. His ruff had been yanked off and dangled from his neck. Philip hoped that meant they would not be pursued, but after Isobel's performance nothing was certain.

They rode hard and didn't stop until they were far from the town. Isobel had apparently fainted and did not wake. Philip carried her before him in the saddle, while Fergus led her horse. They detoured from the route they'd taken south and when night fell found shelter in an abandoned cottage.

Stephen made a bed of their blankets for Isobel, and Philip tucked her into them. Her hands were still deathly cold, though the color had returned to her lips. He chafed her hands between his, trying to warm them. Her chest rose and fell, as though she slept deeply. He hoped it was only sleep. Several times in the course of the day he'd shook her violently. Her eyelids had opened, and though she seemed to focus on him, they only drifted shut again without her responding verbally to his questions.

They built a huge fire in the fireplace, and Philip pulled her close to it. He didn't relax until she began to snore softly. Surely if she was snoring, she was out of danger.

Fergus stood at the open door, scanning the horizon.

Philip came to stand beside him. "I think we're safe. It looked as if they were restraining Ewan Kennedy."

"Aye, but tidings such as these travel quickly. And they know who you are."

Philip nodded. He'd thought of that, but hadn't an answer for it yet.

Stephen joined them. "It wasna my fault this time." It wasn't the first time they'd been run out of a town, but Stephen was usually at fault. Stephen grinned. "She's more trouble than I am, aye?" He shook his head, scratching at the blond whiskers covering his jaw. "I've never seen the like. She knew everything just by touching a piece of linen." Stephen's eyes lit up. He went to the canvas sack he traveled with and came back with a small tattered book. "This belonged to my da. When she wakes, do you think she'd—"

"No," Philip said. "I do not. Look at her. Using this . . . magic, obviously drains her. She's ill."

Stephen gripped the book in both his hands, crestfallen. "I didna think of that."

"That's why she wears the gloves," Fergus said, staring at the lump before the fire. "To protect herself."

Philip watched his friends. It was clear this new side of Isobel did not disturb Stephen. He sat near her, on the stones of the hearth, flipping through the little book of his father's in the firelight. Fergus, however, appeared deeply troubled.

"What is it?" Philip asked.

Fergus shrugged, sighing. He turned back to the open doorway. "It's just that my wife is worried about her sister. Her letters are strange. It would set Fia's heart at rest if Mistress MacDonell could touch a letter and tell her if all was well." He glanced at Philip and smiled ruefully. "But I dinna want to make the lassie ill. Ah, well."

Philip stifled an inappropriate urge to laugh. And he'd worried his friends would react with fear. He crossed the room and sat near her. He couldn't deny his own thoughts had been running in a similar vein. She'd offered to help him find his sister, but he'd not even considered she really could help him.

Her hair glinted in the firelight. It appeared darker in the warm glow of the fire. A coppery curl fell across her cheek. As if sensing him there, her lashes fluttered, and her gaze fell on him. She stared at him for a long moment, then smiled and closed her eyes again.

Philip found his heart was pounding. A look and a smile from her made him giddy as a lad. And he liked it—a great deal.

Chapter 9

Isobel woke slowly from the fog of sleep and peered around the small room, lit only by fire. She was overwarm, bundled tightly in a mound of blankets. She fought her way out, gasping for air. Confusion gripped her until she saw Fergus sleeping a few feet away and Stephen beside him. She remembered now. The handkerchief. The girl, Laurie's, death. A shiver ran through her as the cold memory of death shrouded her again, the stench of moss and decaying leaves, the moist dirt on her face. It was no small effort to put it from her mind, but she had a lifetime of practice. She'd go mad if she let herself dwell upon all the things she'd seen.

She scanned the room, but Philip was nowhere in sight. Something else occurred to her. Once Philip had realized what she was doing, he'd not stopped her. Had he done it out of fear? Or fascination? He was not so different from her. He'd had neither the time nor the desire to help the Kennedys, but once he heard a missing child was involved he'd been unable to refuse.

She got quietly to her feet and tiptoed to the empty doorway. There was no door. The leather hinges flapped lazily in the gentle breeze. The moon was high and bright, but she still saw no sign of Philip.

She took several steps outside when he spoke behind her. "Where are you going?"

She turned. He separated from the shadows beside the house, his arms crossed over his chest. Darkness shaded his face, obscuring his expression.

"I was looking for you. Are you angry with me?"

He considered her a long moment, and Isobel's palms grew damp. She wiped them on her skirt.

"I should be, shouldn't I?"

"I only wanted to help."

"You're going to help us all into an early grave."

Isobel sighed. Though she had underestimated the gravity of her situation in Scotland, she was aware that there was danger in what she did. She accepted that danger—her mother always had, and so she would, too. Lillian MacDonell had felt it was her responsibility to help if she could. That God had given her magic for a reason, and fear was no excuse to refuse to do His will. Though Isobel tried very hard to live her life as she believed her mother would want her to, she had no wish that others come to harm because of her. However, it was inevitable that people would. She was an unmarried woman—it was unlikely she would ever be alone. Anyone associated with her was at risk. It was not a situation she was happy with; nevertheless, it could not be helped. The only alternative was to do nothing. And for Isobel that was not possible.

"I'm sorry I put us all in danger. But I can't just stand by and do nothing—not when I know I can help."

He rubbed at his forehead. Sandy brown hair stirred in the breeze. "Why didn't you tell me?"

"I did . . . in a fashion."

"Deductive reasoning?"

"Perhaps I wasn't completely honest, but you can see why, can't you? How was I to know how you'd react?"

He strolled closer, the strong planes of his forehead and jaw becoming visible, though his eyes were still dark shadows. He was so much larger than she was—broad, hulking. She should be intimidated, but she was not. She felt safe with him, protected.

"Ye say ye're sorry, and yet you still put yourself—all of us—in grave danger over a dead girl."

"I didn't know she was dead until I'd touched the handkerchief. A mother and daughter were lost to each other, and I was their only chance. And after, when I realized she was dead, I couldn't let such an act go unpunished. It betrayed Laurie's memory."

"We never knew the lass. She was no one to us. Is she worth dying for?"

"I know her. Now." She shook her head, looking to the moon. "You can't understand, and I know not how to explain it. I *know* her. She's inside my head now, part of me, and I'll never forget her." She looked back at him. "If left unpunished, Ewan Kennedy would do it again, to some other lass. Laurie knew that."

He didn't respond. She thought he looked at her, but couldn't tell for certain. He seemed enormous in the darkness, looming before her. She shivered.

"The others . . . Stephen and Fergus. I suppose they're afraid of me now?"

"No."

Something eased inside Isobel, and she felt lighter. She counted Stephen and Fergus as friends, and Isobel MacDonell did not have many friends. It pleased her she'd not lost her newest ones.

"What of you?" she asked.

"Me?" He strolled closer until he stood directly in front of her.

Her blood warmed, racing through her. She tilted her

head to meet his eyes. The way he looked at her was odd, his eyes moving over her face as though trying to memorize it. It was too dark to see the clear amber color of them, but she didn't need the light, she knew them now as she knew the psalters. Memorized them, so they came to her unbidden.

"Aye, lass, you terrify me."

She frowned. He didn't look terrified. He mocked her. She sighed, the last weight of apprehension lifting, then smiled. "You jest."

He shook his head slowly. "And you take none of this seriously," he said mildly. "That's what astounds me most."

"I take it very seriously! When I was in England I rarely did it in front of others, and I almost always wore my gloves. People went to Ceri when they lost things, then I helped her find them."

"Why would you even *want* to, when it makes you so ill?"

"Oh, that?" She made a dismissive gesture. "That doesn't happen very often. Only if someone experienced extreme violence—and usually only with people who are dead. And sometimes if the person is very evil." She paused, searching his face. "If you have something of your sister's, I can discover if she's still alive."

He said nothing, staring down at her, his brow furrowed.

"And if she's alive, I can tell you where she is."

"And if she died a horrible death? What then? You relive it until it you're so weak you can do naught but sleep?"

Isobel hadn't considered that. She never did. It happened, when it happened and she recovered. She shrugged. "It won't kill me. Sometimes I sleep a long while—other times I'm better after naught more than a nap. Besides, I can stop it anytime I want to."

He raised a skeptical brow. "Ye can?"

"Yes—I'm almost always still aware of the object in my hand and can release it anytime I wish. So I *am* in control."

"*Almost* always?" he challenged in a slightly teasing tone, but he wanted her to—she could see it in his face. The hope, the fear. And she longed to do this for him.

"Philip, let me help you."

He shook his head. "I have nothing of hers with me."

"Kilpatrick lands are but a day's ride from the MacDonells of Glen Laire. What would one more day matter?" After she said it she thought of her father. The nagging sense of dread had not disappeared, but it had been displaced by a new preoccupation with her protector. She *was* worried about her father and anxious to finally be home. And yet home meant Nicholas Lyon, her betrothed, and saying good-bye to her new friends—friends who in the last few minutes had become precious to her in their acceptance. And most of all she wanted to help Philip—she felt she owed him a great deal. Rather than being afraid of her, or anxious to use her magic for himself, he was more concerned with her health. Even Ceri had not been so thoughtful. If anyone deserved her help, it was Philip. His soul was troubled by the loss of his sister. She wanted to lay his demons to rest. If only he'd let her.

"It's more than a day's journey," he said. "Mayhap two. Three or more if the weather turns."

"It won't."

The dimples in his cheeks deepened as he smiled. "Ye predict the weather now, too? What, did ye touch the sky?"

Isobel smiled back. Of course she could not predict the weather, and he knew it.

His smile faded. "Your father will not be pleased."

"My father need not know."

"Why do you wish to do this?"

"Because you're not afraid of me."

"I told you, lass, you scare me."

Isobel's gaze traveled over him in disbelief, stopping on his impassive face. She could not imagine Philip being afraid of anything. "You don't look scared." She pushed one finger against his chest, as if to shove him away, but he was a rock. "You don't feel scared."

He raised a brow.

"Or perhaps you're just rigid with terror," she teased.

His smile sent a slow burn down to her toes. "That I am—ye've no idea."

Isobel resisted the urge to look down, her cheeks hot. She should walk away, she knew—but couldn't. She felt as though she were suffocating, looking into his eyes. The knowledge that he wanted her—still—though he knew she was a witch, expanded inside her, warming her, making her bold, and pushing all thoughts of Nicholas Lyon from her mind.

"Why aren't you afraid of me?"

He shook his head, still smiling slightly. "You're not listening."

"Very well. Why are you afraid?"

He reached out a hand, tentative at first, then with purpose, touching a curl that lay against her forehead. His fingers brushed her skin. Isobel's body tightened, her breath hitching. The backs of his fingers slid down her temple, to her cheek, and under her chin. She resisted the urge to close her eyes and turn her face into his caress—she couldn't break away when he looked at her in such a manner. His face was fierce with longing, and when he spoke, his voice was rough.

"I want to taste you again. And I know I should not—but . . . right now, I dinna care. That scares me. I should care. Verra much."

Isobel's insides melted, warm and liquid. She swayed

closer to him, her palms settling against his chest. "I want you to."

He lowered his head, his other arm sliding around her waist. Sable lashes fell, as if he were surrendering, and his mouth brushed hers, warm and firm. Isobel's body sighed into his. His arms went around her, and the pressure of his mouth increased. She yielded, her lips parting. His whiskers abraded her skin, his warm scent enveloped her.

His mouth moved over hers, fierce in its tenderness, and she was drowning, her heart wild. His hand smoothed down her back as he shifted, his thigh pushing between her legs, hands pressing her closer, molding her softness to his hard form. His tongue slid against her lips, hot and urgent, his teeth nibbled and scraped at her. Isobel clung to his shoulders, opening her mouth to gasp for air, and his tongue plunged in. Hunger, sharp and deep, flooded her. She opened wider to him, her tongue brazenly meeting his.

He made a sound in his throat, low and hot and resonating through her. His kiss deepened, arching her neck back, but his hand was there, threading through her hair, cupping her skull. Lost in sensation, her body pulsing with each squeeze of her heart, she could think of nothing but *Philip, Philip.*

He tore his mouth away suddenly and buried his face in her neck. His ragged breath blew hot against her skin. She felt dizzy, lights still bursting behind her eyelids, her body aching with want.

She whispered his name, her fingers digging into the leather of his jack, her face turning, searching for his mouth. He stepped away from her, his hands on her shoulders.

"Go inside, Isobel." His voice was harsh.

"I don't want to—"

The hands on her shoulders tightened. "Think for a moment—I wilna long be satisfied with kisses, I vow it."

Isobel wanted to tell him she wouldn't either—her body was tight and trembling with need—but he was right, she was not thinking. Frustration and yearning unhappiness filled her. This could never be, and so it must stop. But she didn't want it to stop. Girlish ideas of love that had withered and died years ago were taking root in his arms. They were not easy to let go, though she knew she must. *She must.* For her father, for Lord Kincreag—what she was doing was unfair to her betrothed. Disloyal. But still she stood, rooted before Philip, unable to leave him.

He turned aside, raking an unsteady hand through his hair, suppressed violence in his movement. "Forgive me—both times it was my fault, I ken. It wilna happen again—so long as you don't seek me out in this manner. Aid me in this, Isobel, I pray you." He tilted his head, giving her a sidelong look. "Bloody hell," he moaned. "Dinna look at me like that."

Isobel quickly averted her eyes, uncertain how she was looking at him. But his silence drew her gaze back. It was hard not to look at him, tall and broad—and warm. She could still feel his strong fingers on her body, her face tingled from the scrape of his beard. She shivered, bereft. She did not know what to say. A hopeless war waged inside her—one she'd already lost—long before Sir Philip had come to fetch her. She would marry Nicholas Lyon and all else was fool's play.

But her will had ever been strong and stubborn. She would marry Lord Kincreag, she'd never questioned that, and she would go to him a maiden still. The earl was her destiny. But she would have her way with Philip until then.

"We'll go to your home? So I can touch something of your sister's?"

He looked to the moon, his mouth flat, muscles in his jaw bulging, but after a long moment, he nodded.

• • •

Philip slept fitfully—too aware that Isobel was but an arm's length away from him. And now he'd sentenced himself to more time in her company. He was a fool. He lay near the fire, refusing to let himself look at her. But it didn't matter—the smell of her was in his nose, the taste of her lingered, tormenting him. He'd spent most of the night arguing the logic of his actions. Take her to his home? Was he mad? But in the end it was not logic that won. If Effie was alive, and he found her, he could make everything right again. Even after twelve years, something inside insisted he could *still* set things right.

He'd spent the first five years after her disappearance searching for her. The last seven he'd spent more time searching for others than for Effie, but he'd never completely given up hope. He still made inquiries, though after twelve years the trail was so cold it was useless, yet he could not help himself. And here Isobel was, claiming that she could set all to rest. Insisting on it. And from what he'd witnessed, it seemed she could.

He should take her home to her father and her earl, and forget about her. But he would not.

In the morning Philip told Stephen and Fergus of the change in plans.

"That's not fair," Stephen protested. "You said she couldna touch my da's book. Why does she get to touch something of yours?"

"Your father is dead, not missing. And everyone knows your father died violently. Would you make her relive that?"

Stephen had not put the book away last night—had slept with it gripped in his hand as he sometimes did—and now shook it at Philip. "He didn't have it when he died. It's not as if he was holding it when he was shot. It was far away."

"I don't think that matters."

Isobel breezed past, plucking the book from Stephen's fingers. "I told you I didn't mind doing it, Philip."

Stephen winked at Philip and followed her outside like a puppy.

Philip stared after them sullenly.

Fergus raised red brows. "It's Philip, now, eh? No 'Sir'?"

"Dinna tell me you were awake last night, too?"

Fergus's brows rose even higher. "No, I wasna—but it seems I should have been." He considered Philip. "What happened?"

Philip looked down at the saddle he was oiling, rubbing it vigorously. "Nothing. And nothing *will* happen."

"That's what you said last time."

"I mean it this time."

Fergus covered his bearded mouth and nodded wisely.

Philip threw down the cloth, grabbed the saddle, and strode outside. Isobel and Stephen sat side by side on a tree trunk. She held the small book between her hands. She spoke too softly for Philip to hear, but Stephen was spellbound, his eyes never leaving her face. Philip couldn't shake the nagging unease he felt seeing her "perform." There was no harm in her helping him, or Stephen, or Fergus, was there? They would never reveal her secret, and each would protect her with his life if it came to that. It was the fact she was so willing and eager to perform that troubled him.

He was more concerned about her future than he cared to admit. He wished she would have a care. He would not always be there to protect her. He tried to remind himself she'd lived four-and-twenty years without his help. But the last twelve were in England, a place that did not kill witches by the hundreds, and before that, Alan MacDonell had protected her—and had felt compelled to send his daughters far away for their safety.

Philip tightened the girth on Jinny's saddle, reminding himself yet again that his responsibilities to her ended once she was in her father's hands. That was as far as he needed to worry about.

When they were mounted and riding north again, Stephen was unusually quiet. Philip inspected his friend's slightly befuddled expression.

"What is it, man? What did she tell you?"

"Nothing really . . . just some things about my father I did not know." He scratched at his head. "Did you know my father and my uncle loved the same woman—my aunt! I guess Da was the loser."

Philip had only met Stephen's aunt once, but she was a striking woman. Philip could see it. Stephen had been a small child when his father died, so his aunt and uncle had raised him. Though the lad was devoted to them, he'd always been preoccupied with his mysterious father. Philip shared a similar childhood, his mother dying when he was very young. His stepmother had been kind to him until he'd ruined it by losing her daughter—after that, nothing had been the same.

"She got all that from your father's book?"

"Aye! That and more," Stephen said, impressed. "She's a most . . . exceptional woman."

Philip's eyes narrowed at Stephen, but his friend didn't notice. His gaze was fixed thoughtfully on Isobel.

"It's a shame," Stephen continued, "that she's to marry Lord Kincreag, aye?"

When Philip didn't reply Stephen glanced at him. "I know she's your charge, but ye canna tell me you haven't noticed."

"She's a wee bit old for you, don't ye think?"

Stephen made a sound of dismissal. "Six years is nothing." He grinned wickedly. "I've had older women than she."

"Ye touch her, and I'll thrash you, lad. This time it's no jest."

Stephen laughed. "Ye think me daft, man? I'll not prick the earl of Kincreag's temper. I value my life."

Philip was sick of talking and thinking about the earl of Kincreag. He had no quarrel with the man and no reason to hate him, but the mere mention of his name had become poison to Philip.

"But I can still think about it," Stephen mused. "No harm in that."

Philip glared at Stephen until the lad raised his brows in amused surprise. Before he could blather any further, Philip spurred his horse forward, catching up with Fergus and Isobel.

"Mistress MacDonell," he said when he was beside her, "ride ahead with me."

She glanced quickly at Fergus, but nodded. The hard ride did nothing to work out the repressed lust plaguing him every time he looked at her or thought of her—and it uselessly tired the horses. Isobel raced along beside him, and when he finally slowed to a walk, she looked at him questioningly, her cheeks flushed from the exercise, her eyes shining.

She looked behind them at Fergus and Stephen, dots on the horizon. "Have I done something wrong?"

Philip had meant to say a great deal to her—all of which sounded foolish now—so instead he said, "Do you plan to tell Lord Kincreag that you're a witch?"

She stared straight ahead, coppery lashes catching the sun. "Not right away . . . if ever. But how am I to know what will happen? He might turn out to be as wonderful as . . . to be wonderful."

He wanted to probe further, to prepare her somehow, but before he could, she said, "Why are you so loyal to my father?"

Philip shrugged, not because he didn't know the answer but because it was at once both simple and complex. "Because I fostered with him. Fostering almost always knits men together. Alan was like a father to me . . . in many ways I look to him more than I do my own father. And as Alan had no sons, I think he often looks on the lads he fostered as *his* lads."

Isobel frowned. "So that's it? Fostering?"

"Aye."

Her brow was furrowed and she chewed the inside of her lip, staring into the distance.

"Why does that trouble you?"

"It's not that it troubles me . . . but in a sense, *I* fostered with the Attmores—and for twelve years. Yet, I feel little loyalty to them, nor they to me."

"Ah." This was what had bothered Philip when he was at Attmore Manor—the lack of feelings between the Attmores and their charge. Now that he realized she truly was a witch, he understood why the Attmores had been so happy to be rid of her. But it didn't mean he liked it. Philip scraped at his whiskers—long and beginning to itch, he couldn't wait to shave—searching for the right words to address what he thought she might be feeling. He was not good at this type of thing and didn't know why he was even trying now.

"It's not your fault, you know, that the Attmores were . . . well . . ."

"Afraid of me?" She laughed softly and without humor. "Of course it was my fault. I *am* a witch."

"Isobel . . . families are strange. I was more comfortable with your mother and father than with my own—even before . . ."

"Before what?"

Philip shook his head impatiently; he hated how things kept coming back to his sister. "Nothing—what I'm trying to say is, your family was very close. I know you were young when you left, but you must remember how your mother adored you—and how your father still does."

Isobel smiled at him, and it was like the sun on his face, warming him and stealing his breath.

"Tell me about *your* family," she said.

Philip shook his head slowly. "There isna much to tell. My mother died when I was five. I hardly remember her, except that she was soft."

Isobel's mouth quirked slightly. "Soft?"

Philip shrugged. "Aye—I loved to sit on her lap, and it was soft."

"What about your stepmother?"

"My stepmother," Philip repeated, thinking about Mairi Kilpatrick. She had been beautiful and kind and loved by everyone once. Philip had adored her. After years of trying to conceive, they'd all come to believe she was barren, and though she became morose, she'd still treated Philip and his brothers as her own. Then Effie had been born when Philip was eleven, and Mairi had thrown herself into raising the perfect daughter. This task had left her very little time for aught else, but she still had kind words and smiles for Philip—unless she thought he was interfering with Effie's upbringing.

His mood darkened. Isobel still stared at him quizzically.

He cleared his throat. "Once, she was a . . ." He paused, then tried again. "Once she was different than she is now."

Isobel frowned. "How?"

Philip didn't know how to explain it. Or perhaps he didn't want to. Either way he shrugged. "It's difficult to explain—but it's my fault."

When he glanced at Isobel she regarded him steadily. "Your fault?"

"She's barren. It was a miracle when my sister, Effie, was born. Effie was her whole life and I lost her."

"I see," Isobel said slowly. "What happened to your sister?"

"That's what you're supposed to tell me, aye?"

She gave him a narrow look, but did not pursue the subject. "What about your father?"

Philip relaxed—his father was a safe subject. "Ah, my father. What can I say about Dougal Kilpatrick? He's managed to sire numerous quarrelsome bastards who think they're as entitled to Sgor Dubh as I am. And my father encourages their plotting and intrigues to amuse himself. I think he believes it will make me take an interest in my legacy. I'm not certain, though, as I never give it much thought." He rubbed the ring on his finger, frowning. "He can give it to them for all I care."

"Your stepmother tolerates this?"

"Tolerates what?"

"His adultery? Shoving his bastards in her face?"

Her indignation amused him. She had been a bit sheltered. Alan and Lillian MacDonell had been deeply in love, and the Attmores had also seemed a comfortable couple who likely honored their vows—a rare occurrence, in Philip's experience.

"He's somewhat discreet. And besides, she has much freedom to do as she pleases. She's not fool enough to complain. I doubt she'd care to have him warm her bed anymore, anyway."

Isobel stared straight ahead, horrified. He knew what she was thinking—imagining Lord Kincreag treating her thus. Philip wanted to assure her she was nothing at all like Mairi and so had naught to fear. But then Lord Kincreag was nothing like Dougal Kilpatrick, so who could know what would happen? The thought of any man dishonoring Isobel sent a surge of hot anger through him so quickly and violently he was startled by it. *I'd kill him.* The thought was strong and fierce—and completely heartfelt. He should not be riding with her. He should not be speaking to her thusly. But he'd already made the error, and so he rode beside her in silence, feeling awkward, wanting to say something comforting to ease the worried lines in her fair brow. But he had no words for her, as her future did not comfort him.

Chapter 10

⌖

The days passed, bringing with them the rougher terrain of the Highlands. A trembling excitement filled Isobel. It had been so long since she'd seen these mountains, seen the heather-covered crags, the glens and hidden lochs, the glistening falls that emptied into clear pools of water. Though it had been twelve years since she'd last set eyes on the Highlands, her heart knew this place. *Home.*

They passed the occasional croft. The men plowing the fields for oats and barley raised their hands in greeting as they passed. Isobel stood in her stirrups to wave back, barely able to contain her excitement. *Home.* Peat smoke spiced the air, rising from holes in the thatched roofs. Women sat on driftwood benches, spinning wool and watching the younger children.

The farther they traveled, the more withdrawn Philip became. Isobel had been surprised when days ago he'd asked her to ride with him, only to be bitterly disappointed he'd only wanted to issue more warnings about Lord Kincreag.

He'd not sought her out since. He took great pains to be certain he was never alone with her. He rarely addressed her directly and was careful not to meet her gaze. But none of that helped. He'd kindled a fire in her that would not be extinguished. She touched his belongings when he was not looking. As he was aware of her ability, he kept his things close to him, so her opportunities were rare, but she took them. They revealed little to her, but she loved the feel of him. Even the most mundane object of his retained something of his essence in it. Strong and male, constantly sorting problems in his mind. Some of the things he pondered surprised her. She caught a memory, once—of him and a young girl, standing calf deep in the shallow water of a cove or inlet. He showed the girl how to catch fish in the weir, a low semicircular stone wall. It was a fond memory, and he recalled it with a touch of sadness.

And sometimes she even felt a shadow of his desire for her, which he worked very hard to suppress. She saw herself once, when touching the rag he used to oil and polish his weapons at night. She saw herself as he saw her. It was a vision she'd never forget—the sun sinking into the horizon behind her. She'd been mending one of her sleeves, her eyes downcast, frowning slightly in concentration. He'd thought she was beautiful—had even felt a sort of frustrated longing, looking at her. She held the memory close to her, something to cherish in the days ahead.

Not that she would need it, she assured herself. It would be this way with Nicholas; she would make it so. With Nicholas she would forget this restless preoccupation with Philip. She'd nearly convinced herself her betrothed had been unfairly maligned. He was a powerful man, after all, people were eager for his downfall. If he really were a murderer, surely the king would have done something. Though she recognized the fallacy of her thoughts—the king never punished noble murderers unless it suited him—she had to tell herself these things, or she'd go mad.

They followed a wending burn until it emptied into a loch. The water was so clear Isobel could see fish darting beneath the surface. Near the bank she spied an elf shot. She plucked the stone arrowhead from the water and dried it on her kirtle, pleased to have discovered such a good portent.

She tucked it in her satchel and inhaled. The scent of the sea had been growing stronger until Isobel felt certain it must be just over the next rise. Goats and sheep dotted the hillside, green with heather and splashed with patches of violets. A shaggy dog trotted around the perimeter of the herd.

They had stopped at the loch to water the horses. Philip stood apart from them, his arms folded over his chest, gazing out at the animals. Isobel stood beside Jinny, her hand on the horse's withers, watching him. A gust of moist wind pushed the dark hair from his face. A frown had settled on his smooth brow. What did he think about? What weighed so heavily on his mind now that they neared his home? Was it his sister? Or something else?

"Sgor Dubh is just over that rise," Fergus said, nodding in the direction Philip stared. "You'll be there in less than an hour."

Isobel looked up at the burly redhead, surprised. "You're not coming with us?"

Fergus took a drink from the waterskin and shook his head. "Nay, Miss. I'm going home for a day or so—but I'll meet you at Sgor Dubh afore ye leave for Lochlaire."

"Sgor Dubh . . . that means sharp black stone, yes?"

Fergus grinned. "Aye, ye ken yer Gaelic, do ye no?"

Isobel shrugged. "I remember some things, if I think on them hard enough." She cocked her head. "Where is your home?"

He gestured with the waterskin to the east. "Dougal has given me a tower house. I live there with my wife, Fia."

"Fergus and Fia. I like that." Isobel smiled. "I'm sorry I won't meet her."

"Och, she'd be honored, she would." He looked uncomfortable suddenly, his mouth compressed, his brow lowered. He frowned at the ground as if he wanted to say something but couldn't find the words.

"What is it, Fergus?"

"It's my sister-in-law . . . Her letters for the past year have been strange, and she doesna want Fia to visit her. Fia is so worrit aboot her. She cries sometimes, when I'm away, and she feels lonely. I was hoping . . ."

Isobel placed a hand on his arm. "Bring something of your sister-in-law's when you return. If possible, something metal, or perhaps a precious stone—or clothing would work, too. Linen is best. Or even the letter, unless your wife has handled it a lot."

"What aboot the spoon she used?"

"Not if it's wood. Wood doesn't give me clear pictures, I don't know why—I just feel things, which are hard to interpret into the type of information you're looking for."

Fergus shook his head. "It's horn."

"Horn is good. But if it's someone else's *now,* and they use it or touch it a lot, it will give me mixed readings. It's best if it hasn't been touched much since your sister-in-law last used it."

He smiled, relieved. "I thank ye, Mistress MacDonell. Ye're a good lass, ye are." He reached toward her awkwardly. Isobel thought for a moment he meant to embrace her and moved forward, but he settled for patting her shoulder.

"God save ye," he said, and turned away. He slapped Stephen on the back and mounted his horse, cantering over to where Philip stood.

They exchanged a few words, then Fergus rode away.

"He doesna like going home," Stephen said from behind her.

Isobel turned. "Who? Fergus?"

"Och, no. Fergus thinks of naught but that bonny wee wife of his. No, I speak of Philip. That's why he's been so foul-tempered the past few days."

They both stared at the lone figure meditating on the far hills.

"Why doesn't he like to go home? Is it because of his sister?"

Stephen shook his head and turned back to his horse, relacing the leather sack to his saddle. "Aye, his stepmother keeps her alive."

Isobel gave him an inquisitive look, but Stephen raised his brows and nodded to something behind her. When she turned, Philip was striding over to them, his face grim, his mouth set.

He swung into his saddle with the air of a man steeling himself to face an army alone. "Let's go."

Since entering the Highlands they had passed the occasional croft, but now the black stone cottages grew more numerous, and they were forced onto the rutted road so they didn't trample freshly planted fields. The mountains had fallen behind them, leaving a clear blue sky that met with glistening blue water.

Sgor Dubh sat on a narrow rocky promontory. The only way to it was by the slender isthmus or by boat. It was a very old castle, added to and expanded over the years until the thick walls reached the very edge of the sharp black rocks it was built upon. A square keep was barely visible over the retaining walls, but soaring high above that were several conical towers.

The castle was quite busy, men and women, all wearing

the wool plaid of the Highlands, came and went across the natural bridge. Many men wore the plaid belted at the waist, so that it draped in folds to their knees. Others wore long tartan breeches called trews, with tunics or doublets and wool mantles. Most of the women wore arisaids, their throats and forearms bare, but others dressed no differently than lowland women, wearing their plaids about their shoulders as shawls. The majority of them were barefoot.

When they were in the courtyard a young man strode over to them. He wore his plaid belted. The weave was finer than anything Isobel had seen yet, the colors a vivid checking of purple and green. He pushed a shock of sandy hair out of his face and laughed loudly.

"Look who decided to grace us with a visit!"

He yelled rapid Gaelic to some men behind him and turned back to Philip, hands on hips and legs planted wide. Deep dimples grooved his clean-shaven cheeks. He grinned broadly, with great pleasure that seemed more inherent to his person than due to Philip's arrival. When his gaze fell on Isobel, one eyebrow quirked. His smile faded slightly, only to reemerge with a wolfish edge. He seemed of an age with Philip, perhaps a bit younger, and was quite handsome.

"That's Colin," Stephen said in a low voice. "Watch him. He's not to be trusted."

Philip swung down from his horse, unmoved by Colin's greeting. He strode toward the man, leading his enormous black horse.

Colin spread his arms, as if he expected Philip to embrace him. "Brother! It's been too long."

Philip slapped the reins in one of Colin's outstretched hands, continuing past him. "See to Horse, will ye?"

Colin's eyes narrowed on the reins in his hand. His gaze darted to Isobel and Stephen. "Take care of that will ye?"

Colin said to Stephen, his gaze riveted on Isobel. He shoved Horse's reins at Stephen. "Let me help ye down, my dear."

Isobel thought Philip had left them in the courtyard, but when she reached to place her hand in Colin's, his hand was knocked aside. Philip was there, his firm grip spanning her waist and swinging her from the saddle. Isobel was a bit breathless when he dropped his hands, but he didn't notice. He stared over her head at Colin.

"See to the horses." His hand curved around the base of her neck. "Stephen?" Stephen handed Horse's reins back to Colin with a grin and trotted after them.

"What was that about?" Isobel whispered. They had caused something of a stir. People had stopped to watch and even now stared at them as they walked to the keep. "Don't you have servants to tend the horses? Surely your brother shouldn't have to."

"That matters not," Philip said. "He needs to be reminded of his place from time to time."

Isobel tried to look over her shoulder, but the fingers on her neck squeezed. "Now don't be looking at him. Can't have him thinking he's caught your attention, or he'll be all puffed-out tonight."

Isobel walked dutifully beside him, facing forward. "I don't understand."

"Nor will you anytime soon."

Before she could ask what that meant, she realized Philip's steps had slowed. A man exited the oldest part of the keep. Tall and broad, he was an older version of Philip, his dark hair and beard streaked with gray. He stopped just outside the enormous double doors, placed his hands behind his back and waited. He wore faded trews, a worn leather doublet, and sturdy boots.

Philip stopped before him. "Father."

Dougal Kilpatrick glanced dismissively at Isobel, then back at Philip. "Where's Colin?" His voice was deep and gravelly, and laced with disapproval.

"At the stables, I imagine, seeing to our mounts."

The lines beside Dougal's eyes deepened with humor, but he didn't smile. His mouth was a hard and uncompromising line in his well-trimmed beard. "Stephen—what am I to tell your uncle when he writes, looking for you, eh?"

Stephen shrugged. "Tell him the truth."

Dougal said nothing for a long while, his flinty gaze fixed on Stephen. After a moment, Stephen lowered his eyes and scratched at his neck, moving behind Philip slightly, as if to shield himself.

Seeing he'd cowed the lad, Dougal turned his gaze back on Philip. He rocked on his heels as he looked Philip up and down dispassionately. "Why are you here?" he asked in Gaelic.

"I'm here for a horse—the gray," Philip answered in English.

Dougal raised a skeptical brow, but continued the conversation in English. "They're your horses, you can take them all for all I care. What do you need it for?"

"A gift."

Dougal turned his gaze on Isobel again. The urge to quail under his piercing stare was great, but Isobel squared her shoulders and returned his gaze.

"What is this?" Dougal asked.

"Isobel MacDonell, daughter of MacDonell of Glen Laire. I'm escorting her home."

Dougal's brows raised in surprise. "The witch's spawn? Hmm . . . we all thought you were dead, lass."

Isobel's smile turned wooden. *Witch's spawn?* Was that how she and her sisters were known? "I'm quite alive, it seems."

"I'd be careful," Philip said mildly. "You're speaking to the future countess of Kincreag."

Dougal turned his sour gaze on Philip. "Lord Kincreag is not my chief."

"He *is* the Colquhoun's overlord. And the Colquhoun is *your* chief."

Dougal grunted, apparently unmoved by this truth. "So you're still serving other chieftains, rather than tending your own inheritance."

Philip cocked his head in mock confusion. "Is it mine? Last we spoke you threatened to name Colin tanist."

Tanist. Isobel searched her memory. Though Highlanders did practice primogeniture, she remembered that tanistry was an old Highland custom that chiefs and chieftains called upon when they either had no heir or found their own heir unfit.

Dougal shook his head disgustedly and began speaking in low, rumbling Gaelic.

Philip cut him off abruptly. "Ye'll not speak the Gaelic in front of Stephen or the lass. Ye ken yer Scots as well as I do."

Though his face hardened, Isobel saw a flash of respect in Dougal's eyes. He nodded at Isobel. "Ye should marry this one. A MacDonell tie couldn't hurt. Things are getting ugly with the MacGregors."

"That might trouble the earl of Kincreag somewhat."

Dougal made a purely Scottish sound, dismissing the significance of an earldom. Philip just shook his head.

"What does it matter?" Dougal said. "Ye've no need for a wife or heirs, aye? As ye've no intention of heading the clan." He started past them, but stopped when he was beside Philip. "Come see me when you've got the lass settled." And he was gone, striding out into the courtyard.

The hand on Isobel's neck had tightened unconsciously.

"He never gives up, does he?" Stephen mused with admiration, watching Dougal's retreat.

Philip's hand slid down to Isobel's back, and the tension seemed to flow out of him. "No, he does not," he agreed, and urged her forward, into the keep.

Isobel blinked when she entered the great hall, momentarily blind in the dark, firelit room. Rushes covered the floor. Two deerhounds squabbled over a bone near the hearth but stopped when Philip entered. They scrabbled to their feet and bounded over to him with excited barks. Philip scrubbed their wiry gray fur as they licked and pawed at him, yipping with delight.

"Lucifer. Daemon. How are the lads?"

Isobel held out a hand so the dogs could sniff at her, but they whined and shied from her, one of them baring its teeth threateningly.

"Hey," Philip said sternly, giving the dog a harsh look. It whined, tail between legs and pressed against his legs, watching Isobel cautiously.

Philip gave Isobel a questioning look, and she shrugged. "I like animals, but sometimes they don't like me. With time, though, they usually come around."

A small smile curved his mouth when he straightened. "I've no doubt of that."

Stephen had left them, heading straight for the kitchens, in search of food.

Philip glanced at her as he led her from the hall. "Why do you look at me so?"

"It's nice to see something about your home makes you happy, even if it's only the dogs."

"They're good dogs, usually," he said.

He led her down a dark corridor, then up a set of curved stairs. They were in one of the newer towers. No torches were lit, and the air was musty and cold. Philip took her hand, moving familiarly through the darkness. Isobel heard squeaking, then something brushed past her foot.

She gasped, clasping Philip's wrist with her other hand. "Don't you have a cat?"

"Used to. But it's been two years since I've been here."

"You haven't seen your family in two years?" She couldn't imagine staying away from home voluntarily. She'd spent twelve long years yearning for her family.

"I didn't say that. Colin sought me about . . . oh, about nine months ago and tried to kill me."

"What?"

He laughed softly. They were on a landing. Isobel only knew that because there were no more steps. There was a soft creaking, and the darkness lessened, narrow strips of sunlight in the room ahead. Philip pulled her forward, then released her hand, crossing the room and throwing the shutters open.

Isobel surveyed her surroundings. An enormous bed, hung with heavy velvet curtains, stood against the wall. The room was sparsely furnished. A chest, a table and two chairs, and a cabinet against one wall. All sturdy and well built, but unadorned. Everything was covered with dust and cobwebs.

He turned, hands on hips, and viewed the room.

"This is your room?" she asked.

"Aye . . . well, yours tonight."

"They obviously weren't expecting you," Isobel said.

"And if they had been, it would look no different."

When she gave him a quizzical look, he explained, "My father uses any means he can think of to remind me of how I neglect my duty."

"Your brother tried to kill you?"

He shrugged. "I told you my father encourages him, thinking it will make me show an interest in Sgor Dubh."

"Your own father encouraged your brother to kill you?"

"Och, no, but he feeds Colin's desire to possess this place. I dinna think he believes Colin capable of murder. At least not of murdering me—and so far he hasn't been successful, so perhaps he's right."

Isobel studied him in the dim light. He seemed more relaxed than he had in days. Perhaps it was because the confrontation with his father that he'd been dreading was behind him. He strolled over to the cabinet and opened a door.

"I don't think I have anything of Effie's in here . . ." He straightened, frowning as he gazed around the room absently. "I'll probably have to go to her room."

"If possible, I need something of hers that has not been handled a great deal. Cloth or precious stones and metals are best."

"That might be a problem."

"Were her things given away?"

He shook his head, still not looking at her. "No. Like my room, hers is probably just as she left it . . . only cleaner. But her things have probably been handled a great deal."

"Really?"

He nodded, distracted. "My stepmother."

"Oh."

His mood changed, and he began to pace the room restlessly, scratching at his beard. He stopped at the window to stare out.

Uncomfortable suddenly, Isobel looked at the bed, then back at Philip. His back was to her, his shoulders wide and strong, and she had an image of those shoulders, naked as they'd been at the burn, bent over her in that bed. Her cheeks burned. She knew he did not mean to share the room with her, and, of course, she didn't want him to. *She didn't*. Why did she think such things?

"Where will you sleep?" she heard herself asking.

He shrugged.

Isobel went to the window and stood beside him. Below them the choppy gray sea stretched away for miles. Two islands were visible in the distance.

"Why do you resist all this? You are heir to it . . . why do you stay away? Your Father clearly longs to give it to you."

"Colin can do it. Father threatened to name him tanist, but he hasn't yet. If Father would just do it, Colin could stop hating me."

Isobel frowned, thinking about his words and how they contradicted his actions. He'd gone out of his way to antagonize Colin. He'd behaved forcefully to his father— in a way that commanded respect from Dougal Kilpatrick. Isobel could see why Dougal persisted. Philip would be an excellent leader. If he really didn't want to be chieftain, why then did he behave so?

"Is that what you're waiting for? Someone to take the decision out of your hands?"

He turned to face her, his brow furrowed. "What?"

"I won't pretend to understand you or your family, but it seems as if you resist your role as heir apparent not because you don't want to do it, but because you think you can't. Or shouldn't."

He said nothing, staring down at her, his expression odd. After a moment he turned his head, looking out the window again, his fingers tapping thoughtfully against the stone sill. "Have I mentioned that you frighten me?"

"I think you might have."

His smile was thin. "It bears repeating." He turned away from the window, his dark eyes shot with amber and unfathomable. "Come, let's see if we can't find something of my sister's so we can finally get you home."

Chapter 11

Isobel rested on the bed in the small room as Philip tore it apart, looking for anything that retained something of his sister. She watched him, her heart heavy. She wasn't quite certain what to attribute her depression to. Everything she touched that belonged to the child was saturated with someone else's thoughts and feelings. Mairi Kilpatrick and her deep, relentless grief. Some of it was old—the heartbreak of a mother who lost her only beloved child—and some of it was fresh, as if the child had just disappeared. Mairi still came to this room and touched her daughter's things, held them, cried over them. Sometimes raged over them—furious at Philip for losing the only thing she loved, furious at her husband for caring more about Philip than their lost daughter.

In this room, Philip's stepmother had even contemplated suicide, had sat with poison gripped in her fist—brought the cup to her lips—before hurling it across the room. Isobel could not tell Philip the things she saw, and yet it broke her heart to see the hope she had put in his eyes dim each time he came to her with something new, something he'd found buried in the bottom of a chest, certain that *this time* it was untouched. And when she touched it, she felt nothing but Mairi's heartbreak and bitterness. The despair was so thick there was nothing of the child left.

Each time she told him that she saw nothing of his sister, she took away what she had given him. *Hope.* And she hated herself for it.

Isobel lay back against the bolster, closing her eyes to block out the sight of him as he shoved a stack of books and trinkets off a cupboard, sending them crashing to the floor. Her heart ached. It was rarely this difficult. But she hadn't anticipated his stepmother. Isobel had felt other's grief so that it broke her own heart, but she'd never felt anything like this before. She placed her palms against the embroidered quilt she lay upon and felt Mairi. She'd lain here, on this very bed, and cried—screamed even. The servants stayed away when she came here, afraid of the state she worked herself into.

The bed creaked and moved as Philip sat on it. Isobel turned her head and opened her eyes. He sat at the end, elbows braced on knees and head in hands.

"That's it," he said. "That's everything. I can think of nothing else."

Isobel had told him she would help him. She felt like a liar, a cheat, a charlatan.

"I'm so sorry, Philip."

"I don't understand," he said to the floor. "It seems so easy with everything else you touch." He straightened, twisting to pin her with an accusing stare. "The Kennedys—hadn't the girl's mother been holding the handkerchief for days?"

"That's because it was only for a few days. Laurie had owned the handkerchief much longer than Heather had held it. And Heather's emotions had not yet become so powerful that they saturated the handkerchief . . . not like this . . ."

"My stepmother is all you feel when you touch Effie's things? Can you not dig deeper? Get beneath Mairi? Effie *must* be there somewhere."

It was sometimes like that, but she was strangely reluctant to go that far, that deep. She feared she wouldn't find Effie at all, but something even more unpleasant about Mairi Kilpatrick. However, she'd never been one to shirk from duty, and she wouldn't start now.

She sat up. It seemed there was a weight around her, dragging her down. She was exhausted, filled with leaden sadness.

She scanned the room, looking for the doll she'd held earlier. "That—bring me the doll."

Philip was off the bed, fetching the doll to her. It had a leather head and body, its painted face faded. The clothes were new—which disturbed Isobel inexplicably. In her mind she'd clearly witnessed Mairi painstakingly sew and embroider new clothes for the doll years after Effie disappeared.

Philip started to hand it to her, then drew back, frowning. "You look faint."

Isobel squared her shoulders and forced a smile. "I'm fine."

"No, you're not." He looked down at the doll. "What *are* you seeing, Isobel? You told me only violence . . . or death affects you so. Are you hiding something?"

Isobel gave him a look of innocent confusion. "What do you mean? I just see your stepmother . . . coming here and touching these things, thinking about Effie."

He held her gaze, searching her face for the truth.

Isobel had to look away. "It's her grief. I feel it as if it's mine."

She glanced at him. He gazed down at the doll, gripped in his strong hands. She'd never thought a man's hands could be beautiful, but his were. Broad and tan, with cords of muscle along the backs and wrists that shifted and moved when he flexed his fingers. She imagined them on her, flexing . . .

She held out her hand. "Give it to me."

"We should stop. For now. So you can regain your strength."

She leaned forward and put her hand on the doll. He didn't release it. His eyes met hers.

"I want to do it, Philip."

"You will tell me what you see—no matter what it is? No matter *who* it is?"

Isobel couldn't look away from him, but she would not promise him that. "I will tell you anything I see about your sister."

His hands tightened on the doll, pulling Isobel closer, so her face was inches from him. "I want to know everything."

Do no harm. That's what her mother always told her. And she would not harm him. *Never.* "Very well," she lied.

He released the doll. Isobel began untying the tiny points on the dress, blocking out the misery that radiated from the garment.

"What are you doing?"

"The dress is new. Your stepmother made it only a few years ago."

Philip was silent. Isobel looked up, and he frowned at the doll as she undressed it, looking slightly ill. He leaned on his knees again, his hands laced over the back of his head. Isobel wished she hadn't told him that.

When the dress was off, she set it aside. She held the doll between her palms and closed her eyes, breathing deeply. "What did your sister look like?"

"Dark hair . . . blue eyes. Uhm . . . she was verra small,

a brownie, I oft called her. She never seemed to eat much—at least not at the table. But I sometimes caught her sneaking food from the kitchens, late. Ye'd never know it, she was so thin. She liked to fish. She wasna afraid to put a sand eel on a hook . . ."

Isobel smiled slightly, forming a picture in her head of Effie, hoping it would be a beacon of sorts, guiding her through the maelstrom of Mairi's anguish. The emotions slammed through her. Isobel tried to close them out, imagining a chest or a door, stuffing the pain inside and closing it, but she could not. Sifting through it all was impossible. She was assaulted with images of Mairi with the doll, rocking and crying, raging against fate. But Isobel persisted, repeating Effie over and over in her mind.

Rage, like a shock filled her. It was Mairi again, but this was different. A child cowered in the corner, small and trembling, clutching the doll to her chest. Mairi yelled at her, "Can you do nothing right? Is it so difficult for you to just do as I say?" She ripped the doll from Effie's grasp. At that moment, Philip pried the doll from Isobel's fingers.

She blinked until his face swam into focus, blurred. Her head throbbed.

"What the hell happened?" His voice shook slightly.

Isobel's face was wet. She touched her cheek, surprised to find tears.

"You curled into a ball on the bed and began to greet."

Isobel shook her head. "It's nothing."

"That's a bloody lie! What the hell did ye see?"

She tried to sit up, but he was leaning over her, his hands on her shoulders. She swiped her sleeve across her face, drying it. "I told you before . . . it just makes me so sad . . . I feel it all, as if it were happening to me."

He stared down at her, his eyes bleak. "I knew I'd broken Mairi's heart. I *knew* it, but seeing you like this . . ."

He started to turn away from her, but Isobel caught his arm. "Philip, it happened a long time ago. You were young—whatever Mairi feels, you cannot keep punishing yourself."

He shook his head, as if she couldn't understand. Perhaps she couldn't, but she wanted to. She put her hand on his face, turning him toward her. He didn't look at her, but allowed her to manipulate him, his long dark lashes lowered.

"I don't know everything that happened, but I know you. You made a mistake, and you are sorry. You would never have willfully hurt your sister or your stepmother. You cannot let this rule you."

He said nothing, holding himself very still. She realized how close they were. She sat on the bed, his face in her hand, the smooth whiskers beneath her palm. One of his arms was braced on the bed for support so that he leaned over her. He had only to turn his face to kiss her—and she could make him. The hand she held against his face began to tremble. Her fingers itched to stroke against his warm skin, to urge him to her mouth. She should not, she knew it, but she could not draw away. His scent filled her, warm and dangerous. And suddenly nothing else seemed to matter.

His hand came up, sliding under her hair. He still did not look in her eyes, though he leaned closer. His gaze was on her mouth. Her lips parted on a silent breath of need. She turned her face to him, her heart fluttering wildly as his mouth brushed against hers, their breath mingling. Isobel's other hand came up to hold him as he pushed her backward, his mouth closing fully over hers.

Her head had hardly hit the bolster when a voice shattered through them both. "What are you doing?"

Philip jerked away from her.

Mairi Kilpatrick stood in the doorway. Isobel knew her

from the visions. Her dark hair was covered with a triangle of fine linen. She wore a pale yellow gown, her arisaid belted at her waist and held together with a brooch at her neck. She surveyed the room—in disarray from Philip's digging. Her eyes lit on the undressed doll. A shaking hand covered her mouth. Philip was off the bed. He picked the doll up from where he'd dropped it on the floor and took it to her, his steps hesitant.

"I'm sorry . . . I . . ." What could he say? He'd brought a witch to help him find Effie? Isobel's throat was tight with the horror of the scene. Books and trinkets were scattered all over the floor where Philip had shoved them in his frustration. Clothes and blankets hung out of the chest.

Mairi took the doll from Philip's outstretched hands and clutched it to her chest like a child, looking at him in hurt disbelief. "Why would you do this? Why would you bring a . . . a woman here . . . in her very *bed* . . . ?"

"I pray you . . . forgive me . . . I . . ." He turned and scanned the room, his eyes wild. "I'll fix it." He went to the cabinet and began picking up the books he'd shoved on the floor, arranging them on top of it. Isobel was still frozen in horrified disbelief. She forced herself to stand.

"It's my fault," she said. "I asked him to show me his sister's things—her room."

Mairi looked at her, her face a mask of cold distaste. She went to Philip, who was trying in vain to fit together a wooden knight that had come apart. Mairi wrenched the toy from his hands.

"Get out! Haven't you done enough? Why do you come back?"

Philip backed away, his face stricken. "I'm sorry," he repeated. When his apology was met with cold indifference, he turned away. Isobel's throat was tight. She searched her mind for something to say, something that would explain this and make it all right. But she could think of nothing short of the truth—and Mairi did not seem the type of woman who would be tolerant of witchcraft.

Philip grabbed Isobel's wrist and dragged her from the room. He pulled her back through the castle, his face set in hard lines. Isobel continued to struggle for words to address what had just occurred, to try to make it better, but this ran deep, deeper than she'd originally suspected. Back at his room, the door stood open. Candles had been lit and the room had been tidied. Her satchel sat on the table.

"I'll come for you when dinner is served," he said, then he was gone, before she could say a single word in reply.

Philip still gripped the latch, even after closing the door. The landing was deserted. Philip lingered there a moment, just to be certain Isobel stayed put, then descended the stairs, skirting through a side door, harboring some insane fear he would meet up with his stepmother on the stairs. Insane because Mairi would never come to *his* tower.

Outside, he headed for the retaining wall and climbed to the ramparts. He looked over the thick wall, to the island where the Kilpatricks buried their dead. The day had turned overcast, the iron gray waves lashing the island. He'd stood here many times, wishing his sister was out there, buried on that island. Then at least he'd *know.* The familiar self-disgust welled up. How craven of him to wish she was dead—to wish for an easy release.

Fishermen were out in their boats, hauling in nets full of herring as waves tossed their small crafts about like toys. He heard the scrape of a boot behind him and straightened, dropping his hands from his head and blanking his face.

"I just talked to Mairi." *Colin*. Philip did not want to spar with his brother now.

Colin strolled to the wall and leaned against it, searching Philip's face.

Philip raised a bored brow. "Aye? And how is she?"

"Jesus God, Philip, what are you thinking? You know how she is about that room. Why would you do such a thing?" Colin shook his head. "It's as if you want to rub her face in it."

Philip hated this. It was why he rarely returned. He had no excuses, no defense. All Colin said was true. However unintentional, Philip persisted in causing Mairi sorrow. He said nothing, staring blindly at the far island.

"Father tries, you know," Colin continued. "He tries to understand why you do these things."

"He shouldn't tax himself over it."

"Easier said. You're his son and heir . . . or you were."

Something coiled tightly in Philip's chest. His fingers went to the ring on his other hand, toying with the topaz stone. So Dougal had finally made good on his threats. Philip should not care. He flicked his brother a disinterested look. "You see? It's not necessary to kill me to get what you want."

Colin laughed. "You persist in that fancy? I did not try to kill you. An unfortunate accident. That is all." When Philip shrugged as if he didn't give a damn, Colin persisted, "You think me so daft I would kill you and provoke Father's everlasting ire? He'd surely not name me tanist then. It would go to Aidan or Niall."

Aidan and Niall. Philip wondered where his other two half brothers were. Likely out reiving kine and raping women and small boys. He didn't ask, as he liked them less than Colin. If either of them ever became chieftain, he might be forced to assert his own claim. They'd be the end of Sgor Dubh.

Philip smiled slightly. "What an amazing coincidence that I was shot twice with your quarrels. Such poor marksmanship, Colin."

"I was hunting—I didn't know you were there."

"So why then did we have to beat you out of the forest, aye? If it were such an innocent mistake, why not come forward and see if I was wounded? And what were you doing in MacDonell's deer park, anyway?"

Colin turned sullen. "I ran because I know you. You'd never believe me. Always thinking the worst."

The conversation was becoming tedious. Philip had other things to worry about. They had to stay the night here, but they would leave at first light. There was nothing for him here. And there was nothing he could do to appease Mairi—he'd tried for years. Isobel had been his last hope. It was best just to leave. Mairi was happier without him there as a constant reminder.

He pushed away from the wall. He would see Dougal and get *that* over with. Then he could leave Sgor Dubh behind him—forever this time. Colin would be so pleased.

As Philip passed his brother, Colin said, "What about the lass? What is she to you?"

Philip faced his brother. He could see the wheels turning in Colin's head. If Philip married her, and they had a son, Colin could say good-bye to ever being chieftain. Dougal would name Philip's son his heir. Dougal knew his boys. Colin, Aidan, and Niall were not moral men. They were drunk more often than sober—and everyone suspected Niall had the pox—though he denied it vehemently. They were weak-minded and easily swayed. Colin was the best of the three, with some will of his own. But still, when with Niall and Aidan, he showed little common sense. That was why Dougal had badgered Philip for years—even when Philip repeatedly refused, willingly stepping aside for Colin.

"She is nothing to me," Philip said. "She is, however, soon to be the countess of Kincreag."

"Then what is she doing here?"

"I'm giving the gray mare to her and Lord Kincreag as a wedding gift. We're here to fetch it. We leave in the morn."

Colin raised his brows. "That's a fine gift."

"He is an earl."

"I'm surprised Lord Kincreag would have her. Wasn't Lillian MacDonell burned for witchcraft?"

Philip's gaze narrowed. "What has that to do with Isobel? Women are burned for naught more than the accusations of their enemies anymore. It means nothing."

Colin laughed incredulously. "Nothing? Perhaps there are so many burnings because the evil in this country runs deep. Witches must be rooted out, exterminated—not married to earls! I'd not want to wed that crone's daughter—"

Philip grabbed his brother by the front of his shirt and slammed him hard against the wall. "You speak ill of the MacDonells again, and you'll wish your arrow's aim had been true, for I'll not show you mercy this time."

Colin tried to push Philip off. "Bloody hell, Philip— surely you've heard the rumors. It's said her daughters are fey—that's why MacDonell hid them."

Philip leaned close to Colin's face. "I find out you're spreading such tales, and I'll track you down and kill you."

"The tales hardly need me to spread." His brother's brow twitched in sudden understanding, and he smiled. "Oh, that's the way of it. I'm certain MacDonell of Glen Laire will be pleased to hear how well you've taken care of his daughter. And the earl of Kincreag! What would he think? That, along with a few accusations of sorcery and . . ." Colin shook his head sadly. "I fear things would not go well for the lass."

Philip had miscalculated. How had that happened? He rarely lost his temper with his half brothers—always careful to impress how little he cared about Sgor Dubh or them. Not that it mattered, they'd always held a powerful weapon—his guilt over Effie, his remorse toward Mairi, and though he'd striven to take even that power from them, he'd never been entirely successful. And now he'd played right into Colin's hands and revealed yet another weakness. Isobel.

Colin thrust Philip away from him and made a show of straightening his shirt and plaid. "Just remember that when you talk to Father. So long as he names me tanist, you can do what you like with your little witch."

Philip's hand was on his sword hilt, his jaw rigid. Colin saw it and backed away, still smiling his oily smile, and disappeared down the ladder. Philip's hand still clenched the hilt, itching to cut his bastard brother down. That Colin would be chieftain of Sgor Dubh chafed. He'd wanted Colin to have it—or so he'd endeavored to convince himself for years—but now, to give it to him under threats of blackmail, when it had been his all along . . . Philip was tempted to go down to his father and announce he'd changed his mind and would take his place as heir apparent.

But no. That would mean living with Mairi and the ghost of his sister. And besides, he didn't doubt Colin's sincerity—he would find a way to inform Lord Kincreag of Isobel's alleged crimes. And unfortunately, too much of it was the truth.

Philip's hand relaxed on his sword. He could not wait to be quit of the place. He wished they'd never come. Tomorrow. All he must endure was an audience with his father and a meal with the rest. And on the morrow they would be gone.

Chapter 12

Philip did not come for her. Isobel spent several hours in his room, trying to wrap her arisaid about her shoulders in the manner of the women she'd seen in the courtyard earlier. She thought of Mairi's. It had extended from shoulders to ankles. No wonder Isobel's had looked ridiculous—it was far too short to be worn so, but she could still wear it as a wrap. She'd seen some women do that, though their arisaids had been wider and longer. But no matter how she fussed with it, she couldn't seem to make it look as the Highland women's.

When finally she'd shoved it back in her satchel in disgust, she'd decided to go through Philip's room—gloves on. She was drained from touching Effie's things and needed to rest. She knew she should lie down until dinner, but though her body was tired, her mind was not.

The scene in Effie's room played over and over again in her head, and still she could find no way to make it right. She knew from touching Effie's things that Mairi's feelings toward Philip were poisoned. It was not mere dislike, or even hate, it was far more complex than that. She wanted him to suffer. And even more disturbing was that Isobel understood it. Who could blame her? It was clear Mairi had loved her daughter, that the loss of Effie had destroyed her life, and Philip claimed to be responsible for it all.

But Isobel's feelings for Philip ran deep—deeper than she cared to examine—and she couldn't bear that he continued to punish himself for something that could not be changed. She knew him well enough to understand that whatever happened, it had not been intentional and that he'd paid for it—was still paying.

But who was Isobel MacDonell to fix anything, even if she could? She was nothing to Philip—his charge. Once he delivered her to Lochlaire, he would go on with his life and she with hers. She would marry Nicholas Lyon and have a whole new set of problems. She should not involve herself in Effie's disappearance. But she couldn't help herself.

She was digging through a chest filled with nothing more than warm woolen blankets and animal skins when Stephen arrived to take her to dinner.

"Where's Philip?" she asked, disappointed.

"He's been closed up with his father for hours now. There's been some shouting—the servants are frightened. I dinna think we'll be staying here long."

"Is it always like this?" Isobel asked.

"Worse, sometimes."

She looked Stephen up and down. He wore a belted plaid, his legs bare from the knees down, his feet bare. His long blond hair hung loose about his shoulders, and his beard was becoming thick. He looked a proper barbarian.

"I thought you weren't a Highlander?" she teased.

"I'm not—but the lassies here sure like it when I put one of these things on."

Isobel laughed. "You stopped eating long enough to notice?"

"Och, I can do both." The sound of a clanging bell drifted through the window. "That's dinner."

"Stephen, wait."

He raised an inquisitive brow and came further into the room.

"You must tell me what happened to Philip's sister."

"He lost her."

"I know that—but *how?*"

Stephen's brows drew into a troubled frown. "So ye didna learn aught today?"

Isobel shook her head.

"I dinna understand. She has a whole room full of things."

Isobel sighed and sat on the wooden chest. "Remember when I touched your father's book? The first things I saw were of you, but beneath all that I discovered your father. But your father had owned that book for a very long time and kept it close to him. Effie's things . . . well, they've been Mairi's for longer than Effie was even alive. And Mairi's feelings are so strong, they overshadow anything else."

Stephen crossed his arms over his chest. "How did Philip take it?"

Isobel just shook her head. She would not discuss what happened with anyone. "I must know, Stephen. Tell me."

Stephen was thoughtful, no doubt wondering how much trouble this would get him in. But his natural loquacity won out. "If Effie were alive, she'd be my age, so I wasna even here when it happened. My uncle sent me to be fostered here five years ago."

"Five years ago? That seems a long time."

Stephen shrugged. "Aye, I should've gone home by now, 'tis the truth, but I do well with Philip, and so I'm his man. My uncle isn't happy about it, but he does like Philip, so he doesna complain too loudly. Anyway—about Effie. Philip doesna talk about this, though I ken he thinks about it a lot. All I've heard has come from others."

"You said once before that Mairi told you things. What did she tell you?"

Stephen raised his brows and looked away as if it weren't something he wanted to share. "It's not as if she ever sat me down and told me the story. It was other things, things she said. I pieced it together from there, and asked Fergus to fill in the holes."

"Stephen!" Isobel cried impatiently. "Just tell me!"

He came to the bench and gestured for her to scoot over. When he was sitting beside her he frowned at the wall. Isobel was ready to bludgeon him when he finally spoke.

"They were in Edinburgh for some reason, I dinna know why, and Mairi was shopping. There aren't lots of shops out this way, I'm sure ye noticed, so if ye like books and comfits and such, ye best get them when yer in Edinburgh or Stirling or—"

"I understand, Stephen."

He nodded. "Anyway, from what I've heard, Effie could be a . . . difficult bairn. Mairi was in the apothecary— Philip was following her about, I dinna know why, as I cannot see them off about town together, but it seems they got on well back then—she's his mother, after all. Effie was grabbing bottles off the shelves and touching things— just being a bairn—but Mairi wasna so tolerant of childish behavior and told Philip to take her somewhere else so she could shop in peace.

"So he did. Things were going fine, until a lass caught Philip's eye, and he set to work on her. All thoughts of his wee sister apparently fled and when he did recall her, she was nowhere to be found."

Stephen shook his head. "It was a quarter day, so the streets were packed with servants itching to spend their money. A bad time to lose a child. Fergus says Philip didn't sleep for days—wouldn't leave Edinburgh, even when Dougal had given the child up for dead. He walked the streets, calling for her."

"He was seventeen?"

"Aye." He gave her a sideways look. "She was six—old enough to know better than to run away, or leave with someone she didna know—to my way of thinking. He's too hard on himself." Then he raised a shoulder, as if conceding a point. "But Fergus also tells me Effie did try to get his attention—no one knows for what purpose—because he became irritated with her for bothering him and spoke harshly."

"What does Mairi say?" Isobel asked softly.

Stephen stood. "I wouldna repeat some of the things that woman said to anyone . . . and doubt Philip would want me to." Before Isobel could press him further, he was heading for the door. "Come on, I'm starving."

The hall was warm and fragrant from fresh, herbed rushes, roast meat, and the press of bodies. Stephen led her to the head table. Philip was already there, beside his father and opposite his stepmother. Colin sat beside Mairi, and there was an empty space on the bench beside Philip. Stephen led her to it and after she'd slid in, he squeezed in beside her, pressing her close to Philip's side.

But he didn't seem to notice. He was drinking something from a square wooden tankard. His plate was empty. Platters filled the center of the table, but Isobel didn't have a plate. Everyone was engaged in loud conversation—in Gaelic—no one taking notice of her dilemma. Stephen didn't have a plate either, but he simply ate directly from the platters.

Isobel tapped Philip's arm, then gestured to the empty table in front of her. He shoved his plate at her.

"I don't want to take your plate," she said hastily. "We can share."

"I'm not hungry." He grabbed a bottle and refilled his tankard with amber liquid. Whisky. It seemed he was drinking his dinner. Isobel looked up to see Mairi watching him with narrowed eyes and thinned lips.

She turned her sharp gaze on Isobel. "So, you are MacDonell of Glen Laire's daughter? Colin tells me you're promised to the earl of Kincreag."

Isobel's cheeks burned, remembering the scene Mairi had interrupted—and knowing she was remembering it, too.

"Yes."

Mairi smiled, her gazing darting to Philip. "Amazing Philip found time to stop by before taking you to your father and betrothed. Surely Lord Kincreag is eager to proceed with the nuptials. He is still without an heir."

Isobel glanced at Philip for help.

He was looking at his stepmother oddly. "I don't know why I came. I shouldn't have. I'm . . . sorry."

"Colin says it was for a horse. Do you remember now?"

"Aye," Philip said tightly, and stared into his tankard.

Mairi cut a piece of meat. "When I heard you'd arrived, I thought perhaps you had welcome news."

The muscles in Philip's jaw bulged. "It's been a long time. It's not likely I'll ever have welcome news."

Mairi put her knife down purposefully. "That is what you keep telling me. But then I see how much it really means to you, don't I, when you desecrate her memory as you did today. I don't believe you're looking at all anymore. Perhaps you've never looked."

Philip's gaze was locked on his tankard. His chest rose and fell with emotion, but he spoke not a word in his own defense.

"That was my fault," Isobel said suddenly. Colin and Dougal were still talking over them. In fact, no one paid any attention to Mairi and Philip's conversation. Perhaps these scenes were common. This saddened Isobel. She lowered her voice. "I've been known to . . . find things. I offered to help. I'm sorry I could not. The rest . . . what you saw. That was all my doing."

Mairi looked her up and down, then turned her stony blue gaze on Philip. "Is this true?"

Philip shook his head wearily. "No."

"Philip?" Isobel said, confused.

"That's what I thought," Mairi said. "Don't waste your time trying to protect him, Mistress MacDonell. He'll only repay you with heartbreak."

Philip started to stand, but Dougal laid a hand on Philip's shoulder. He said something in Gaelic, gesturing to Colin, who looked up from his meal.

Philip ignored his father, though he remained seated. Dougal's mouth thinned and he repeated himself in English. "Colin has some interesting ideas on breeding those horses you sent from France. I'd like to hear what you think."

"I'm sure Colin knows better than I do."

"Whether he does or not, I think you should hear it. They're your horses."

"No, I sent them to you."

"I'll tell ye what I think," Stephen said, leaning across Isobel to look at Dougal. "That big stallion, the black one . . ." He trailed off when Dougal just glared at him. "Maybe later." He grabbed a roll.

"He doesna care!" Colin said, his face red. "Why do ye keep trying? *I* care, Father."

"He only cares for himself," Mairi said, pinning her husband with a withering look. "And you only care for him."

"I'm not going to listen to this, wife."

"Since when do you listen? Certainly not when Philip comes home. None of your other children matter when Philip is here. Colin is here every day trying to please you— but you fall all over yourself as soon as Philip comes home."

Philip drained his tankard as Dougal and Mairi dissolved into vehement Gaelic. He stood, grabbing a bottle from the table. "Then I'll just go, aye?"

Dougal stood angrily, but Philip strode from the hall. Colin and Mairi's angry stares followed him out.

Isobel hesitated, then slid off the bench and followed him. She didn't care what the others thought. She should, she knew. Though the Highlands were remote and far removed from England and the lowlands, and even the king's court, information did have a way of traveling. Her father or her betrothed could hear of her behavior, and she'd have some explaining to do.

She would deal with that when—if—the time came. For the moment all she could think of was Philip. She passed into the dark corridors, lit at far intervals by torches, and saw no sign of him. That was where he'd gone, though, so she followed the corridor and came to an open door.

Outside thick clouds shrouded the moon, but torches lit the bailey. Stones crunched under her feet. She scanned the open yard. Wooden buildings lined the edges of the walls. There was a shadowy recess between two buildings and she caught sight of Philip, disappearing into it. Isobel lifted her skirts and hurried after him.

She came to a crude arched doorway cut into the stone, with steps leading downward. No lights were lit, but a rope rail was tacked to the wall. She descended, clinging to the rope. She heard movement below. She emerged into a cave of sorts, facing the sea. An old wooden chest sat against one stone wall. Coils of rope littered the floor. Water lapped against the stone, and several oared boats were tied to posts driven into the rock. Philip was untying one of the boats.

"Philip?"

He turned, surprised. She knew then he was drunk—otherwise, he would have known she'd followed.

He turned back to the boat. "Go to bed."

"I don't want to . . . I've told you before, I don't sleep much."

"Then go inside."

"You can't go out alone."

"I've done it before."

"Drunk?"

He shook his head. "I'm hardly drunk."

She went to him. "Nevertheless, I'm coming with you."

"Isobel, I really dinna think that's a good idea."

She was already in the boat, sitting on a wooden cross plank and staring up at him expectantly.

He sighed, hands on hips, then shrugged. "I care not. Just keep yer mouth shut, aye? So I can pretend I'm alone."

Isobel clamped her lips together and nodded.

He took an oil lantern and handed it to her to hang from the hook on the bow of the boat. He sat on a plank facing her and began to row.

When they were clear of the cave and heading into open sea, she asked, "Where are we going?"

He said nothing.

"Why do you still wear lowland attire? Stephen changed."

When she still received no answer she pointed to the bottle of whisky rolling around in the bottom of the boat. "Could I have some?"

He paused in his rowing to regard her with a severe expression. Then he shrugged again. "It's damn hard to pretend I'm alone when ye wilna stop talking."

Isobel smiled at him. She took the bottle and pried out the cork. He watched her, his face shadowed, but she could see the dimples denting his cheeks. She sniffed the contents and shuddered. She'd not drunk whisky since she was a child. She and her sisters would steal drinks from their father's cup when he wasn't looking. Lord Attmore had forbidden it, allowing the women to drink only watered wine or ale.

She took a swig. The brew burned going down, and, she sputtered, clamping a hand over her mouth. Warmth moved through her whole body, and she shuddered with a mixture of revulsion and pleasure. She looked at the bottle. "Faith!" she said, and Philip laughed. She took another drink, and another, until he snatched the bottle away.

"That's enough," he said. "I canna have ye falling oot of the boat." His Scots had grown broad. He took another long drink himself, before stuffing in the cork and placing the bottle in the bottom of the boat.

When he was rowing again, she asked, "Why did you lie to Mairi? Maybe if she knew why we came, she wouldn't be so sour."

"And tell her you're a witch? I think not."

He was always protecting her. It warmed her more efficiently than the whisky.

"Where are we going? To one of the islands I saw from the window?"

"Aye."

"Who lives there?"

"No one. The chieftains of Sgor Dubh and their families are buried there."

Isobel looked up at the approaching island. A deserted cemetery. A shiver of apprehension slid over her.

When she glanced back at Philip, he grinned at her. "Scared?"

"Of course not. They're all dead."

"Och, it's said the Kilpatricks are restless in death—that's why they're buried on an island, so they canna haunt the living."

A frisson of unease went through Isobel, but she kept her face bland. "You're just trying to frighten me."

He only smiled.

By the time they reached the island, Isobel's limbs felt warm and heavy—an interesting and pleasant sensation. She wanted more of the whisky and said so as he dragged the boat ashore. He fetched the bottle from the boat and considered her a moment before passing it to her again.

He grabbed the lantern as she took another deep pull. This one went down much more smoothly. She started to take another drink, but he plucked the bottle from her grasp.

"I dinna want ye to bock all over me or the boat—or someone's grave."

"I've never bocked in my life!"

He slanted her a skeptical look, taking another drink. "Never?"

"Well, perhaps when I was wean. But not that I remember."

He grunted and started up the beach. Isobel started to follow and stumbled, surprised at how wobbly her legs were. He turned to look at her, and she giggled. "I haven't got my land legs back yet, it seems."

"We werena in the boat that long. Ye're sotted, lass. If yer father could see ye now, he'd thrash me." He caught her arm and led her to a trail worn in the windswept grasses.

"It'll be our secret, aye?" she said, and giggled again.

He just shook his head at her, but he was smiling, and that filled Isobel with happiness.

There were no trees on the island, and the damp air blowing across it was cold. Isobel wished she'd brought her arisaid or cloak. They arrived at a well-tended plot of land, bathed in muted moonlight. Long slabs of stone littered the area, some standing upright, others partly submerged in the earth. Isobel paused before one, barely able to make out a carving of a warrior in a pointed helmet and chain mail, wielding an enormous cross hilt sword. Philip continued on to a stone cross. He held the lantern high. The cross was decorated with a knotwork of braids. Isobel stopped beside him.

"My mother," he said.

Isobel said nothing, staring down at the overgrown plot.

"I wish I remembered her better."

"How soon after your mother died did Dougal wed Mairi?"

"It wasna even a year."

"So she is the only mother you ever knew?"

He nodded.

And Mairi hated him now. She hadn't always. Stephen had said they got on fine before he'd lost Effie. Isobel didn't know what to say, so she touched the leather sleeve of his jack.

"I dinna ken why I come here." He started back for the beach.

Isobel watched him go, troubled. She turned back to the stone cross. She thought of her own mother, buried somewhere near Lochlaire. She didn't even know where, had never seen her mother's grave. Everything had happened so quickly after her mother had been burned. Alan MacDonell had sent his best men to deliver his daughters away to different places. Isobel didn't even know where her sisters were. Hadn't spoken to Gillian and Rose in twelve years. She remembered Rose's face as she screamed for her mum and da—arms outstretched and tears dripping from her chin as the big knight had carried her off before him on his horse. Alan had wept, too, and told them all they must be brave. Isobel had not cried, though she'd wanted to. She'd seen how it hurt her father.

She returned to the beach. Philip sat in the sand, elbows on his knees, bottle dangling from his fingertips. The lantern flickered near his feet. Isobel sat beside him and took the bottle. After taking a drink, she turned to him. He had placed a palm behind her and leaned toward her, looking at her. Her pulse fluttered and set to racing.

"I want to talk to you about something," she said.

"Hmm . . . ?"

"It's about your stepmother."

"I dinna want to talk about my stepmother."

"I know, and that's why we must."

His dark eyes were on her face, searching it, drinking her in, it seemed. Her mouth had gone dry, and she licked her lips, trying to recall what she'd wanted to say.

"You dinna belong here," he said, his voice low and rough. "Ye're too good for this place."

Isobel didn't know how to respond, couldn't look away from his thick-lashed eyes. She found her lips trembling on his name, a whisper. The moment spun out, and Isobel was snared in it, powerless to break away from his heated gaze.

"Will ye forget me when you are a countess?" he asked, his voice low and husky, resonating through her.

Isobel's breath caught, and she managed to whisper, "I will try."

He looked away, to the waves washing the shore. Isobel longed to touch him, to stroke the strong line of his jaw, feel the firm, sensual set of his lips against her skin.

She swallowed hard, and said, "But I do not think I will succeed."

He turned back to her, a feverish light in his eyes, and leaned toward her until his mouth touched hers. He kissed her gently, then murmured against her mouth, "I should not do this."

Isobel leaned into him, sliding her arms around his neck. "Then I will." She ran her tongue along his bottom lip, tasting whisky and desire. His arms came around her, crushing her close, his tongue plundering her mouth as he pushed her down into the sand.

His mouth was hot and demanding, and she answered it, pressing her body up against him. Her mind was a fog of desire, but she knew she wanted this, wanted him this way. His hand slid up her waist and ribs, to the laces of her bodice. He worked them free, his mouth never leaving hers. When his hand slid inside, closing over her breast, Isobel gasped and stiffened, shocked at the intimate touch. His hand was warm and his thumb, rubbing over her hardened nipple, sent a nearly painful arrow of lust through her.

He drew back to look at her, his hand sliding up to cup her face. He seemed about to say something, but instead he kissed her again, holding her face so he could explore her mouth with tongue and teeth until she was breathless, clinging to him and whimpering. Though his kisses and touch swept her away, her mind could not forget that this was transient, that it was all she'd ever have. It lent an urgency to her, her fingers tracing the strong lines of his face, the dark silky brows, the powerful corded muscles of his neck and shoulders.

His mouth left hers. He pushed her shift from her shoulders. His mouth scorched her skin, moving downward. She trembled when the cold air blew over her naked breasts. And then his hands and tongue were there, and need, fierce and aching, blossomed inside her, curling deep in her belly.

His hand was beneath her skirts, sliding up her thigh— and his knee was between her legs, pressing them apart. She yielded, consumed with these new sensations, afraid at any moment it would stop, and she would be left alone with this desperate need.

Her hands slid inside his jack and around his back, the long, hard muscles shifting and bunching beneath her fingers. The heat of his mouth on her, the feel of his strength beneath her hands was more potent than the whisky that spilled into the sand beside them. His hand brushed the damp curls between her legs, and she gasped, her legs closing involuntarily. His mouth covered hers again, his kiss wet and drugging, as his open palm stroked her quivering belly. Her limbs went weak from the bold stroke of his tongue and the sharp answer that pooled in her loins.

When his hand returned, cupping her, his fingers stroking deeper each time, ribbons of pleasure rippled through her. She made a sound against his mouth, as exquisite sensation ripped through her, tightening her muscles, shattering her senses.

Philip dragged his mouth away, staring down at the flushed and writhing woman beneath him. Her red-gold hair was spread around her like fire, and the heavy throbbing in his groin increased. He wanted to drive into her— she was ready for him, he'd seen to that, could still feel her body clenching around his fingers with the aftermath of her pleasure. He closed his eyes, trying to force some semblance of control over his whisky-thickened senses.

He withdrew his hand as her long, reddish lashes lifted slowly to gaze at him, her eyes foggy. She smiled, sated and warm, and it sent an answering surge of lust through him. She was all soft, heated skin, fragrant and beautiful, and he wanted to rip open his breeks and to bury himself.

How had this happened? He certainly hadn't planned it. Why could he not keep his hands off her?

Her bodice and shift gaped, round breasts, rosy from his body pressed against her, from his mouth . . . He rolled away, his hand coming down in a patch of wet sand. The empty bottle of whisky rolled away, waves washing over it and dragging it out to sea. What the hell was he doing?

"Philip?" she said, her voice soft and sensual, drawing him back.

But one look at her and he averted his gaze. "Cover yourself."

He could not look at her and not touch her. The hands he scrubbed over his face and into his hair shook. She was still a virgin, he reminded himself—and decided he should be canonized on that point—the evidence of his heroism still strained painfully against his breeks.

When he chanced a look at her she was fumbling with

the laces of her bodice, decently covered again. Her hair was wild though, red-blond curls spilling down her shoulders, framing a face flushed red with shame.

He pushed her fingers aside and pulled the laces tight, tying them quickly, but letting her tuck them into the top of her bodice. When she finally looked up and met his gaze, she held it for a long moment.

"I am sorry," he said.

"I'm not."

He had to look away, couldn't bear to look at her when she said such things. Was he mad, bringing her to this island, alone, and plying her with whisky? And now all he could think of was Nicholas Lyon, Earl Kincreag, finishing what he had begun here in the sand. He had awakened the woman in her for someone else, and it made him sick with jealousy.

He saw himself then, as her father might. A man who denied his inheritance and lived like a nomad, tracking villains for money. He could not even find a small child—or protect Isobel from his own base lust. If this didn't stop, it would cost him his friendship with Alan MacDonell—a man he respected and loved—and he still would not get Isobel. Alan wouldn't allow it, and Lord Kincreag would never stand for such an insult.

At the thought of Alan, he knew they must delay no more. He should not have brought her here. She should be with her father, spending what little time they had left together.

He heard movement beside him, felt the soft touch of her hand on his sleeve, and felt himself waver, wanting to kiss her again, his hands itching to touch her skin, and wondering what could it possibly matter now? What would one more kiss or fondle matter after what he'd just done? He stiffened himself against this infernal weakness and stood, grabbing the lantern.

"Let's get back before these clouds turn into rain."

Chapter 13

The row back to the cave at the base of Sgor Dubh was silent. Torches blazed on the castle walls, lighting their way, even as the damp mist encroached on their small vessel. Isobel tried not to look at Philip, but it was difficult. She imagined the smooth pull of muscle beneath shirt and jack as he rowed, remembering the feel of his body, so much larger and warmer than hers.

He hardly looked away from her the entire time, which was disconcerting, considering what had occurred between them. She wasn't quite certain exactly what *had* occurred on that beach. Oh, she knew she was a maiden still—she'd seen enough of men and women rutting in her visions to understand he had to put more than his fingers inside her to make a child. But she had never imagined the things they'd done could bring so much pleasure. Her loins still ached from it, warm and liquid.

It had to be wrong. She was promised to another man. Doing these things with Philip was disloyal. Knowing that didn't banish the dull throb of want every time she looked his way. Still, she didn't know what it all meant and felt a sliver of apprehension in her blood that she had begun something she could not finish. He had been right. She really didn't know what she played at. It was so intense, so painfully beautiful, that it frightened her.

It was a relief to finally be back in the cave. Philip tied the boat to a post and stepped out. Isobel scrabbled from the boat before he could help her. They stood in the gloom, the lantern giving them a dim circle of light. He watched her, silent.

She wasn't sure what he wanted, what he expected. Her own thoughts were scrambled and uncertain. But she latched on to what she knew in her heart. Her father had promised her to Lord Kincreag—to disregard that promise would not only shame her father, but it could harm his relationship with the earl, clearly not a man to be trifled with. It was extraordinary that an earl would deign to wed a mere baron's daughter. This could mean great things for her father and her clan. Lord Kincreag was the way of her future, and she must stop this flirtation before it went any further. Besides, there was Philip to consider, not just her father and family. Lord Kincreag would not countenance such an insult. He would ruin Philip—and perhaps the Kilpatricks of Colquhoun, or even kill him. And what of herself? If he really had killed his wife for cuckolding him, what would he think of Isobel's little beach tryst? She shuddered to imagine it.

"Philip," she finally said, "we must talk."

He nodded slowly. "Aye."

He was so quiet, so intent on her she could not stand fast, facing him. So she walked slowly across the cave. A chest was against the wall, the wood warped, but service-able. She stopped in front of it and took a deep breath.

"This . . . the, er . . . we cannot . . ."

The light followed her, alerting her he was behind her. "I won't touch you if ye dinna wish it, Isobel."

Isobel clasped her hands, staring blindly at the chest. "I know it—you are not to blame. It's my fault . . . I feel wanton with you. And before . . . when it was just kisses, I thought mayhap there was no harm in it—though I admit now I was wrong. . . . And you did warn me. But now . . . now I know I've done wrong. I must think of my father and Lord Kincreag. And I should not wish for you to come to any harm because of this."

"Kincreag." His voice was strange.

Isobel still couldn't look at him. "Yes. To continue on like this . . . well, it's just not fair to him." She finally turned and gave him a beseeching look. "I do not go into this union expecting great love and happiness; however, I do hope for it, as we grow to know one another. But with this . . . whatever it is, between you and me . . . I fear it will poison my life with Kincreag, and that's not fair to him."

He didn't speak for a long moment, and her heart beat into the silence, its pulse in her ears. Did her words hurt him? She didn't want that. She suddenly wished she could take it all back—her words, their kisses—anything to end this misery.

Then his lips curled into a bitter smile, unpleasant and empty. "You're such an innocent," he said quietly. "Everyone is poisoned. The whole world. You put too much weight on something of little significance. Your virtue is intact. And I'll wager my life Kincreag has done what we have and more. So lay your tortured conscience to rest. You've done nothing wrong—yet."

Her chest was tight. She'd not expected him to scorn what she felt—what she'd thought they both felt. "Yet?" she echoed, her voice barely a whisper.

"You're far too bold in your innocence. I warned you—don't blame me if you got burned." He lifted one shoulder and looked away as if bored with the conversation. "These . . . wanton feelings of yours. Save them for your husband and spare me your regrets, aye?"

Isobel's face did burn, with shame and anger. Why was it so difficult to hear him say this? Her eyes stung, and she blinked rapidly, mortified that she was about to cry. When she thought of life before him, it seemed empty—and life after? Without him? Joyless. *But it wouldn't be.* She must take heed of what he said to her. This would fade. It was nothing to him. And she'd never even met her betrothed. It could be this powerful with Lord Kincreag. *It could.* She must believe that or she would die inside.

His gaze slanted back to her, but his face was shadowed, his expression hidden. As she fought to control her emotions, to save herself a shred of dignity, his head tilted, looking at something behind her, his brow creasing. He walked past her, setting the lantern down beside the chest and dropping to his knees.

Isobel was even more hurt by this, and irritated, too. She'd never guessed she meant so little to him. She'd assumed, by his manner on the beach and the things she'd seen when touching his belongings, that he was as affected by their liaison as she was, but apparently not if he suddenly had an urge to rummage about in an old chest.

He held the lantern out to her. "Hold this, would you? I can't see what I'm doing."

Isobel took the lantern and held it over his head, contemplating dropping it. This was important to her. She was hurting. And now she felt foolish. That he could dismiss her and her feelings so easily cut deep, carving a hollow in her chest.

Her thoughts were interrupted by an odd, shuddering breath from Philip. "It's here." His voice was a whisper.

Isobel caught the urgency and knelt beside him. "What is?"

"Everything—the hooks, the line, the creels—Effie and I used them to fish. They look as if they haven't been touched in years."

He started to lift a wicker creel out of the trunk, but Isobel said, "Don't touch it."

Her despair was replaced with excitement, and when he looked at her, she saw it reflected in his eyes. The hope was back—along with fear that this, too, would come to naught.

"These might not even be the same ones," she cautioned, though something inside told her they were. "It's been twelve years—surely others fish."

Philip shook his head. "No. Fishermen fish. The Kilpatricks are not fishermen—at least not the ones who live in Sgor Dubh."

"What about servants?"

"They would have their own gear. No—this is it. *I* brought this chest down here—so we'd have a place to store our things. Taking Effie to fish was an indulgence— one Mairi forbade. So it was a secret between Effie and me. We had to keep these things somewhere Mairi wouldn't look, and she never came down here. No one has moved it since Effie disappeared."

"Well then," Isobel said, her voice slightly breathless. She set the lantern on the floor beside her. "Shall I give it a go?" She surveyed the contents of the chest. "The creels are made from wood—so they won't be too helpful. What of the hooks?"

"Bone."

Isobel nodded. "Good. Give me one."

Philip selected one with an unsteady hand. Isobel had slipped her gloves on in the boat, so she pulled them off and tucked them into the garter at her waist.

He held the hook away from her, frowning at the sharp curve. "You behaved oddly last time. I fear you'll hurt yourself with this."

Isobel didn't mention that in the past she'd hurt herself.

It was part of what she did, and she accepted that. She kept her hand facing downward so he didn't see the narrow silver scar that slashed across both palms. She'd grasped the blade of a warrior's sword to determine for his grieving father how he'd died. It happened sometimes. Her mother had said it was a price that must be paid. She couldn't deny aid to people because she was frightened she might wound herself. Lillian MacDonell's own hands had been crisscrossed with scars; a testament to her unselfish nature.

"It will be fine. Give it to me." When he still hesitated, she said, "This could be our last chance to discover what happened to Effie. When you deliver me to my father, I may never see you again, so even if you did find something else of hers, it wouldn't matter." She reached for the hook that he held away from her. "Give it to me, Philip."

He did not hand it to her, but when her fingers closed over it and drew it from his grasp, he let her take it.

Neither visions nor feelings assaulted her immediately, so she sat back on her knees, leaning against the chest. She slid the hook over her finger, the sharp edge lying against the back of her finger so it was less likely to puncture her should the vision become violent. She then pressed her palms together as if praying and closed her eyes.

She focused on Philip, together with his sister. A scene slowly crystallized behind her eyelids. Philip as a young man—handsome still, but leaner, all hands and legs, his hair long as the Highlanders wore it. He wore a plaid, too—his feet bare. He was on the beach with a young girl, and they scoured the sand for sand eels, laughing as they chased after them. She smiled at this, but knew she must dig deeper. She focused on the girl, asking the hook to tell her more—*What became of the girl? Where is she now?*

The scene on the beach clouded over. She strained to see through it. As the mist slowly cleared she found herself in a house. It was warm and rosy with firelight, redolent with the scent of lamb stew. A woman sat before the hearth, her belly round with child, sewing a wean's gown. Isobel knew immediately it was Effie. A woman. Isobel dug deeper—where was she?

She instinctively sensed the woman's happiness—also that the woman no longer went by Effie, but Isobel could not grasp what her name was now. She felt it began with an "S"—Starla or Sunny—but she could not be certain. Then she was drawn rapidly away, until she was outside the house, above it. She saw a church, and many buildings. This was not a little hamlet but a good-sized town. The farther she was pulled back, the more she saw, until she was above it, as if suspended like an angel. Walls surrounded the town, and in the distance was a group of ancient cairns on a hill.

She focused on the town, and it drew her in like a fishing line. *Where is this? What is its name?* The town's name was clear to her now, and with it came more information, in a flood. "Wyndyburgh. Rose Lane, fourth house on the right. She goes by Summer. She's married to the cooper and expecting a child in . . . June, she believes."

Isobel tried to dig deeper but only returned to visions of Effie and Philip on the beach as children. But she had enough to lead him to his sister. She opened her eyes, a wide smile on her face, and found Philip staring at her in horrified disbelief.

She looked down at the hook, still wrapped around her finger. She handed it to him, stained with a drop of her blood. "Your sister is alive and well, and quite content in her life."

When he didn't take the hook from her, she took his hand and placed it in his palm. "Go to her. I was unable to discover how you lost her, but she'll tell you . . . if she remembers. She doesn't go by Effie anymore, so I don't know how much she remembers of her life here. She was only six when you . . . when she was lost."

He stared down at the hook in his hand.

Isobel placed her palm against his cheek. "This is real, Philip. I wouldn't lie."

"I know." The words were said so softly that she almost missed them.

She hesitated, wanting to say more, to do more. The idea of leaving him now—of going to her betrothed while he went to find his sister—tore at her. She wanted them to see this through together. She wanted to be there when he saw Effie again. "Take me with you," she said impulsively. "We can go to Lochlaire after."

He shook his head against her hand, still staring down at the hook. When she would have drawn her hand away his came up, covering it, holding it against his face.

"You must go home." His lips moved against her sensitive skin, so soft, and the rasp of his beard tickled her. His breath was warm against her, sending a shiver of pleasure throughout her body, weakening her.

"What if you get there, and she remembers nothing?"

"Then at least I'll have found her."

Isobel's other hand came up, holding his face, forcing him to look at her. "We both know that will never be enough for you. There, her things will surround her. I *will* be able to discover what happened—I vow it."

The eyes he raised to hers were bright, and her heart felt swollen and bruised from the emotion she saw there. He did care. *He did.*

He swallowed hard, his throat working. The thick dark lashes fell as he closed his eyes. "No. It's too dangerous. Wyndyburgh is near where it all began—it spread from there like fire. They've burned more witches than any other area. I can't take you there."

Isobel smiled. "I will not be in danger, so long as I'm with you. I trust you to protect me. And I'll keep my gloves on. I promise."

He still shook his head, his eyes shut hard, but she knew she had won. He would still protest, but she would wear him down. She had to do this, had to finish it with him. She had to reunite him with his sister and make certain all of his questions were answered. Only then could she go on to her new life, letting go of this one.

His arms slid around her and crushed her against him. Her breath left her as she clung to him, holding him and the moment close. Something cracked inside, exquisitely painful, and Isobel knew it was her heart.

Colin stood on the bottom step, pressed against the stone wall. From the walls of Sgor Dubh he'd watched Philip and Mistress MacDonell's return from the island and had come down with the intention of berating his half brother for his careless stupidity—taking a boat out in the dark with a storm coming. If he cared for nothing else, he should at least think of Father's boat. But Colin had been halted on the bottom step by the scene he'd found in the cave.

Philip and Mistress MacDonnell had left the boat, only to stand there, staring at each other with such longing Colin almost felt compelled to avert his eyes. Almost. He'd hidden in the shadows, determined to glean as much information as he could, to use later to blackmail Philip if it became necessary. It was just as Colin had suspected—there was something between his brother and Isobel MacDonell, something he could report to Earl Kincreag if necessary. But the rest, when they'd moved to the chest . . .

that had shaken him to the core. He hurried back up the steps, trying to step quietly, his mind racing.

Isobel MacDonell was the daughter of a powerful chieftain and one did not make accusations idly—retribution would surely follow. Colin had only called her a witch to annoy Philip, knowing his brother would never tell Alan MacDonell. But now . . . it seemed Philip *was* consulting with a witch—a crime nearly as grievous as being one.

If that wasn't shocking enough—it got worse. Mairi's daughter was alive. Colin didn't even want to consider what this meant for him. If Philip returned Mairi's daughter to her, he would have no reason to stay away from Sgor Dubh. Mairi would finally forgive him. And Philip would happily accept his inheritance, leaving Colin with nothing.

Colin entered the keep, and the dogs ran to him, jumping and licking. He shoved them away, impatient. Something must be done, and before Dougal or Mairi learned that Effie lived. And he must find a way to end Philip and Mistress MacDonell's affair before something dreadful happened—if Philip got her with child, his honor would compel him to marry her, and if that child was a boy . . . Colin's head pounded from the possibilities, and he pressed his fingers against his eyelids to relieve the pain. It felt as if everything he'd worked for was about to be demolished by this MacDonell woman. He *must* do something, but he didn't yet know what.

Then he remembered the messenger that had arrived that morning—just before Philip. Colin had managed to get his hands on the missive before his father had read it. It had been from the elders in some village—something about a murder and needing Philip's presence for the trial. They also requested the *seer's* presence. The seer had to be Isobel MacDonell. Dougal had burned the letter after reading it—muttering about hysterical elders, but Colin remembered the town's name. Hawkirk.

Isobel MacDonell was certainly a witch, and if there were already accusations leveled against either Philip or Mistress MacDonell, it wouldn't take much to turn the tide against them—even without the witch's presence. If they believed Philip had been consulting with a witch, his fate was sealed. The past few years had seen many folk burned for that crime.

He smiled, rubbing his hands together. He would need help. He would have to find Niall and Aidan—they would do whatever he asked, so long as he promised them rewards. Pleased with himself and this new development, he left the castle to fetch his brothers.

Chapter 14

Fergus had not yet returned, not that Philip had expected him, but still, it was inconvenient. He left instructions for Fergus to follow when he arrived at Sgor Dubh, then Philip sought out Isobel and Stephen.

He found them in the great hall breaking their fast. He carefully avoided meeting Isobel's gaze. "We're leaving. Now."

Isobel looked up at him with a wide smile. "I told Stephen where we're going."

Philip looked quickly around the hall, relieved no one was nearby. "Have you told anyone else?"

"Of course not."

"Could anyone have overheard you?"

She looked around, confused. "No."

"Good. Speak of it no more. Do you understand?"

She frowned at him, but said, "Aye, but why?"

Philip shook his head in disbelief. Would she never understand? "So the Kilpatricks dinna decide to use you for kindling in their May Day bonfire, that's why. Christ, woman—think!"

Isobel looked at Stephen helplessly. "But it's good tidings for your family."

Stephen nodded, speaking around a mouthful of bread. "She has the right of it, Philip. A white witch, she is. White witches are not burned."

Philip cuffed the back of the lad's head. "Of course they are—as soon as someone perceives something they've done as evil—or as soon as someone dies, folks suddenly recall how that *white* witch once happened to touch or look at the deceased. It doesna matter what good deeds they've done in the past when a scapegoat is needed. Now leave off with all this talk of witches. I dinna want to hear either of you say that word again."

They both nodded, though Isobel clearly thought him unreasonable. It would drive him mad, leaving her with Kincreag. She would be strapped to a stake and lit like a candle in a sennight.

He mustn't think of it. Not his place.

They set out, heading northwest. The pink heugh daisies and lus an rois of the coast gave way to violets and heather blanketing the ground in a soft carpet that muffled the horses' progress. But the terrain would grow difficult soon, as Lochlaire was nestled in a glen surrounded on all sides by mountains. He wondered how long it would take Isobel to notice they were heading deeper into the Highlands, rather than southeast, where the town of her vision lay. It seemed luck was with him and her sense of direction was poor—that or Stephen's incessant chatter kept her from noticing. To give her a reprieve, Philip and Stephen took turns riding ahead to scout out their route. There were a lot of broken men wandering the western Highlands.

The gray he'd fetched from Sgor Dubh as a wedding gift was high-strung and still nervous around Isobel, so they had to be kept apart—the gray had a nasty habit of biting anything that annoyed him. Philip hoped the horse found the earl highly irritating.

When they stopped to rest the horses and eat, Stephen took him aside.

"We're not going to Wyndyburgh are we?"

"Aye, we are. Right after we deliver Isobel to her father."

Stephen glanced over to where Isobel knelt beside a burn, washing her face. "She will be vexed. She thinks she's going with us."

Philip shrugged. "Not my problem."

Stephen looked back at Philip speculatively. "You seem . . . discontented of late."

"Do I? Well, I'm not," Philip answered sourly.

Stephen made a few thoughtful noises, but wisely said no more.

Philip tried not think of his cowardly behavior. Isobel would be upset when she found out he was not taking her to Wyndyburgh with him, but it couldn't be helped. He was not strong enough to withstand her entreaties to join him. He knew that if she kept at him, he'd eventually give in and he'd be forced to spend even more time in her company, which would be disastrous for both of them. No, it was better this way.

When they were traveling again, and Stephen was scouting ahead, gray in tow, Isobel made an effort to engage Philip in conversation. He'd been quiet most of the day, thinking it better to have as little contact with her as possible. The situation had somehow gotten away from him, and he didn't like that. He liked being in control of things, but she set him off-balance.

"Tell me about some of the people you've located," she said. "You must have some very interesting stories."

"I canna speak of most."

She raised her brows. "Really? Were you sworn to silence?"

"Something like that."

She seemed to be thinking on that, so he said, "I would do the same for you—take a vow of silence that is, about all I've seen you do."

She smiled, turning the full force of her pleasure on him. "Would you?"

"Aye, if you would do the same. Vow to never speak of it. Never to exercise it in the presence of others. To rarely take your gloves off."

Her smile faded, and she looked away from him. She did not make any vows.

"Mistress MacDonell? I pray you to consider it."

"It's Mistress MacDonell now?" she hissed at him, pinning him with a green stare. "After last night I'd think we were more familiar."

"We should not be so familiar, and you know it. Last night is something else we must both take a vow of silence about."

She looked at him steadily, proudly. "I can vow never to speak of it—but I'll never vow not to think of it."

Heat washed through him at her words and her look. Bloody hell, but life was cruel. Now he could imagine her in her marriage bed with Kincreag, but thinking of him. He shut his eyes to force away the image that provoked.

He sighed deeply. "You'll never learn to stop playing with fire, will you?"

A slow smile spread over her face. "Maybe I like getting burned."

Philip shook his head. "That is not amusing." He was thinking of bonfires, of course, but she just continued to smile impishly at him.

"Tell me," he said, to change the subject. "When did you realize you were a seer? Were you born this way?"

"No, I remember many years where I could touch

things and feel nothing at all. But once it started, the whole household was in an uproar." She gave him an abashed smile. "I was something of a teller of tales—discovering things about my sisters or the servants and tattling on them. There was a period when Gillian and Rose didn't speak to me for months without it dissolving into a spitting and hair-pulling brawl."

Philip smiled, remembering his own vicious fights with his brothers—though they'd been out to cause each other serious harm more often than not. "Did it frighten you, the first time you saw something?"

Isobel exhaled thoughtfully, her brow furrowed. "No— it seemed . . . right—just like any other sense I possess— seeing, touching. I was seven when I first had a vision."

"So you've been like this since you were seven?"

"Aye, my mother was also a seer, just like me. Well, not *just* like me, she was far better. She only used it for good. She taught me ways to control it. She had planned to teach me much more, but . . ." She trailed off. They both knew the remainder of her sentence—her apprenticeship had been cut short by Lillian MacDonell's death.

"You said your mother only used her magic for good. When do you use it for evil?"

Isobel shrugged, obviously reluctant to talk about this, but he pressed her. He had seen no evidence that she used her magic for anything but good and so was curious as to her definition of evil.

"Tell me—what evil have you wrought in the world?"

She caught the teasing in his tone and gave him a sheepish look. "I've seen things I should not have—and I've oft gone looking for them—so it's not always a mistake. And when I was younger I would sometimes use what I learned to get my way or get revenge on those who'd wronged me . . . even if others got hurt."

"You're too hard on yourself. Surely when your mother was young she did such things. No one is born a saint."

"I don't know," Isobel said, not convinced. "She was quite adamant in her teachings."

"Perhaps that's why—she didn't want you to learn the hard way. She meant well, but it's an impossible task. Bairns will be bairns—naught we can do about it."

She looked at him slyly from beneath her lashes. "Just as lads will be lads—flirting with lassies and becoming annoyed at their little sisters?"

He reined in hard, staring at her in shocked surprise. Not just that she knew, but what her words made him feel. When she said such things, he wanted her so desperately nothing else seemed to matter—not her father or her betrothed—he just knew he didn't want to be without her. She filled an emptiness in him that he hadn't known existed.

But how did she know? It was certain any number of people could tell her of how he lost his sister—but was that how she'd obtained her information?

"Have you been touching *my* things—digging around in my mind?"

She looked away quickly, guiltily, and his chest tightened. He didn't want her to know what he felt. It served no purpose.

When she looked back her chin was set. "What if I did?"

"Is that how you know about Effie?"

"No—I've seen little of her, only what I told you. I vow it."

He rode his horse closer to her, so they faced each other, their horses muzzle to tail. "Well then, what *did* you see?"

She bit her bottom lip as he held her gaze, unwavering. What had she seen? That not a moment passed without her haunting his thoughts? That he lay awake at night, cursing fate for betrothing her to an earl—for making him some fool without a future to offer her. That right then he'd give up everything just to touch her again. His hand tightened on the reins and he leaned forward to drag her off her horse, into his arms.

The sound of hoofbeats halted him. "It's clear ahead," Stephen called. "Nothing but heather for miles—though I did see Ben Nevis in the distance."

Philip turned his horse to face Stephen, faintly shaken by what he'd been about to do—after all the vows he'd made to himself not to touch her. He could not honor them. And if he didn't take her to her father posthaste, he doubted he could honor his promise to Alan MacDonell.

"Ben Nevis?" Isobel said. "But Ben Nevis is north . . ."

Philip glared at Stephen.

"I could be mistaken," Stephen said hastily. When Philip continued to stare at Stephen furiously, the lad said, "Let me look again—I'm probably wrong." He swung his horse around, yanking on the gray's tether, and galloped ahead.

Philip spurred his horse to follow.

"You're taking me to Lochlaire," Isobel said in disbelief, catching up to ride beside him.

"Aye."

"But I thought I was going with you to find Effie. I thought we were in this together."

He took one look at the betrayal in her beautiful eyes and looked away, hardening himself to it. "We're in nothing together. You have an earl waiting for you at home, and it's past time I delivered you to him."

She didn't say another word, and when he glanced over, her face was sad and lost. The fist wrapped itself around his heart again, and he resolved they would not stop for the night. They would not stop until they were at Lochlaire, and she was safe with her father.

Chapter 15

The terrain they traveled through all looked the same to Isobel. It became mountainous and difficult, yet when Isobel expected Philip to stop he kept going. Dark fell, and still they rode on. He seemed to know his way instinctively and never slowed. Isobel and her horse were exhausted. After a time she found herself dozing in the saddle for stretches, when the ground was relatively flat—and thought by Jinny's stumbling that the horse was dozing as well.

Isobel kept her silence as long as she could. When her horse stumbled again and whinnied plaintively, she said, "Please, we must stop. Jinny needs rest."

Philip's and Stephen's horses were similarly exhausted, but the gray Stephen led tossed its head irritably. Philip's gaze raked over her and Jinny dispassionately. "Very well. Those trees ahead will give us some cover."

Philip and Stephen galloped toward the trees, but Jinny continued plodding like an old mule. She wasn't used to such a trek. Isobel spoke soothingly and rubbed her neck. When Isobel reached the stand of rowan trees, she dismounted and gave Jinny some water. Then she sank down herself, her back against a tree trunk, and closed her eyes.

It would not be long now. She felt it. The sensation of dread that she was sure had to do with her father had never left her, but she had grown accustomed to it, had begun to ignore it—but in the past hours it had grown and gnawed at her. She wished for Ceri as she hadn't in days. She needed someone to talk to, to sort it all out in her head. Her thoughts were so jumbled and miserable. All she could think about was Philip and the fact he was leaving her, going off on his own to find his sister. It made her feel empty, left out. What if he needed her there? What if Effie remembered nothing, or she was hostile toward him? Isobel couldn't bear it, *needed* to be there to help him. But he didn't want her. He was finishing the task of delivering her to her father. She'd never been any more to him than a duty and a tool.

She opened her eyes. Dawn streaked the sky with pink and orange. He was a dozen feet from her, drinking from the wineskin. He looked beautiful in the soft light, his forehead and nose, straight and clean, his dark hair curling about his collar. He still wore lowland clothes, and she wondered why, now that they were in the Highlands. Had he not expressed a desire to blend? Stephen still wore his Highland costume.

Isobel looked down at her own dull green gown, travel-stained and worn. This was how she'd be presented to her father—like a common Englishwoman. Philip turned toward her suddenly, his gaze raking her from head to toe. Then he went to his horse and opened a leather sack, withdrawing a bundle of cloth.

He walked over to her with the bundle. "Fetch me your brooch."

Isobel did as he bid, stealing curious glances at the cloth he carried. It was a plaid of the type the women at Sgor Dubh wore—finer and lighter than the men's, the colorful checks woven onto a white background, rather than green or brown. When she returned to his side he shook it out. Isobel gasped with pleasure. It was at least six feet in length and more than half that in width.

"Turn around," he instructed.

Isobel obediently put her back to him. He lifted her braid, sliding the arisaid beneath it.

"Turn." He held it together at her throat as she turned back toward him. "Give me the brooch." She handed it to him, and he secured it at her throat. Then his hands were at her waist, unhooking her garter. His touch was impersonal, efficient, and yet Isobel's heart raced, her blood simmering already from his nearness. He was so close she could see how fine and poreless his skin was, and though his hair was sandy brown, his beard was darker, and, upon closer inspection, she counted several gray whiskers. He glanced up at her, as if he sensed the intensity of her perusal. Whisky-dark eyes held hers a heartbeat, the air about them thickening, then he returned to his task.

Perhaps he was right to take her home. No good could ever come of these feelings. She reasoned with herself that she hardly knew him. These feelings would fade. After all, she had fancied herself in love before. True, she'd only been a girl, but her heart had been in agony—she'd feared she would die from it. But she hadn't. She'd lived through it, and though it felt as if losing Philip would devastate her, she would continue on. That was the way of the world. She wondered how many great ladies had loved deeply before they married their lords and earls and dukes. Marriage was not about love, it never had been, and sensible ladies made the best of their lot. That was just what Isobel would do. For her father.

Philip had gathered the material at her waist, folding and belting it with her garter so it did not drag beneath her feet. Then he stood back and looked at her. Isobel looked down at the beautiful arisaid, her hands smoothing over it. She looked like a true Highland woman. Her father would be so pleased.

"Thank you, Philip." Her voice was thick with emotion. That he would do this for her, that he knew what it meant to her to go to her father looking like a true MacDonell, made her love him more. She blinked back tears at the realization that she'd fallen in love with her protector. It seemed the most natural thing in the world to love him and yet it was so wrong that it left her heart in shreds.

He came forward and adjusted how the arisaid fell over her shoulders. "If it rains or snows, you can just pull up the back and cover your head. The colors are not right. MacDonells use local dyes, which are different from the dyes near Sgor Dubh."

"That is fine—it's still beautiful," she said, her eyes never leaving his face. He fussed with it some more before letting his hands fall away and finally meeting her gaze. The loneliness she saw there tore at her.

"Philip," she whispered, reaching for him, but he backed away.

"Rest now." He nodded to something beyond the trees. "That break in the mountains—that's the pass that leads to Glen Laire. You'll be home before noon."

He started to turn away, but she asked, "Will you just deliver me, then leave?"

He looked away, a muscle in his jaw bulging. "It's what I should do, God knows, but I expect Alan will not let me go until the morn."

Isobel looked to the rising sun. One day. That was all they had left.

• • •

They rode through the dangerous mountain pass until it opened into a valley. Isobel drew rein and stared down at it. Mountains surrounded Glen Laire on all sides, green and purple and dotted with sheep and kine. The river, a glimmering ribbon of mercury, snaked through the valley, emptying into a loch. Lochlaire Castle sat on a small island in the center of the lake, its gray stone walls disappearing right into the water on the south side. A cluster of crofts surrounded the eastern and northern shores, then fanned out so they dotted the entire valley. The north end was covered in thick forest that climbed the mountains, supplying the inhabitants of Glen Laire with game year-round.

The castle was impregnable. The only way into the valley was through the narrow mountain pass. It was nearly impossible to bring any sizable cannon or siege machines through unless dismantled, and even that was a challenge, with MacDonell archers picking the enemy off as they emerged from the pass.

Isobel's gloved hand clamped over her mouth, muffling her sobs. Her vision blurred, making it all a jumble of grays and greens. She heard movement beside her, then a hand patting her back. She blinked the tears away, using the corner of her arisaid to wipe her eyes. Stephen was beside her, smiling encouragingly.

He winked at her, giving her a harder pat on the back. "Come on—they've sighted us by now and are waiting."

Isobel smiled back, her lips a bit wobbly, and dug in her heels, sending Jinny racing past both of them. The trail leading down the mountain was dangerous and rocky. Philip bellowed after her, but Isobel couldn't wait. She was too excited. The anticipation of this moment had built until she felt ready to burst with it. *Home*. Her father. Her sisters. Would Uncle Roderick be there? Father had said he spent more time at Lochlaire since Mother died.

Rocks showered down around her, but she urged Jinny faster until they were at the base of the mountain, then she sent her flying. Philip soon overcame her—his horse was much bigger and faster—and grabbed her reins, pulling her to a stop.

"What the hell was that?"

"Not now, Philip! I'm almost home!"

"Aye and until we get there, ye're still my charge, and I say slow down!"

"I've taken that hill a million times—and faster!"

"That is not a God damned hill, but a mountain—and ye havena taken it in twelve years. Now slow down before you hurt Jinny and kill yerself."

Isobel ground her teeth, but said, "Very well."

They cantered along at a more sedate pace that nearly drove Isobel mad. They passed several crofts. The men and women came out, yelling greetings to Philip and Stephen—and amazingly, to her. They called to her in Gaelic, but she understood. *Bless your sweet face, Mistress Isobel,* they called. *Welcome home.*

A large stable sat near the shore. A man waited just outside the stables, his plaid and his long red hair billowing in the wind. When she was close enough to hear, he called, "Iseabal!"

Isobel slid down from Jinny's back. "Uncle Roderick!"

He was so much older—so much more mature. He'd been two-and-twenty—younger than Isobel was now—when last she'd seen him, but he was still handsome as ever—handsomer. She ran to him and threw herself in his arms, tears streaming down her face, unable to believe she was home at last.

Her uncle's arms were strong and smelled of sandalwood and wool. He lifted her and swung her around before finally setting her away from him. He was only slightly taller than she, but heavily muscled, his neck thick and corded. His grin was wide and contagious, exposing a set of blindingly white teeth. He spoke in Gaelic, and she just stared at him—his speech was too fast. He saw her confusion and reverted to Scots.

"Look at you! Twelve years it's been—and ye're as beautiful as yer mum."

She smiled and clasped at his hands.

He looked at them meaningfully, copper brows raised. "I see ye still wear the gloves."

"Aye—I must."

He smiled, his own dark blue eyes bright with tears. He slung an arm around her shoulder, pulling her into his side, and turned to Philip and Stephen, who had dismounted and turned the horses over to the stable hand.

"Sir Philip, ye brought her home in one piece. We canna thank ye enough." He looked down at Isobel again, giving her a quick squeeze. "I hiv no children of my own—yet—so I've taken Alan's to heart and have missed these lassies sorely."

Philip's smile was thin. "It was my pleasure, Roderick. How is Alan?"

Isobel looked up at her uncle. Why was her father not there to greet her? She'd been so happy to see her uncle, she'd not even thought of it.

Roderick glanced down at Isobel, his expression grim. He tilted his head toward the shore, where several boats were beached. "Why dinna ye come see for yourself."

The only means to Lochlaire was by boat and so Roderick and Philip set to the oars, rowing them across the loch. Isobel shivered, worried about her father. It must be bad if he couldn't come to greet her.

They had traveled in silence for a time when Roderick turned to her, and said, "Guess who awaits you?"

"Who?"

"The earl of Kincreag waits within Lochlaire's walls. Alan sent him word right after Sir Philip left to fetch you, and the earl answered by coming personally." He glanced apologetically at Stephen. "You'll have to bed down with Sir Philip tonight, the earl brought a score of men with him. We found rooms for the most important, but Lochlaire is not so grand as Castle Kincreag, and many have made do with the hall." He winked at Isobel. "The girls' room is safe, of course, as is yours, Sir Philip."

Isobel was frozen, a polite smile of interest nailed on her face. Her betrothed was there. It was upon her already, and she was not ready. She was ready to be with her family, but not to let Philip go, and accept this strange new man. Her gaze was drawn to Philip. He pulled savagely on the oars, his stare fixed on the approaching castle. When she looked back at her uncle he had been watching the two of them, a speculative gleam in his eye. But once Isobel's gaze was on him again, he smiled the familiar smile she remembered, comforting and friendly. The girls had always loved him dearly. He'd always sought to amuse them and loved to play games, sing, and dance—things Alan and Lillian MacDonell had little time for.

"God, it's good to see ye Isobel! Yer sisters wait most impatiently for you."

Isobel gasped. "They're here already?"

"Aye—Rose has been here a sennight, but Gillian arrived yesterday."

The tears welled in her eyes again—she could not help it. It had been so many years since she'd had sisters that she barely remembered what they had looked like. Both of her sisters were witches—just like her. They'd been sent away for the same reason Isobel had—to protect them. She would never be alone again, not with her sisters there. She only hoped their marriages did not take them far away. But even if that happened, at least now they'd be able to write each other and visit.

A metal gate yawned before them, the bottom dripping dark water as they passed beneath it. "Where have ye been these twelve years?" Roderick asked as he pulled on the oars. "Ye dinna speak the Gaelic, and yer own tongue sounds a bit strange, like a sassenach."

"Da did not tell you?" Isobel asked, surprised. She'd assumed that Uncle Roderick knew, even if no one else did.

Her uncle shook his head gravely. "Och, no, my dear. Yer father told no one. He wouldn't chance anyone slipping up and revealing yer whereabouts."

"Not even *you?*"

Roderick leaned forward, an eyebrow raised. "Not even me." Then he grinned, settling back into the rowing. "I'm the heir remember? What if I sought to eliminate any possible contenders?"

"That's absurd!"

Her uncle shook his head sagely. "No, it's being careful, lass, and I canna say I blame him. Not that I ever would, mind ye, but Earl Kincreag is a verra powerful man, and if he decided to push the claim to Glen Laire—as well as Alan's holdings that came through *my* mother—he could be named chieftain. The king favors him, after all. It all goes to him through you anyway if I die withoot issue—as it seemed likely I would for some time. Three wives I've had and every damn one of them barren, till Tira. She is finally with child. I wilna let that woman leave her bed—they'll be no more miscarriages!"

"Three wives?" Isobel asked, aghast.

"Aye, I finally found something fertile to plow, thank the saints, which is more luck than yer father has had."

"What do you mean? He has three daughters."

"Och—Lillian was a childbearer, make no mistake—but she didn't give him any sons, and Alan still tried for them. He remarried, but she, too, died in childbirth. It seems we MacDonell men are cursed."

This information was such a shock to Isobel she could not form an adequate response. She'd never known her father had remarried.

"Why did he never tell me?"

Roderick shrugged. "God knows he loved yer mother to his very bones—it nearly killed him to lose her. And then to have to send you girls away . . . she was naught to him—he likely didna think to mention her."

Isobel thought this a rather callous explanation and not like her father at all. It was all so extraordinary. She'd expected things to change, but this was not what she'd anticipated. Her father widowed? Her uncle—on his third wife? He'd not even been considering marriage when she'd left—or at least not to her limited twelve-year-old awareness.

The bowels of the castle were dark and permeated with the smell of mold. Torches lit their way to a landing of stairs. Philip stepped into the shallow water of the lower steps and secured the boat to the landing. He held his hand out to Isobel. She placed her hand in his and let him help her from the boat. She watched him as she stepped onto the landing. He was so quiet, so serious. Did this tear at him as it did her? She didn't wish him to hurt, and yet it seemed important to know he shared her feelings. But why? Nothing could come of them. Nothing. Why did she persist in torturing herself?

He stepped back toward the boat, and the moment was over. Stephen tossed him her satchel and the rest of their sacks, while Roderick led her up the steps. Isobel barely listened to her uncle, nodding in the appropriate places as he filled her in on recent castle news. It felt as if the sands of her hourglass were slipping through her fingers, and she could not grasp them. She wanted to hold on just a bit longer.

Roderick led her up another set of stairs that opened into the hall. His arm went around her again and he tilted his head close. He was speaking of her father. Isobel shook off her despairing thoughts and attended his words.

"Alan is very weak. He seems better since Rose arrived—she still has the healing touch—but we must be careful not to overtire him, aye?"

Isobel nodded, a fist of fear squeezing her heart. They crossed the great hall, Isobel in a daze, recognizing her old home, the scents, even the very feel of the air on her skin and in her lungs, but did not remark on it even in her thoughts. Her father's chambers were right off the great hall, and that was where Roderick led her.

At the doorway he drew his arm from around her and let her move ahead of him. Isobel hesitated, looking to her uncle for support. He gave her a sad little smile and nodded to the open door.

Isobel stepped over the threshold, her gaze on the enormous bed that dominated the room. She gasped, tears welling in her eyes, but she hurriedly swallowed them and stiffened her spine. There were others in the room, women who stood when she entered, another man, and a dog, but her gaze was focused on the man in the bed.

It had been two years since she last saw her father. Alan MacDonell visited his daughters every year—not all of them, of course, but one each year, so that they each saw him every third year. It had been two years since Alan's last visit to Isobel, and he had changed dramatically.

He seemed smaller, sunk into the great sea of his fur-covered bed. Isobel was rooted to the threshold until he called to her. "Isobel? Is that you?"

"Da . . ." She ran to him and fell onto the bed, her face buried in the fur over his chest, unable to look at his face—a shadow of the Alan MacDonell she remembered. "Oh, Da, what has happened?"

"Isobel," he murmured, his voice cracking. "Look at me, child."

Isobel raised her head. His face was blurred from her tears, and he wiped them away. He was only eight-and-forty and yet his face was lined and pale-grayish above his beard. More silver threaded the rich auburn of his hair and beard. His eyes were still clover green, though, and they smiled at her.

"My beautiful Isobel. I have you all now. My strength," he said, gripping Isobel's hands in his and squeezing. "My heart and my soul," he said, nodding across the room. Through her tears Isobel made out the figures of two women, clinging to each other, one dark and the other with hair as flaming auburn as her father's had once been. "All will be well now," he said, his hands falling away, his eyes closing, as if those words and the strength of his emotion had exhausted him.

Isobel wiped her eyes and gazed down at him. "What ails you, Da? Why did you not tell me you were ill?"

He opened his eyes. "To what end? So you could fash the entire way here? Why would I wish that? And I know not what ails me. None of the healers know. I just waste away. Even Rose is at a loss."

Isobel felt a presence behind her and turned to see that Philip had joined them. She fixed him with an accusing stare. "Why didn't you tell me?"

"He could not," her father answered. "He vowed he would not tell you of my illness, and Sir Philip does not break his vows—that is why I sent him to fetch you. There are few I can trust. Philip, Hagan—" He nodded across the room at the enormous black-haired Irishman who'd been Alan MacDonell's personal guard since Isobel was a small child. "I sent Hagan for Gillian. And Davie MacLeod, who I sent for Rose."

"Da," Isobel cried. "There are more than three men you can trust! What of Uncle Roderick?"

Alan smiled. "Of course I trust my brother—but your mother never did, so I could not send him for my most priceless treasures. And you are right, there are others." He smiled at someone behind her. "Stephen, of course, but he rides with Philip, and so they are one. The earl of Kincreag—but a chieftain does not send an earl to do his bidding."

At the mention of her betrothed's name Isobel looked away from her father, down at the dog who snuffled at her and nudged her hand. How odd that it was unafraid. It must have become accustomed to witches, with Rose and Gillian there. Her father was fey, too, but never so much it troubled the animals. Her mind turned back to her betrothed as she scratched absently at the dog. "Lord Kincreag is here?"

"Aye, and he waits for you. He wanted you to have time with me and your sisters, so said he would see you after dinner." One of her father's hands covered hers, and the other touched her chin, raising her face to look at him. "I ken ye're afraid. 'Tis a common thing for a lass to be anxious, but he is a good man and will care for you."

Isobel chewed her lip, then said, "What of the stories that he killed his wife?"

"Do you think I would wed you to a murderer?"

Isobel's lips trembled as she shook her head. "But I'm a witch," she whispered. "What if—"

He hushed her and shook his head. "He knows all that and is jaded as they come, my dear. He does not believe in magic or witches. You are safe with him, so long as you do as I have always urged you. He knows why I sent you away. I meant to marry you long before now, but then the king began burning witches like they were cheap candles, and I couldn't risk it. I've always wanted Lord Kincreag for you. Only he can offer you true protection. As a countess, no one will question you. And he has promised to speak for your sisters as well, should any harm befall them. I have chosen good men for them, too, so there is naught to fear. I leave my greatest treasures in good hands."

Isobel had known that her marriage to the earl was important, but she had not realized to what extent. It was not just land and titles, but protection—and not just for herself, but for her sisters as well. The importance of her responsibility weighed on her. There were no excuses left. She looked over her shoulder at Philip. He stared at the floor, his hands clasped behind his back. As if he sensed her gaze, he looked up, his eyes resting briefly on her before moving to Alan.

"Philip, come," Alan said.

Philip stepped forward and knelt beside the bed, his shoulder brushing against Isobel's thigh. He tried to dislodge the dog, but it was stubborn and remained by its master's bedside.

Alan searched Philip's face, frowning slightly.

"You have never failed me, and you have done well in this. I thank you. How can I repay you? If there is anything I have that you desire, you know you have only to ask."

Isobel stared at Philip's profile, her heart pounding painfully against her ribs. What would he ask for? She had a vision of him looking her father in the eye and saying, *Your daughter is all I want.*

He was silent for a long moment, staring down at the bed, his long dark lashes hiding his eyes. His jaw clenched, then he met Alan's gaze. "You owe me naught, you should know that, but I would ask that you consider very carefully your daughter's marriage to the earl."

Isobel gasped. Though she'd longed to hear him say such a thing, she'd not really expected it.

Alan frowned thoughtfully. "Why do you say this?"

Philip inhaled deeply. "You say the earl is jaded, that he doesn't believe in witches and magic. I've seen your daughter's magic, and when he does, he'll no longer doubt. Can you be certain of how he'll react when he discovers the truth?"

Alan smiled slightly. "Your concern touches me, Philip, but as I know your heart, so I know Lord Kincreag's. A man couldn't ask for better friends than I have, and I'm proud to count Kincreag among them. He'll protect my daughters with his life."

Philip nodded, his jaw locked. Isobel's heart sank. She'd hoped for something else, something more, but she should have known. If he hadn't the courage to take the home he so obviously loved and wanted, why would he ask for her?

"I can see your concern is true," Alan went on, "And so here is what we'll do." His gaze moved to Isobel. "Have you your mother's charm?"

Isobel nodded and turned to Stephen, who quietly passed her the satchel. Isobel dug through it until she found the bone casket and removed her mother's peridot.

"Now put it on," Alan said.

Isobel looked from the charm to her father uncertainly. She didn't know if she wanted it on at all times. Sensing her hesitance, Alan said, "That's why you must wear it. It will be a constant reminder of your mother's fate. Be sure you dinna repeat it."

Isobel fumbled with the ribbon until Philip moved behind her and tied it at her nape. His fingers were warm and sure, and her loins clenched, deep and painful. She closed her eyes briefly. She must get through this somehow. Her father was dying, and it was clear he wanted nothing more than Isobel married to the earl of Kincreag. She *must* do this.

When she opened her eyes Alan was smiling at her. He sighed deeply and sank back into the pile of pillows behind his head and shoulders. He looked drained and so frail he might blow away, but content.

His gaze cut across the room and he held out a hand that shook slightly. "Come Rose, Gillian. Help me welcome your sister."

Chapter 16

After giving their father a quick examination, Rose MacDonell shooed everyone except Hagan and the dog from the room, including Isobel. She stood in the cavernous great hall, looking longingly from her father's closed chamber door to Philip's retreating back. Where was he going? Surely, if he were leaving, he'd say good-bye? But she wasn't at all certain he would, and her belly twisted with anxiety.

She became aware of the questioning eyes on her and turned to her sisters. "Look at you two."

The last time she'd seen Gillian and Rose they'd been children, ten and eight, respectively. They had both blossomed into beautiful women. Though they'd changed dramatically, Isobel could still see the sisters she remembered. That dreamy look still lingered in Gillian's smoky gray eyes. Her hair was a mass of mahogany curls, braided at the crown to keep it from her face. She had been a plump child, dimpled and precious. The plumpness had moved to all the right places, so that she was voluptuous, while her limbs and neck, as well as her face, were delicate as a dove.

Rose was tall and slender, like Isobel, but sturdier. Her features held none of the delicacy of Gillian's, but were sharp and fierce, her blue eyes brimming with passion, and surrounded by a sleek fall of deep auburn hair.

They both examined Isobel with the same intense scrutiny. "You have changed," Rose said. "You look just like Mother." Then her strong face crumpled, and she threw herself into Isobel's arms. Gillian came close and rubbed at Rose's back, making soothing and sympathetic noises.

"It's true," Gillian said in her soft sweet voice. "You look just like Mother . . . at least as I remember her, so beautiful—her hair such an unusual color."

Rose sniffed and drew back, wiping her eyes, blue as midnight. "I'm sorry . . . it's just that I've waited so long, then Davie showed up with a letter . . . and now I'm here and Father is dying and we're all together—but getting married. . . . And then I see you and feel like I truly am home—looking at you is like seeing mother here again." Rose covered her face suddenly. "I canna even think straight."

"Father is dying?" Isobel whispered. "Are you certain?"

Rose dropped her hands. "Aye—but from what, I haven't an inkling. Something saps away his strength and causes painful marks on his body—like bruises and welts, sometimes even in odd patterns. Hagan is beside himself. He rarely leaves Father's side—so the marks trouble him greatly. They look as though he's been beaten, but Hagan can attest that no one enters or leaves the room without his knowledge." Rose stared down at her hands, the fingers spread wide, then curled them into angry fists. "Even if I lose someone, I always kent what was wrong with them and why I couldna save them. But this . . . this disease eludes me!"

"Is there no hope?" Gillian asked.

Rose's fine pale brow creased with worry. "I know not—though I am still trying—I vow it. I'll not leave him until he is healed . . . or gone."

The dread in Isobel's belly intensified, and she finally understood what it was—a premonition of her father's death. It had to be. That he should die now, when they were all together again, was so wrong, so unfair. She looked down at her own hands, useless to her father.

Gillian covered Rose's hands with her own. "You cannot heal everything, Rose."

Rose spoke with a Highland Scots accent—which told Isobel she'd been in the Highlands for the past twelve years and found Gaelic more comfortable. Gillian, however, spoke with a lowland lilt.

"Where have you both been the past twelve years?" Isobel asked.

"I've been on Skye," Rose said. "She's been on the borders—right in the thick of the witch-hunts!"

Isobel looked at Gillian, alarmed. "How did you manage?"

Gillian shrugged, eyes averted. "I . . . I don't know."

Isobel exchanged a look with Rose. "Has something happened, Gillian?"

Gillian's expression grew strained, her nose pinched. Then she sniffed, and a tear fell over her thick lashes. "I am not a witch."

"What?" Rose scoffed. "Of course you are—but you have the right of it. Just keep saying that. I will, too." She eyed them both with wide-eyed intensity. *"We are not witches."*

Gillian looked up at her sisters, her gray eyes wide and sad. "You don't understand. I truly have no magic."

Isobel removed her gloves and took Gillian's hands. "But you did, didn't you? Before you left Lochlaire?"

Gillian shook her head miserably. "No . . . Mum said it would come, in time, and we'd know what my magic was. But the magic never came."

There was a long moment of awkward silence, then Isobel put her arm around Gillian's shoulders. "Be happy, sister, you're the safe one. I go to a husband who does not believe in witches. How I will turn his world upside down."

Gillian nodded, her gaze on their joined hands. "Earl Kincreag. I think he's not as horrid as everyone says."

Rose snorted. "He's a sour, surly, unpleasant man. I know—I've been here a sennight now, and he almost as long." Then she smiled weakly at Isobel's worried frown. "Sorry. Gillian's right, he's probably not so awful."

"He's very handsome," Gillian offered.

"He'd likely be prettier," Rose said, "if he wasna always scowling."

These tidings did nothing to ease Isobel's anxiety over meeting her betrothed. It was all too much. Her father's illness, meeting Lord Kincreag, losing Philip.

At the thought of Philip, Isobel wondered aloud where he'd run off to so quickly.

"You got Sir Philip," Rose said, and waggled her eyebrows enviously. "Lucky you! Da sent Davie MacLeod for me! Can you imagine?"

Isobel tried to place Davie MacLeod but could not. "Who is Davie MacLeod?"

Rose looked at her incredulously. "The bard? The harper? He who always sang cloying love ballads to Mum? *Alas for him whose sick in love, Whatever the reason I should say it!*" she mimicked in a warbling falsetto.

"Oh!" Isobel covered her mouth and laughed. "Has he changed?"

Rose shook her head, rolling her eyes. "He's still in love with Mum—even though she's dead." She looked at Isobel consideringly. "Just wait until he gets a look at you!"

"Davie means well," Gillian admonished gently. "And he was never in love with Mum. Da wouldn't have stood for it. He *admired* her. Da sent Hagan for me. He's as sweet as ever—he takes care of Da now."

Rose nodded. "Aye, he's become more than a personal guard—he's Da's nursemaid. Hagan is a good man if ever there was one. But still—he's no Sir Philip!"

Isobel smiled thinly. "Yes, well . . ." Her cheeks were burning as she fought to change the subject. "Who has Da betrothed you to?"

Rose's expression softened. "Jamie MacPhereson." She dug into the folds of her arisaid and removed a miniature. It was secured to her brooch by a ribbon. "Here he is—do you remember him?"

Isobel and Gillian leaned close to scrutinize the tiny portrait. It was of a blond man, his face narrow and handsome in a fine, English way.

"He doesn't look like a Scot," Isobel commented.

Rose frowned, looking down at the miniature. "Of course he does. His father was a great friend of Da's. He's chief now—and he remembered me." Her face was pink as she stared down at the miniature. "He asked for me. He's written me letters, saying he's loved me since we were children."

"You were eight when you left here," Isobel said.

"I know! Isn't it wonderful?"

Isobel smiled. She was glad one of them would marry a man of her choosing. "I do remember Jamie now. He was a very nice lad—his father, too. Da has done well for you."

"He's no earl," Rose teased, but it was clear she much preferred her Jamie. She would marry the man she loved. A twinge of jealousy stabbed Isobel. It seemed childish to whine that it wasn't fair, but inside, she couldn't help it.

Gillian sighed. "You are both so fortunate. I remember Jamie. He was a kind and comely lad, and his lands are not far. And you, Isobel—Earl Kincreag is dark and mysterious and so beautiful I vow you will swoon when you see him. Even if he is sour as an old goat—he's disgustingly rich and has a dozen castles. You'll never have to see him if you don't want to. And you also will not be far from Lochlaire or Rose."

"Where will you be?" Isobel asked, disturbed by the wistfulness in her sister's tone.

"I am to marry an old man in France."

Rose frowned indignantly. "Father is marrying you to an old man?"

Gillian lifted one shoulder. "Well, he's not *ancient.* Nearly fifty. Still that seems very old to me—like marrying my father."

They all made faces of disgust.

"Maybe he will be kind," Isobel said hopefully.

"Or maybe he will die quickly and leave you a rich widow," Rose added.

Gillian's mouth turned down at the corners. "I wouldn't care if he was eighty so long as he lived in Scotland." She gripped Isobel and Rose's hands. "I've missed you both desperately, and now our time together is so short. What if I never see you again?"

"Don't say that!" Isobel cried.

Rose just frowned, deeply disturbed.

"Have you told Father how you feel?" Isobel asked.

Gillian shook her head. "Oh no! He mustn't know. He's dying, and these marriages are so important to him. My Frenchman is an old friend of Father's. I cannot protest— not now, when it's his dying wish. That is why he brought us here now—to see us married to these men so he can die in peace."

Isobel understood just how trapped Gillian felt and she squeezed her sister's hand reassuringly. She knew what it was to be torn between duty and desire—but there was no help for it—for either of them.

Rose raised a speculative brow. "You still have time.

Has a man caught yer fancy here? Encourage him. Better to lose your maidenhead to a lad of your choosing than to some old stranger."

Gillian shrugged. "I couldn't do such a thing."

Rose nodded across the hall to where Stephen stood, stuffing his face and talking animatedly with Davie MacLeod—who looked as if he wanted to escape. Stephen noticed that they were all looking at him and winked.

Rose wiggled her fingers and smiled flirtatiously. "What about him? He's uncommonly handsome."

Gillian moved in front of Rose before she enticed Stephen to approach them. "Stop it! I don't even know him!"

Rose laughed. "What matter? You'll hardly know your Frenchman when he mounts you on your wedding night. Should your first coupling be with a stinking old carcass, or someone young and beautiful that might bring you pleasure?"

Gillian shook her head. "My betrothed expects a virgin. I cannot soil myself and dishonor Father."

Rose rolled her eyes and made a rude noise. "Honestly, Gilly! Do you really believe that every lady goes to her marriage bed a virgin?" Her fine auburn brows arched knowingly. "Virginity, my wee innocents, is so very easy to fake."

Isobel and Gillian looked at their sister curiously. She seemed to know of what she spoke, which intrigued them both.

"What if she were to get pregnant?" Isobel asked.

Rose dismissed this with a wave of her hand. "There are ways to prevent unwanted pregnancies—but in our case it doesn't matter overmuch. Father is rushing us all to the altar, so anything you do in the next fortnight or so can easily be attributed to your husband so long as he beds you immediately."

"Really?" Gillian breathed, fascinated.

"Aye. Ye should grab what ye can, while ye can," Rose continued. "Ye never know what the future holds. And by the look of that young buck yonder, methinks it might be worth your while." She winked conspiratorially and looked around the hall. "Later I'll give you something—"

"I don't want it!" Gillian said, starting to sound hysterical, as if she feared Rose might somehow force her into it.

"Leave off," Isobel said. "She doesn't want to—and besides, Stephen is a good friend—leave him out of your schemes."

Rose squared her shoulders and put on an obedient face. "Aye, mum!"

They all laughed and moved to the enormous fireplace. Isobel hadn't felt so warm and wanted in years. She had missed her sisters and her home desperately. But although an easy rapport was quickly established between them, Isobel did not share her feelings about Philip. She was not yet ready—and besides, what Rose had said would not leave her. *Better to lose your maidenhead to a man of your choosing, than to some old stranger. Ye should grab what ye can, while ye can—ye never know what the future holds.*

Lord Kincreag was not an old carcass, but neither was he Sir Philip Kilpatrick, the man she loved beyond reason. Better to have one night with Philip, than to always wonder, to always wish and want.

Virginity, my wee innocents, is so very easy to fake.

Her heart beat faster at the very thought, and it lingered, took root and blossomed, filling her with excitement and delicious fear.

Tonight, she would pay Philip a visit.

• • •

She was distracted all through the dinner hour. It was an odd meal, besides. Uncle Roderick presided over it as if he were already chieftain, and though that was not wrong of him, considering her father's condition, it still made Isobel feel slightly resentful. Rose was not present, and Roderick informed Isobel that she tended his wife—the pregnant Tira. He confided that he was stalling Rose's wedding until after Tira gave birth. He feared that without Rose's superior healing skills the baby, and perhaps his wife, would be lost. This was a very important baby, as Alan had already verified that it was a boy.

Isobel immediately felt chagrined for her cross feelings at her uncle. He had suffered much in the past twelve years—being twice widowed could not be easy on anyone, certainly not a kind man like Roderick MacDonell. It was amazing he'd managed to preserve his good humor.

There was still no sign of Philip, though Stephen came to the table late, looking as if he'd been up to no good. Davie entertained them with music from his harp and some rather tame ballads. Isobel wanted to ask Stephen about Philip, but he was seated farther down the table. She tried to get his attention, but he was bolting his food down as if he were starving, his concentration completely on his meal.

When Stephen finished, he stuffed more food in a sack and hurried away from the table without a word to anyone. Isobel stood to follow him, but Roderick caught her arm.

"It's time, lass."

"Time for what?" Isobel asked impatiently, straining to follow Stephen, who promptly disappeared through a doorway.

"Time to meet your betrothed."

The air left Isobel in a rush, and she forgot Stephen. She turned to her uncle. "Now?"

He nodded sympathetically and propelled her across the hall, his hand on her back. "Best not to keep him waiting."

Isobel's mind was a whirlwind of fear and apprehension. Before she could make any sense of it, or even prepare herself for meeting Lord Kincreag, they stood before the door to his chambers—the finest in the castle, besides her father's. But her uncle didn't knock. He frowned at the door for a moment, then turned to her, and whispered, "Have ye tried to use yer magic to discover what ails yer father?"

Isobel shook her head. It hadn't even occurred to her. He was ill, after all, and she was not a healer—Rose was.

Roderick nodded, the frown easing from his brow.

"Should I try?" she asked.

"No—ye best not chance it with the earl here." He took her shoulders and looked deep into her face. His gaze dropped to her mother's charm that lay against her breasts. "Your father has spoken to you of the importance of concealing your magic?"

Isobel nodded miserably.

"Well, I will be redundant then, but just the same I must. Do nothing to make him suspect. You have heard the rumors of what he did to his first wife?"

"They're just rumors. Father would not wed me to a murderer."

"Of course not. But what happened to the countess remains a mystery—one the king didn't care enough to investigate."

Isobel blinked. "Are you saying he *did* murder her?"

Roderick shook his head emphatically. "I *am not* saying that. Your father certainly believes him innocent, and Alan is a good judge of character. However, I have always found the man cold and—"

The door swung open. Isobel jerked guiltily toward the

man who now filled the doorway. He stood with one hand on the doorframe and the other gripping the edge of the open door. He was as dark as Philip had said—black hair, black eyes, skin so dark he must have Spanish Moor in his blood. He was dressed almost entirely in black as well. And the room beyond was dimly lit, so the broad expanse of his shoulders seemed to melt into the darkness beyond.

His black devil eyes were currently fixed on Roderick. "And?" he drawled, his voice deep and chilling.

Roderick smiled charmingly. *"And* here she is, my lord. Isobel MacDonell."

Lord Kincreag continued to stare at Roderick. Finally, his gaze flicked to Isobel, examining her with disinterest before scanning the corridor.

"She comes alone?"

Roderick placed a palm on his chest. "What am I, my lord? I'm here to vouch for her maiden safety."

A dark brow arched slowly, sardonically. "And who will vouch for her maiden safety on her journey from England to Lochlaire?"

"My lord?" Roderick queried. "I dinna understand."

"I've been told she traveled with three men—and no one else."

Isobel's face flamed. "What do you accuse me of? Are you doubting my—and Sir Philip's—honor? My father sent him because he could be trusted with my life. He would not have sent someone who would debauch me at the first opportunity."

That cold gaze moved to her, eyes narrowed. "It's not always the men who are doing the debauching."

Isobel let out an incredulous breath, but her cheeks and neck burned. He insinuated she was some whore who debauched men? And just what had she been doing with Philip—with her eager kisses and wicked thoughts? What was she contemplating doing that very evening? She fought to keep her expression insulted, rather than revealing the horrified embarrassment she truly felt.

She looked at her uncle for support, but even he seemed at a loss. Finally, he said, "I assure you, Isobel comes to you a maiden—innocent of the ways of men. Sir Philip Kilpatrick would never dishonor Alan in such a fashion." When Lord Kincreag still eyed them skeptically, Roderick said, "Perhaps we should come inside so you might become acquainted with Isobel."

The earl put his back to them and disappeared into the room. Roderick urged Isobel forward, giving her a grimace of sympathy.

No candles were lit. Only the light from the fireplace. But seconds later a candelabra slowly came to life. The earl tossed the tinderbox on a table and turned to her.

"Let us be clear. You are a witch, and I am a murderer."

Isobel's mouth went dry. What did he mean? "I . . . I am not—"

"I have no intention of talking to you about my first wife, so do not bother asking. Nor will I ask you why everyone believes the MacDonells of Glen Laire are witches. I don't care."

"If you think I'm a witch, why would you want to wed me?"

"I did not say I think you're a witch, I'm merely repeating what everyone else says. If you . . . *think* you are, once again, I do not care to know."

Isobel clasped her hands tightly before her. This was not going as she'd imagined. In spite of the warnings she'd received about him, she'd never expected him to be so cold and unfeeling. "But . . . but we are to be married," she protested. "Am I not allowed to ask about your life before me?"

His sleek black hair was tied back at his nape. Neat, severe almost. Just like his attire. For a man who was disgustingly rich, he dressed simply. Black breeches that fit close to his lean and muscular body, black hose and shoes, a black doublet relieved only by small silver buttons. Only a simple falling collar, smaller than any she'd seen, tempered the oppressive blackness of his clothes, fitting close to a dark, corded neck. His glacial and uncompromising features were undoubtedly handsome, as Gillian had said, and they did make her swoon—but with dread. She saw no kindness in this man. No warmth. He was heartless and cruel. He would never love her, and he would never welcome her love. She was not at all certain she was interested in giving it to him.

"This is a marriage, not a friendship," he said. "I offered for you, and your father accepted. You are mine now. You will live by my rules."

Isobel placed a surprised hand on her mother's pendant. Waves of fear and agony—her mother's—washed through her, but she held the emotions at bay, searching for her mother's strength, the courage she went to the stake with, to bolster her in this.

"You offered for me?"

"Well, one of you. I did not care which. Your father is my friend—one of the few I have. He fears greatly for you and your sisters' safety. I offered for you because I can protect you—all of you—if you are my family. No one will harm you while I live."

Isobel was not comforted. She was deeply dismayed. The hope she had tried desperately to preserve—that she could somehow find happiness, or even a sort of contentedness, with Lord Kincreag—was crumbling before her eyes.

"Uh . . . thank you, my lord."

He dismissed her thanks with an indifferent nod. "Very well. We are finished then. We'll be wed in a week's time. The banns are being said already."

It was moving too fast, her heart cried. A week? "But . . . that's May—it's bad luck to wed in May."

He looked at her as if she were a foolish child. "Luck will not make this bearable, Mistress MacDonell. For either of us."

When she just stood there, gaping at him, he said, "You are dismissed."

Roderick ushered her out the door, closing it behind them. Isobel let him lead her to the hall, but she held back at the entrance, unable to bear the sounds of laughter and music. She could not join in—not now. She feared she might be ill.

She looked up at her uncle, feeling betrayed and miserable. "Father loves this man?"

Roderick rubbed his temple. "He is not like that with Alan, you'll see." He took her hands then, and said, "I'm sorry, lass—your father knows how he is, but thinks it's because of his first wife. He believes the right woman will thaw him."

"And that woman is me?" Isobel shook her head. "I don't think so—he hates me!"

"I can talk to Alan . . ." Roderick said, but it was clear from his expression he thought it would do little good.

Isobel shook her head. Her father had good reason for doing this—the earl of Kincreag could protect all three of the MacDonell girls. She could not let her personal unhappiness ruin it. She would manage to get on with the earl well enough . . . one day . . . if he gave her a chance . . .

She squared her shoulders. "No, I pray you, don't trouble Father with this. Tell him . . . tell him I liked Lord Kincreag and will marry him as planned."

Her uncle hesitated, then nodded. "Very well. But perhaps you'd rather tell him yourself?"

Isobel couldn't lie to her father with the memory of Lord Kincreag's cruel eyes still fresh in her mind. She would likely burst into miserable tears—she was close to doing so at the moment and turned partly away from her uncle.

"I cannot. I'm unwell."

Roderick made a soft clucking sound. "Of course ye are, lass. Shall I send Rose to look in on ye?"

"No, that's not necessary. I just want to go to bed." She could feel him watching her as she walked away, but she didn't care. She would marry Lord Kincreag, as her father wished, but tonight was still hers.

Chapter 17

Philip's chambers at Lochlaire were very fine—finer than his chambers at his own home. Alan had always treated him like a son, always kept a room for him, as if this was as much Philip's home as anyone else's. So why did Philip suddenly feel so betrayed? He rolled over on the fragrant, heather-stuffed mattress and stared at the fire from between the fall of velvet curtains. He had left the keep immediately after he'd seen Alan. He'd toyed with the idea of just leaving, but instead he'd stood on the castle walls and looked out over the glen, waiting for the feeling that someone had punched him in the chest to subside.

But it had not.

Even now, lying in bed, he felt bruised and angry. He recalled when Alan had sent for him several weeks ago. Philip had been shocked at his friend's condition, trying to hide his own grief at losing a dear friend, and so was ready to agree to anything. But when Alan had begun speaking of his daughters and marriage, Philip had nearly run like a frightened hare. He'd been greatly relieved when Alan had only asked him to fetch his eldest daughter, not marry her. He'd not wanted to hurt or insult his friend by saying no. But now . . .

Why had Alan not asked him? He didn't trust Philip to care for his daughter? To protect her? Or perhaps he just didn't think Philip was good enough. It rankled and festered, making him more angry and misused by the moment. Had he misinterpreted his friendship with Alan? Stephen had brought him some dinner and told him about Alan's choices for his daughters. Jamie MacPhereson wasn't so bad, Philip thought, but still, how was he any better than Philip? And some old Frenchman! He'd send his daughter away, across the sea, rather than wed her to someone like Philip. Not that Philip wanted Gillian or Rose—it was the principle of the matter.

The only husband who was acceptable and understandable—on the surface at least—was Isobel's betrothed. An earl. Philip could not compete with that. It ate at him that she'd been with Lord Kincreag tonight. He wanted to know how it went, what was said—but then again, he did not. What if she'd found the earl all she'd hoped for? Philip should be happy, should hope for that—but he did not.

He should just leave. He turned onto his other side, staring morosely into the darkness. He couldn't leave without seeing her again. But then what would he say? He could think of nothing except good-bye and well wishes; empty, meaningless phrases that minimized how he truly felt. He wanted to tell her so much more, to warn her, to somehow continue to protect her. But it was no longer his place.

He violently threw back the covers and strode to the fire. He rubbed at his forehead, trying to think of what to do. How foolish of him to try and puzzle this out when he knew exactly what he must do. Leave and travel to Wyndyburgh. There he would find his sister and take her home to Sgor Dubh, where she belonged. Then he would kick his bastard brothers out of his home and take his place as heir. And then what? Marry? Provide heirs? The notion held no appeal for him. He only wanted one woman, and he could not have her. Her father—one of his most beloved friends—did not think him good enough.

He sat there, becoming increasingly aggrieved with Alan—and with himself. Could he really blame Alan? After all, the chieftain of Glen Laire was well aware that Philip had refused his inheritance, that he spent more time wandering about finding strangers than tending to what was his—that he'd set his own life aside twelve years ago when he lost his sister. Alan knew all of this. Of course he wouldn't want Philip for any of his daughters—and certainly not the one who would bring Glen Laire to her husband should aught happen to Roderick MacDonell. He'd done this to himself, and yet he'd never before cared.

Philip's thoughts were interrupted by a soft knock on the door. "Aye?" he called, expecting Stephen, who was supposed share Philip's room, but had likely sought a more agreeable bed to share.

The door creaked open. At first it was too dark outside the door for him to see more than a slender shape, dressed in pale colors. But then the door closed, and she came farther into the room, her red-gold hair, reflecting the fire like sunlight, spilling over shoulders and framing her pale, fragile face. She was wrapped in the arisaid he had given her, wearing it like a mantle.

He was stunned into silence, his throat tight, his mouth dry.

Isobel paused, eyeing him warily, then drifted closer. Bare hands peeked from the folds of the plaid where she held it closed. What did she wear beneath? His heart seemed to stutter at the thought, then raced, sending heat rushing through him. Feet encased in velvet slippers peeked from beneath the white of her shift.

When she was but an arm's length away, he asked in a hoarse voice, "What are you doing here?"

Red-blond lashes lowered, catching the firelight like burnished copper. "I knew you would not come to me."

His groin tightened. This felt like a dream—or a fantasy—and he still couldn't seem to move. "Why would I do that?"

Her expression turned slightly sad. "Because you're leaving tomorrow, and I'm getting married in a sennight. We may never see each other again . . . and even if we do, it will never be the same."

"Isobel . . ." But he couldn't seem to say anything more. She should not be here, in his room, but he did not want her to go, could not send her away.

She released the plaid and it puddled to the floor. Beneath she wore an indecent shift, all lace and lawn, and he could see the weight of her breasts pressing against the material, the dusky thrust of her nipples, and farther down, a dark triangle. He looked back to her face.

She looked fearful, her pale green eyes wide, her teeth worrying her bottom lip.

"You are beautiful," he said, nearly choking on the words.

"When I went to the room I'm sharing with my sisters, I found three chests, each full of new clothes. This"—she gestured to the filmy garment she wore—"is for my wedding night. I would wear it for you, before I ever wear it for *him*."

She spat out *him* as if it were a dirty word.

Power returned to his limbs and he stood. He placed his hands on her shoulders and looked down into her eyes—silver-green eyes that begged him not to send her away. Her hands came up, resting against his chest. She had bathed. Violets and musk drifted from her skin and hair.

"Please don't send me away . . . I . . . I want to be with you tonight."

"Isobel, do you realize how dangerous this is? What if someone saw you? Or someone finds out?"

"No one saw me—I was careful. And no one will find out. I latched the door behind me."

When he said nothing, tears welled in her eyes. A fist squeezed at his heart as he watched a single tear track her cheek. There was a tremor in the hand he used to wipe the tear away. He framed her face with both hands. "What happened?"

"I met him tonight. I will never find happiness with him, Philip—I know it in my bones. It's you I love." And then she began to weep silently. Tears coursed freely down her face, and she squeezed her eyes shut as if she could stop them, but they fell anyway.

He pulled her against him, wrapping his arms tightly around her shuddering body. His mind raced desperately, wondering what he could do to help her, to protect her from this unhappiness. And then he knew, with calm certainty, there was only one thing he could do, only one answer, Alan and Kincreag be damned.

Isobel rubbed her face against his shirt, drying her tears, and gazed up at him. Though he held her and comforted her, he seemed oddly restrained. She feared he didn't want her here, didn't want this. She flexed her hands against his shirt and felt that he did desire her, faintly from the linen that lived against his skin. But wanting with your body and wanting with your heart and mind were two separate things, she knew. He was a good and honorable man and would not want to deflower another man's betrothed, under her father's own roof. But there was no help for it. She would not leave his room a maiden.

His gaze burned into her, but his hands were still, gently cupping her shoulders. She lowered her gaze to his muscular neck, corded and strained. His pulse beat rapidly in the hollow of his throat, and crisp brown hairs were visible above the white of his shirt. She pulled the top tie, breathless and warm with a shyness she was determined to overcome. She pulled the next, and the next, until the linen parted, exposing a lightly haired chest, hard with muscle. He was so beautiful and strong. Her hands slid beneath the linen. He tensed, but did not stop her. Skin warm and smooth except for the dusting of coarse hair soothed her palms. She leaned forward and pressed her lips against the pulse that throbbed in his neck.

He groaned and murmured something in Gaelic, a curse perhaps. His hands slid from her shoulders, one to the small of her back, the other tangling into her hair, forcing her head back. His gaze moved over her face possessively, fiercely, until her knees nearly buckled with want. Then he kissed her, his mouth warm and demanding, parting her lips, and plunging inside.

His kiss was long and slow and drugging. His hands moved over her body, stroking her through the thin material of her nightrail. His fingers slid between her thighs and buttocks, brushing against her sex, and desire rent her. She gasped against his mouth.

His chest heaved beneath her hands. She slid them up, sifting the silk of his hair. She could stay like this forever, their bodies pressed close, straining to get closer, hands seeking and stroking, mouths mating hungrily. Then he dropped to his knees before her. He pressed his face against her belly, and she felt his warm damp kisses through her nightrail. Sharp arrows of lust pierced her loins. His hands slid down her thighs until he reached her ankles and circled them, stroking gently upward, beneath her gown. When his caresses slid up between her knees, to her inner thighs, her breath was coming in short gasps, and her eyes fluttered shut. He would feel the dampness there, and though she should be embarrassed, she could not care. She only wanted him to touch her as he had on the beach.

Her nightrail was bunched up at her hips, and he turned his face, nuzzling the curls at the top of her sex as his finger stroked across it, sending a jolt through her. Her hands dropped to his shoulders, curling into the soft linen. He made a deep sound of male approval that resonated through her body. Her legs were water, and she could barely support herself, but when she tried to slide to the floor, he held her up, one hand rubbing and stroking her bottom, the other, stroking between her thighs, forcing them farther apart.

And then she felt his mouth *there*. She tried to back away, surprised—and appalled at the rush of damp warmth that flooded her lower body. "Wh—what do you mean to do?" she stuttered, straining away from him, even as he held her firmly, refusing to allow her retreat.

Whisky brown eyes simmered up at her. "What does it look like I'm doing?" He lowered his head and she felt his tongue there, laving at the sensitive folds, and she could no longer think enough to be appalled or embarrassed. She clutched at his hair and shoulders, her body opening to him as waves of exquisite sensation washed over her, more devastating with each wave. She whimpered from a pleasure so great it was painful. She could not make her limbs work. And when his fingers slid in to join his flicking tongue, she cried out, her body convulsing as it had on the beach, only this time far more intense, shattering her from within.

Her heart hammered loudly in her ears, her blood roared, and her body sagged, blissfully drained from his attentions. She felt more than saw him move and shift, then he swung her into his arms and carried her across the room. Her eyes drifted open, gazing up at him.

The fire was behind him, casting part of his face in shadows, all straight lines and hard angles. His square jaw was set with an odd determination, considering what had just passed. But when she touched the silky hair of his short beard, he looked down at her, and his eyes softened, his mouth curving slightly.

He shouldered the bed curtains aside and deposited her among a froth of furs and sheets, then disappeared, the curtains falling back to close her in. She pushed up on her elbows, then fell back when she heard the rustle of fabric as he undressed. The sensual excitement returned, thrumming through her blood as she waited. She tried to not to consider that this was all she would have of him, that she would live the rest of her life with someone else—and he would, too, eventually. She would not think of that tonight.

The curtains parted, and the bed dipped beneath his weight. He looped the curtain around the bedpost and turned to look down at her. She could only stare at his body, sculpted with muscle that slid and shifted beneath honey-tinged skin as he leaned over her, bracing an elbow on one side of her head.

He leaned close, dark eyes intent. He whispered, his lips brushing against her skin, "Did I frighten you? I could not help myself." He kissed the corner of her mouth, his breath and beard tickling her.

"Shocked . . . but not frightened." She held his face between her hands and looked up at him, her heart in her eyes. "I could never be frightened of you."

Philip was undone by the utter trust he saw in her eyes. He vowed to himself he'd never abuse her trust, or let her down. She held his heart in her eyes. In that moment he knew he was no longer ruled by the same passions that had bound him for the past twelve years. Now it was only Isobel and this love she had given him—more precious to him than lands or castles—or even finding his sister.

He kissed her, gathering her close and lifting her off the

bed. Her arms went around him. He stopped long enough to pull her shift over her head, then enfolded her in his arms again, reveling in the softness of her, the silkiness of her skin and hair against him, warm and supple. He laid her back on the furs and kissed her neck and breasts, wanting to go slow for her, but his heart strained with the desire to plunge inside her and relieve the burning ache that had plagued him since they'd first met.

She tasted of the violet-scented water she'd bathed in and her own, soft musky flavor. He slid his hand between her legs and found her ready for him. He positioned himself between her legs and took her face between his hands. Her lashes slowly opened and her eyes were dreamy, dazed.

"This will hurt for a moment, love," he whispered, kissing her chin, licking away the dew of perspiration. "But then it will be over."

"I know. Just kiss me, and it will be fine." She urged him with her hips, seductively sweet and untutored, and he had to grind his teeth, forcing himself to go slow.

He kissed her slowly, his tongue swirling lazily against hers, rubbing himself against the damp curls, caressing her hips and thighs.

She whimpered and tore her mouth away. "Please, Philip, do it now." She wriggled beneath him, somehow sliding him into position as her thighs tightened on his hips. He was powerless to do aught but her will, and pushed into her, through her barrier. She cried out, but he kissed her, swallowing her pain until she strained against him again, her hips moving. He pinned her hands over her head, tasting the salty sweetness of their sweat on her breasts, and rocked slowly into her, reining in the violent urge to take her fast and hard.

She clung to him, her breath ragged, her hips finding his rhythm and urging him on, faster, and he could not stop himself. He lost himself, thrusting into the tight hot grip of her, their lips clinging, tongues tangling in ardent accord. For him there was only this moment, this woman. He crushed her against him as his climax ripped through him, tearing a cry from him that he muffled in her neck.

He lay there for a long moment, his chest working like a bellows, his mind sluggish and muzzy. Her hands stroked at him, slicking damp hair from his face, even as her hair clung to them both like a web.

He rolled to his back, taking her with him, and held her tightly, his hand petting over the thick mane of curls.

It was done. A great weight seemed to have lifted from him. Everything had changed with this one act, and he was not sorry. She was his now, and no one could change that.

Chapter 18

Isobel was afraid to sleep. This night was all she had, and she wished it wouldn't end, but knew it must. Dawn would come, and she would sneak back to her room and Philip would leave to find his sister. Life would go on.

Philip wasn't much interested in sleep, and that was fine with her. He'd shown her things this night that even in her visions of others she'd not seen, and certainly never imagined on her own. With him she was free. He knew she was a witch, and he did not care—he desired her anyway.

They lay quiescent at last, and Isobel felt herself drifting, his arms hard and warm around her. Her gaze strayed to the window. Darkness still held sway. But how far away was the dawn? She must not worry on when it would end, she told herself firmly.

She pushed up on her elbow, refusing to allow herself to sleep away their short time together. His eyes were closed, the thick tangle of lashes lying against his cheeks, but his arm tightened around her, aware of her movement, the corners of his mouth deepening into a self-satisfied smile.

Isobel gazed down at him, wanting to remember him like this. "Only a short time ago I could not imagine myself lying here, naked with a man."

His eyes opened, one brow arching slightly.

She leaned closer, resting against his chest. "Aye, I vow I thought I'd end up some old witch, living in the woods, telling fortunes and making love philters, never knowing the touch of a man."

He shook his head slightly, his gaze traveling over her face. "What did the Attmores do to you, Isobel, to make you feel that way?"

"What do you mean? They were good to me . . . as good as could be expected."

" 'As could be expected'? What does that mean? Considering how much your father paid them, I would expect them to care for you as well as a child of their own. They had you for *twelve* years."

Isobel shook her head. "No, no—I was clearly not a child of theirs and a bit of an inconvenience at that. They were very good not to send me away."

He pushed himself up on his elbow and she fell back on the pillow. He frowned down at her. "Why is that?"

She stared at his chest, heavy with muscle, hard and sleek as steel. "Well, they were afraid of me. The villagers were, too—and yet they still sheltered me and protected me. That was good of them, don't you think?"

When he didn't respond she met his eyes again. His brows were drawn together in consternation, as if he still didn't comprehend what she was saying.

She chewed her lip thoughtfully, then said, "The first few years I was with them, I hid my magic well. The Attmores thought I was just very perceptive. I would see things, and if it seemed significant, I would bring the subject around to whatever concerned me and give advice. Sometimes they took it, sometimes not. But I never saw anything truly hurtful or frightening . . . until I was fifteen."

"What did you see?"

"I saw their youngest son's death. I touched something of Benji's and saw him struggling against a rush of water—it was a time of heavy rains, and the rivers and streams were swollen and dangerous. It was awful— clogged with dead animals—stinking of rot. Then I saw Benji, floating about beneath the water, his face bloated . . . the fish feeding on him."

She closed her eyes, forcing the memory away. They were all part of her; every horrible—and wonderful—thing she'd ever seen was engraved in her memory. She had to work hard to recall only the good.

"I tried to warn them—I had a feeling time was short. They thought me hysterical—and I was. That was the first time I'd seen something like that. I finally told them how I knew. Rather than think me a witch or even heed me, they thought I'd gone mad . . . at first."

She looked toward the window, remembering the horror on their faces when they realized she had foreseen their youngest son's death. When they realized she was *different*. They had also wondered, with fear and dread, what else she could do—if she was dangerous.

"I tried to go after him, to find him before it happened, but it was too late. I could not find him, and the river was treacherous. As the days passed, they began to believe that perhaps I *had* seen his death. So they searched the river."

She closed her eyes and let out a shuddering breath. Philip's hand was on her arm, rubbing. She firmed her mouth, willing herself not to cry over this. It was over, fin- ished, truly behind her now. When she felt in control again, she said, "And they found him . . . just like I'd seen. He was almost unrecognizable, except for his clothes. *He was only five.* They were scared then . . . they acted as if I'd somehow *caused* his death, that I'd had a hand in it. Some people even said I brought the storms." She opened her eyes then and shook her head. "I cannot do that kind of magic—call storms and such, I vow it."

Philip pressed his mouth against her forehead, and whispered, "I know."

She sighed, relieved to have told someone, but also anxious that her story had changed things between them. "Philip? Does this bother you? That I cannot fix some of the things I see? Sometimes it's not the future I see, but the present or past—and I don't always know that immediately . . . I wish it was always clear—"

He hushed her with a soft kiss. "You are not to blame. The Attmores are like my stepmother. She canna look at me without remembering what I did. But you aren't deserving of it, as I am. You tried to help, and they have to live with the knowledge that they dismissed your aid and lost their son for it." She still stared at the dark hairs scattered across his chest. He touched her chin, lifting it so she had to look at him. "They are angry with themselves—but if they admitted that they had a hand in their son's death, they might not be able to live with themselves. You were a convenient scapegoat. Just because you have this gift, doesna mean you shouldna be loved or well treated."

Isobel kissed him then, her arms going around his neck. She didn't know how she would ever be able to say goodbye to him. But somehow it was enough to know that he felt this way about her, that he was somewhere in the world, caring about her.

The kiss deepened, and his arms came around her, enfolding her in his strength. He made love to her, softly, sweetly, and afterward, Isobel continued to fight the satiated fatigue that possessed her limbs, but finally gave in to sleep.

When she opened her eyes again, she was alone among the furs. Faint light spilled through the window.

Panic surged through her. She sat up, clutching the sheet and furs to her body, and searched frantically for her nightrail. Why had he not awakened her? They might be discovered! What if someone was looking for her—or him! What if someone became suspicious that they were both missing at the same time! She'd asked her sisters to cover for her—though she didn't tell them why, she knew they suspected it was a tryst of some sort—and they had readily agreed. Still, it was morning and her betrothed was *in the castle!* How could she be so foolish? She might ruin everything. If her father found out . . .

Dread twisted her gut. That could not happen. She would not have him die in disappointment, thinking her a faithless whore.

Isobel spotted the filmy puddle of lawn at the end of the bed and snatched it up, pulling it quickly over her head. She parted the curtains and put her feet out, only to pull them back when they encountered cold wood.

She scanned the room for her slippers and froze when her gaze passed the fireplace. Philip was there. He sat on a bench before the fire. But it wasn't his presence that shocked her into immobility, but what he wore and what he did. A plaid was wrapped about him, pleated expertly and flung over his shoulder, secured with a brooch that glinted topaz. He wore leather boots, laced up to his knee, with a dirk hilt peeking from the top of one.

At the moment, he was shaving. He'd secured a polished silver mirror to the fireplace and currently scraped the whiskers from his face with a wicked-looking blade. Isobel watched, transfixed, as the clean line of chin and jaw was exposed.

He set the blade aside, wiped his face off with a damp rag, then turned to her, grinning. Her breath caught. She had always thought him handsome, but the absence of the whiskers exposed the clean cut of chin and jaw, strong and square, and set with determination. He looked a true Highlander. What had brought on this transformation?

He straightened and came to her, grabbing up her slippers and ariasad on the way. Kneeling before her, he slid her slippers on her bare feet, and all the while, she could not take her eyes from him.

When her slippers were on, his hands slid up to cup her calves. He tilted his head from his position kneeling below her and cocked a brow. "Well?"

Isobel was speechless. She put out a hand to touch his face, to trace the dimples that ran beside his mouth. "You are the perfect Highlander. But . . . why?"

He took her hands and stared down at them. The hair at the top of his head was slightly wet, and she caught the scent of sandalwood soap. "If I'm to ask yer father for yer hand, I must look like a proper Highlander."

Isobel's heart lodged painfully in her chest. The air seemed to leave her as her eyes blurred with tears. Surely she had heard him wrong—he could not have said what she thought she'd heard. She pulled her hands away and covered her mouth in horror—but it was mixed with the bittersweet happiness that he *wanted* to marry her, that he had done this for her.

He looked up at her, smiling still. "Ye didn't think I'd do right by you, after last night?"

She shook her head slowly. No, she had not thought he would. Had not dreamed he would do such a thing. Had never imagined he'd even want to—or thought it could possibly be. And if she had suspected he meant to do something like this, she'd have never come to him last night.

"Philip—" she began, but he moved to the bed beside her.

"Alan will not be happy . . . at first, but what we did canna be undone—he'll see that we did not do it lightly. And he respects and trusts me. He'll come to see that this is good—"

"It can be undone . . . It must be undone . . . I cannot marry you."

The way he looked at her—puzzled by her words, ripped at her heart. She had thought for certain he understood what this was, that he had no wish to ever wed, and that even if he did, it could never be Isobel MacDonell. She'd truly thought he *understood*.

"What?" he finally said.

"I *must* marry Lord Kincreag. My father is dying, and it's what he wishes. I have to honor his dying wishes. I couldn't live with myself if he died disappointed with me."

He looked away from her, as if he couldn't believe what he was hearing.

"Listen to me—my sisters and I are witches—and he is an earl. Not just any earl, either, but one in the king's favor. The only thing the king hates more than Highlanders are witches. We *need* Kincreag—the protection his name and title will afford us. If it were only me, I would marry you, but it's not, there are others I must consider. My union to Kincreag is important."

The gaze he turned on her was like an icy blade. "What we did *cannot* be undone. Why did you come to me last night?"

The tears she'd kept banked began to fall. "Because I love you, because I wanted one fine memory to hold close."

He looked so angry; she was desperate to make him understand. The last thing she'd ever wanted was to hurt him.

"You must understand," she begged, catching his arm when he tried to stand. "You cannot offer the same protection the earl of Kincreag can—you won't even accept your own inheritance. My father will not see this as good, and he will be disgusted with me—think me a whore for throwing marriage to the earl away simply to lie with a man."

"It cannot be undone," he repeated forcefully, his gaze hard.

"It can," Isobel said softly. "You must know virginity can easily be faked."

He stood, ripping his arm from her hands. "Get out."

Isobel squeezed her eyes shut, unable to bear the look of bafflement and fury on his face. Suddenly what she had done no longer seemed like a good idea—but a selfish, hurtful one.

She went to him. "Forgive me—I should not have come . . . but I never imagined you would want to marry me, I vow it."

He looked at her, his dark gaze traveling over her body. Then he closed his eyes and turned his head. "I canna even look at you. I pray you, leave before I do something I will regret."

But she could not. Indignant anger began to warm her. How could he not understand? How could he have thought anything different?

"Philip? You're being unfair."

"I'm a bloody fool to have believed your words of love."

"I meant them! I still do, but when has marriage ever been about love or desire?"

He exhaled, a bitter, rueful smile curving his lips. "When indeed? That's what lovers are for, aye? Well, dinna think I'll be hanging around Castle Kincreag to satisfy your needs, my lady."

"You think I would cuckold my husband?"

He whirled around, grabbing her arms and shaking her

slightly. Her eyes widened in alarm and she put her hands up to ward him off.

"What do ye think we did last night? You are *betrothed*—as good as married. You're right—I did not think for a minute you'd cuckold him—which is why I thought you'd come to me to save ye from a miserable marriage."

"I do not need to be *saved* or protected—that wasn't why I came. I just wanted to be with you, one last time."

He released her abruptly, as if she'd burned him. "My mistake, my lady," he said, his voice pouring over her like acid. "One I will not make again, I assure you."

Isobel could not respond, her throat was clogged with tears and hurt anger. He glared down at her for a moment before turning away wearily.

"Go—before someone discovers you've been here. I'll burn the sheets."

He strode to the bed and began yanking them savagely off the mattress. Isobel saw the blood on them—evidence of what they'd done. She picked up the arisaid he'd given her from the floor and wrapped it around herself. He crammed the sheets in the fireplace and grabbed the tinderbox.

When he saw she still stood there, he said, his voice cold, "Good-bye, Countess."

She flew to the door, flung it open, and ran straight into Stephen. He caught her arms and opened his mouth to speak, but froze, his pale blue eyes traveling over her in shock.

"Isobel . . . ?" he said, scandalized.

She wrenched her arms away and hurried down the deserted corridors to her chambers.

Her sisters were still in bed, and she slid beneath the covers beside Gillian, burying her face in a pillow to muffle her sobs. How could her plans have gone so awry? Philip hated her now, and her beautiful memory was ruined by how it had ended. How could she ever bear Lord Kincreag as her husband, knowing Philip wanted her, and she had turned him away? Knowing he now despised her. The despair and hollow regret washed over her again and again until she felt weak and empty.

She felt a hand on her shoulder and looked up to see Gillian gazing down at her, sleep-tousled and muzzy, but her brow creased in concern.

"Tell me who hurt you, and I'll have Hagan flog him."

Isobel laughed softly, but it quickly dissolved into more tears. "It doesn't matter. It's over—he hates me."

Gillian drew Isobel into her arms and spoke soothing words until Isobel was coherent again. When she lifted her head Rose was sitting up, watching with an auburn brow arched.

"I see you took my advice last night."

"Promise me you'll tell no one I was gone? If anyone asks, I was here all night."

Gillian and Rose exchanged worried glances.

"What?" Isobel breathed, fear gripping her.

"Well," Gillian said, "Uncle Roderick came here last night to fetch Rose to see to his wife."

Rose rolled her eyes. "If she farts, he's in a lather, thinking it's a miscarriage."

"Anyway," Gillian continued, giving Rose a stern look, "he noted you were gone. But we swore him to secrecy, and you know Uncle Roderick will never tell."

Isobel nodded, slightly relieved. She knew her uncle would not betray her, but still, it made her nervous that more people knew of her perfidy. Stephen knew, too, and though she knew she could trust him, she still felt ashamed, wondering what he thought of her now, what Philip would tell him.

"It will be fine," Gillian soothed. "No one will ever know. Now lie down and rest. You look tired."

"She looks like hell," Rose said. "Have ye been up all night?" Her gaze moved over Isobel's hair critically. "Jesus God—it'll take hours to get a comb through yer hair. Did ye do it on yer head?" She raised her brows suddenly in appreciation. "Was it good?"

Isobel groaned and fell back onto the pillow, closing her eyes. "I cannot speak of it." She held her hand up.

Gillian caught it and stroked the back of it. "Then do not," she whispered. "I'll make Rose shut her mouth so you can sleep. Don't worry about your hair now, it looks fine."

Isobel nodded and tried to force herself to sleep. That's what she needed, she told herself, a few hours of peace, then she could put all of this in perspective.

Unfortunately, she feared she would never know a moment's peace again.

Chapter 19

In less than an hour, Philip and Stephen were ready to leave. Philip had burned the sheets and swept out the fireplace—disposing of the evidence over the castle walls, into the loch below. As if it had never happened. That was what she wanted. For himself, he could not pretend it didn't happen and so he would have to stay away from Glen Laire and anywhere else she might be.

After an abortive attempt to scold Philip for bedding Kincreag's betrothed, Stephen was wisely keeping quiet. He waited in the great hall as Philip strode across the castle to Alan's chambers.

Philip hammered on the door until Hagan opened it. Hagan's black brows were lowered dangerously until he saw who it was. "Sir Philip? He is still asleep."

"Then wake him. I'm leaving, and I do not wish to go without speaking to him, but I will."

Irritated, Hagan opened the door wider to admit them. Philip strode in, only to stop when he noticed the earl of Kincreag slumped beside Alan's bed, asleep. Philip looked at Hagan questioningly, and the big Irishman motioned him close.

"He offered to keep watch so I could get some sleep."

"Keep watch?"

Hagan shook his head with a mixture of weariness and despair. "Sometimes . . . things happen at night."

"Things?"

"He has dreams . . . nightmares I cannot wake him from. And when he finally wakes, he is covered with bruises as if someone beat him—and yet *no one is here* but me. I cannot explain it. But I will not leave him unattended at night. I fear what would happen if someone is not watching over him."

Hagan's description of Alan's illness was unsettling, and Philip felt a new twinge of guilt over what he'd done last night. Isobel was Alan's daughter; he should have controlled himself and respected that. Hagan woke the earl and said something to him in a low voice. Kincreag stood, rubbing a hand over his face. Hagan woke Alan. The earl leaned down, whispering to Alan, and they gripped hands.

Philip still stood near the door, and when Kincreag turned to go, he kept his gaze steady on Philip until he stood before him. They were of the same height—Kincreag perhaps a bit taller. Philip did not like him, despite his obvious devotion to Alan. He didn't think he could ever like the man who married Isobel, but especially not this one.

"Thank you for bringing Mistress MacDonell home safely," Kincreag said. "Alan assures me you executed your duty with honor, despite the lady's lack of female companionship."

Philip nodded stiffly. *With honor.* He felt ill. A liar and a cheat.

"If there's anything you need . . ."

Philip shook his head. "No. Nothing."

Kincreag stared at him a moment longer, his eyes narrowing slightly, then gave him a crisp nod and left. Philip wanted to follow and threaten him to be kind to Isobel or he'd have Philip to answer to. But he restrained himself. She didn't need him to protect her—she'd told him so herself. She'd needed something else entirely from him. He gritted his teeth against the furious pain and humiliation that assailed him when he thought of this morning. What a bloody fool he'd been to think for a moment that *she* had considered him good enough.

"Philip?" Alan called.

Philip went forward, taking the chair Kincreag had vacated. "I'm leaving. I've come to say farewell."

Alan frowned. "So soon? You just arrived."

Philip looked down at his hands, fisted against his thighs. "I must."

Alan sighed. "You'll be back?"

Philip shook his head slightly, his jaw clenched. "I know not."

"Always running, you are. When will it end?"

Philip ground his teeth at the reminder of his instability.

Alan was silent for a long while. "What is wrong? You are vexed."

Philip stared hard at his hands. He would not have Alan know it was over one of his daughters. He'd never before believed Alan was a witch, but now, after seeing what Isobel could do, he wondered. Women from miles around came to the chieftain to find out if the child they carried was a son or daughter. Such things had amused Philip before, but now they worried him. He hoped that was the extent of Alan's magic.

"It's my sister," Philip said. "Isobel used her magic to find Effie."

"I see." Alan's voice was distant.

Philip looked up.

Alan's mouth was flattened in his beard, his eyes staring at the far wall in annoyance. "She will not refrain from using magic will she?"

Philip shook his head. "No . . . I'm sorry. I know you have warned her—I have also. She knows her own mind and will not be swayed from it."

"Aye. Like her mother she is. We can do naught but pray for her." Alan looked back to Philip. "So your sister is found. It has been a very long time—I assumed she was dead. This must mean great things for you at last. Will you finally go home and accept that you are heir apparent? Your father will think the angels have smiled upon him."

Philip laughed softly. "Aye."

"Damn, damn, and damn again," Alan muttered. "Ah, well. It's too late now."

"What is?"

Alan opened his palm on the thick pile of furs. "I wanted you for Gillian. I even thought to talk you into accepting your inheritance, but when I summoned you, I could see in your face you'd chew off your arm afore you'd marry. But now that you've found your sister . . . ?"

Alan's gray deerhound sniffed around Philip's feet. Philip scratched the dog's ears, staring down at it, a dangerous flush suffusing his neck. He knew what Alan asked—now that he'd found Effie, would he settle down? Oh, he'd wanted nothing more just a few short hours ago. But he would not give Isobel's secret away. "Effie *has* been unfinished business for a long time. Now that the end is in sight, I likely will take my place, and that means taking a wife . . . eventually."

Alan fell silent and when Philip finally had the courage to look up he saw his friend was deep in thought.

"Jacques is a good friend of mine, but if I tell him I want to keep Gillian close, perhaps he will agree to break the betrothal off amicably. He has daughters, he must know what it is to lose them. And with Gillian at Sgor Dubh, she would be close to her sisters—and me, too. I would hate for her to be so far from her sisters when this illness finally takes me."

Philip fought to keep his face expressionless. Part of him was sick with horror. Alan *did* think him good enough—but dammit—he was choosing the wrong daughter! He didn't want Gillian. It clawed at him, the desire to suggest Isobel. But part of him wanted to take Gillian anyway—just to hurt Isobel as she'd hurt him that morn. It was *she* who didn't think him good enough to protect her family. Alan clearly thought him capable.

He smiled at Philip, looking less ill, happy even. He pushed himself up and Philip leaned forward, adjusting the pile of pillows around him so he could sit.

"Ye'll have Gilly, aye? She's a beauty, that one." He gripped Philip's arm. "It's what I'd always hoped for, lad, to bind you to me with blood and make us family. For your sons to be my grandsons. I'll have the papers drawn up and sent to Sgor Dubh for you to sign when you get back with your sister."

Philip did not know how to refuse Alan. He felt a trap closing on him. He stared down at his hands, searching his mind for a graceful way out of this. He didn't wish to alienate Alan—especially when his friend was so near the end. But when Alan died, Philip wanted nothing more to do with the MacDonells. He would never be able to bear seeing or even hearing about Isobel—and to marry to her sister? Jesus God. He would not consider it.

Finally, he said, "Let me think on it."

When he looked up, Alan stared at him, disappointed. "You do not want Gillian? She doesn't please you?"

"That's not it . . . she's lovely . . . it's just that this is very fast. I have not even found my sister yet—or spoken

with my father. Just let me think on it, I pray you."
Coward. He would find himself married if he didn't just
tell Alan no. He understood Isobel's reluctance to disap-
point her father—he shared it. His heart was heavy, not
wanting to understand why she'd done what she had. It
was easier to think poorly of her.

Alan's gaze narrowed on Philip, then he smiled smugly.
"You do that, lad. I'll get to work on those papers." He
winked. "Just in case."

Philip tried not to smile sickly as he stood. He quickly
said his good-byes and strode out of there as if Satan were
on his heels. Stephen was waiting for him just outside the
door and followed silently.

Philip was headed straight for the stairs that led down to
the quay when he saw Gillian sitting before the fire,
sewing. He put out a hand to Stephen. "Wait here."

Gillian had seen him leave her father's room and was
watching them. Her welcoming smile turned to a small
frown as Philip approached.

"Sir Philip?" she said, setting her sewing aside. "You
look as if you're ready to depart. Isobel will be disappointed if you don't bid her farewell."

"Er . . . we've said our good-byes."

"Oh." Her dark brows raised slightly. "I see."

He sat on the hearth near her. "I wish to have a word
with you." He looked down at the ring on his finger. "A
few words actually. First—your father wishes us to wed."

When he looked up Gillian's eyes were wide.

"Really? That's wonderful! Now I won't have to go to
France!" She blushed and looked down. "Of course, marrying you rather than an old man would be pleasant, too."

Oh God. Philip wanted the ground to open. This was
not why he'd mentioned it to her. "Gillian, I cannot marry
you. But I haven't told your father that."

The joy faded from her face, but she still gave him a small smile of understanding. "It's difficult to tell my father anything these days, isn't it? No one wants to upset him." She patted his hand reassuringly. "Don't fret. I'll simply tell him I won't have you, that I find you uncouth and repulsive."

Philip laughed softly. "My thanks—I think." He removed his ring and held it out to her.

She took it, raising her brows quizzically.

"Give it to Isobel for me. Tell her if she needs me, she has only to look. And please, tell no one of this."

Gillian looked at the ring, her face grave, then she tucked it away in her bodice. "I promise."

"And tell her . . ." He looked down at his hands, clenched hard on his knees, and sighed, releasing the anger that had bound him up. "Tell her I understand."

Isobel's sleep was fitful—filled with images of her night with Philip, yet colored with a film of sorrow, as if she watched through a frosted glazed window. When she finally woke she continued to lie in the darkened bed with the curtains drawn, staring at the carved wooden top of the bed. Was he gone? Traveling south to find his sister? Would she ever see him again? Somehow she knew Philip would go to great lengths to avoid her, perhaps even severing his friendship with her father, and her heart broke a little more. She never meant to make such a mess of things.

Slowly, she became aware of a soft humming and turned her head vaguely to stare at the back side of the curtains. Gillian. Relief washed through her that she must not endure this loss living in empty, loveless Attmore Manor, where everyone was afraid to touch her.

Isobel slid through the curtains into the sunlit room. Gillian looked up from her sewing and smiled. "Good afternoon! You are lazy—you must not have slept at all last night."

Isobel's face flushed as she shuffled to her chest, muscles she hadn't know she possessed aching and protesting her movement. She rummaged about until she found her gloves. Her own feelings were raw; she couldn't handle anyone else's just then. She slipped on her gloves and turned to Gillian.

"I suppose I must face Father today."

Gillian nodded sympathetically. "Aye, I'm afraid you must. But worry not—he suspects nothing and is actually quite well this morn." Gillian set her sewing in her lap and raised her brows. "Father doesn't want me to marry the Frenchman anymore. He has someone else in mind."

Isobel came to the hearth and sat beside Gillian. "A Scotsman?"

Gillian nodded.

Isobel caught her sister's hands and squeezed. "That's wonderful!" When Gillian didn't smile, Isobel asked, "Is he old?"

"No—he's young and handsome."

"Then why aren't you happy?"

"He wants me to wed Sir Philip Kilpatrick."

Isobel gaped at her a moment before averting her eyes, staring at their joined hands. Her head spun and she felt as if she might bock. "What did Sir Philip say to this?"

"He did not say nay."

Isobel's hands tightened involuntarily on her sister's, unable to even consider Philip wed to her own sister. Unthinkable.

"But I offered to do it for him," Gillian said.

Isobel looked up, confused.

Gillian smiled. "Like you, he can't seem to tell Father how he truly feels. Everyone is so afraid of disappointing Da—has anyone thought for a moment that what our father truly wants is for us all to be happy?"

"What about you? You're going to marry an old man in France—would you dare tell Father that you'd rather die?"

Gillian sighed. "I know, I know—but after speaking with Sir Philip, I have reconsidered. I'm going to tell Father that I want to marry neither the Frenchman nor Sir Philip. I'll beg him to find someone else, someone more like Rose's Jamie or your earl." She squeezed Isobel's hands. "And I think you must tell Da that you want Sir Philip."

Isobel shook her head. "It doesn't matter anymore. Philip won't have me . . . he hates me. And my marriage to Kincreag is very important."

Gillian made a scoffing noise.

"I am serious, Gilly. Lord Kincreag can protect us from what is happening in Scotland. We are witches, and the whole world hates us for what we are. Father is right to wed me to him. It's not just about my happiness. It's about all of our lives."

Gillian looked down. "Forgive me. I forget that because I'm not a witch."

Isobel knew the difference tore her sister up. She didn't know what to say. Despite the danger, Isobel would not trade the magic she'd received from her mother to be normal. It was a part of her mother, and she cherished it.

"Magic is not everything," Isobel finally said.

"When you're a MacDonell, it seems like it is."

They sat in silence for a long while.

"Oh," Gillian said. She unbuttoned the top of her bodice, reached inside, and withdrew a ring. Philip's ring. The topaz stone glinted at Isobel in the sunlight.

Gillian offered it to Isobel. "He told me to tell you that if you need him, you have only to look. And that he understands . . . whatever that means."

Isobel took the ring reverently, glad for her gloves, knowing she couldn't bear to feel him. It would break her heart all over again. It was breaking anyway, from this final gesture of protection. A tear dripped from her chin onto the ring.

"What difference does it make which of us he weds?" Gillian said. "Father approved him for me, why not for you?"

Isobel shook her head, unable to look up from the topaz ring, even as it swam in and out of focus with her tears. "I can't!"

Gillian made a rude noise. "Fine. If you won't marry him, I will."

Isobel's head jerked up, pinning her sister with a look of astonishment. "You wouldn't!"

Gillian nodded determinedly. "I will. I *do not* want to go to France. I *do not* want to marry an old man."

"But . . . but you said he didn't want to wed you!"

Gillian shrugged. "What matter? He won't say nay to Da, so if I say I want nothing more than to marry Sir Philip, I shall have him. Sir Philip is cowardly enough to go along with it. And you will sit cowardly by and say naught."

"He is not cowardly," Isobel mumbled through stiff lips.

Gillian ignored her. "I refuse to be miserable if I don't have to be."

Isobel just stared at her sister in disbelief.

"Don't look at me like that." Gillian picked up her sewing again. "If you are afraid to grab him, you have to live with the consequences."

Isobel was speechless. Her sister was right. Why should

she miss a chance to change her fate just because Isobel was afraid to change her own? And the only reason Philip said nothing was because she'd made it clear to him she didn't want him to—that she was determined to do her father's will—regardless of the cost to them both.

Isobel's gaze turned on her sister, who stared at her expectantly.

"What about Kincreag?" Isobel whispered, excitement edging her voice.

"What about him? He's a fine-looking man—powerful and rich—he'll not suffer just because a MacDonell lass jilted him."

Isobel grabbed Gillian's arm urgently. "No—that's not what I mean! Why don't you marry Kincreag? He told me he didn't care which of us he wed. He's doing it for Father."

Gillian's gray eyes widened, and her hand fluttered on her breast. "Oh! I hadn't thought of that. Mmmm—yes, I'd like that."

Isobel tilted her head, observing the flush that rose in her sister's cheeks with fascination. "You *like* him!"

Gillian shrugged casually. "I certainly like the look of him. And I think he's all gruff and growl, really. Beneath that scowl is a decent man. I'm sure of it."

"What about the rumors that he killed his wife?" At that thought Isobel wondered if perhaps it was a bad idea to send sweet Gillian into the dragon's lair. "Mayhap this a bad idea."

"No!" Gillian gripped her arm back. "It's a perfect idea. It behooves us to go to Da with a plan. As for the rumors—that's all they are. It's foolish to give them more weight than they deserve. Perhaps that's why he's so sour—because everyone believes the worst of him."

"I don't know," Isobel said uncertainly.

"You don't have to. I *know* what I want. Do you?"

Isobel nodded, Philip's ring clutched in her gloved hand. She was happy suddenly. If Philip hated her, he would not have sent her his ring. She would not ruin the gift of a second chance. "Yes. I love him, Gillian. I don't know how I would go on without him."

Gillian smiled. "Then don't."

Chapter 20

Isobel spent the day with her sisters, trying to decide how best to approach their father. It wasn't that they feared his anger. He'd never raised a hand against any of them or spoken harshly to them. They feared upsetting the delicate state of his health with unhappy news. Rose was especially uneasy about it as she felt their father was finally showing some improvement.

"Can't this wait until he's stronger?" Rose asked again, frowning stubbornly.

They were closed up in their chamber, the door bolted. Earlier, Rose had removed her bodice and rolled up the sleeves of her linen shift to mix a philter for their father. She hadn't bothered to dress herself again and paced the floor half-dressed. Gillian sat calmly before the fire, sewing, not a fold of her emerald silk gown or a glossy sable curl out of place.

Isobel slouched on the hearth, dressed, but still struggling to work a comb through her hair. "How much longer?" she asked. "I'm to marry Earl Kincreag in a sennight!"

Rose sighed. "Can't we stall the wedding? You don't understand how ill Father was when I arrived just a sennight ago. He looked as if he were ready to die at any moment, and now . . . now there's some hope. What if he doesn't take this news well?"

Gillian made an exasperated sound. "That's what we're trying to do—to make it sound good. It will be a bit of a shock to him, but it's not the end of the world. One of us is still marrying the earl, and that really is what he wants, after all."

Rose shook her head. "No—it will not play out so perfectly."

"How do you know?" Isobel asked, throwing down the comb in disgust. Her arm ached, and her hair only seemed to be becoming more tangled. She'd have to get Gillian to comb it for her later. Rose would no doubt rip her hair out by the roots if she tried.

"Because," Rose said, "these things never do. Let's just consider for a moment the foul temper of the earl." She pinned Isobel with a hard look. "You spent a great deal of time practically alone with Sir Philip—no lady's maid or any other type of proper accompaniment. Now you want to marry him. It looks to me as if you are damaged goods— and it's going to look to Kincreag as if he's been cuckolded."

"But we're not married!" Isobel cried.

"But a technicality. That betrothal contract makes you as good as married, and he will be sore vexed. Will he even want Gillian after such a game? He might not trust any of us if he discovers we are all in on it."

Isobel looked at Gillian hopelessly. Rose made too many good points.

"So what do you suggest I do? That I marry him anyway? I *am* damaged goods!"

Rose shook her head, irritated. She looked fierce as a Viking, her long sleek auburn hair spilling about her shoulders and her midnight eyes flashing. "Think, you two ninnies! Stall the earl! Gillian, charm him—make him think he wants you, rather than Isobel. Isobel, be a shrew. Make yourself undesirable."

Gillian and Isobel exchanged a dubious look.

"He's not going to reconsider in a few days, dear," Gillian said. "I appreciate your confidence in my charms, but they are inflated. Besides, as the eldest, Isobel has an additional enticement I do not posses. If Uncle Roderick dies without issue, Glen Laire passes to Isobel's husband."

Rose nodded thoughtfully. "Yes, yes, I'd thought of that. But as you said, he is filthy rich. What's one more estate to him if he could have you in his bed?"

Gillian looked at Rose incredulously. "You must be jesting. Isobel is beautiful—and she comes with the possibility of lands. *She* is more desirable."

Rose rolled her eyes. "You're not listening to me. She will be rude and unpleasant to him. She'll make herself look like a hag. You, on the other hand, will be as stunning as ever, kind and gracious, hanging on his every word."

"What words?" Gillian said, becoming more distressed by the moment. "He hardly speaks!"

"He doesn't seem the type of man to be swayed by flirtations and pretty faces," Isobel offered. "I don't think he views marriage that way. He clearly said he didn't care which of us he got, and by that time he'd seen all three of us and preferred not a one of us over the other."

Rose glared at them both. "Very well, if you two continue to be blockheads, I will devise the plan. Isobel—you are deathly ill. In my exalted position of castle healer, I will assure him it is impossible for you to stand up, let alone go through with a ceremony or bedding. If he insists on seeing you, I have something guaranteed to make you vomit all over him. In the meantime, Gillian will try to seduce Kincreag."

"Seduce!" Gillian protested. "You said charm a moment ago!"

Rose directed her gaze to Gillian's ample bosom, and said, "You have only to rub against him, darling, and he'll be charmed and seduced, both."

Gillian flushed and plucked at her bodice, hunching her shoulders slightly.

"I'm not discounting Gillian's obvious attributes," Isobel interrupted. "But I've met the man. I think he's frozen both above and below the belt."

Rose frowned thoughtfully. "That may be . . . He doesn't seem to fancy women."

Gillian's hand went over her mouth and her eyes widened. "Do you think he fancies men?"

"No. I don't think he fancies *people*." Rose paced the room, her arms crossed over her chest. "Let's see. Perhaps seduction is a bit drastic. Why not just . . . keep him distracted—so that the feels he knows you better than Isobel, and when Father is stronger and we propose the new matches, he will not be so . . . offended. I'll make sure he hears the most awful stories about you Isobel, so that he's sure to be repulsed. After all—whether he fancies men or women, he'll prefer to wed a lass like Gillian than the horror he'll think Isobel is." She turned to them, auburn brows arched. "Well? What do you think?"

Isobel shook her head slowly. "Where did you get such a devious mind, Rose?"

"It was a necessity for survival on Skye." She turned to Isobel. "Get ye into bed. I'll tell everyone there will be no wedding until you're well."

Isobel had just slid beneath the covers when there was a rap on the door. Rose hurried to the door and opened it a crack.

"What?"

Isobel heard some muffled argument, then the door was forced open, and Uncle Roderick burst in, looking extremely annoyed. Isobel quickly shut her eyes, trying to feign illness. It wasn't hard—the deception made her stomach queasy.

She heard him stride quickly to the bed and stand over her. "What the hell is going on here?" His hand was on her forehead, then her cheeks. "She hasna got a fever."

After a moment he tapped her cheek lightly. "Open yer eyes, lass."

Isobel didn't know what to do. Should she be insensible? Babble incoherently? She decided to pretend unconsciousness and simply lie there.

"Leave her be, Uncle! She's very ill!" Rose was there, Isobel could smell the faint scent of mint that drifted from her sister's hands as she tucked Isobel in more securely.

"My arse she's ill," Uncle Roderick said. "What are you three up to?"

"Just what are you accusing us of?" Rose asked indignantly.

He was silent a moment, then Isobel heard him stride across the room. She cracked one eye and saw him standing over Gillian. Gillian calmly placed her sewing in her lap and looked up at him inquiringly.

"Gilly, don't you lie to me. What are you and yer sisters up to?"

"Nothing. Isobel is ill. She caught a chill last night."

"Last night," Roderick scoffed. "You'll all catch hell from me if ye dinna tell me what's going on. Isobel is to marry an earl in a few days. She canna be ill."

"But alas, she is. The wedding will have to be postponed." Gillian stood and smiled prettily. "Shall I inform the earl?"

Uncle Roderick placed his hand on her shoulder and

pushed her firmly back into her chair. "No. Someone had best be forthcoming right now, or there'll be trouble."

"Oh, you used to be fun!" Rose said.

"This is not a game, little girl." He came back to the bed. "Out with it, Rose."

The sisters were stubbornly quiet.

"You're not too old for a flogging—I'll wield the strap myself if someone doesna talk now!"

When Rose and Gillian still refused to speak, Isobel opened her eyes and sat up. "I don't want to marry the earl! They're trying to help me . . . to stall the marriage."

He stared at Isobel in confusion. "Stalling wilna help you, lass. What's the point?"

"The point," Rose said, "is Father. Since I've arrived he is doing so much better. We want to wait until he is stronger before we give him such a shock."

Gillian had come to the bed, too. She touched their uncle's arm. "That's not all. Father wants to marry me to Sir Philip now—but Isobel and I have decided that we'd like to trade husbands. She prefers Sir Philip, and I prefer the earl."

He blinked down at Gillian. "They are men—not a box of sweetmeats to be tasted and traded about."

"Why not?" Rose asked. "That's how they see us. Besides . . . Sir Philip *prefers* Isobel, and the earl cares not so long as it's a warm body."

Roderick looked at each of them with frustrated disapproval before sitting on the edge of the bed in defeat. "Very well." He sighed thoughtfully then looked up at Rose with a frown. "Alan's getting better, ye say? Are ye sure of that?"

"Aye," Rose said quickly.

Roderick rubbed at his forehead, his frown deepening. "Yer certain he's not pretending to feel better? For your benefit?"

Rose put her hands on her hips and gave her uncle a condescending look. "I'd know."

He rubbed his forehead some more, then pinned Isobel with a suspicious look. "I gather this has something to do with where you were last night?"

Isobel nodded. Roderick's eyes narrowed on her neck, and he reached out, fingering one of the ribbons that dipped into her bodice. He drew it out until he held Philip's ring in his palm. He exhaled loudly.

"Will we be feuding with Clan Colquhoun if your little scheme fails?"

Isobel started to shake her head when Rose said, "Aye."

Isobel glanced up at her sister uncertainly, then nodded agreeably. Why not?

Roderick stood. "Well. Sir Philip isna much of threat, unless he can get his clan behind him. Doubtful, that. Ye dinna desert your people for more than a decade, then expect them to rally to you when you need them."

Isobel winced at her uncle's honesty.

He turned to Rose. "Is there any way you can make her *look* ill."

Gillian gasped and clutched their uncle's arm. "So you'll help us?"

"Aye, I'll help you devious wee witches. Though I'm not certain this is the way to do it."

Gillian clapped her hands together.

He raised a brow at her. "Ye're awful keen on the earl. Is there something else ye should be telling me?"

Gillian blushed a deep rose. "No! I'm just happy for Isobel, is all. She and Sir Philip are in love—isn't it beautiful? And now I don't have to go to France!"

Roderick shook his head. "Married to Kincreag, you may wish ye had gone. Blasted witches—made me forget why I'd come. Your father sent for you, Isobel, but I suppose I must tell him you're too ill." He did not seem pleased about that at all.

Isobel's heart sank. She'd only seen her father once since she'd returned. She'd missed him so much and now she had to continue to stay away. It made her feel selfish again. If Rose was wrong and their father wasn't recovering, then the little time she had left with him was slipping away while she spent their precious time trying to deceive him.

Roderick gave each of them a censorious look. "You dinna think Isobel being so ill she canna leave her bed will distress Alan? This might do him a worse turn than your fickle tastes in men will."

Isobel looked at Rose, alarmed.

Rose licked her lips uncertainly. "I hadn't thought of that."

Roderick raised his brows at her—as if perhaps she ought to think on it.

Isobel kicked the covers off her legs. "Forget it. It was a stupid idea anyway."

"Wait, wait," Roderick said, placating. "Just let me talk to Alan, aye? Your father wants to see ye happy, above all. As do I." He put a hand on Isobel's shoulder. "If it's Sir Philip ye want, then I'll help ye get him. Let's just not frighten yer father to an early grave."

Isobel nodded. She was glad they'd told their uncle. He would help them do this right. He knew their father far better than they did. He'd been at Lochlaire the past twelve years while they were all far away. He would make everything right.

Roderick looked at them all. He nodded, satisfied that he'd changed their minds, and they wouldn't do anything foolish. "I'll talk to him now." He jerked his head at Rose, who stood, arms crossed over her chest and mouth set stubbornly, apparently not pleased her plan had been so thoroughly ruined. "Ye'd best come with me."

Rose sighed and followed Roderick out of the chamber. When the door shut behind them, Gillian sat on the bed beside Isobel. She reached out and touched the ring that dangled from Isobel's neck.

"Where's Mother's charm?"

Isobel pulled another ribbon from around her neck, letting the peridot fall beside Philip's ring with a soft tink of metal.

"Have you touched it yet?" Gillian asked. "To find him?"

Isobel shook her head. "I'm afraid of what I'll see."

"What do you mean?"

Isobel swallowed. "He never said he loved me. He only wants to marry me because . . . because of what we did last night. He wants to protect me. He's like that—he wants to take care of people, thinks it's his responsibility. Besides, he doesn't like the earl. He thinks if Kincreag discovers I'm a witch, it would go bad for me."

Gillian smiled gently, knowingly. "It sounds as if he is very protective of *you*."

"I don't know. What if I look and see he doesn't love me? Or worse, what if I see his future, and I'm not in it? That we failed and Father makes me marry Kincreag? And he is . . . he is wed to someone else?"

"Aye, that could be frightening. But don't you want to know? I don't think I could help myself. Besides—is the future set in stone? Maybe you ought to look. If you do see that you're not together, perhaps there is still time to fix things, aye?"

Gillian was simply too sensible. Isobel wished she'd had her around the past twelve years.

Isobel was not wearing her gloves. She looked down at the ring. "Maybe I'll just have a peek."

Gillian scooted closer. "Oh, do."

Isobel took a deep breath and rubbed her palms together. She tried to prepare herself for whatever she might see, but knew it was impossible. Her heart was too fragile when it came to him. Finally, she just wrapped her hand around it and closed her eyes.

She did not have to probe the ring for visions as she often did, this one unfolded before her so vividly she fancied she could smell the burning pitch and something else—overcooked meat and another unpleasant odor that was familiar, though she couldn't place it. The smoke burned her eyes and she squinted, peering through the thick smoke rolling around her.

The air was hot. She willed herself to move and realized in this vision she had a body. Oddly, she didn't know whose it was, though she assumed it was Philip's, as she was holding his ring. A crowd surround the fire. They talked amongst themselves, and she heard the word *witch* spat out several times. She was at a witch burning, and the elusive scent was burning hair. Isobel's stomach hitched involuntarily, but she forced herself to move closer, to identify the victim.

She was so close to the stake now that it felt like a furnace on her face. The figure tied to the stake was unidentifiable, black and twisted, its head hung at an odd angle. The Scots strangled witches before they burned them. Live burning was reserved for the most evil witches.

Perhaps this wasn't the future she was seeing—or maybe it was some random snatch from Philip's future that had nothing to do with anything. That happened sometimes, but usually she was able to locate a context within the vision, something to help her understand what she was seeing. The context to this one continued to elude her.

The hum of conversation around her changed tone, rose in anger and scorn. Isobel turned. A public building was nearby and something pricked her. Recognition. She knew this place, had been here before.

She peered around the crowd, looking at the faces. Some were vaguely familiar, though she could not place them, until her gaze lit on a man and woman standing together. Her blood froze and the air left her. Heather and Ewan Kennedy. Ewan was unrestrained, his face triumphant as he gazed at whatever spectacle everyone else currently jeered at. Heather, however, stared with a face carved of stone, dark circles beneath her eyes. Ewan slid his arm around his wife and leaned close, whispering something in her ear. She did not react, but for an odd moment her gaze seemed to lock on Isobel. She frowned, shaking her head slowly. She crossed herself and mouthed, *Forgive me.*

The crowd was becoming ugly. Isobel turned away from Heather. She was in Hawkirk, the village they'd passed through, where Isobel had found the body of Heather Kennedy's daughter, Laurie. Why was Philip there? And who had burned?

Isobel swung around to stare at the charred corpse again. That's when she noticed a second stake, near the first. Several men were crowded around it, securing someone to it. Isobel moved forward quickly. The men backed away and began piling bundles of pitch-drenched faggots around the stake.

When she saw the lifeless body bound to the stake Isobel's heart stumbled as a silent scream started in her head until it filled like a storm.

The vision dissipated, and Isobel found herself staring into Gillian's gray eyes.

"My God, Isobel—you're white as a sheet." Gillian dabbed at Isobel's face with her sleeve. "And in a cold sweat, at that. I had to pry the ring from yer hand. Whatever did you see?"

Isobel couldn't speak. She couldn't cry or scream as she did in her head—wailing over and over, *no, no, no, no!*

Gillian shook her, hard. "Breathe! What is wrong? What did you see?"

Fragments of coherent thought began to return to Isobel's mind. "They . . . they left this morning . . . so they cannot possibly be there—they weren't even going to Hawkirk. It was the future. It hasn't happened . . . yet. There is still time." She closed her eyes and took a shuddering breath. "He's not dead. *Not dead.*"

"Who's not dead?" Gillian cried, her voice taking on a note of hysteria.

"Philip . . . I . . . I saw him—strangled . . . dead—they were going to burn him."

Isobel clenched her hands in fists until her nails cut into her palms, forcing herself to not to see it anymore. She had to find him and warn him that he must never go near Hawkirk again. *I will stop this. I will. It will not be like Benji Attmore.* But how? Philip had nearly a day's head start. But they were probably traveling at a normal pace, stopping to sleep. If Isobel rode hard, not stopping, she might be able to catch them. But she didn't know which way they had traveled, didn't even know how to get to Wyndyburgh, where his sister lived.

Isobel grabbed her sister's hand. "Gillian—you've lived in the lowlands for twelve years. Did you know your way around? Particularly in the east—the Lothians?"

Gillian nodded vigorously. "Aye, aye, that's where I lived—with the Hepburns."

Isobel stood, dragging Gillian off the bed with her.

"Change into something for riding. We must leave now."

"Where are we going?" But Gillian didn't hesitate, throwing her chest open and rummaging through it for suitable clothing.

"We're going to change fate."

Chapter 21

Isobel and Gillian made it out of the keep with little incident. They left a note for Rose, so she wouldn't worry. They'd considered bringing her, but decided her healing skills were needed here at Lochlaire.

They were below the castle, in the dank quay with only the sound of dripping water. Fog seeped through the water entrance, winding about them like seeking hands. Half a dozen boats bobbed in the gentle current. There were more, but they wouldn't be so easily gotten at as these. Isobel and Gillian untied them all, climbing in one, and letting the rest drift away.

They rowed in silence, both of them edgy, waiting for someone to discover them. Soon, they feared. It would be difficult to make it to the shore without someone seeing them from the walls. It was evening and not yet full dark, but they had the fog for cover. If MacDonells were sent after them, they would not make it. They had not the strength of the men, who could easily overtake them. As it was, they were barely out of the arching cavelike water entrance to the castle and Isobel's shoulders ached. She felt blisters forming on her hands from plying the oars.

The boat glided through the water. They had not lit the

lantern on the bow of the boat, but they could see lights twinkling from the cottages near the shore, drawing them near. They had both chosen to wear their dark lowland mantles rather than arisaids. With the hood of her mantle pulled over her head, Gillian's face was completely hidden from Isobel.

They reached the shore undetected. Isobel removed her shoes, stuffing them in her satchel, and pulled up her skirts, securing them like breeches at her waist. She waded into the water, pulling the boat along behind her until it nudged the coarse grass. They were too far from the small wooden dock and could not pull the boat onto the shore as the men seemed to do so easily, and this irritated her. A sense of desperation infused her. She had no patience for her own shortcomings—it reminded her of the difficulty of the task she'd set for herself, and she could not consider that she might fail.

Gillian hopped out of the boat, and after Isobel had her shoes on again, they hurried along toward the stable. No one was in sight around the building. When Isobel cracked the door she heard the soft nickering of horses and their rustlings about in their stalls. They slipped inside and the warmth from horses enveloped them. A table and stool were near the far double door. A single taper burned and a man, his plaid wrapped around him like a blanket, slept, leaning against the wall, his boots propped on the tabletop.

Isobel saddled Jinny as quietly as possible and led the mare out of her stall. Gillian joined them a moment later, leading the gray Philip had brought for a wedding gift. As soon as it spotted Isobel it tossed its head and snorted testily, pawing the ground. Isobel frowned at her sister. Whyever would she choose that thing when there were much more docile mounts to be had?

Gillian's eyes shone when she stroked the gray's neck. "Isn't he beautiful?" she whispered.

Isobel raised her brows, but there was no time to swap horses, and the gray was already saddled and ready to go. They stared across the stable at the sleeping man guarding the horse entrance.

They couldn't hope to escape the stable without waking the guard, so they didn't even try. After heaving off the heavy bar locking the stable's double door, they both mounted. Isobel spurred Jinny forward, bursting through the doors as the guard woke, falling off his stool in surprise.

And then they were free—the only MacDonell wise to them was the stable guard. He would soon alert the castle, but they had a good head start. They raced across the glen, letting instinct and the horses lead them to the mountain pass. They were halfway to the narrow mountain pass that led in and out of Glen Laire when Isobel finally looked back. It was too dark to see anything, though Lochlaire glowed with torches and she thought she discerned the glare of firelight reflecting off the loch's surface, moving to shore.

She spurred Jinny faster. The day before she'd been filled with excitement, racing to her home—and now she raced away from it, terrified of being stopped. Stones dislodged and fell beneath the horses' hooves, but they kept at it, climbing their way to the mountain pass.

Once through the pass, Isobel reined in Jinny. Gillian's gray stopped beside her, shaking its head and snapping at Isobel's mount.

"You know which direction?" Isobel asked. "Because we can make no mistakes."

Gillian nodded. "I remember the route Hagan and I took—and once we reach familiar landmarks, I know the way to Wyndyburgh."

Gillian's confidence eased some of Isobel's fear. "How long will it take?" she asked, as they started down the other side of the mountain.

"If we don't stop unless absolutely necessary, a day and half—maybe two days. But it will take them three or more if they're stopping to rest the horses and sleep. Fash not, Isobel, he's going to Wyndyburgh, not Hawkirk. We'll reach him in plenty of time."

Isobel nodded, but didn't share her sister's confidence. She needed to touch the ring again, to see what else she could discover. Already she had a sense that time was running out and that there was something more that she was not seeing. But she could think of no reason why Philip would be anywhere near Hawkirk when his destination was so much farther east. *There was still time.*

They did not stop riding through the night. When the blush of dawn lightened the sky, Gillian said, "I have to stop—just for a moment."

They hobbled their horses at a cluster of bushes. When Isobel emerged from the bushes she rubbed her aching belly. They'd brought very little food and water, and so would have to ration themselves. Gillian, however, had a good deal of coin, so when they reached a village that evening, they were able to eat a decent meal at the tavern.

"We should stay the night here," Gillian said. She was exhausted, her dark curls springing free from her tight coiffure. "We're two lone women, and this is the only weapon I have." She held up the small sharp knife she used to cut her meat.

They did need to rest. They'd ridden all day and the night before. They couldn't continue running the horses at that pace—even the gray was showing signs of fatigue. Isobel gripped her own knife with impatience but nodded her assent.

That night she touched the ring again, with fear and apprehension, but also with determination to squeeze every bit of information out of the vision that she could. She knew what to expect this time and was prepared. So was Gillian, who sat close.

But there was nothing more to see. Isobel emerged from the vision with tears streaking her face, unable to understand how or why such a thing could happen.

"He's not a witch," she whispered to Gillian, as they lay on the narrow straw-filled tick, arms around each other to keep warm.

"It doesna matter," Gillian said softly. "Half the village saw him with you, protecting you, and it was clear to them that you *are* a witch." Isobel had told her what had happened in Hawkirk and how they'd escaped. "Many people have been burned these past years for nothing more than consulting witches."

Isobel knew that was true, but could not think of it. It made her sick that mere association with her could be someone's death sentence. She had known it, but it had not been real to her until now. More tears leaked from her eyes as she wondered if the burned corpse in the vision was Stephen, or even Fergus, who must surely be making his way to join them. Philip had left instructions for Fergus to follow at both Sgor Dubh and Lochlaire. He could be following them straight to his own death.

Gillian hushed her, whispering softly and telling her she must sleep or she'd not be able to stay in the saddle on the morrow. Isobel did sleep, but her dreams were filled with nightmares and burnings, and this time it was she who was strapped to the stake, her neck bruised from being strangled. But she wasn't dead, and the fire surrounded her as it had her mother as she screamed and screamed.

• • •

It took them three days to reach Wyndyburgh. It looked just as it had in her vision of Effie, with the added odor of rotting garbage and horse offal filling the streets. Isobel dismounted and led Jinny through the narrow streets as if in a trance, Gillian close behind. She stopped before a small house, packed in close with its neighbors.

"He must've been here by now," Isobel said. "He might even be in there now." Her heart sped with hope at the thought, and she shoved Jinny's reins at Gillian.

She knocked on the door and suddenly became aware of her appearance. She'd not even bothered to tidy her hair when they woke that morning, and hadn't washed since the previous day. Her gown was travel-stained, and she probably smelled awful.

The door swung open, and Philip's sister stood before her, her stomach huge with child. She wore an apron over her dress and her hair was tucked up under a white, starched cap. She was wiping her hands on an old towel. The scents of fresh bread and roasting fowl drifted from the open door.

"Aye?" Effie said, inspecting Isobel curiously.

"I'm looking for a man. Sir Philip Kilpatrick. He was coming here to see . . . you . . ." As soon as Isobel said Philip's name Effie's large dark eyes widened with dismay.

"He's not here, Miss, and God willing he'll not be back." She started to shut the door, but Isobel put up her hand, stopping it midswing.

"But he's been here?"

She looked Isobel up and down, her mouth pinched in a way that reminded Isobel of Mairi, then she nodded reluctantly. "Aye, he was."

"Do you know where he is now?"

"No." She tried to shut the door again, but Isobel was bigger than the diminutive pregnant woman and kept pushing against the door.

Isobel was very confused, but it was becoming clear that things had not gone well when Philip had found his sister. "What did he say to you?" she asked.

"I'll not speak of it. I wish you'd go."

"He said that you were his sister, Effie Kilpatrick, didn't he?"

"I am Summer Cooper—no Highlander, as you can see for yourself. Now go, before my husband comes home."

Isobel's heart sank as she stared at Philip's sister. And it *was* Philip's sister, Isobel knew it. "Did you say that to him?"

Effie finally quit trying to close the door. "Aye, I did, and when he insisted, I asked him to go away and not return. I'm telling you the same. Effie Kilpatrick is gone."

Isobel gasped and this time inserted her body in the doorway when Effie tried to close it. "What do you mean? Gone?"

"I didna even remember him or that place until he turned up at my door—and I dinna welcome the memories now! There was a reason I forgot."

The door latch was digging into Isobel's ribs, and Effie was pushing at her, trying to shove her back through the opening, but Isobel held fast to the doorframe.

"You don't understand. Your father is a chieftain, your family has mourned your loss for twelve years—how can you deny them—"

"Mourned my loss?" Effie hissed, coming close to Isobel now, eyes so fierce she resembled Philip. "You know nothing. Now go away!"

Strengthened by her anger, she gave Isobel a hard shove, dislodging her from the doorway. The door slammed before

Isobel could say another word, and she heard the bar drop on the other side, locking it.

Isobel stared at the door incoherently, her mind a blank wall of panic. What now? Where could Philip be? How would he react to Effie's denying him? Had he lost faith in Isobel? Decided she'd led him astray? That she was a charlatan? Or had this been the final blow to his dream of finding his sister?

She started to turn away from the house when she caught sight of something caught in the door. The towel Effie had been wiping her hands with. Isobel grabbed it and tried to pull it out of the door, but it was stuck. She fumbled about in her skirts until she found her knife. She sliced a hunk off the towel and carried it back to Gillian.

"From where I was standing, it didn't go well."

Isobel shook her head, stuffing the piece of towel into her satchel.

"What is that?" Gillian asked.

"Something for me to look at—but not now. Now we have to find out where Philip and Stephen are."

"She didn't know?"

"She denies that she's his sister."

Isobel was suddenly afraid. She had dragged Gillian far from home, and they were alone as they'd never been before. And Isobel did not know what to do. They stood in the street with people milling about them. Gillian watched her, waiting patiently for her to reveal her great plan for finding Philip.

Finally, Isobel said, "I can't imagine Philip giving up so easily. I'll wager he's still here somewhere, trying to decide how to approach her again."

Gillian raised a dark brow. "So what do we do? Go to every inn and alehouse until we find him?"

"Aye, I think we must." She felt better for having a plan.

They found a public stable and boarded their horses. The day wore on, one stinking alehouse dissolving into the next. They visited scores of public houses that day. At each one Isobel went through the speech she'd practically memorized by now, describing Philip and Stephen.

It was full dark when she stood before the ostler at the White Hare, one of the cleaner establishments, and finished up her description with, "They might also be with a third man—he's not as tall as the other two, but he's big. Red hair and beard."

The ostler shook his head. "No, Fergus hasna been here."

Isobel started to turn away, dejected, then realized she'd never mentioned any names. "How did you know his name was Fergus?"

The ostler hesitated, then said, "I was told, if a big red-headed man named Fergus came looking for them, I was to send him up."

Isobel and Gillian exchanged excited looks, but the ostler shook his head. "They gave no instructions on sending anyone else up. And the young one, he's in no condition for trouble, lassies, so get you gone."

Isobel caught the ostler's arm as he tried to turn away. "No, we mean them no harm—we're—we're family. We're their sisters. We've been looking everywhere for them."

The ostler frowned. "Well, it's just the one now. I do fear he'll be wanting some family close soon. The other was killed or he left, or some such."

"What do you mean?" Isobel cried, her voice rising. "One was killed?"

Gillian took Isobel's hand and squeezed. "Just take us to our brother, I pray you."

The ostler led them up a flight of narrow steps and down a dark narrow corridor. He hammered on a door at the end of the corridor, and, when no one responded, he tried the latch.

"He's not always in his head, ken? And he canna get up to answer the door."

It was dim inside, a single candle lit near the bed. The small window was open, letting in fresh air. Isobel followed the ostler across the room. An anguished sob clogged her throat as she stared down at the man on the bed. He lay on his stomach, shirtless, bloodied linens piled on his lower back.

The ostler was trying to light a lantern, but Isobel pushed him aside, falling to her knees beside the bed.

"Stephen," she said, her voicing shaking. She touched his shoulder and drew back. He was on fire. She glanced over her shoulder at Gillian, who stared down at Stephen wide-eyed.

Isobel looked to the ostler. "How long has he been this way?"

He shook his head grimly. "Night afore last. He and his friend paid me well, so I've been keeping him, hoping his Fergus friend or his family showed up. I'm glad you lassies are here now. A man shouldna die alone."

"What happened?" Isobel breathed.

Stephen's face was turned away from her and she could only see a tangle of blond hair. But his shoulders rose and fell as he breathed. She leaned over him, moving his hair aside and saw his face, bruised and scabbed as if someone had taken a club to him.

"I dinna know, Miss. Someone shot him and gave him a fair beating . . . dinna know what happened to his friend, the dark one, but was told he was beaten pretty bad, too. I saw this one lying in the street all bloody. Thought he was dead, but once I realized he wasna, I brought him back here. The barber removed the bullet. He's been babbling something about the earl of Irvine and I would hiv sent a message, but I dinna even know the lad's name. He keeps saying Sir Philip, but I didna think that was him. I think that was the other man."

"Has he been delirious?"

"In and out. He's a big lad, so I fear he'll go slow." The ostler shook his head and made a clucking noise. "A damn shame. Nice lads, they were—paid in advance." He sighed and started for the door. "Is there aught I can bring ye? Any messages ye'll be needing sent?" He looked at Stephen's motionless body meaningfully.

Isobel tried to force herself to think clearly. "Yes . . . bring me fresh linens and clean hot water . . . And send a message to the earl of Irvine. Tell him his nephew is dying."

"Nephew?"

When Isobel nodded distractedly, his eyes widened, and he hurried out the door.

After a moment Gillian joined Isobel beside the bed. "What are we going to do?" she whispered. For the first time since they'd been reunited, Gillian sounded scared. "We should have brought Rose."

"We'll send for her," Isobel said. "And Uncle Roderick, too."

Gillian put a hand out, touching Stephen's skin experimentally. "Jesu. There's no time for that, Isobel. He's practically steaming."

Isobel covered her mouth with a gloved hand and shook her head. "There *is* time. There must be." Isobel felt the beginnings of hysteria and firmly reined it in. She could not fall apart. "The first thing we'll do is re-dress Stephen's wound and discover how severe it is. He's the only person who can tell us what happened to Philip." Because Philip couldn't be dead. Not yet. Though the ostler's words had given her a start, Isobel knew from experience that unless she intervened, Philip would die in Hawkirk, strapped to a stake; therefore, he could not have died in Wyndyburgh.

"You could touch something of his," Gillian offered. She began to look around the room. "Look—some of this stuff might be Sir Philip's"

Isobel peeled her gloves off, not so that she could divine things, though that often was a by-product, whether she wanted it or not, and she was adept at blocking most visions she didn't want to see. She couldn't tend Stephen's wound with the gloves on.

She gingerly unwrapped the linen, hissing when the dried blood stuck to him, though he seemed oblivious. A knock sounded on the door, and a boy entered with hot water and clean linens. Another soon followed with a platter of food.

When they were gone, Gillian said, "Mayhap you should mention you're betrothed to the earl of Kincreag and see what the ostler does for us next."

Isobel was too busy cleaning the wound in Stephen's back to answer. It was a gunshot wound—right at the small of his back, beside his spine. It was once probably small and circular, but no longer. The barber had removed the bullet with no finesse, and the skin around it was ravaged and swollen.

"Who would do this?" Isobel said under her breath. What enemies did Stephen have? Isobel thought of all Philip's warnings about how Highlanders were hated. Could that be what happened? But Stephen wasn't even a Highlander. As Isobel cleaned the wound, Gillian knelt near Stephen's head and washed his face and neck with a cool cloth, then tied his hair back.

Isobel had just rewrapped his wound with clean dry linens when Stephen groaned and tried to turn his head.

"Get water," Isobel said.

Gillian leapt to her feet, returning with a tin cup full of water.

He was a big man, and moving him was out of the question, but between the two of them, they got his head turned. Gillian held the cup to his lips and tilted it, but it just ran down his face.

"Dammit, Stephen, drink!" Isobel said, frightened and upset by his condition.

To her surprise he did. A blue eye cracked open. He blinked a few times, as if clearing his head. "I'm dreamin' again," he murmured, and closed his eyes.

Isobel grabbed Stephen's chin. "No you're not. It's Isobel and Gillian, and we're really here."

His eyes opened again, and he squinted at them. "What the bloody hell are you doing here?" He tried to move his arm, but it was pinned awkwardly against his side, as if he'd been shivering and brought his arms up to warm himself.

He gritted his teeth and managed to get his arms under his head. He was breathing hard when he finally lay still, but he gave them a weak smile. "Everything hurts." He frowned at them a moment, then asked, "Why are ye here? I thought you were wedding the earl of Kincreag?"

"I had a vision."

Stephen closed his eyes, sighing deeply. "Oh, aye?"

"Of Philip, in Hawkirk."

Stephen's eyes snapped open. "In Hawkirk, ye say?"

Isobel nodded. "They . . . they'd strangled him and were burning him."

Stephen cursed rather obscenely and pushed himself up.

"Stephen, no!" Isobel cried, trying to hold him down. "Your back—you shouldn't even move."

It didn't seem as if he really could move . . . at least from the waist down. The muscles of his arms and back trembled and strained as he tried to push himself to sitting. Finally, he collapsed back onto the bed.

Gillian knelt beside him again, wiping his brow with a cool cloth. "Can you feel your legs?" she asked softly.

"Aye, I can—it feels like they've been stabbed by bolts of fire, right down from my back."

"Try to move them."

Jaw rigid, he did as she bid, grunting horribly with pain and sure enough, his legs moved.

Gillian touched his shoulder as he lay exhausted on his folded arms. "I think you'll walk again."

"If I live through the infection," he murmured. "That's how my da died, ye ken?"

Gillian and Isobel exchanged a grim look. The infection had already clearly set in. All they could do was wait it out.

After a moment Stephen lifted his head again. "You've got to get help . . . that's where they're taking him—to Hawkirk."

"Who, Stephen? Who did this to you?"

"Colin. Aidan. Niall." His head rolled against his arms as he shook it. "Don't know how they knew we'd be here, but they were waiting for us. Didna want me. Shot me afore I even knew what happened—right in the back, the bastards. All three of them beat Philip unconscious and dragged him off. I couldn't move after they shot me— thought I was dead at first—kicked me in the head, too, the damn cowardly bastards. They were taunting him, say- ing that there's a witch pricker looking for him in Hawkirk and that he was going to burn." Stephen's eyes squeezed shut, and a tear tracked down his stubbled cheek. "God bloody damn it! I just lay there, and now he's going to die and I still canna do aught but lie here."

Gillian patted his head, her brow lined with worry. "You were shot in the back. You can't even walk. What were you supposed to do? At least you're alive."

Stephen just shook his head, becoming increasingly distressed. "Fergus should be here. Where the hell is he?" He seized as pain from his back gripped him, then went limp.

Isobel touched his shoulder, hot and damp with sweat. "Stephen?" There was no response. Isobel sat back on her heels. "Well, we know what happened."

She stood and went to Stephen's and Philip's sacks, which were tossed carelessly on the floor. She came up with a primed dag, bullets, gunpowder, and a wicked-looking dirk. She transferred them to her own satchel.

"Where are you going?" Gillian asked, when Isobel swung her mantel on and secured it at the throat.

"To Hawkirk."

"What? You can't go alone!"

"There's no one else. No one is coming to help us."

"We're sending for Uncle Roderick, remember? And Stephen's family will surely seek retribution—and what of Philip's clan? We should send for them, as well."

Isobel shook her head. "There's no time for that. I feel it."

"But what about Fergus?"

"I don't know where he is. You have to stay here with Stephen. If Fergus arrives, send him to Hawkirk."

Gillian clamped both hands over her mouth, tears welling in her eyes. Then she threw her arms around Isobel's neck and held her tight. "Please, please, have a care, sister. I'm so frightened for you."

Isobel hugged her sister back. "I am, too," she whispered. And it was more than fear for Philip and fear of doing this on her own. It was also fear of her vision. Though she'd never had a vision of her own future, she couldn't help wondering if *this* was the source of the foreboding she'd been feeling for so long—that the charred body bound to the stake, stinking of burned hair and flesh, was Isobel MacDonell.

Chapter 22

Philip sat in the dank, dark cellar, trussed up like a Christmas goose, still unable to believe he was being tried for witchcraft and murder. He worked at his bindings some more, but it was no use. Colin made certain he was guarded carefully. Every time someone came into the cellar, his bindings were checked and tightened. It still amazed him that Colin had managed to convince an assembly of men—men who had apparently been convinced of Ewan Kennedy's guilt until Colin's arrival—that the deaths of Laurie Kennedy and Roger Wood was all Philip and Isobel's doing.

Currently they were going through the motions of a trial, but as Philip wouldn't tell them who the woman he'd been traveling with was, it was going nowhere. The conclusion, however, was inevitable. He would burn—probably within the week. The odd thing was that Colin knew it was Isobel, and yet pretended he knew as little as the elders. Philip decided he should be happy for small favors.

There was a jangle as someone unlocked the door. It swung open, and he turned his head, closing his eyes against the blinding light of the lantern. They untied the rope binding him to the pole and pulled him to his feet.

He was being held in someone's cellar, he didn't know who. He'd stopped attending to his own trial after the first day. No one listened to his protestations of innocence, and no one seemed to care that he was the son of a Highland chieftain—in fact, that seemed to count against him, especially after Colin revealed how he'd been disinherited. And the scratches and bruises on Ewan were not seen as proof of his guilt but as evidence of witchcraft. They believed Isobel made them appear to incriminate Ewan and remove guilt from Philip.

Philip was shoved onto the street. He squinted against the dull sunlight. A storm was coming, but the sun fought it, sending down shafts of light through the thick clouds. Colin, flanked by Niall and Aidan, waited for him on the street.

"They have a surprise for you today," Colin said, falling into step beside him as they pushed him up the main street. Philip didn't respond; he'd tired of Colin's taunts. He should have expected something like this, but he'd underestimated his brother. He'd not thought him capable of something on this scale. Of course, in retrospect, it was just his style—using others to do his dirty work while keeping his own hands clean of murder.

"I've been trying to help you," Colin said. "I vow it. I told them to just burn you and get it over with, but they want the witch, and they're not through with you until they get a name."

"Why don't you just tell them, then?" Philip asked, loud enough for his jailers to hear.

Colin sighed. "You should know by now lying won't work. I have no idea who she is."

Something hit Philip in the back of the head. He looked over his shoulder, and Niall grinned at him. His pocked face was sporting fresh boils. He snapped a leather strap at Philip again, catching him in the neck this time.

"Stop it," Colin said irritably, snagging the strap out of his brother's hands. The idiot twins, as Stephen called them, were becoming a bit of a liability for Colin, causing problems in Hawkirk. Though the elders seemed to like Colin well enough, they didn't appreciate Niall and Aidan's drunken brawling every night in the tavern, or the way they bothered the local women and boys when they were drunk.

They stopped outside the blacksmith's forge. Three of the elders and a small group of spectators had gathered around. One of them was Ewan Kennedy. Though Heather was frequently absent from the proceedings, Ewan never missed a minute of it. He stared at Philip now with stony eyes. Philip wondered how he could live with himself, but didn't particularly care. He was tired of all this. Stephen was dead, he'd lost Isobel forever, his sister wanted nothing to do with him, and Colin had won. These things pressed down on him until he found he cared about little that went on around him.

The man at the forge, however, did manage to catch his interest. It was the blacksmith. His enormous bulging arms were currently pumping the bellows. He turned his head and fixed Philip with a wicked, toothless grin.

A tremor of unease went through Philip, and he looked quickly to the elders.

Colin leaned close, and whispered in Gaelic, "Hawkirk has burned several witches in the past few years, but they've never had need to . . . er, forcibly persuade them to confess. Though it's done all the time elsewhere, it never occurred to the good men of Hawkirk. Luck is with them, however, as I'm here to advise them." He sighed ruefully. "But unfortunately they don't have a formal place for such diversions—so I suggested the blacksmith could manage in a pinch. Look at him—he seems right willing to fill in."

"How fortunate they are to have you," Philip answered in Scots.

"What's that?" one of the elders called out to Colin. "What did he say?"

Colin sobered. "I believe he's frightened. Perhaps he's ready to talk?"

Philip stared straight ahead blandly, sighing as if bored. He was far from bored. Although he was not afraid to die, he was afraid of what the blacksmith had planned for him and prayed he was strong enough to hold his tongue. He would never voluntarily reveal Isobel's name, but he'd never been tortured and was afraid he'd lose control. That was the point—to make someone so mad with pain he'd say anything to stop it.

"Bring him here," the elder named Ramsay said. He seemed to be the leader. He wasn't the oldest, but he had the longest beard and the tallest black hat.

Philip was pushed into the forge and forced to sit on a stump. One of the other elders came forward—Andrew, Philip's only friend in all of Hawkirk it seemed—and said, "He's a knight, Ramsay. I dinna think we should be doing this."

Ramsay looked down his nose at the little man. Andrew was the youngest elder, he had the shortest beard as well—black and well trimmed—and he wore no hat. "We have the commission, Andrew. The king has put the power in our hands."

Andrew nodded patiently. "I ken—but we've never tried a *knight* before."

Ramsay seemed to waver, thinking on this, until Colin spoke up. "I've seen lairds tried, and the king hasn't become angry. He's glad to be rid of another witch. Think on it. What of the wizard earl of Bothwell? Aye—I wager he wishes someone burned him when they had the chance.

Worry not. I'll speak for you if it comes to aught." Colin
looked Philip up and down as if he were covered in dung.
"Besides—he may be a knight, but he is nobody. Our
father disinherited him because of his perfidy. Not a farthing to his name."

That wasn't true, but Philip didn't bother to correct him.
He had considerably more than a farthing.

"Sir Philip Kilnobody," Aidan said, and Niall snickered.
"No one'll miss the farthingless knight."

"Shut up," Colin said.

Ramsay nodded wisely at Colin's words. "We'll continue."

Andrew backed away, still looking unhappy with the
proceedings. Philip sighed. *Sorry, lad, I was rooting for
you.*

The smith was at the fire, rolling a rod about in it. When
he turned, it glowed red at the tip. Philip's heart sped as he
looked from the smith's grinning face to the glowing
metal. He swallowed and braced himself.

Ramsay came to stand before him, the expression in his
eyes condescending, as if Philip were naught more than a
recalcitrant child in need of discipline. "Now, Sir Philip.
I'm going to ask you again. Who was the witch traveling
with you?"

"I told you. I dinna know any witches."

The elder sighed deeply and regretfully, his mouth compressed to nothing in the thicket of his gray beard. He nodded to the smith. Philip's hands were bound behind his
back. Niall and Aidan appeared on either side of him and
grabbed his arms to hold him in place.

With his free hand, the smith grabbed the front of
Philip's shirt and yanked, ripping the fabric until it hung
from his shoulders like a rag, his chest exposed. Though
Philip fought to show no emotion, his chest heaved. He
was sweating, though the air was cool. The smith moved

slowly, as though to prolong the moment, bringing the glowing cherry of the rod ever closer. They were waiting for him to break, Philip realized, giving him a chance to save his skin.

He *would not,* he vowed to himself. He would not say her name, no matter what they did to him. He closed his eyes when the fiery rod seared him, and endured.

Colin waited impatiently as the guard unlocked the cellar door. It was night—which meant Niall and Aidan were drunk and probably causing trouble. He should be keeping an eye on them, but as he'd paced his room at the inn, he'd become more and more convinced he must speak with Philip alone. This had gone on long enough.

The elders trusted him completely, so no questions were asked when he visited Ramsey and told him he wanted to talk to his brother. No one but the smith—and Niall and Aidan—had really enjoyed the torture session that day. Colin had been especially surprised that it had turned his stomach. He hated Philip, but he didn't seem to have the stomach to watch him tortured. But Ramsay felt it necessary. The elders would not rest until they had the witch who was behind the murders. Thanks to Colin, they believed Philip had been utterly bewitched by her— not that a plea of bewitchment would save him from the stake—but it made Isobel the true perpetrator.

Though Colin had anticipated that they'd try to discover her identity, he'd not believed it would go this far. He didn't know whether she was married to the earl of Kincreag yet, but he was not so stupid as to be the one to name her. She was a bonny lass, and, witch or no, the earl might fancy her enough to seek retribution.

Colin had come to urge Philip to tell the elders her name. He'd suggested to Ramsay that Philip might still be bewitched—and perhaps if they told him he would be set free, he would give her up. They would not set him free, of course, but it was perfectly legal to lie during interrogations.

The guard passed Colin the lantern, closing and locking the door behind him. Colin lifted the lantern high and descended the damp steps. Something dripped, and there was a scuttling near his feet as the rats scattered.

Philip was tied to a pole near the far wall of the small cellar. He sat on the ground, knees up, his head leaned back against the pole, his eyes closed; though Colin was sure he was awake and fully aware he was not alone.

He'd been given another shirt, but it was too small and was tight across his shoulders and chest. The bulk of the bandages wrapped around his chest made him look bumpy and odd. They'd cleaned and dressed his wounds immediately after the torture—couldn't have him dying from infection—not when their questions were still unanswered. Colin felt a wave of involuntary revulsion for the whole affair.

True, he had orchestrated it all, and true, he wanted his brother out of the way for good, but he'd never wanted *this*. Truth be told, if Philip managed to escape—which surely, surely was impossible—Colin was scared. It had gone too far, and Philip would see him dead for it. All of which brought Colin to the cellar that evening.

"If you don't tell them tomorrow, I will."

Philip smiled, and Colin was amazed he still could. Though Philip had spoken not a word, made not a sound throughout the torture, no one there had assumed he was unmoved. His jaw had been rigid, and when he'd bared his teeth in pain, blood had coated his teeth from biting the insides of his mouth to keep from crying out.

"What? Are you growing a backbone, Colin?" He straightened his neck and opened his eyes, fixing them on Colin. "Willing to stand up to the earl of Kincreag? What if he finds out you're pointing fingers at his wife? What happens if he brings his power and influence to the trial, and she's acquitted? False accusations of witchcraft are not treated lightly."

"I have no intention of accusing her. Just of revealing her name. It is indisputable that she was traveling with you. I'll say no more."

Philip's lip curled. "Why? What do you care so long as I'm dead?"

"I want this to be over—I've other things to attend, and I can't do that while you still breathe. So let's just get the burning over with."

Slowly, Philip leaned his head back against the pole, exposing a neck thus far unmarked. "Here's my neck. If you're so impatient, why don't you just cut it."

Colin stared at his brother, wishing it were that easy. He could not kill Philip with his own hand. If their father ever found out, he'd see Colin dead for it. It was already looking bad for him. He'd had quite a story planned to tell Dougal, about how he came too late and tried to save his brother, but alas, the commission had the king's power in witchcraft trials. There'd been naught he could do but comfort his brother at the end. But sitting back and watching his brother tortured would not be so easy to explain.

"I don't understand why you're so keen to protect her. She *is* a witch. She deserves the stake."

Philip didn't move, but the air seemed to still around him. "Untie me and say that again."

Colin exhaled loudly. "Do you *want* to be tortured? Did you *like* the burning rod?"

A small smile curved Philip's mouth again. "Why,

Colin—is that concern I hear in your voice? Are you actually feeling regret?"

Colin snorted. "Hardly, but the stench of burning flesh
has ruined my dinner."

"It's a poor chieftain who has such a weak stomach."

"You're one to talk. You haven't even the stomach to be
chieftain. At least I want it. It's yours by birth, and still
you're too cowardly to take it."

Philip opened his eyes then, his jaw rigid. "If that's true,
why am I here?"

"Because you found Effie. I knew that would change
things . . . and I want things to stay the same."

Philip shook his head and started laughing. Colin
scowled at him, but Philip didn't seem to care—it started
as a rough chuckle and dissolved into helpless laughter,
tears streaming down his face.

"You find that amusing?"

When Philip could talk again, he said, "Ah, I do, I really
do. It's all a bit amusing if you look at it just so."

Colin shook his head in annoyance. "And how is that?
From the ground, tied to a stake, and covered with burns?"

"No—it's just that you are right. Everything *has*
changed." The humor left his face as suddenly as it had
appeared. His eyes grew fierce and he strained against the
stake, as if he were trying to spring free. "I vow on Sgor
Dubh, which is mine by right, you thieving murderer, that
if you speak her name, I will find a way to kill you."

Colin should not have been unsettled. Philip was tied to
a pole for Christ's sake—weak from torture. There was no
escape for him. He could not hurt Colin. And yet unsettled
Colin was as he quickly retreated up the stairs, Philip's
threats following him out of the cellar and into the night.

Chapter 23

Isobel's journey to Hawkirk was uneventful. She'd not been bothered by any broken men, and the few times she'd stopped to ask directions, the farmers had been very helpful. She'd arrived in Hawkirk in the evening and rented a room. She wore a scarf over her hair and her mantle hood pulled low over her face, just in case someone recognized her, but so far no one had said a word.

They were too busy talking about the withcraft trial. The man accused wasn't a witch exactly—though he was accused of consulting and aiding a witch. The problem was, he wouldn't give her up. Everyone agreed he was still enchanted. It was obvious, they claimed. That very day the smith had burned him with a hot iron and he just smiled and laughed. He couldn't even feel pain. The devil's work, it was.

Such talk made Isobel ill. When she inquired about the prisoner, she was told he was locked up for the night. She'd be able to view him on the morrow when the smith took the tongs to him. Would she like a basket packed for her—in case the questioning went on overlong, and she became hungry?

Isobel declined and retired to her rented room. She spent a restless night pacing the floor, wringing her hands and praying to God for divine intervention. Come morning, she was no closer to a plan than she'd been when she arrived. The dawn found her waiting outside the smithy with a crowd of other villagers, many carrying baskets packed with refreshments, waiting for the witch to arrive and the amusement to begin.

Isobel had debated whether or not to come armed. She couldn't fire a gun—did not even know how to reload. But in the end she brought the whole satchel anyway. She might as well be prepared for anything.

Isobel backed to the edge of the crowd when Ewan Kennedy arrived on the scene. He stood apart from the others, looking very grave and dignified. Soon men drifted to him, to speak quietly and respectfully to him.

A surge of hatred shot through Isobel. He played the part of martyr well, acting as if he was only grudgingly forgiving the villagers for wrongly accusing him, for believing the witch's lies. Isobel wished then that she did have the power to give the evil eye—for she'd strike him down in his tracks for letting an innocent man suffer for his crimes.

"Here he comes," someone shouted.

Quiet fell over the crowd and they all turned. Isobel turned with them and saw a group of men coming up the street. She covered her mouth, biting her finger through her gloves to keep from making a sound when she saw Philip. Though his face was unmarked, he looked haggard, whiskers covering his jaw and dark circles beneath his eyes. The shirt he wore was too small and bulky from the bandages beneath it.

Colin was with him, looking very grave and important. He was dressed as a lowlander, in leather breeches, doublet, and a cap tilted rakishly on his blond head. Isobel's attention went back to Philip. The relief she felt at seeing him alive and walking under his own power was tempered by the fact he was about to be tortured. Again. They sat him on a stump and removed his shirt. His upper torso was wrapped with bloody and fluid-crusted linen, and when they began removing it, he hissed with pain. It had dried to the wounds, and skin ripped off with the cloth.

All sound from Philip stopped as he went rigid. Isobel raised her horrified eyes to his face, unable to bear watching him suffer, but unable to stop it. Her breath caught. He stared into her eyes, his so mournful it nearly broke her heart. Then he looked away and his gaze did not pass her way again. She wondered if she'd imagined it, then decided she'd not. If he'd not mentioned her name throughout his torture yesterday, he certainly wouldn't give her up now.

The smith was at his forge, rolling a pair of tongs around in the fire. An elder with a long beard and tall black hat came to stand before Philip.

"Must we do this again today?"

"You can just let me go," Philip suggested. When the elder only stared at him reprovingly, Philip sighed. "Let's get on with it then."

"Tell us the name of the witch, and we will set you free. It's that simple."

Isobel's breath hitched in her chest. *Set him free?* She started forward when Philip said loudly, "That's a lie— you'll burn me no matter what I tell you."

She paused. Would they lie? They were elders, church members who administered the village. Surely they didn't tell blatant lies such as that.

The elder stroked his beard, watching Philip. "We are not lying. Tell us her name, and you are free to go."

Philip rose suddenly from the stump. "Let's just get this over with, shall we? There is no witch, and no matter what you do, I'll not say different."

The elder backed up quickly. Two men stepped forward, grabbing Philip's arms and forcing him back to the stump. They remained holding his arms. His bare chest gleamed with fresh blood and scabs from where they'd burned him the day before. They'd burned him at least a dozen times, all over his torso.

Isobel choked, her eyes blurring. The smith was coming forward, carrying tongs that glowed crimson. Philip turned his face away, his jaw hard as he braced himself.

Isobel held her breath, unable to look away as the tongs drew closer to him. She couldn't do it—she couldn't just stand here and watch. She threw back the hood of her mantle and pushed through the crowd. "Stop!"

The crowd parted for her. The smith stepped back, withdrawing the tongs and frowning at her. Philip turned, trying to stand, his eyes furious.

"Stop this at once!" She moved in front of Philip and turned to the elder. "You said you would set him free if you had the witch. Well, here I am!"

"That's not her—she's lying," Philip said. "Go away you stupid woman and leave me alone."

The elder looked her up and down, frowning slightly, then turned to Ewan Kennedy. "This is she, is it not?"

Ewan Kennedy nodded, his face paling. "Aye, she's the one."

"No—you've got it all wrong," Philip was saying. *"She's* not a witch. *I'm* the witch. I bewitched her."

No one paid him any mind. All eyes were on Isobel. She held the elder's gaze steadily. "You said you'd set him free."

"If he revealed your name. He still has not done so."

Isobel turned to look at Philip expectantly.

He shrugged. "I've never seen her before in my life."

"I am Isobel MacDonell, daughter of Alan MacDonell

of Glen Laire and betrothed to the earl of Kincreag. Now set him free."

The elder sighed regretfully. "Well, I would, Mistress MacDonell, except we all heard him confess to being a witch."

Isobel shook her head incredulously. "No—he was just saying that, to protect me. He's not a witch. *I* am."

"She's insane, actually," Philip said. "I canna get rid of the stupid cow, following me about everywhere. She's harmless, though, I vow it. Not a witch at all."

"It looks as if we have two witches," Colin said. "And they've both confessed. I'd say the trial is over."

The elder nodded thoughtfully. He gestured to someone, and, moments later, Isobel's arms were grabbed and her satchel confiscated. She looked at Philip, and he was shaking his head at her, glowering furiously.

"Take them to the cellar while we vote," the elder said. The other elders who had been gathered at the forge set off toward the tavern, black hats of various heights bobbing.

Isobel and Philip were shoved in the opposite direction. Philip didn't say a word to her until they were forced down into a moldy cellar and tied to a pole, their backs to each other. When the others left and the lock clanked, he said, "Was that your plan? Because it was bloody brilliant."

"He said he'd set you free!"

"And you believed him?"

Isobel's throat tightened and her eyes burned. When she could finally speak again her voice was hoarse. "They were going to hurt you . . . I didn't think . . . I just . . ."

He didn't reply but she fancied she could hear him shaking his head in the dark. She'd really mucked this up. It seemed her suspicions that she was the other witch in her vision were right. She and Philip would burn together.

Their hands had been bound behind their backs, but

they were secured to the stake with rope wrapped around their upper bodies, their backs to each other. Isobel felt Philip's hands seeking hers around the stake. She clasped his fingers in response. They'd removed her gloves and the warm touch of his skin was reassuring somehow, despite their dismal situation.

"Isobel," he said wearily, the sarcasm gone from his voice, "why did you come? You're supposed to be at Lochlaire, getting married."

"Gillian gave me your ring, I had a vision."

"So you came to save me."

"I guess I didn't do so well."

His fingers tightened on hers. "You were verra brave to come forth like that."

She shook her head, tears blurring the dark. "No, I'm a coward—I couldn't bear to watch them hurt you. Perhaps if I'd just waited, we'd not be here."

He sighed heavily. "I'm glad you mentioned the earl. They might not care about burning a knight, but they'll think hard before burning a countess."

"Do you think that will save us?"

He was quiet for a long while, then he said, "I think it will stall your burning, aye. Time enough for your uncle and the earl to hear of it and come."

Isobel understood what he didn't say. It wouldn't stop them from burning Philip—and the fact of it was, she *was* a witch, and countess or no, she was in deep trouble.

They sat in silence for a time, their fingers clasped, listening to the sounds of footsteps on the boards overhead. She had no sense of the size of the cellar. She'd only seen it briefly when they'd been brought down. There was the stake they were tied to, near the back of the cellar, a table against one wall, and some boxes and casks. She couldn't remember seeing any alternative means of entry.

Isobel fell into deep thought, wondering how Lillian MacDonell had felt near the end. Had she any time for thoughts or regrets? Isobel realized she was more fortunate than her mother, for she had Philip with her. Lillian had died alone, unable to say good-bye to her husband and children. Alan hadn't even known Lillian had been taken until it was too late.

Philip's fingers tightened on hers. "Isobel," he whispered, "listen to me very carefully. You must tell them you're with child."

"What?"

"They won't burn a pregnant woman—they wait until she's delivered of the child. It will be months before they can prove ye're lying . . . if it even is a lie. Enough time for your uncle to come."

Isobel said nothing. He only spoke of her, not of himself. She couldn't bear that his situation was so hopeless. Anger suffused her. What good was her magic if it couldn't save them? Why show her a future she couldn't change?

"Isobel, promise me you'll tell them."

"And who am I to say the father is?"

"If you say it's mine, you'll have my father at your service."

"But our child will be a bastard."

His hand tightened on hers. "Not if we handfast."

Tears spilled down Isobel's cheek. They didn't even know if she was pregnant. It all seemed such a horrible, horrible waste.

"Promise me, Isobel MacDonell, that your plight is trothed to me, and we'll marry proper afore a pastor when this is over."

When this is over. Isobel could barely speak through her tears, but she managed a strangled, "Aye."

"Say it, Isobel," he urged, his fingers squeezing painfully, his voice urgent.

"I promise, before God, that I plight thee my troth—but only because I love thee more than my own life."

Philip sighed, and his fingers gentled on hers. Isobel soon understood his sense of urgency. The pounding of footsteps overhead had grown louder—as if there were many more people above them. Then there was the sound of a key in the lock, and the door swung open. Isobel was behind Philip, so she couldn't see anything, but she knew it was the elders, with their verdict. Her fingers clung to Philip's.

Philip faced the cellar stairs and door. Isobel was behind him, facing a moldy stone wall. In the light of the lanterns she was able to see the cellar's interior. Her heart sank. She sat on a dirt floor. All four walls were of stone. They were completely underground. Not a door or window to be found.

"Philip Kilpatrick, you are sentenced to be worried by the neck until dead and your body burned at the stake tomorrow morning. Isobel MacDonell—"

"Mistress MacDonell," Philip interrupted, "pleads her belly."

The was a heavy silence and some feet shuffling, then, "I see. And who is the father?"

"Her husband."

Another pause. "She is not yet wed to the earl of Kincreag."

"Nor will she ever be. She plighted her troth to me but a few minutes ago. We're handfast and she is my wife. Send word to Dougal Kilpatrick to collect his grandchild when he is delivered."

"There were no witnesses to this handfasting."

"You're witnessing it now. Did we plight our troth, Isobel?"

"Aye, we did," Isobel answered readily.

There was another long pause.

"Once she is examined," the elder said, "and your claim confirmed, your father will be notified."

The group shuffled out, taking the light with them.

They sat in silence for a long time, Isobel too frightened to think or speak.

Out of the darkness Philip suddenly spoke. "Know this, Isobel MacDonell. I've loved you since I first set eyes on you, I think—but I did not lie when I said I was afraid of you. I've been a fool and a coward, and if I could go back . . ." He trailed off and after a moment his voice came back to her, stronger, "If I could go back to that morning at Lochlaire, I'd never let you walk out on me."

"And I vow that I'll never walk out again, Philip." She would have said more, but the lock jangled again.

Isobel had expected her "examination" to take place in a private room somewhere, so she was shocked when an old woman was brought down to the cellar. She shoved her filthy hands up Isobel's skirts and groped around. Isobel cried out in mortified pain once and Philip's fingers gripped hers reassuringly.

When the old woman straightened, she said, "She's a virgin."

"What?" The word exploded from Philip and the entire stake shuddered as he tried to lunge at someone. "That's a bloody lie!" The cellar door slammed, plunging them back into darkness, but Philip lit a blue streak of swear words. From that Isobel gathered her "examination" had obviously been funded by Colin. Even if she was pregnant, Colin had no intention of letting another rival be brought into the world.

"It's all right, Philip," Isobel said. "I'm not afraid to die."

He said nothing, but she heard a shuddering sigh in the dark.

"I'm just sorry you're tangled up in it. You didn't do anything but what my father asked of you, and now you have to die because of it."

"I would gladly die protecting you." Their fingers twined tighter. "At least we don't face this alone."

"What will happen?" Isobel asked. Though she'd read about witch burnings and heard the gossip, living in England half her life, she'd never seen one.

"They will send a man down—the executioner—to strangle us. He'll bring a witness. It's a merciful death, not having to burn alive."

Isobel nodded into the darkness, hoping they strangled her first and knowing Philip hoped the same. She didn't want to be alive even a moment without him.

"So they'll just tie our bodies to a stake and burn us?"

"Aye, they'll sew us up in a shroud. At least that's what they usually do."

Isobel thought of her mother and how they'd shown her no mercy. She had not been strangled first, and it had taken her an agonizingly long time to burn to death. But still, the thought of being strangled and shoved in a sack brought Isobel no comfort.

Neither of them slept that night. When the key in the lock sounded again, hours later, they both stiffened. It couldn't be morning already! Isobel wanted to scream. She was not ready to die yet. Just a few more moments.

Several sets of footsteps echoed on the cellar steps, one ominously heavy. The footsteps stopped in front of Philip. "Colin," Philip said, his voice strained and rough. "Have mercy, man, let her go. She did naught to you or anyone."

"Mercy is not mine to give, brother. I'm only here as a witness, to be sure the deed is done."

They'd brought lanterns down and Isobel turned her head, straining to see what was going on behind her. She saw the executioner. He laid several implements out on a wooden table near the far wall. He wore a black leather mask over his head, and when he turned, she saw small holes had been cut for the eyes.

"What's he doing here?" Philip asked, contempt lacing his voice.

"Och, Mr. Kennedy paid for the privilege."

Isobel heard the soft scraping footsteps before she saw him. Then Ewan Kennedy was before her, staring down at her with his close-set eyes.

"You tried to ruin my life, witch. I'm here to make sure you're good and gone. It's not unheard of for families to pay the executioner to stick some other corpse in the shroud." He leaned down so his face was close to hers. "It ain't going to happen this time."

The executioner was standing in front of the table now, watching. Ewan nodded at him. "Ye can do her first. I want to watch."

Philip jerked savagely at his bindings, muttering something incoherent.

The executioner started forward, but Colin said, "Wait. One of the elders sent something . . . laudanum." Then to the executioner, "Give her the laudanum. She'll not be in pain at all then, aye? You see, Philip, I'm not completely heartless."

"Oh, you will be when I'm through with you," Philip growled.

Colin tsked. "Still making threats—to the very end."

"Laudanum?" Ewan said. "She doesna even deserve to be worried first. She tried to ruin my life. My wife still wilna lie with me." And then he spat on her.

The executioner knelt beside Isobel, his back to Colin

and Ewan, blocking out Ewan's hated face. Isobel looked at the huge mask, through the eyeholes, for some sign of justice. Dark blue eyes peered back at her, laugh lines crinkling beside them. A frisson of surprise ran through her as she became certain this was a good man before her, despite his awful job.

"Give Philip the laudanum, too," she pleaded.

"Here you go, lass," he said. "Just you drink up." But he pressed nothing to her mouth. In fact, his hands moved swiftly to the pole between Philip and Isobel. She felt the nick of a cold blade on the back of her hand, drawing blood.

But she didn't move. The eyes that stared into hers were familiar. She caught the subtle raising of his brows through the mask's eyeholes, then he straightened and turned.

"It'll take a bit for the laudanum to work," the executioner said, and went back to his table to wait.

Isobel kept her hands behind her, as if they were still secured. They were still trapped. The rope that secured them both to the stake was still there, wrapped twice about their upper torsos. But their hands were free. Philip gripped her full-handed.

Ewan was still talking to her, but Isobel's blood pounded in her ears so she could barely hear. The executioner was a friend. This was not the end.

Ewan squatted beside her. "Are you feeling sleepy yet, witch?"

Isobel blinked at him, trying to look groggy. She didn't know what the plan was, but then neither did Philip. Was she to use her freed hands, or wait for the executioner to do something? Her heart continued hammering insistently in her throat, her body tense and ready to spring at the slightest signal from the executioner.

"Why don't ye kill the redshank so we can get on with the lass," Ewan said.

Philip released Isobel's hands. "What did he say?" Philip asked, his voice deathly quiet.

There was a scrape of a boot, then Colin's voice was close, too, as he squatted down beside Philip. "Oh, that's another thing Mr. Kennedy paid for. A wee bit of fun with Mistress MacDonell afore her worrying." There was a long pause, then, "I was going to pass, myself, as I dinna fancy witch quim . . ." Colin's face appeared before her as he leaned around, his eyes traveling over her body and lingering on her breasts. "But I just might reconsider."

The entire pole moved as Philip surged forward, his hands on Colin's throat. They were still attached to the pole and it shuddered with a splintering crack as Colin struggled to escape. The executioner ran forward, and their bindings were cut. Someone's head slammed into Isobel's, and she tried to scramble out of the way. Philip and Colin rolled about on the floor. Ewan tried to hop over them, making for the stairs.

Isobel was still on the ground, but she snagged the edge of his cloak, jerking him backward. She still had no idea what their plan was, but she knew well enough that Colin and Ewan could not leave the cellar, or the whole town would be breathing down their necks.

Ewan turned and kicked at her. Isobel caught his foot, throwing her weight on it. He tried to shake her off, but she held tight. The edges of her vision began to fragment. "No!" she cried, but she couldn't let go, and before she knew it, a vision was upon her.

Ewan was trapped. The thick homespun of the sack sucked into his mouth every time he tried to breathe. But still he could get no air. He just sucked in more smoke, making his throat raw and his eyes water. The smell of pitch surrounded him; the oppressive heat grew thicker until it licked through sack, frying his skin like pork fat.

Ewan shook her off. Isobel blinked, back in the dank cold of the cellar. Philip had subdued Colin and the executioner guarded the cellar door. Ewan looked between them, then turned and grabbed Isobel by the hair, dragging her up in front of him.

He drew a small dirk from his belt and held it to her throat.

Philip came closer, looking between Ewan's face and the knife. "Drop the dirk, or it'll go bad for you, I vow it."

"Let me out, or I'll slit her gullet," Ewan said.

The executioner removed his mask. It took Isobel a moment to recognize him; without his beard he looked quite different. "If we let you out, you'll bring the whole village down on us," Fergus said. "So that doesna make much sense, does it?"

"I won't," Ewan said, but they all knew he lied.

The knife pricked into Isobel's skin. They were at an impasse. Ewan would not give up his only bargaining tool, and they could not let him out of the cellar alive. So Isobel did the only thing she could, considering the circumstances. She was sure her mother would have approved.

"I've seen your future, Ewan Kennedy," Isobel said, her voice low and trembling.

"What?" he said, distracted.

"You will not go unpunished for your crimes."

He grabbed a handful of her hair, yanking her head back so more of her neck was arched and exposed. "Shut up!"

"Isobel," Philip said, a warning in his voice. His eyes pleaded with her to stop, but she could not. She could smell Ewan's fear—the sharp tang of sweat. The blade trembled against her throat, and his stale breath beside her face shuddered with each labored exhalation. She was scaring him.

She continued, "I saw you . . . your mind is thick from

the drug . . . you're not sure what is going on at first, except that you can't breathe because of the smoke. It will almost kill you, but not quite, not before you realize it's you burning rather than the witches. It's the fire that finally does it, burning through your shroud—"

"Shut up!" He yanked her around and hit her. Pain exploded in her head. The moment the knife was gone from her throat Philip sprang at him, knocking Isobel aside. She rolled out of the way and struggled to her feet. When her head cleared she saw Philip standing over the limp body of Ewan Kennedy.

He turned, catching Isobel as she flew into his arms. He grunted when she squeezed him hard.

She drew back. "I'm sorry. I forgot about your burns."

He pulled her back against him and held her tightly, his face buried in her hair, his muscles quivering.

"There's time for that later," Fergus was saying. "For now, we've got to do something with these two."

Philip broke away from Isobel reluctantly and looked down at the men on the floor. "Colin is dead." He leaned down, pressing his fingers to Ewan Kennedy's neck. "He's still alive." He stared down at his brother's body silently. Finally, he turned to face them. "Three men came in, so only three men can go out."

Fergus gave Isobel a meaningful look. "Well, that's going to be something of a problem, methinks."

"No—Ewan is small for a man. Isobel can wear his clothes. I'll wear Colin's. And you . . . you can go as yourself. But first, we'll make sure Mr. Kennedy doesn't wake up." He took the vial of laudanum and, grabbing Ewan by the nose, poured it down his throat.

After they exchanged clothes with Ewan and Colin, Philip said, "Come on, let's get out of here."

Isobel followed him to the stairs, but Fergus hung back.

He grabbed one of the shrouds he'd brought with them. "The elders of Hawkirk expect a burning in a few hours, and their executioner is indisposed. If they dinna get their burning, there'll be trouble."

Philip gave him a curt nod.

"There's horses at the edge of town," Fergus said, leaning down to fit the shroud on Ewan. "Take them and ride. There's a burn to the east and a hillock just above it. Wait for me there."

Philip nodded tightly, and they started up the stairs again.

"Mistress MacDonell—wait." Fergus came to her, his dirk out and Isobel felt a moment of fear. He removed Ewan's cap from her head and cut off a hank of her hair.

He looked down at it, then back at her. "I'll sew it into the shroud so it's hanging out. Then they'll be no questions."

Isobel's nod was jerky. She stuffed her hair back into the cap and, taking Philip's hand, left Fergus and the cellar behind.

They waited for Fergus on a distant hill. The sun rose and was soon followed by two trails of smoke climbing into the air above the buildings of Hawkirk. Isobel sought Philip's hand as he stood beside her. He squeezed it, his face grim. An hour later Fergus joined them, his face smudged with soot and his eyes hard as stone. They spurred their horses east, back to Wyndyburgh.

Chapter 24

The crowd at the White Hare Inn in Wyndyburgh was Isobel's first clue that something was amiss. Villagers huddled outside, peering in the windows and through the door. Philip made a hole for them, dragging Isobel along by the hand.

There were shouts of greeting inside as half a dozen lads hurried over to say hello. As Philip introduced them, Isobel realized this was Stephen's family—the legitimate side.

The oldest, a dark-haired, fetching lad elbowed Philip, gesturing to the window with a tankard of ale. "Ye'd think they'd never seen an earl before."

Philip followed his gaze. "Likely they haven't."

"Well, they'll not be satisfied soon—he hasn't left Stephen's side since we arrived."

Philip's hand tightened on Isobel's. "He's alive?"

Fergus's report on Stephen's condition had been even grimmer than Isobel's. When he'd arrived in Wyndyburgh, Stephen had been so fevered he was delusional. He didn't even recognize Fergus. Gillian had been the one to tell him everything.

"Oh, aye, he is. We canna shut him up."

Isobel let out the breath she'd been holding. When she

looked up at Philip he grinned at her, as profoundly relieved as she was. They followed Stephen's cousin up the stairs. The room they were led into looked significantly different from the last time Isobel was there. The floor was covered with fresh, sweet-smelling rushes, chairs and benches crowded the room, all with beautifully embroidered pillows, and Stephen's bed was covered with furs. The lad himself was still on his stomach, but propped on several plump pillows, looking clean and quite healthy. A large basket filled with comfits, florentines, sweetmeats, and tarts sat on a chair near the bed. He'd obviously regained his appetite, for there was another basket on the floor filled with nothing but crumbs.

"Philip!" Stephen yelled, excited. He looked to the man sitting on a chair beside his bed, and said, "D'ye see? I told you they'd be fine." The older man nodded patiently. "Uncle Bren sent some men to Hawkirk yesterday, just in case ye needed a hand."

The earl of Irvine stood to an impressive height and stretched. He was in his late forties and quite handsome, with graying auburn hair and beard. He clasped Philip's hand with both of his. "I told you to keep the lad out of trouble." Though his tone conveyed a reprimand, his eyes were warm and friendly.

Philip shrugged. "I try."

The earl just grinned. "You can mind him while I go see what my other lads are up to." He disappeared out the door, and Philip took his chair.

Isobel put her hand on Stephen's forehead, just to check, and was relieved that it was cool and dry. She gave him a kiss on the cheek.

When she sat beside Philip, Stephen gave him a knowing look. "Did ye see that?"

"Keep yer plaid down—she's my wife."

Stephen's jaw dropped and he looked up to Fergus for

confirmation. His eyes widened when they rested on the big redhead, and he burst out laughing.

"What is so damn amusing?" Fergus asked, scowling.

Isobel had to admit Fergus did look rather strange without a beard. He'd been forced to shave it off, since Hawkirk's executioner was blond and beardless. Half of Fergus's face was ghostly white, and the rest was a ruddy tan. But already he was growing it back and in the sunlight the red whiskers glowed like a halo.

"Fia will have apoplexy when she sees ye. I'll be sure to be there to console her." Stephen stroked his own short blond beard suggestively.

"Ye'll not be swiving aught for a while, ye bacach bastard."

"Hey," Stephen said. "What did ye call me?"

"A bastard," Philip said. "Ye are illegitimate."

"Not that—the other—ba-bac—"

"Bacach," Isobel supplied, giving Fergus a censorious look. "It means crippled."

Stephen made a face and a rude hand gesture at Fergus, who just grinned wickedly at him.

"I'll have you know," Stephen said, "the surgeon said I'll be walking in no time. I might not run, but I'll surely be swiving. Tell Fia not to fash."

Fergus just shook his head, trying to hide his grin.

There was a soft knock on the door, and Gillian peeked around it. "Isobel!" she cried. They hugged each other, then Isobel filled Gillian and Stephen in on all that had happened. When it was over they were quiet, until Stephen said, "I canna believe you went and got married withoot me."

Fergus looked heavenward.

Philip's eyes met Isobel's, warm and full of promise. "Och, don't fash on that. We still have to do it proper, before a pastor."

The earl came back and shooed them all out of the room, claiming Stephen needed his rest so he could travel home to his auntie. Isobel peeked back at him over her shoulder before she was out the door and saw him look sourly at his uncle. No doubt he was hoping for something more exciting than being nursed by his aunt.

Philip and Isobel spent the night at the White Hare, comfortably ensconced in each other's arms. Philip trailed his fingertips over the bare skin of Isobel's back, and she shivered, unable to remember ever being happier. She was free as she'd never been before. Philip had married her, given her his name to protect her. She knew she'd made the right choice. Her father might not agree, but Philip was right. In time, he'd come to see it was for the best.

His hand covered hers where it rested on his chest. "What do you see for us, my *taibhsear?*"

Isobel smiled, her fingers flexing against hard muscle. "It doesn't work that way. I don't see anything when I touch a person's skin—it only works with objects. But now, when I touch your things, I sense feelings, but see nothing. No visions." This development pleased her immensely. Since she'd never been able to see her own future, the fact Philip's now eluded her, too, must mean their future was together.

"That's a relief."

She propped her chin on his chest and gazed at him. "Why is that?"

He quickly rolled her over, pinning her beneath him. "I'd rather it all be a surprise."

Her agreement was muffled by his mouth, brushing against hers, then lower, planting warm kisses on her chin and neck, before lavishing her breasts with his attention. She arched against him, her hands moving over him gently, careful of his wounds. Lord Irvine had brought with him the best physicians for Stephen, of course, and they had seen to Philip's burn wounds. A fresh linen bandage was wrapped around his chest, smelling faintly of herbs.

His mouth returned to Isobel's, kissing her urgently, his knee pressing her thighs apart. He pushed into her, and she gasped and clutched at him, unable to help herself. It did not hurt, but the invasion was still such an exquisite shock, it sent tremors of intense pleasure through her every time. He grunted softly, then rolled onto his back, taking her with him so she was astride him like a horse.

She stared down at him, her lips parted as she panted, her body still spasming around him, not certain what he wanted her to do. He was still hard inside her, and when she shifted slightly, it sent waves of delicious sensation through her so that she did it again, whimpering slightly each time.

"Wait," he hissed through gritted teeth, then his hands slid to her hips. "Now." He lifted her, then thrust into her. She gasped, her hand gripping his wrists to anchor herself as he moved into her again and again. She caught his rhythm, and rode him, her palms against the iron muscles of his belly, his hands moving over her breasts, the pleasure swelling inside her.

Her breath came in small, constricted gasps, her muscles drawing taut as the sensations shivering through her grew sharp. His arms went around her, drawing her down to his chest. The pleasure spilled over her, and the world grew dim around them. There was only his arms around her, his body hot against hers, enveloping her, loving her.

They lay there a long while, Isobel dozing in the circle of his arms. She woke sometime later, sensing that he was awake—that he had not slept at all. All was right in Isobel's world, but the same was not true for Philip. She leaned up on her elbow and looked down at him in the flickering candlelight.

He raised a questioning eyebrow. The light played over his face, casting part in shadows.

"Something's troubling you," Isobel said. "Is it your sister?"

He brought his hand up to toy absently with her hair. "I can accept that I lost her and can never get her back . . . I think. And I'm ready to go home and take my place—and even to tell Mairi I've had enough . . ." His mouth flattened as he stared at the curling copper-blond hair he'd spread out over his chest. "But I just want to ken why."

"Why what?"

"Why she refuses to speak to me. Why she denies who she is."

Isobel gave him a secret smile. "Good thing Fergus managed to snatch my satchel. The benefits of being an executioner, he said—the privilege of rifling through the condemned's effects."

"And what's in your wee satchel?" His fingers trailed over her shoulder, his mind already moving on to other things, she noted by the heat in his gaze.

"Let me show you." She leaned over him, feeling about on the floor until she felt it, then drew it onto the bed, dropping it onto his chest.

"Oomph!"

"Sorry," she said, digging through it.

"What the hell is in that thing?"

"Your gun, your dirk . . . some other things." She removed the section of towel she'd cut from Effie's door. Already she felt things from it. Distress and unease—a deep, alarming fear that caused Isobel to frown at the piece of cloth.

"What's that?" he asked, dumping her satchel back on the floor.

Isobel told him how she'd gone to Effie's house looking

for him and how his sister had sent her away. "But I did manage to get this. She'd dropped her towel and closed it in the door. So I cut this off."

Philip pushed himself up on his elbow so they faced each other, his eyes fixed on the towel.

"Damn," he said softly, then met her eyes, waiting.

Isobel held the towel in both hands and focused on the small pregnant woman on Rose Street. *What was she afraid of?* She saw Effie, knees pushed back, straining and crying out as a midwife urged her to push. Isobel felt the deep cramping pain about her middle as Effie worked her baby out. Yes, she was afraid of childbirth, but that wasn't what Isobel was looking for.

Why does the thought of Philip distress you? The image of Effie giving birth was gone, replaced by her bedchamber in Sgor Dubh. Effie was a child, five or six, and Isobel sensed it was a short time before her disappearance. She played with the doll Isobel had held such a short time ago. Mairi came in and began sniffing the air. It led her to Effie, who watched her mother anxiously. Mairi grabbed Effie, jerking her to her feet and snatching up her hands to smell them.

"Fish," she said, her lips curling. "What have I told you about this?"

"I'm sorry, Mum," Effie began, but Mairi dragged her to the basin. She poured water in and began scrubbing Effie's hands savagely. Effie said nothing for a time, but as it went on, she began to cry softly.

"It hurts."

"Shut up," Mairi said, absorbed in her task. "My daughter cannot be stinking like a common fishwife. This water just isn't hot enough. I can still smell it."

She dragged Effie down to the kitchens and ordered the cook to boil water. Effie cried, straining to escape her mother, but Mairi held her daughter's wrist in a vise-like grip.

"We'll get that smell out, just you see."

Isobel pushed it away, not wanting to see any more. She was back in the candlelit bed, Philip watching her intently. Isobel set the towel aside with trembling hands. Suddenly everything made sense.

Philip looked from the discarded towel to Isobel. "What did you see?"

"You didn't lose your sister, Philip. She ran away."

Philip stared at her blankly for a long moment, unable to believe what he was hearing. "What?"

"She didn't intend to—not that day at least, though she'd been entertaining the idea for some time. She dreamed of it, actually, being away, somewhere she could eat what she wanted, to play and be dirty. Somewhere no one expected her to be the perfect child. She dreamed of having a mother who looked at her with approval and love rather than disappointment."

Philip just shook his head. None of this made sense. He hadn't been aware that Effie had felt that way. "Lots of children have such fantasies. Hell, I know I did—but they dinna really run away!"

Isobel sighed. "I know, and Effie might never have either."

"I'm listening."

She took up the towel again. "That day in Edinburgh, while in the apothecary, she stole a piece of marchpane. She was not a thief, so please don't think poorly of her, but her mother would not let her have candy and comfits, and she so wanted one. But she knew if her mother found out, she would be severely punished. She became scared. Mairi was a nightmare when she was angry—and she was often angry with Effie. Once, after she'd gone fishing with you, Mairi made her wash her hands until they were raw."

Philip was speechless. He'd been so much older than his sister. He'd not been aware that these things occurred. But he did recall now that she had refused to fish with him for a time. Of course, he'd had other things on his mind—lassies and friends, fighting and hunting, learning to be a chieftain, and didn't always notice her.

His heart was sick. He rolled onto his back and stared at the low ceiling. "So she ran away."

"Well . . . not exactly. She did run, but soon enough came to her senses and realized she had naught but a piece of marchpane. She became frightened and tried to find you—but by then she was well and lost." Isobel paused, her eyes faraway. "Your sister grew up happy, with people who loved her. A kind woman who'd lost her husband and daughter in a fire found her. She meant to find Effie's family, but she fell in love with your sister and from some of the things Effie told her came to believe her home life had been a very unhappy one. So she told Effie her mother had given her away. Effie believed her. After all, Mairi had always looked at her with disappointment and punished her harshly—it made sense to Effie that her mother had finally gotten sick of her and given her away. She was very sad for a time—and yes, she missed you and Sgor Dubh—and even Mairi—the only mother she'd known . . . but soon she grew to love her new family, for they treated her very well. And then she just . . . forgot. Her new mother took her away and married a wealthy barrister—a man who accepted Effie as his own. She was well loved, Philip. The day she ran away was the best day of her life."

"She just forgot." Philip laughed humorlessly. "I canna believe this."

"She never blamed you."

"Why didn't she come to me for help?"

"I don't know. She was a small child—her mother ruled her whole life, seemed all-powerful. I don't think six-year-olds think very logically. And you were young, occupied with whatever things young men think on—lassies and war, most likely. Perhaps she thought you wouldn't believe her. Mairi made her think she was a very bad child."

"I should have seen. I should have stopped it."

Isobel leaned over him, planting her palms on either side of his head. Her hair spilled down around them, a curtain of burnished red-gold curls. "Stop it. You said you wanted to know, to understand. Now you do. You did not lose her—she ran away. Stop searching for something else to blame yourself for. You were just a lad."

He thought of all the years he'd spent searching for a sister who did not want to be found—a sister who was better off lost. And thanked God he'd never found her. Thanked God for Isobel and her gift. He knew, had she not told him all this, he wouldn't have given up on Effie and one day might have forced her to acknowledge him, or worse, told Mairi her daughter was alive.

"But that's not all," Isobel said softly, her eyes intense, a secret smile on her face.

"What?" Philip asked, his chest tight, afraid to hear any more.

"Your sudden appearance has caused Effie no small amount of distress. She is remembering a great deal about her childhood. Some of it is giving her nightmares."

"Wonderful," Philip said acerbically.

"And some of it makes her very sad and wistful." Isobel placed a gentle hand on his shoulder. "She is sorry for how she treated you—but she's not yet ready to behave any differently." Isobel paused, looking deeply into his eyes. "But if you wait, Philip, she will be ready, one day." She looked down at the towel, and said, "I'll tell you when."

Philip closed his burning eyes as emotion washed over him. His slid his hand beneath the fall of warm, heavy curls to the soft nape of Isobel's neck, and drew her against him, holding her tightly.

"Do ye know how bonny you are?" he whispered, his voice uneven.

He pulled back to look at her face. He stroked at the velvety skin, drawing her closer to his mouth. He saw her small, impish grin just before he kissed her.

Philip and Isobel were married before a pastor in Wyndyburgh so Stephen could be present—though both knew their fathers would be displeased. Then they traveled to Lochlaire to return Gillian and face Alan.

Philip was apprehensive. He was reluctant to face Alan's disappointment. After all, Philip wasn't an earl. And though he was confident that he could protect and care for Isobel better than anyone else, it troubled him that Alan might not agree. He also didn't relish a confrontation with Kincreag. Jilted men could be quite ugly. But Kincreag had quit Lochlaire, and though Alan assured them that the earl would not seek retribution for the insult, he was not at all sure Kincreag was still interested in marrying a MacDonell lass.

But as for Alan's disappointment, Philip didn't have to worry. The moment Alan saw Isobel he forgot anyone else was in the room.

"What in the bloody hell were you thinking?" he cried, trying to rise up off the bed, his face red and mottled. "You could have been killed—oh, aye—Gillian told me all aboot it. Nearly gave me apoplexy, it did. How would that have been, aye? Giving yer poor father's heart such a fright?"

Rose was hovering around Alan, trying to get him to sit back and calm down, but he was having none of it. "Thank God for this laddie and his quick thinking. Pleading the belly. Splendid idea!" He clasped Philip's hand and looked up at him with damp eyes. "I owe you a great deal . . .

Gillian told me *everything.*" He closed his eyes and sighed deeply. Gillian had been with Alan first, and had already told him the whole story. When Alan opened his eyes, he fixed them both with a severe expression. "I do not have the sight, so I cannot help you if you don't talk to me. If one of you had just told me ye fancied each other, all of this unpleasantness could have been avoided."

When they both started sputtering at once, Alan held up his hand to quiet them. "I know, I know—everyone thinks I'll pass away if I hear the milk has gone sour, but truly, I'm stronger than that."

Philip was relieved and confused, stammering out some unintelligible response. He exchanged a bemused glance with Isobel, who only shrugged and sat beside her father, apologizing profusely. Philip looked over her head and saw Rose watching him knowingly. She arched a dark auburn brow at him, and he understood who had smoothed his way with the chieftain of Glen Laire. He owed Rose a great deal.

"Where is Uncle Roderick?" Isobel asked.

"He's out looking for you," Alan said, giving Isobel a hard look, even as he held her hand so tight he must've been cutting off the blood flow; but Isobel didn't complain.

"I canna wait until he returns," Rose said. "He'll not believe how much Father has improved just since he left."

"Aye," Alan said, grinning. "Lately I think I just might be out of this bed one day." He directed his gaze at Isobel's belly. "I hope, in time to see my grandson."

Isobel looked up at Philip guiltily, then back at her father. "But Da, I'm not really pregnant—we just said that—"

"Are ye sure?"

"Well, no, we're not sure . . ."

He winked at them both. "Well, I am."

• • •

They arrived at Sgor Dubh a week later. Philip had written
to his father, explaining he'd wed Isobel and was coming
home to stay. The heavy wooden doors leading into the
keep stood open, and Dougal was just inside, hands
clasped behind back, waiting.

He looked stern and unforgiving as his gaze raked over
them both. Philip had a sudden fear that he'd pushed his
father too far the past twelve years, and he would not forgive him.

"This is for good, aye?" Dougal said skeptically.

"Aye," Philip vowed solemnly. "You'll not get rid of me
this time."

Dougal's gaze flicked to Isobel and back. "So ye finally
decided to listen to me." He shook his head wearily. "It's
about damn time."

Dougal had prepared a feast to celebrate their wedding
and Philip's homecoming. Mairi sat stiffly on Dougal's
right, staring hatefully at Philip. Isobel was excessively
solicitous of him, and Philip knew she feared Mairi's bitterness still hurt him. But Philip was finally free of her. He
felt nothing but pity for the sour old woman sitting across
from him, and joy and relief that Effie had escaped her.
And hope, that one day soon his sister would be ready to
welcome him back into her life.

"You'll likely have to deal with Colin when he finally
shows up," Dougal warned. "He'll be sore wroth when he
hears of this."

Philip and Isobel exchanged a secret look, and Philip
replied that he wasn't too worried about Colin's ire. "I'm
more concerned with Aidan and Niall—where are they?"

Dougal shook his head sadly. "Stupid culls—I canna
believe they're mine sometimes. They came here, looking

for Colin, complaining he'd deserted them in some wee village. When I told them I hadn't seen Colin in a week or more, they took off again. Not a day later the earl of Irvine's men arrived, looking for Aidan and Niall. They shot Stephen in the back. The back! God's eyes." He shook his head. "I ken ye already know this, and one day I hope to hear the whole story. Anyway, what could I do? We've been fostering that lad for years—he's like one of my own—hell, better than one of my lads. I'm just glad to hear the asses didn't kill him. So I just told Irvine's men where to find the fools. I wash my hands of them."

Mairi threw down her spoon and stood. "Aye, what care you now that Philip is back? God forbid anything should happen to *Philip*. You'd sacrifice every one of your children for him, as if he is Joseph, with his coat of many colors. Do you wonder that his brothers hate him?" She looked down her nose at Philip. "*I* know what you really are." She turned and stalked from the hall.

"I have heard enough!" Dougal's voice raised in an angry curse. He started to stand to go after her, but Philip placed a hand on his father's arm. "It's all right. I think that's the nicest thing she's ever said to me—comparing me to Joseph."

Dougal sat down but was not mollified. "It's not all right, and I'm sick of the evil shrew. She's going away, Philip. I have other houses—she doesna need to be here. And I'll not hear another word about it."

Philip shrugged. "If you insist."

Dougal gave him an appraising look before turning his gaze to Isobel. "Well, good, then," he said, set off-balance by Philip's easy acquiescence.

Later, Philip saw his father take Isobel aside. They spoke softly, then Isobel rose on her toes and kissed his cheek. Dougal watched her return to Philip's side before retiring to his chambers.

Philip took her hand and led her to their chambers. "What did he say to you?"

"He thanked me for giving him his son back."

He pulled her into their chambers, shut the door, and pressed her up against it, so she was trapped between his body and the wood. "Now it's my turn to thank you."

She moved her hips against his, looking up at him suggestively beneath her lashes. "Thank me for what?"

"For giving me back my life."

She smiled, her arms sliding slowly up his chest and around his neck, sending tremors of anticipation through him.

"I didn't do that."

He brushed his mouth against hers, loving the way her breath quickened, the way her lashes fluttered down, veiling the sage green of her eyes.

"Aye, ye did, my *baobh le suil uaine.*" His hand went to the pendant around her neck, the peridot her mother had worn.

Isobel looked down at the watery green stone he held. "You're not afraid to be wed to a witch? It did not go well for my mother."

"Afraid? Woman, do you never listen to me? I've told ye, I'm terrified of you."

She smiled, pressing herself against him. "I can tell. You're absolutely rigid with terror."

"That I am." He lowered his head to kiss her. "But I think it will go well for you."